LEGEND OF THE TRIFO

1

THE CADENCE

OF CROWNS

R.V. WILBUR

THE CADENCE OF CROWNS

Ebook ISBN: 979-8-9878180-5-3

Paperback ISBN: 979-8-9878180-6-0

Hardcover ISBN: 979-8-9878180-7-7

Edited by: The Editor & the Quill

Cover Design by: Selkkie Designs

Interior Artwork by: Selkkie Designs

❀ Created with Vellum

To A + B
for reminding me that all of the best
bedtime stories start with
"once upon a time"...

AUTHOR'S NOTE

This book has scenes depicting grief and loss, violence, blood, and war. Death is both on page and discussed, and there is mention of terminal illness. There are some suggestive scenes and kissing, but no spice...yet. No children or animals are harmed in this book.

PLAYLIST

POMPEII by Cavendish Masters, Joep Sporck
DANCE OF THE SUGAR PLUM FAIRY by Lindsey Stirling
MARJORIE by Taylor Swift
CAROL OF THE BELLS - THE DARK KNIGHT VERSION
by L'Orchestra Cinematique
WHERE IS YOUR RIDER? by The Oh Hellos
WEIGHT OF EVERYTHING by ill Factor, Katie Garfield
WHERE THE LONELY ONES ROAM by Digital Daggers
NATURE'S ALTAR by Peter Gundry
O HOLY NIGHT - EPIC VERSION
by L'Orchestra Cinematique
CAN YOU HEAR ME? by Fleurie
STORM SONG by PHILDEL
PERSEPHONE IN THE GARDEN by Aidoneus
THE ROSE by Ola Gjeilo, The Choir of Royal
Holloway, 12 Ensemble
LONG WAY DOWN by Steelfeather
WAKING UP (ACOUSTIC) by PVRIS
SILENT NIGHT - EPIC VERSION
by L'Orchestra Cinematique
DANCING IN A DAYDREAM by Roses & Revolutions
DANCE WITH THE DEVIL (AURORA VERSION)
by Breaking Benjamin, Adam Gontier
GOTHIC BALLROOM by Derek and Brandon Fiechter
LIAR by The Arcadian Wild
GOOD LOOKING by Suki Waterhouse
CITY OF THE DEAD by Eurielle
NIGHT OF THE DAMNED by Peter Gundry
SOLDIER, POET, KING by The Oh Hellos
MIDNIGHT WALTZ by David Garrett, Royal

Philharmonic Orchestra, Franck van der Heijden
MAKE ME BELIEVE by The EverLove
WE HAVE IT ALL by Pim Stones
TRANSCEND by Peter Gundry
MARBLE FLOORS by Ivan Izak, Juniper Vale
WILDEST DREAMS by Chris Richter
A WEEKEND IN MAINE by Zealyn
THE VIOLET HOUR by The Civil Wars
AVE MARIA by Tommee Profitt, Stanaj
A NOSTALGIC DREAM by Peter Gundry
COME FIND ME by Emile Haynie, Lykke Li, Romy
THE WOLF IN YOUR DARKEST ROOM
by Matthew Mayfield
THE END by JPOLND
ESMERALDA by Adriel Genet
ARE YOU WITH ME? by nilu
DANCING AFTER DEATH by Matt Maeson
WE THREE KINGS - EPIC VERSION
by L'Orchestra Cinematique
CEILINGS by Lizzie McAlpine
RADIOACTIVE - ACOUSTIC VERSION by Sofia Karlberg
SIX FEET UNDER by aeseaes
FOR THIS YOU WERE BORN by UNSECRET, Fleurie
WHEN DARKNESS SPOKE by Peter Gundry
SLIP AWAY by UNSECRET, Ruelle
TEARDROP OF THE SUN by Yoko Shimomura,
Shotaro Shima
THE WRECK OF OUR HEARTS by Sleeping Wolf
LOW THREAT by Gothic Storm
IMMORTALIZED by Hidden Citizens, Keeley Bumford
RESTLESS HEART by Jessie Early
END OF THE WORLD by Yoko Shimomura
DARK WINTER EPIC - PIANO by Gothic Storm
SORCERER FATE by Gothic Storm

ATRIUM OF HELL by *Gothic Storm*
CAN YOU FEEL IT COMING by *Steelfeather*
YOU ARE IN LOVE by *Minnz Piano*
FOREVERMORE by *Broken Iris*
NIGHT OF WONDERS (ORCHESTRAL) by *Gothic Storm and Christoph Allerstorfer*
HOW VILLAINS ARE MADE by *Madalen Duke*

THE WORLD OF BRETERIA

THE STARS:
Isteriaeth (is-ter-ee-aith)

THE AWDURON (AW-DUR-RON):
Mage
Form Forger
Faery
Elfin Folk
Einherjar

THE KOLLAPSAR (KOHL-LAP-SAR):
Axion
Vacare
Eoten
Hrotesk

THE ELÉRYND (EL-LAE-RIND):
Humans with magic living in their hearts/souls (who believed in magic) who were sent with the Awduron to Breteria.

THE FIVE STRANDS OF MAGIC

ATMOSPHERIC MAGIC
Bestows the ability to conjure items from the air itself.
MAGIC OF FORM
Bestows the ability to forge the bearer's physical form into
whatever animal or creature they wish.
ELEMENTAL MAGIC
Bestows the ability to control and manipulate the four elements.
TEMPORAL MAGIC
Bestows the power to defy time and the ability to halt and bend
it at will.
TENEBRESCENT MAGIC
The strand of magic, carried by beings of darkness, that ushered
in the end of the Age of Stars and brought about the fall of the
Trifolium Thrones.

GLOSSARY

TRIFOLIUM: (Try-foal-ee-um)
The clover that represents the four Thrones and rulers united to serve the realm of Breteria.

INFLAMEL: (In-fla-mell)
The kingdom at the heart of Breteria.

OBARIAN: (Oh-bar-ee-an)
The northern kingdom of Breteria.

GRIMOIRA: (Grim-oy-ra)
The western kingdom of Breteria.

TAURIELLIS: (Tar-ee-ell-is)
The southern kingdom of Breteria.

CRYSTAL: (Cris-tal-lum)
A relic crafted from one or multiple strands of magic for a specific purpose. Often sacred, passed down from one generation to the next.

GLOSSARY

DHUST: (du-st)
The visible representation of magic.

STRAND: (Str-and)
The form of magic.

BESTOWED: (Bee-stow-ed)
The point of time within an Isteriaeth's first decade of life in which their strand of magic is revealed to them.

PRONUNCIATION GUIDE

WREN KLAVER: (Ren Clay-ver)

TIMOTHIUS DROSSEL: (Tim-oath-ee-us Dross-elle)

ELRIC: (Ell-Rick)

NELLUENYA: (Nel-lou-en-ya)

PHILLIPAE VASILEIO: (Philli-pay Vas-ee-lio)

MUSANNULOS: (Moo-san-new-los)

KATHRINA POULTNEY: (Kath-ree-na Poult-knee)

MILO PENRITH: (Migh-low Penn-rith)

REGINALD BUXTON: (Reg-inn-ald Bucks-ton)

GERARD FLUGÉ: (Gare-ard Fluj-ay)

PRONUNCIATION GUIDE

MAURITANIA FLUGÉ: (Maur-ih-tain-ya Fluj-ay)

ISPERI MAGE: (Is-pair-ee Mage)

MARIONALDI: (Marry-on-al-dee)

VINCIENTI: (Vin-see-en-tee)

SIR SHELBURNE: (Sur Shell-burn)

Inflarian Strait

Borealis Ocean

Inflamel

Taurian Strait

THE LEGEND

Once upon a forgotten time, there was magic upon the earth. Magic so brilliant it rivaled the sun. So powerful it could shift mountains and carve valleys. So gentle it danced upon the air itself, drawn into every lung and whispered across every surface.

Until it was no more.

Until it was rejected by humanity. There was no room for magic amid progress. No place for fantastic beings within reality. Its hosts, discarded by fate and time, were purged from a society that had outgrown its enchantment and become numb to its wonder.

But....

What is life to tell a dream to cease breathing?

What is reality to inform wishes of their doom?

What is the world to suffocate the very thing that might restore its life?

Five eternal strands of magic fought their way from the earth, beyond the clouds, through galaxies, piercing the constellations until they were reduced to no more than dust strewn across the heavens. They collided with dying stars and bound together as one, creating a realm that had not existed before—opening a world of perfect impossibility. Four kingdoms formed of stars and magic where they alone could thrive.

Beings that were once cast aside, unwanted, opened their eyes to a second life after dancing a short time with death. Elfin folk, winged faeries, beings able to shift their appearance, mighty conquerors and their legendary descendants—each one unable and unwilling to relinquish the magic coursing through their very souls—awoke to a new existence, the authors of their own freedom.

But with them came beings of a different sort of magic—a power drawn from the darkness left in its wake, pulled from a cold ruin and brought to life with the promise of violence. They were monsters carved from stone and shadow, demons existing only to feed the insatiable lust for power that magic alone could satisfy. They rose unbidden, ready to usher in an endless collapse.

But all was not lost.

A ruler was chosen from each of the four kingdoms, and together they stole away into the mountains high in the northernmost reaches of their realm. Together they raised a stronghold—a castle laden with bricks of each magic, forming a foundation strong enough to withstand the test of time. And there, with the greatest sacrifice, they poured out the very magic that had given them life to forge four thrones. Each ruler bound their fate to their crown, forsaking their own flesh and blood in order to cleave to one another.

Joy and prosperity, peace and providence reigned over the realm in the middle of the stars. The lands thrived, magic was cultivated, and its people flourished under the rule of the four thrones. Within each kingdom, a field of clover bloomed. Each bore four delicate leaves—the very world itself paying homage to the united rulers who poured themselves into the realm to preserve it, just as the strands and stars had once done for them.

The Trifolium Thrones, as they were then known, reigned through time from their Keep high in the mountains, their mantle passed down from generation to generation, no two strands of magic alike sitting on the Throne at one time. But while their power flowed deeper into the land, delving through rock and sediment to the remnant bones of the fallen stars themselves, the darkness at its core began to shudder and grow.

Beings in every form of malice rose under the banner of Kollapsar and burst forth. Having grown cunning over time—not resting while peace reigned but strengthening and waiting—they waged war on the four kingdoms, cutting down life, land, and creature with no discrimination. The greater the battle won, the more magic they consumed, and the more infallible their power became. One by one the kingdoms began to crumble, and still they marched, undaunted, daring the High Kings and Queens to come down off the Thrones and save their people.

The first Throne to be lured away was the conqueror, the mighty Einherjar, from the kingdom of Obarian. But rather than be consumed for the very magic he had protected and saved, the King of Obarian sought to save his own life. He turned his back on the world and led the demons to the foot of the mountain itself. And so the first leaf of the Trifolium blackened and died.

Weakened by their loss, the remaining Thrones held fast to one another until the great Trifolium Keep was breached, only fleeing at the final moment to their own kingdoms, each to take one last stand for their people.

The second to fall was the Elfin Queen, from the continent of Grimoira. She stole away with her kind, weaving their magic like a shroud to conceal their presence—vanishing from time itself. And so the second Trifolium leaf broke from the stem.

The third to fall was the King of Faeries, delicate wings and wishes doing nothing to stop the full-scale slaughter of his people. Fleeing into the depths of the forest, into the trees of Tauriellis so thick that no man could carve a path, the faeries retreated to the source of their strength—forever to be hunted. And so the third Trifolium leaf curled into itself before crumbling to dust.

The final Throne rallied what forces they had left to the city within the kingdom of Inflamel. Isteriaeth, mages, beings who could forge their form at will, all came together to defend the final tie to their world, and beneath a rain of stardhust and magic, they fought until they could give no more. Until they had no choice but to take one final action. And there, under the banner of the clover sigil with death breaking through their door, the last force of magic threw their saving grace from the world. The final Trifolium leaf froze, neither living nor dying, forever preserved in time.

The Kollapsar overtook the world, swallowing everything in their path. Faeries, mages, and form forgers alike either fled or were consumed, and each kingdom was set to rule by a new crown under a new banner. Inflated with power and believing themselves to be untouchable, the Kollapsar marched upon the four vacant Thrones at long last. And when the most powerful, malevolent, and darkest of terrors rose to devour them, the great Thrones sent a surge of magic through the realm—shaking the stars and time itself—and shattered the Kollapsar leader into shards.

With their figurehead felled and their stolen magic broken, the Kollapsar retreated, weakened and desperate to regain power.

Silence descended upon the four kingdoms, desolate and cold as an unrelenting winter. The Thrones stood empty, high in the mountains over the world, their magic alive but dormant.

Waiting.

The fields of clovers in each kingdom withered and died,

their ashes strewn through the skies and into the heavens themselves, floating on the air, desperately seeking their lost rulers.

But none could be found.

For nearly four centuries, the realm of Breteria plunged into a bleak existence devoid of magic, lost and forgotten, where it remains to this day.

Some now recall the Thrones as legend. Others as tragedy. But they are all correct, for what is there to live on after tragedy but a story to be told?

PART I
THE REVELRY

CHAPTER ONE

Ten minutes. Wren Klaver had been staring at the house for ten minutes. It wasn't in dread of what she knew would come next—though she did, in fact, know and dread it—so much as it was the reticence to leave the quiet serenity of her car.

Ah, the joy of family holidays.

It had taken a small miracle to reach her destination. Only two days after Christmas, a drive that was supposed to be four hours took nearly double the time thanks to the post-holiday traffic, a few unplanned stops on the side of the road to field calls from her office, and the practically unplowed roads she had faced since exiting the highway. But she had made it.

Now to make it through the door.

She visualized the scene ahead, rehearsing answers to the questions she knew she would encounter.

"How is work going?"

"Fantastic! I was just promoted."

Translation: I've sold my soul to the gods of corporate America because I'm addicted to success and don't know how to say no to anything.

"They better have given you a hefty raise for the hours you put in..."

"Oh, they did. That's why I gave myself a car for Christmas."

Translation: There was no point in gifting myself anything else. Everything I have is either work-issued or new.

"Do you still like your apartment?"

"Oh, I love it! It's in an amazing part of town. I can walk to any restaurant I want."

Translation: I'm never home. And when I am, I'm exhausted, so I order takeout from whichever place is still open by the time I arrive.

"Are you still seeing Brian?"

"I'm not, actually. We decided we weren't a good fit for one another."

Translation: We're both workaholics who loved the idea of a relationship more than we liked each other.

"You should feel so proud. You're practically running a business, have an apartment in the city, you own a car, and you're making six figures. You've it made."

"I am. It's a lot, but I'm so happy. I wouldn't have it any other way."

Translation: I'm almost thirty and have nothing to show for it. I have no friends—no one thinks to extend an invitation to the woman they all seem to forget when she walks away. I haven't felt alive in years. I'm hollow, but I'm stuck and there's no way out.

Wren's phone rang, interrupting her thoughts, and she answered it without even looking at the name.

"I'm still on vacation, Carter," she said in a sing-song voice that her annoyance bled through.

"ABW wants out of their contract."

Wren sat up straight in her seat. "I'm sorry, what?"

"They called, said budgets have been reevaluated and they won't be moving forward."

She paused, tapping the button on her console until the orange lights illuminated and heat began to warm the seat at her back. "They already paid us."

"They did not, actually. The payment was processed but canceled before a check was issued from the bank."

Calculations flew through Wren's head. The loss of the deal truly didn't mean anything in the larger picture. They didn't need it or the money, but to take the loss of one of their biggest clients with mere days left in the year meant missing their goal —and the bonus that each employee counted on.

"Sales won't be able to make that up in four days. And I don't have any more contracts we can draft early," Carter confirmed on the other end of the line, as if he knew what scenarios were running through her mind.

"I'm aware," she said, her tone all business. "Send me the number, I'll give them a call."

"It's in your inbox as we speak."

"Thanks, Carter. And I guess since I have you, did you happen to draft the new policy we talked about before I left yesterday?"

The silence on the other end of the line was the only answer Wren needed. He wouldn't remember because he never did. She was a phone number, an email address for the individual he knew would bring a resolution. Nothing more. Never anyone more.

"Don't worry about it. Happy New Year, Carter."

Wren hung up without another word. Pulling up the email, she inhaled long, exhaled deep, and pressed dial.

A forty-minute conversation about the holidays, deadlines, budget goals, commitments, and due diligence later, enough of the deal had been salvaged to keep their record earnings for the year firmly intact. ABW would stay on board with the promise of a renegotiation call in the spring to revise the contract to better suit their budget needs. And this is why she was paid the big bucks.

She replied to Carter's email, though she didn't know why she bothered. While she was in the forefront of everyone's mind to navigate difficult negotiations and hairy discussions, as soon as she put out those fires, she disappeared once again into obscurity. Most of the time she liked it that way—the solitude, the independence of being alone and self-sufficient. But it was also the bane of her existence.

She had been the odd man out her entire life. The piece that didn't fit. The one grandchild who stood all on her own. Never old enough to stay with the grown-ups, but never young enough to fit in with the children. And it didn't help that even her own parents seemed apathetic to her existence. Summers were spent at a variety of camps, and the school year was filled with so many extra-curricular activities and sports it was a miracle she remembered what her parents looked like. Her only bright spots had been the weeks she was able to spend here—at her grandparents' house.

She loved this house. Loved the magic it still held for her, every year a memory for as far back as she could remember. She loved its smells, the deep berry from the tri-wick candle in the living area and the rich spices drifting from the kitchen. She loved its ease. The way she always had a seat that belonged to her, the way it felt more comfortable than any other house she had inhabited, the way being there filled her cup in a way that nowhere, no one, and nothing else did.

But now it was crammed full of all sixteen of her cousins, their families, and all of her aunts and uncles. Tomorrow the house would be filled with even more people—friends who were like family and others who had simply just been invited. Her grandparents never knew a stranger and always had an open door and a home-cooked meal waiting for anyone who was in the neighborhood and decided to stop by.

And she needed to get out of her car.

Another five minutes passed, for good measure, and Wren was shoving her wheeled suitcase through the front door when she came face to face with her first family member.

"Mother," she said, startled.

At the sound of Wren's voice, her mother nearly missed a step on the staircase into the foyer. "Oh, Florence. I didn't realize you would make it this weekend."

Wren stiffened at her given name. "I texted you last week and told you I was able to take a few hours so that I could leave early and be here."

Her mother's brow furrowed. "It must have slipped my mind. Anyway, I'm helping your Uncle Cas with dinner in the kitchen. You're more than welcome to give us a hand. Otherwise, I'm sure your aunts and cousins would—"

"I'll be right there," Wren cut in. "Which room am I in?"

She saw the answer on her mother's face before she spoke a word. "I forgot you would be here so there isn't one for you. You'll have to take the chaise in the family room. You can sit your bag in the attic where the younger girls are staying. But be quiet on those stairs, your grandmother is resting."

The skin along the edges of Wren's face prickled in awareness, but she ignored it and moved past her mother toward the stairs. "I've got it. Will she be awake soon? I really want to see her."

Her mother nodded. "She will, but for now it's best we let her be."

Wren climbed the first flight to the second floor, and ascended to the house's spacious attic. On her way back down, she could not help but pause at the bottom of the stairs in front of the only bedroom door that was shut. It took everything in her power not to go inside.

Yes, this year will be different.

7

CHAPTER TWO

The following day blew by in a blur of wrapping paper, toys, glittered bows, food, and enough noise to sate Wren for the next twelve months...if not longer. But now the grandfather clock in the corner of the room was chiming the hour and the lamps in the house had fallen dark.

It would have been eerie had the remaining decorations not shone so warm. The pale-yellow glow of the candles in each window reflected off the paned glass, disrupting the snow-crusted night with their incandescence. Their beams of light reached across the knotted wood floor to the enormous, plush rug in swirls of red and gold—its woven strands serving to carry the light like veins to the center of the room where a chaise disrupted their flow.

The high back of the lounge was only a minimal shield to the ten-foot tall Christmas tree erected in the corner, its green, red, blue, and orange bulbs illuminating the shadows of the room. After countless holiday seasons spent gathered in this very house, one knew to leave the lights alone or else their timers would fall off schedule.

Wren, however, trying to sleep, was tempted.

This home was magic, yes, but like all good things, this too would come to an end, and as much as she willed her heart to still and take in every moment of goodness that another year had brought, she could not allow herself to ignore the fact that it would end. The magic would die. The decorations would be put away. And she would make the trek back through the snow and ice to the city and reality. Only this time, she didn't know if she would ever return to this moment.

We don't know how much time she has left.

Those were the nine words that had frozen her world. The ones that had sunk into her bones. The goodbye she had dreaded all her life was somewhere in the imminent future. And just like that, another year, another holiday, another gathering, another memory would become another ending.

It wasn't the kind of thing people thought about during such happy times. Normal people, at least. But Wren had thought of nothing else all through their celebrations that day. She remembered the sudden loss of her beloved Grandpa Vince when she was seven, the sting still fresh in her mind. That was the moment she realized the price that could be paid if one did not pay close enough attention to the possible endings all around them.

"Wren Klaver, it is past your bedtime," came a lilting yet strong voice from across the room.

Wren's heart leaped and she sat up, draping an arm over the back of the chaise.

Her grandmother crossed the room with a small limp to sit beside her and, like she had so many times before, Wren nestled into her side. The scent of citrus and geranium clinging to the elder woman's butter-yellow sweater enveloped her instantly and she smiled to herself.

"*My* bedtime?" she asked. "It was a full day, I thought you turned in hours ago."

Her grandmother feigned offense. "Of all the stories I've

shared with you, you still haven't learned enough to know that I will not turn into a pumpkin at midnight."

Wren's smile faltered, the fairytale image conjuring visions of her grandmother slowly fading away.

We don't know how much time....

As if it heard her thoughts, the clock chimed again, fifteen minutes past the hour.

Wren's grandmother rose and moved to the clock, opening the glass door on the front before carefully inserting a golden key and winding it up.

We don't know....

"I'm sorry I haven't been here to see you more," Wren said steadily, absentmindedly picking at the pilling on her leggings. "I was thinking maybe I could stay an extra day or two after everyone leaves."

Her grandmother smiled but her eyes were knowing. "You have too many responsibilities to be sticking around here. But I also won't stop you from visiting whenever you'd like. With fewer people here, maybe you'd earn a bed and not the chair."

Wren forced a smile. "I know, I just...." She stared across the room at nothing. She didn't want to worry her grandmother. She wouldn't worry her grandmother. Not now. Not when they didn't *know*.

Her grandmother nodded but instead of sitting, she held out a hand for Wren to take. "Let's turn this around."

Not to be deterred by age or ailment, she stubbornly helped Wren shift the chaise until it faced the tree towering over the room. The same tree that Wren had looked upon in every last one of her twenty-nine years of life. She knew it all by heart. Every globe, every bauble, every plastic reindeer and picturesque chapel and group of tiny carolers.

We don't know....

"I have something for you," her grandmother said, and when

Wren looked, she noticed a small box resting in the woman's palm.

"You've already given me enough, Gran," said Wren, her dismissive words trying and failing to mask the emotion tightening her chest.

Her grandmother only handed her the box. "This isn't another Christmas present. This is a gift from me to you. Something special of mine that I'd like you to have."

A knot lodged itself in Wren's throat. Her mother had warned her there would be things passed down this weekend, she just hadn't had time to adequately prepare for it.

The box was a perfect square, smaller than a carton of tissues and wrapped in plum paper with a silver silk ribbon. Wren let the bow fall apart, and it drifted into her lap as she removed the lid.

Her brow furrowed. Inside the box, resting on a padded pillow, was—

"An ornament?" she asked, bemusement causing her lips to tip up.

"Not just any ornament," her grandmother said. Her smooth fingers, gnarled by time but still so beautiful, lifted it carefully from the box. Wren looked into it, marveling at the beveled crystal in a shade of deep garnet.

She cupped her hands around the orb, and when they blocked the light, she saw something more than her own reflection. Her blue-gray eyes and tawny, face-framing locks bled into the likeness of her grandmother. She watched the sunspots —the only signs of age that the woman carried—disappear from her skin. The softness of her permed, ashen hair faded into dark curls worn against a younger, freckled complexion....

"This," her grandmother said, interrupting her thoughts and breaking her gaze on the crystal, "was the ornament your grandfather gave me our very first Christmas together. He brought it home from the war—something beautiful out of something so dark. And I want you to have it."

Words stuck in Wren's mouth, but she nodded and wrapped her grandmother in the tightest hug, that faint scent of citrus, floral, and a sweet spice clinging to Wren even after she pulled away.

Another hour of sitting, reminiscing, and simply being together passed by under the watchful eye of the grandfather clock before they both turned in for the night. Wren lay alone, staring at the ornament that she had hung from a vacant branch at the highest end of her reach. Her eyes were heavy but her mind would not stop racing.

What would life be without her grandmother? A younger Wren would have cried. Maybe, possibly, if she were alone in her apartment, she would have allowed herself that moment of weakness. But here? No. It didn't mean she could keep from thinking, though.

From regretting.

She let her eyes fall shut and one tear slid down her cheek, the sensation oddly cold, like ice trailing across her skin. Elsewhere in life she was a leader. A strong, successful, independent woman. But here she was just Wren. A girl who grew up with the sweetest memories and watched them fade one by one. She had outgrown them all and was left with none of her own.

A loud slam made her jump up and nearly fall off the chaise. A freezing wind licked with frost roared in the house and whipped about the room. Wren sprang to her feet and tugged her tunic sweater down around her thighs, rushing to close the front window that had blown ajar.

The wind shoved back against the glass, resisting its exile like a prisoner fighting for freedom. She hadn't known there was a storm coming, or that there had even been one going on outside, but when she wrestled the window nearly shut, a few flurries of snow made it in the house and onto the rug where the electric candle lay, still glowing.

One last gust of wind tore into the room and she threw all of her weight behind her shoulder to lock the window shut with a *snap*. She leaned against the windowpane, panting, but the rustling of tree branches snagged her attention, and with a sinking feeling, she knew exactly what was about to happen.

Wren turned to see the crystal orb falling, almost in slow motion, drifting and rolling from tree branch to tree branch, down, down, down to the floor. She ran to reach it, desperately trying to get there before it hit the floor, but the sound of glass shattering brought time rushing back to full speed the same moment that her world crashed to a halt.

But when she came around the chaise, surveying the shards of red shed like blood all over the rug, her mouth fell open. In the midst of the pieces lay another orb. It was cut in the same crystal, reflecting everything around it the same way it had when she first held it, and hanging from the same ribbon, but the ornament was slightly smaller in diameter and a now radiant emerald color.

"How?" Wren whispered. A frigid wind suddenly wrapped around her, as if every window and every door in the house had flung open to the winter night. It stole her breath, and the world spun—turning on its axis and sending her stomach into her chest. The ground vanished beneath her feet, and she hurtled through the air, falling and flying all at once.

Wren opened her mouth but could not form a scream against the pressure reinforcing her plummet. The world grew dark around her....

And then there was nothing.

CHAPTER THREE

*I*t was the shout of voices that stirred Wren first, but it was the steady *thud* vibrating the ground against her cheek that rattled her to consciousness.

She opened her eyes, the dim light bringing the branches above her into focus. A little uneasy at the thought of randomly passing out beneath her grandmother's Christmas tree, she forced herself to sit up slowly—minding the now-green ornament in her hand—and leaned on the thick root of the tree for purchase.

She strummed the rough chips of bark beneath her fingernails, and something about the motion grounded her, allowing her dizziness to subside until a chilling thought prompted her to freeze.

What kind of artificial tree had bark?

Wren shot to her feet and caught her cheek on a tree branch. The cool pine needles brushed against her skin, soft and abrasive all at once, and its potent scent served to rouse her senses entirely.

She looked about wildly, taking in the sight of the shriveled brown leaves and pine cones scattered beneath her feet.

17

Looking up, she saw nothing but trees—towering pines and oaks bared for the winter—for as far as the eye could see. Weaving past her through the forest was a rudimentary path covered in stones and littered with pine straw and twigs.

It had been years since she dreamed of anything outside of workplace nightmares and commonplace chores, but this seemed more real than any dream she'd had before. The vividness of it was striking, and while it felt like her body had separated from her head somewhere in her fall, she couldn't help but take a deep breath of the crisp air and savor it.

Gingerly, she took a step forward, and while her toes crunched against the forest floor, she did not feel the slightest bit of pain or fatigue in her head any longer. She felt more awake and alert than she had in years.

She took another step and winced when her toes found a stone. Glancing at her feet, she saw that she was still wearing her slipper socks. In fact, she was still wearing her pajamas entirely.

Unease set in—the premonition that something was not quite right. If she were dreaming, *truly* dreaming, why would she be wearing exactly what she had gone to bed in, right down to her socks?

Think, Wren.

She needed to keep her wits about her. Logically, her reasoning was flawed, but she could not come up with any other explanation. Regardless of how beautiful this place was—and it *was* breathtaking—it had to be a dream.

The ornament in her palm caught what little light filtered down through the trees, its sparkle drawing her eye. Where cushioned bevels had decorated the red before, small etched four-leaf clovers now embellished the entire green orb. She ran her finger along the raised flourishes. They felt the same way the previous design had—as if this had been the ornament in her possession all along.

"How?" she whispered to herself.

The sound of voices carried on the air, jarring her from her thoughts. Uncertain where to go or what to do but knowing that an encounter with an enemy would be better than a nightmare where she slowly froze to death in the forest in her pajamas, Wren began to move carefully through the trees in the direction she hoped they were coming from.

Silent steps, however, became an issue for her knit socks that seemed to attract every bit of debris they came in contact with. She crept forward as best she could until the trees thinned to form a clearing in the wood. When she approached, she heard the voices grow angry, and though she felt confident that she could manipulate the outcome of her dream, something in their tone made her pause behind a tree.

She glanced beyond its trunk and caught sight of what appeared to be three soldiers in the clearing, but it wasn't until one of them turned that she felt panic set in. He wore the uniform of a soldier, down to his armor, leathers, and sword; however, in place of a helmet, he wore a mask. But not just any mask....

The full face of what looked like a gilded wolf.

Squeezing her eyes shut, Wren decided she did not want to be seen after all. She would rather be as far away from here as possible.

"He can't have gone far. Find him and bring him to me," uttered wolf-mask to his companions. When they slipped into the trees, Wren took the opportunity to leave in the opposite direction.

Afraid to make noise but terrified to walk so slowly with her back to people she did not wish to cross, Wren took painfully exaggerated steps past where she had awoken and toward.... Well, she wasn't sure where she was headed.

After a few moments, the sound of flowing water rang in her ears, bringing her to pause. Though it was terribly cold, walking along a riverbank would be easier than traipsing through the forest. Maybe then she could get some distance between herself and whatever those men were.

With all her focus on her next steps, she was not aware of the soldier behind her until they grabbed hold of her arm and whipped her around, causing the ornament to slip from her fingers and into the leaves.

A sword pressed beneath her chin, but somehow the notion of the blade at her neck was not the thing that wrenched a half scream from her lips. The mask inches from her face bore an elongated snout, enormous ears, and golden whiskers carved into the leather along with wickedly pointed teeth peeking from its snarling maw.

This was not a wolf.

It was a rat.

"The rebels will take anything now, won't they?" a man's voice hissed from within, rough but muffled save for the slits left in the snout for breathing. His eyes glared out of the small holes cut from the center of the rat's own bulbous orbs. "A woman, unaccompanied, in men's clothing with bindings for shoes. One would take you for a harlot were you not so hard on the eyes."

Harlot?

Wren let out a short, humorless laugh that would have signaled danger if this man knew her at all. When she tilted her head to tell him exactly what she thought of his insult, the blade nicked her chin, leaving a sharp pain and a warm, sticky wetness in its wake.

Her skin stung and begged her to cover it—to block the air from reaching it. A cold terror spread across her chest, and she began to think of ways to shift the dream.

To change the narrative, or at the very least to wake up.

The soldier made a sound that resembled a sneer, and he lowered his blade a fraction of an inch. "No falling on your sword today, rebel. One way or another, you will all face our great king."

Wren's mind spun. Nothing was changing. The blade felt real. The cut felt real. The blood felt real. And the way this creepy mouse man was cutting off circulation in her arm *definitely* felt real.

"I'm not a rebel. And I don't have anything. What the hell do you want from me?" she stammered.

The soldier sheathed his sword and jerked her forward before pulling a length of rope from his belt. "You know nothing of Hades yet, rebel."

Wren struggled, desperate to get away from the man who was binding her hands, until she caught sight of a tall, hooded figure standing just over his shoulder. His face was shrouded in shadow, but she could see the strong definition of his jawline, which was all she needed to confirm that he was not another masked soldier.

He pressed a single long finger to the darkness where his lips would be, and Wren's eyes widened when he stepped forward, raised his broadsword, and brought it down hilt first onto the back of the mouse man's head.

Having just tightened the final knot on her bindings, the soldier fell into Wren and knocked her off balance. Unable to catch herself with the hands bound in front of her, she let out a small scream and braced for the fall. But instead of slamming her head against the ground, she froze in midair and was gracefully pulled upright. The hooded man gripped the opposite end of her rope, steadying her, though she could see no more of his face than she had from a distance.

"What king sits on the throne?" he uttered in a voice so low and deadly it sent chills down her spine.

"I...I don't—" she stammered, truly afraid, but before she could form a full thought, the glint of a gilded snarl caught her eye beyond the man's cloaked head.

"RAT!" Wren screamed.

The hooded man dropped the rope and spun, his cloak billowing out behind him when he stalked forward with his sword raised.

The men met in a clash of metal on metal, each contact reminding Wren of what it sounded like to drop two baking trays on the floor in her grandmother's kitchen, only this was more metallic and impossibly loud when you were unable to cover your ears.

She inched away from the ensuing fight, but something caught her foot and she tumbled backward. This time there was no hooded stranger to steady her. Her tailbone cracked on impact, sending a shock of pain up her spine when it met the root of a tree. Wren groaned, closing her eyes against the nauseating pain, and when she rolled to her side, she felt something slide beneath her.

A flash of green in the leaves caught her eye, and she shifted the ornament toward her, barely able to cup it between her fingers. She held it up in front of her eyes, her mouth falling open. The crystal was still in perfect condition. She wasn't what society would consider heavy, but she was certainly weighty enough to shatter an ornament that had already broken from a simple fall to floor, yet here it was without so much as a crack in it.

"How?" she whispered as the pain-ridden cry of a man broke the even collision of the blades. Wren's head whipped up, and her mouth fell open in horror watching the hooded man rip the length of his sword from where he had thrust it up into the soldier's gut.

Grasping the wound, the soldier fell to his knees and then ultimately the ground where he ceased moving.

The hooded man sheathed his sword and rushed to her side, effortlessly hoisting her to her feet with the orb still firmly locked between her palms.

"Come," he said, hardly winded. "We must move, the rest are surely on their way."

Wren had barely nodded when the man grabbed one of her bound wrists and started to run through the forest, half-pulling and half-steadying her beside him.

She fumbled in her socks and saw him briefly glance down at her feet, a dark curl sneaking from beneath the hood riding back on his head. His brows tightened in confusion but he focused forward once more and led them out of the forest and toward the embankment.

Running along the river to a narrower crossing, he plunged them into the rapids, but when the water seeped into Wren's clothes, she found it surprisingly warm—not the bitter cold she had braced herself for.

On the other side, they did not continue far into the wood before the man stopped. Wren pulled away from him and looked around, her chest heaving. Glancing back to him with questioning eyes, she opened her mouth to speak, but he stepped forward and gently grasped the crook of her elbow in a soft, wordless command. His fingers were frigid even through her sweater—a firm and steady ice calming the adrenaline racing hot in her veins—but his touch was gentle and disarming.

She stared for a moment at where his thumb rested gently over her pulse, but when she moved to speak again, the man released her arm. He turned away and stalked toward a massive oak tree that he began to climb.

She nearly pointed out that it would be difficult for her to follow with bound hands when the bark on the tree suddenly moved before her.

Rippling.

Leaping to the forest floor, the man landed in a crouch and rose fluidly, extending his arm through the bark of the tree to pull it back like a curtain.

"After you, my lady," he said smoothly, gesturing forward with the other hand.

Wren hesitated, but at the sound of shouts echoing from the other side of the river, she ducked into the darkness of the tree's trunk.

"What in the Keebler elf is—"

Her words cut off in a scream as her legs were swept right out from under her. She flew downward at an alarming speed and then was spit out onto the soft, clay floor of what appeared to be an underground compound.

No, not a compound.

It looked like a home.

CHAPTER FOUR

*W*ren had barely moved out of the way when the man's legs and torso appeared at the bottom of the slide, but the instant his head came into view, she swung her clasped hands like a mallet toward his face. He leaned back and caught her fists in one hand, standing straight and tall before taking a menacing step forward.

His hood had fallen when he ducked, revealing a dark mop of curls flattened against his fair skin and hazel eyes that shone, the flecks of green in them fiery and wild. A smattering of freckles dusted his flawless complexion, and though his stare was hard, his features were soft—youthful, even. He did not appear to be any younger than her.

"Care to inform me why you would assault the man who just saved your life?" he asked.

Wren blinked and quickly regained her composure. "You killed someone right in front of me, how do I know I'm not next?"

Holding her fists with one hand, the man's other hand deftly untied the rope at her wrists and let it fall to the ground. "Are you or are you not one of us?" he asked stonily.

"It would be so nice to wake up right about now," Wren muttered under her breath, ignoring the question.

Not to be deterred, the man's hand tightened around hers, holding them immobile. "Do you or do you not stand opposed to the Rat King?" he demanded.

Wren's lips parted and her head spun. Every strategy she had learned over time, every tactic she knew, all the negotiations she had ever mediated, and yet she could not work out a single word in response. How could she when she was unable to stop this madness?

"And what in Trifolium's name is on your feet?" the man demanded.

Spell broken, Wren's eyes fell to her once cream, sherpa-lined slipper socks. "They're thirty-dollar socks that are now ruined, thank you very much," she retorted.

The man's eyes remained stern even while his brow furrowed. "What is a dollar sock that you must wear thirty at one time?"

Wren closed her eyes to keep from rolling them and let her shoulders sag. "That's not— Look, it's been a long night, okay?"

"'Tis morning," the man replied suspiciously, causing Wren's eyes to snap open.

"Whatever. Can you please let go of my hands? I'd really like to think for a minute, if that's okay with you, and I can't with you standing so close to me."

He released her hands, and a look of concern flashed over his face, shadowed by a hint of shame. Walking past her, he crossed the room to a table and pulled out a chair before lighting a fire in the small hearth. It was not until he had placed a cauldron of water above the kindling fire that the man turned to face her once again, his features softened.

"I apologize, my lady. Sometimes I forget in the midst of this war what it is to be a gentleman. If you will forgive me, I wish to begin again." He rushed the last line, and Wren could see the nervousness beneath his dashing facade.

Wren made a point of considering his words for a moment and then offered a single nod. She moved to the table, slid her own chair forward, and then sunk into it. "Starting over is good. Starting at the beginning is better. Who are you and what is this place?"

His brow creased deeper, and she noticed how he kept a hand on the pommel of his sword when he spoke. "You are in Breteria, my lady, in the Brumal Forest within the Kingdom of Inflamel. My name is Timothius Drossel, and I am at your service," he finished, bowing with a flourish.

Wren's pulse pounded in her ears, and she could not keep her jaw from dropping at his words. This wasn't a dream or a nightmare, it was delusion. Had she been under more stress than she realized? Could she be trapped in some sort of state? Was she hallucinating? The frantic need to escape rose in her chest, tightening her lungs and gripping her throat.

Enough was enough, she needed to wake up.

She closed her eyes, squeezing them shut before opening them again, but nothing changed. She repeated the motion, this time holding her breath and pinching her skin until she felt it break between her nails. Yet she was still in the same spot. She glanced around the room, taking in every inch, from the earth-covered ground to the dirt walls to the water boiling over the burning hearth. Her breaths began to heave, faster and faster.

"My lady, are you well?" Timothius asked, appearing at her side.

"I-I don't know," she answered honestly. What could she even say? "What..." She fumbled over the words. "What year is this?"

"It is the year three hundred eighty-six since the Fall of the Thrones," he answered.

The world spun around Wren and she swayed in her seat, then, as gentle hands caught her, there was no more.

※

"Do you think she's a form forger?" a slightly familiar voice spoke above her.

"No, she seems to have no power whatsoever," another voice answered. "But she may have encountered a foul spell."

"She seems to have no idea where she is. She even wished to know the year," the first voice added.

Wren's eyes flew open to meet a pair of bright-blue ones staring back at her. Waves of auburn hair rustled against the man's forehead when he sprang away from her. "Who the hell are you?" she demanded, sliding until her back was pressed against the wall. She surveyed the men standing before her—Timothius and another stranger—and realized that she had, at some point, been laid on a bed.

She was lying in bed with two strange men hovering over her.

Taking quick inventory of herself, her panic eased. She was, in fact, perfectly fine. The only thing missing—aside from her sanity—appeared to be her slipper socks.

"Are you sure she is not a mage?" Timothius quietly asked the man beside him. "She has invoked Hades upon us."

"I haven't invoked a thing," Wren scowled, giving him one of her most scathing glares. "And what have you done with my socks?"

She saw a light bulb go off in Timothius's head, and as she took in the small space lit only by the hearth and a few candles spaced out along the wall, she realized that light bulbs probably didn't exist here. "I removed them before laying you upon the bed," he answered. "I was curious, but there are not thirty of them. Forgive me, I was concerned they might have aided you in feeling faint. They were…quite foul. And they are not suitable for the forest. We shall find you a pair of boots."

Wren could feel the storm clouds gathering around her head. "Where are my socks?" she all but growled. She truly didn't care that much for them, but she had reached the end of her rope with the entire situation and their loss seemed to be the easiest way to vent her pent-up frustration.

Both men had enough sense to look nervous. "We, ah… We burned them, my lady," the auburn-haired man replied, not directly meeting her eyes.

"You *burned* them?" Wren shrieked, flying up off the bed at the man.

Timothius lurched forward, catching her around the middle, but the auburn-haired man still took a step back, his hand gripping the hilt of his sword.

"I think you ought to go, Elric," Timothius said in a calm but strained tone while holding the raging Wren at bay.

The man called Elric nodded, moving toward the wall. "I shall return after nightfall and bring more supplies for the lady." A rope appeared in his hand, trailing down from the ceiling, and he pulled on it, testing its hold. Using it as leverage, he planted a boot on the wall and scaled it, scrambling out of sight and leaving behind nothing but the candle sparkling through a small cloud of smoke.

Wren froze in Timothius's arms, blinking wildly at the place where a man had stood only seconds before. "How?" she all but cried.

No, she was crying. She had no control over where she was or what was happening to her, and now she couldn't even control her own emotions. Burying her face in her hands to hide her immature tears, she felt a hand awkwardly rest on her shoulder.

"It is—ah—all well, my lady," Timothius spoke.

He sounded so unsure of what to do that Wren's near sob

turned into manic laughter. "Well? How is any of this well? I believed I was dreaming, then possibly hallucinating, and now I think I've lost my mind, but none of it matters because I'm still here. With you. In my pajamas. I don't know how any of this is *well*."

Timothius released her, and she fell backward onto the bed, laughing hysterically as the wide-eyed man stared at her. She knew how crazy she looked. How crazy she sounded. She would bet money on the fact that she *was* crazy. But what did any of it matter at this point?

Burying her head in the pillow, she laughed until she felt the sting of tears again. Then she fell silent and still, not wanting to move. Not wanting to open her eyes. Not wanting to lift her head to the strange place inside the ground beneath a tree in.... What had he called this place? Infa-what? She had experienced enough. She wanted to go home.

A warm hand touched her shoulder and with a sigh of resolution, Wren turned her head.

Timothius hunched over the bedside, a steaming mug in his hand. His eyes were soft and kind when he held it out to her. "My lady, I am not sure what brought you here or what you may have encountered beyond our forest, but I want you to know that you are safe now. No harm will come to you while you are here. I will make sure of it."

Wren stared at him. His words were so earnest, so honest. A normal man would have some underlying motive, some *catch*, but this man...this *Timothius*...she could tell he meant what he said. It did not make sense, this place was even more confusing, but there was an aura of strength about him. Instinctual honor and duty. He felt responsible for her, and though there was not much that she trusted, she found herself believing him.

She sat up and accepted the mug, gingerly taking a sip. The bitterness of the herb hit the back of her throat and caused her to cough. His brow tightened again, concern stretching across his face, and she forced a smile. "This is good. Thank you. I just wasn't expecting the flavor. I— I'm more of a coffee drinker."

His eyes lit up slightly. "I have heard of the drink. It is native to Tauriellis. Is that where you are from?"

Wren hesitated before taking a smaller sip and resting the mug in her lap. "No, I'm from America."

It was Timothius's turn to look wary. "I have never heard of such a town."

"That's because it isn't a town," Wren replied. "It's a country."

Timothius shook his head. "We have but four kingdoms, my lady. How far have you traveled to come here?"

Wren mirrored his motion. "I didn't travel here. I was in my grandparents' living room, and I—" A realization struck her and she gasped. Looking around wildly, she asked, "My ornament. Where is it?"

"Ornament? My lady, I have already told you, we burned your—"

"The crystal," she said, pushing the mug into his hands and standing to search the room. "I was holding it. Where did it—"

"Ah, the crystallum. It is safe. I placed it above the hearth." He looked at her curiously. "How did you come to possess such an object?"

Wren did not answer until she laid eyes on the bright-green orb shimmering where it sat on the mantel, secured safely between two books. She let out a sigh of relief and sank back onto the bed.

"I'm sorry," she said honestly, meeting Timothius's curious eyes. "I don't know what's happening right now."

Timothius nodded. "I believe you need rest, my lady. Truly. Take your leave until supper. Allow Elric to return with some suitable clothing for you. Then, if you are ready, we will hear your tale."

It was Wren's turn to frown. "Until supper? You said it was morning."

Timothius nodded. "You were asleep for quite some time. It is midday now."

Wren's eyes widened, but this time when they welled with traitorous tears, her head also began to pound, and she laid back down in the bed.

Hours. She had been here—wherever here was—for *hours*. Had her family woken up to find her gone? Was her grandmother worried that she was missing?

"I have to get back," she said, thinking aloud.

Timothius sat the mug on the table and pulled a chair to the bedside. Though there was uneasiness in his motions, he clasped one of her hands firmly in his and the scent of suede and a dark amber surrounded her. Shutting her eyes, feeling the drowsiness set in and welcoming it with open arms, she heard him whisper, "You are safe, my lady. I will make sure you find your home."

CHAPTER FIVE

*I*t was the pangs of hunger and the rich, herby scent of roasted meat that roused Wren from her slumber next. She opened her eyes and saw what appeared to be a chicken now over the fire on a spit. The rest of the room came into focus, and Elric was there once again, sitting at the small table on the adjacent wall, opening a bottle.

Timothius stood beside the hearth with his back to her, and her eyes widened when he lifted his shirt over his head, leaving him standing before her in only breeches. Deep, grooved lines stretched in a series of scars over the expanse of his back. They stopped at his shoulders but extended well below his belt, and though they had long since healed, she could not help but feel ill wondering what trauma would leave scars like that.

Unfolding a fresh tunic, he turned, and the air caught in Wren's lungs. He was beautiful, his entire torso sculpted in lean muscle, like he had been built in the likeness of a statue. In fact, he put every statue she had seen in any museum to shame.

He tossed the shirt over his head, poking it through the v-neckline, and Wren closed her eyes, feigning sleep, until he spoke from across the room. "Are you well, my lady?"

She cursed herself but yawned and stretched as if just waking. "I am. But I'm starving."

Timothius continued to tuck his shirt in, glancing up to smirk at her, letting her know without words that—much like her own—his eyes had missed nothing.

It was Elric who replied, "The bird is nearly done. May I invite you to some wine while we wait?"

Finally, a language she spoke. "I would love some," Wren exhaled, rising from the bed.

She took the seat across from Elric at the table, and he poured her a glass. She could tell from the smell that, much like the tea, it was highly fermented and strong, but she didn't care one bit and drained the glass.

The sight of both men staring at her nearly made her laugh, yet when she recalled her already concerning emotional range, she swallowed it back down. "So Elric, is it?" she asked, extending her hand. "I know this is probably a little late, but it's nice to meet you."

Elric stared at her hand for a moment before taking it and tipping his brow forward. "I am pleased to make your acquaintance, my lady."

Wren pumped his hand once and released it, the look of confusion on his face bringing a small smile to her lips. "So, are you a magician or acrobat or something? Belong to a traveling circus or stage show, maybe? Because you climbed the wall over there like it was nothing. You were there and then you were gone."

The silence and wide, discerning eyes that answered her were more sobering than the reality that she was the odd man out. She was the splotch of paint dripped from a brush at the corner of a canvas, not meant to belong but placed there nonetheless. The thought chilled her, and it could have been the wine already affecting her addled brain and empty stomach, or the weight of silence in the room, that dissolved the bitter pill of acceptance on her tongue.

Wren glanced down at the cup in her hands, the taste of mead thick on her lips. She stared at her feet resting in the cool dirt of a home beneath a tree. She smelled the earth around her, felt the place where a sword had been pressed to her throat and her back had broken her fall. And then she finally raised her face to the living, breathing people before her and spoke the words she was loath to admit out loud. "This is somehow real, isn't it?"

The men glanced at each other again before fixing her with nearly identical stares. "We are real," answered Elric. "But to say we did not wonder the same of you would be a falsehood."

"Oh, I am real. I have a real family, a real job, a real life. I just don't know how to explain, well, anything. I don't know how I came here. I don't know how to tell you where I'm from. I don't even know where to start," she admitted, not knowing what else to say. She always knew what to say. And words failing her made her even more uneasy.

Timothius pulled a stool up next to Elric and sat. Giving the same reassuring smile first to Elric and then to Wren, he said, "Then we shall start at the beginning. What should we call thee, my lady?"

Wren smiled then, shoulders relaxing. "My name is Florence Klaver. But I'd like you to call me Wren."

❋

WREN HAD TRAVELED OVERSEAS ONCE on business. In preparation, she had attempted to learn enough of the language to communicate on her own. However, her regional dialect had not been quite accurate, and she'd found herself grasping wildly for common descriptions and ways to explain what she was trying to say without using words.

Telling her story to the men before her was nearly the same experience.

"So you were residing in your grandmother's village two moons ago to celebrate Yuletide when a great wind broke the crystallum and you fell asleep to then awaken within our forest?" Elric's eyes were so keen to understand that Wren had to bite her tongue to keep from laughing at his innocent expression, despite his refined posture.

"Close enough," she replied. "And why do you keep calling it a crystallum?"

"A crystallum is a relic formed from many strands of magic," he replied. "It is sacred to families and often passed down. Some carry no more than sentimental meaning, but others contain things that may only be released by the one who carries it."

Wren blinked slowly. "I don't.... It's just an ornament. It was a gift from my grandfather to my grandmother on their first Christmas."

Elric stood then, crossing the room to the mantle and peering closely at the ornament. Carefully, delicately, as if afraid it might bite, he ran the tip of his finger along the etched clovers. He stepped back and turned to Wren. "Has your grandmother always been in possession of this?"

Wren shrugged. "I would assume so. She said my grandfather saw them hand crafted in a village he was stationed near during the war. So it was made, given to him, then gifted to her."

"And then to you," Elric confirmed, and Wren nodded.

He made eye contact with Timothius and gave him a small nod. Timothius sighed, then turned to Wren. "Has it always looked as it does now?"

Wren's shoulders stiffened. "What do you mean?"

"Has the crystallum always been the same color and carried the same markings? Or has it adapted over time?"

"It— Well, I'm honestly not sure I ever saw it on the tree. But when it fell, before I ended up here, it wasn't green. It was red."

The men exchanged glances again, and Wren grew impatient. "What are you not saying? I can see you, you know. I'm sitting right here."

Elric turned back to the fire and started to clear away the remnants of their dinner. Timothius stared at a worn spot on the table for a moment and then finally spoke.

"It is not that we seek to keep things from you. It is simply that we are trying to make sense of this. I can say with certainty that I believe you did not come from here, though I'm unsure how. Yuletide occurred almost a fortnight ago."

Wren's brow furrowed. "Isn't that like two nights?"

Timothius shook his head. "A fortnight is two weeks, my lady."

Wren's lips parted. "I lost almost two weeks?"

Timothius smiled wanly. "I fear you've lost far more than that. We believe that the crystallum you carry—when it broke— summoned you here, but for what purpose none can say."

"But where is *here*?" Wren asked, slightly exasperated. "You don't understand Christmas or vacation or even my socks, but I don't understand anything you're saying either. The year? 386? The Roman Empire hasn't even fallen yet, and you've referred to thrones and a king and magic. You're living in a tree? None of this feels real, it all feels like... like a...."

"A tale?" finished Elric.

"Yes. A very tall tale."

The men glanced at each other. "There is...one explanation," the auburn-haired man said slowly.

"Elric," Timothius said, tone warning.

He raised a hand. "I know. But it bears cautioning her."

"Cautioning me of what?" asked Wren, looking between them both.

Neither man moved to answer, but Wren would not be deterred. "Look, I know you don't trust me. I can't blame you, I don't trust you either. But you said I was safe here," she said, staring pointedly at Timothius. "So am I or not?"

He sighed, and with barely a movement, nodded to Elric.

His friend inhaled deeply. "There is one explanation for your crystallum. But it in itself is a tale. A tall one, as you say. A legend."

"A legend about a Christmas ornament?" Wren snarked, unable to keep her tone congenial.

"Crystallum were used widely when the stars walked freely in our realm," Elric pressed on. "The stronger the magic, the more power contained in the crystallum. Each one was unique to the individual it was created for. Some served menial purposes. Honing skill during a hunt or allowing crops to double in size, but others had larger uses. Protection, transportation, things of that nature. One has not been seen since the Thrones fell."

"So we find some stars to break it and send me back?" Wren asked skeptically.

"I am afraid it is not so simple," Elric replied. "Forging a crystallum required more than one. That same number would be needed to unmake such a relic in order to find its purpose. There is no telling how many would need to gather in order to perform the unmaking. And the stars no longer gather here."

Wren frowned, thinking for a moment. "It fell and shattered. And when I picked it up, everything spun, and the next thing I knew I was lying in a forest. If I break it again, it should take me back home, right?"

Elric considered this and rose, crossing the room to the hearth and gazing intently at the ornament still secured on the mantel. "May I?" he asked, turning his attention back to Wren.

She nodded, and he carefully lifted the ornament. Allowing it to dangle by the hook pressed between the pads of his fingers, he raised it to the light and gazed into it intently. Then—to Wren's horror—he threw it directly into the fire.

"What are you doing?" she screamed, jumping up so quickly that she hit the table and nearly knocked the bottle of wine into Timothius's lap.

Elric said nothing but grabbed a poker from the hearth and used it to roll the ornament back out of the fire.

Wren snatched it up off the floor, cradling it to her before realizing that it was cool to the touch. She looked at it closely. The hook had been lost to the flames, but the ornament itself was untouched. Not a single marking was flawed, every piece of glitter was in place, and the surface held not so much as a dimple or scratch.

With all her might, she threw it to the floor. The ornament landed with a loud *crack*...and then it rolled harmlessly away. Timothius picked it up this time, eyeing both Wren and Elric incredulously, and gazed at it for a long moment. Finally, he handed it back to Wren. "It is flawless."

Wren felt the question rise within her, but she refused to ask it again and turned to Elric instead. "I'm tired of asking how. Tell me what I need to do to use this thing. What do I need to do to get back home?"

Elric pursed his lips. "If it is the relic I believe it is, then it will respond to you alone. What magic it contains, that is to be seen. We cannot know for sure, but should it break again and reveal a new layer underneath, it would be safe to assume that each magic must be broken to reveal its full purpose."

"So when they all break it will take me home?" Wren confirmed.

Elric gave a small nod. "That would be my hope. However, there is one person who may know for certain."

Wren felt Timothius stiffen more than she saw him do so, and she glanced at him, matching the level of suspicion he was using to regard her. "A journey north would be a great risk. She cannot fall into the wrong hands," he said, addressing Elric.

"What do you mean *wrong hands?*" Wren interjected. "Does this have to do with the man you killed thinking I was a rebel?"

Elric's eyes widened. "You killed a—"

"Yes, my lady, it does," Timothius said over Elric. "You have managed to find yourself in a kingdom balancing unrest between crown and country upon the edge of a sword. Here, you are guilty until proven loyal. A risk until your side has been declared. It is no place to trust anyone, let alone strangers."

"Which is why we should help her in whatever way we can," Elric said, addressing him. "What harm can there be in accompanying her to the Guardian if it is a means for her to leave this place?"

Wren listened to the men bicker back and forth. She knew it would be in her best interest to take in their words, to analyze what was being said and learn more of her surroundings and the company she kept, yet she could not focus beyond the cold nagging in her chest. It could have been mistaken for homesickness, but the old familiar pang reminded her of every summer spent in a different place. Its chill brought back the memory of each friend, of her own family, remembering her long enough to forget her again. She had made something of her life, accomplished all that she had, leaning on self-reliance and her own instinct. She had learned to be bold when others were passive, and while some would say her risks were aggressive, if she was successful in the end what did it matter? They wouldn't remember it anyway.

"You're as much a stranger to me as I am to you," she said, talking above the men and bringing their disagreement to heel. "If you offer me protection, if you ask me to trust you, then I'm going to do the same in return. This is a risk I am willing to take. The question is will you give me the same chance, or am I doing this myself?"

Timothius considered her words for a long moment before

finally standing down. "Well then, my lady, I would take your rest and ready yourself. Tomorrow we shall venture on a rather long walk."

CHAPTER SIX

*T*he next morning arrived with a hearty breakfast of eggs on fresh bread, and though Wren longed for a proper shower, she decided that if she had to choose between being clean or well fed, she would happily accept the latter. She had just finished washing her face in a bowl of tepid water when the men excused themselves, leaving behind a parcel of clothing and stating they would return with the final supplies needed for their journey.

Wren scooped the last bit of eggs from the plate into her mouth and then crossed the room to unwrap the clothing. She remembered her grandmother teasing her once about wearing so many layers and couldn't help but wonder what she would think if she saw this ensemble.

There was a short linen shift with thin straps that she realized were meant to suffice as undergarments, but there was a snowball's chance in hell that she would be giving up her underwear and bra any time soon. The layer that came next appeared to be of the same color and material, though longer and with capped sleeves. Next came a heavier dress of dark gray with sleeves that fit snugly over the preceding layers, followed by a thick, woolen dress in a slightly darker shade of gray that cinched her in nicely at the waist before flaring out to her ankles. The skirt's long slits made it easy for her to move while also allowing her underskirts to rustle gracefully as she walked about, and she couldn't help but twirl like a child playing dress-up.

The neckline was too wide to hide the straps of her bra, so she reluctantly shimmied out of it, pleasantly surprised at the way the layers held her in place.

The scrape of metal against wood prompted Wren to turn and Timothius appeared at the bottom of the slide. "Here," he said, jostling three knapsacks to the side in order to hand her a pair of ankle boots. "They should fit well, but if not, please let me know. We may have another stashed around the forest somewhere."

The boots fit perfectly, but when she turned to face him again, he frowned. "Your hair is...uneven. And oddly colored. I have never seen gold spun into brown in such a way."

Wren reached up, tugging on the ends that just brushed her shoulders, and returned his frown. "What do you mean it's uneven? It's a bob, it's supposed to be shorter in the back, longer in the front. And I love my color. I pay a lot of money for it, thank you very much."

A smile teased his lips. "It accents your face perfectly; however it will be noticed. It is not common for women to have more than one color or length in their hair."

Wren hesitated, realizing that it had not been a criticism, but merely an observation. "Should I...cover it?"

Timothius shook his head vehemently. "Never. Never hide a source of your pride to suit another. Carry it proudly and with your head held high."

"Right, but in this case also keep a cape on at all times," said Elric, appearing out of nowhere to Wren's left and causing her to jump. "I'd recommend keeping your hood up as well. It is not for lack of pride or beauty, but we cannot have you coming to harm before we learn how to aid your return home. This world is no place for a woman with her entire life waiting ahead for her."

Wren blinked, looking between them slowly. Why *were* they going out of their way to help her?

"Do you two always know all of the right things to say?" she prodded. "Because some would call it fake."

Both men only stared at her, confusion marking their eyes.

"Fake," she repeated, eyes darting between the set of sapphire blue and flecked brown. "Disingenuous?"

"You will find, my lady, that we always speak truth," Elric replied smoothly. "Which is why *I* did not deign to comment on your hair."

It took a moment for his words to sink in, but when they did, she whipped around. "Wait a minute," she snapped, but he was already gone.

"How does he do that?" she asked Timothius. "Can you put a bell on him or something? Maybe a leash?"

He cracked a smile. "Elric has a good heart. He is a historian of sorts and has seen much in his days—more than any should have to. But what he says is true. And you will come to find that just as much may be said in unspoken words as those that are voiced."

He turned away, and Wren watched him pull a long, spindly vine off the wall. Instead of plucking it all the way, however, he gave it a tug, like a tassel, and a ladder unfurled from above. "I will go first and ensure that all is clear. Stay close, but do not leave the tree until I confirm. If there is trouble you must return underground."

Wren nodded but did not move as she continued to stare at the ladder, a cold anxiety seeping into her bones.

"My lady?"

She blinked out of her stupor, realizing that whatever had

taken ahold of her was also displayed on her face. "I— I'm right behind you."

Timothius paused with his hand still on the ladder's rung and turned to face her fully. "I would say that you have nothing to fear, but you have already seen that is untrue. What is it that concerns you most?"

Wren was surprised by the simplistic kindness in his question. He was earnest, yet not curious nor prying, and the way he stood before her with his entire attention fixed on her led her to be honest. "Most? I'm not sure. I don't understand where I am. I was attacked by masked guards. I watched you kill a man and then let you lead me to an underground house where you fed me, gave me clothes, and promised help. Somehow, I'm not afraid, but I don't know who or what I can trust. I don't know how to prepare myself for what comes next. And being unprepared? That is what scares me."

Timothius nodded, then asked, "Is there a weapon in which you feel adequately trained? Anything from your world that may be useful to you here?"

Wren laughed. "I'm horrible with sharp objects and the only gun I've ever fired had foam darts, not that you even know what that means. Or probably what a gun is." She paused then, remembering something. "When I was younger, I spent every summer at camp. We learned a lot of things, different skills. I loved archery. It was something I always had fun doing."

Timothius moved in broad steps across the room to a wardrobe and swung the doors open to reveal an array of weapons. He unhooked a bow and a quiver full of arrows from inside the door and returned to Wren, holding the strap out from the quiver. "May I?"

Wren nodded, and he slipped it over her head, allowing her to tuck one arm through the loop. He then tightened it across her chest and secured the quiver to rest firmly between her shoulder blades.

Handing her the bow, he paused before releasing it to her. "I cannot tell you who to trust. I would not ask you to take the word of a stranger and a murderer, even if it was one who sought to save your life. I cannot remove your fear, but what I can do is give you a means to protect yourself against who or whatever may come against you. Use it with confidence."

"Thank you," Wren said around the lump in her throat. Moving away quickly to hide the rawness creeping into her eyes, she crossed the room to the mantle and removed the ornament. She dropped it into the deeper pocket of her skirt and then turned back to face Timothius fully and with more confidence than she had felt since arriving in this strange new world. "Let's do this."

CHAPTER SEVEN

*T*heir small company had only walked a handful of miles before the air began to bite at Wren's cheeks, its chill devouring her ears from the top down and causing her nose and eyes to drip. It was mere moments later that the sky high above them—still concealed by the treetops—started to drop flakes of snow in large wafers, covering the ground and resting on the hoods of the men to either side of her like confetti during a New Year's Eve celebration.

Is it the New Year at home yet?

She pushed the thought away and focused on the present and what she was grateful for—and right now, more than ever, it was for her boots. The snow collected in drifts that grew higher the farther they traveled, making her steps more difficult. It wasn't until she adjusted her hood and looked forward that she truly absorbed the world around her.

It was beautiful. The wood felt like Christmas, or at least the idyllic white Christmas that children dreamed up and songs were written about. The way the snow fell in perfect intervals, how it nestled onto the boughs of the pines surrounding them, made it feel as though she were walking in a winter fantasy. Not a park or a wonderland—a pure, unadulterated fantasy. A daydream full of myth and magic.

Suddenly aware of her surroundings, Wren glanced behind them and was shocked to find that they were leaving no footprints. Even now, every time her foot left the ground, the snow would shift within its shadow, leaving not a single trace of her shoe behind.

"Are these boots magic?" she asked, her voice sounding louder in the barren wood than she had intended.

"You can say that," replied Elric, his tone hushed and his head moving in wide sweeps across the surrounding forest.

"How does it work?"

"Yes, E, how do the magic boots work?" asked Timothius, and Wren's eyes narrowed at the mirth both in his voice and on his face as he glanced past her at his friend.

Elric sighed. "They were formed with or are blessed by magic. That is how an item becomes magical, which I'm fairly certain we already covered while discussing your...item."

"You know someone with magic, then?"

It was Elric's turn to smile mischievously. "I don't, but T does."

Wren's head whipped back to Timothius just in time to watch him school his features from a glare into a look of boredom. "I did in my early years. In any case, we should be more silent. You know better than to engage with small talk in the middle of the wood, E."

Wren nodded, looking back at the ground before her, tracking her own movement across the earth even if the snow did not. A smile toyed at her lips. "T and E. Very cute nicknames."

She felt the uneasiness more than she saw it, but when she glanced back and forth at the men, she was met with puzzled, confused, and even slightly frustrated concentration.

Elric spoke first. "What do you mean when you say 'nickname'?"

Wren allowed a small smile, keeping it contained so as not to embarrass the men further. They were clearly leaders, strong and seldom unnerved by what they didn't know. But she could already tell that Elric was the more curious of the two, even if Timothius's attention was also on her, awaiting an answer. "A nickname is something you call a friend. It's a short form of their name. For instance, Wren is my nickname, though only my grandmother uses it. My real name is Florence."

"We use our first letters for safety," explained Elric. "But why would a friend not call you Florence if it is your given name?"

"Because I hate it," Wren responded flippantly before thinking for a moment. "And a nickname is something you call someone close to you. Something personal. Something informal that says 'I care about you' in just one word."

Elric nodded, a smile tickling his lips. "I believe I like that."

Timothius huffed. "You will have plenty of time to educate E in the ways of your world once we reach our destination. And trust me, if there is anything he loves second best in life, it is learning. But if I may remind you both, we are traipsing through the wood and wish to remain undetected. Further conversation that does not involve pertinent information or a request to relieve yourself must wait."

Elric fell silent, but Wren narrowed her eyes. "Yes, Dad," she muttered.

Timothius shot her a look out of the corner of his eye, but Wren pretended not to see. And she especially pretended not to notice the way his eyes danced with amusement, though his tone tried to be firm.

They stopped only briefly for a bite to eat and then continued on, the sun soon falling in the sky and plunging the wood into a cold so bitter the very air burned in Wren's lungs.

"We shall stop to rest until the sun is once again in the sky," said Timothius, his eyes perusing the trees before landing on a small clearing beneath a canopy of branches. "It is not safe to travel this forest at night. Not even the guards would dare."

Wren slowed beside him and released a sigh of relief. The first day of walking was done and she was more than ready to stop moving. Timothius looked down at her, a small grin tipping up the corner of his lips. He reached out and gently grasped the crook of her elbow, guiding her to the base of a tree where he produced a blanket from his pack and handed it to her.

"And how long until we reach the other woods?" she asked, sinking into the snow and resting her back against the trunk.

"The Elfin Domain is on the northern boundary of the Vernal Wood, nearly a sennight away," he replied, packing down a portion of the snow with his boot. "If we make haste, I dare say we might cross the highway in two nights' time. Once we are well into the Vernal Wood, it will be safer to make a proper camp."

Wren stared in silence at the snow, searching her brain for the meaning of sennight and coming up empty.

"A sennight is half of a fortnight," Elric said quietly beside her.

She glanced at him and then through the dimly lit forest to Timothius who had walked a few paces away and was stripping worn bark off a nearby tree. "Thank you," she murmured.

Elric nodded. "It is...not easy to face so much unknown. At least I would imagine it that way. You show much courage, if I may say so. Though my word means little as a stranger."

Wren couldn't help but smile. "There is strength in knowledge. And it is hard. This is not exactly my forte here, in the woods, lost somewhere in time."

Elric returned a grin. "I would like to offer you a bargain. If you teach me of your world—of your time—I will teach you of ours. For as long as you are here."

Wren considered the man before her. He carried maturity like a mantle upon his shoulders, but the boyish gleam in his brilliant cerulean eyes made his face light up with youth. "I think you have yourself a deal," she replied.

Timothius returned and within a few moments he had used the bark as kindling for a small fire. He fed twigs to the flame, tenting branches above it with Elric beside him and Wren opposite the fire, their bodies encasing its warmth and blocking its light from the rest of the forest.

"Shouldn't we be afraid of the fire attracting unwanted attention?" Wren asked around the blanket cocooning her body, the scent of amber and suede warming her from the inside out.

Timothius shook his head. "Nothing dares traverse these woods at night and we will be back on the move well before daybreak. Which is why you should rest now."

"But won't the snow eventually melt and put out the fire?" she asked.

Timothius eyed her keenly over the flames, and an odd sensation passed across her skin, as if she were being studied under a microscope. "You truly are not from here," he said finally, musing almost to himself.

Wren found she could not voice words, the familiarity in his tone clogging her throat with emotion. It was the same resigned acceptance she still felt surveying the world around her, filled with shock and disbelief, yet also wonder. She brushed the feeling aside and shook her head proudly, even with glistening eyes.

Something akin to softness flickered in the depth of Timothius's eyes but he blinked it away and nodded in stoic acknowledgment. "We *will* ensure your safe passage home, my lady. You have my word."

"But you do need to take your rest," Elric interjected. "We still have far to travel before we can find answers."

"I will try. It's just…. It is hard for me to slow my brain

down. I have too much in my head, too many things I'm thinking about. I can't relax." She realized how vulnerable her words were and rushed to add, "I'm sorry, I'm rambling."

They glanced at each other in bewilderment and then Elric spoke. "There is nothing to apologize for, my lady. My K, she says very similar things. It is natural and the way you were formed as a person. There is no shame in that."

Her brow furrowed. "K? Who is she?"

Elric's eyes practically radiated warmth. "She is my greatest love. We are to wed soon."

Wren couldn't help but smile, recognizing the same pride in his face that she had always seen reflected in her grandparents' when they spoke of each other. "Will I meet her where we are going?"

The light still burned, but a shadow passed over it, dimming Elric's eyes subtly. "I am afraid not. But I look forward to telling her of you. She would have liked you very much, I know it."

Wren turned to Timothius who was poking the fire absent-mindedly. "Do you have a great love, Sir T?"

Timothius snorted and snapped a twig to feed the flames. "I do not. My life is a solitary one. It is best for me to remain that way."

Wren didn't know why but the thought made her sad. "That is a hard choice to make," she said softly. She understood it—knew it intimately—but it was never something she would choose for herself. Not voluntarily.

Timothius's eyes met her own over the fire. "I did not say it was a choice, my lady. I said it was best."

Her skin prickled and she found that neither one of them were ready to break their stare, each recognizing something in the other.... A vulnerability they'd never dare to admit. A truth too hard for words.

"Tell me about your K," Wren finally said, diverting her eyes to Elric.

He hesitated. "I must be wary of what I say. Even the trees have ears. I can say, however, she eases her brain with books. Her stories sing her to sleep."

Wren smiled. "Well, unless you have a book hidden in your cloak, that isn't much help to me."

Elric's eyes gleamed once again. "Not in my cloak, but in my memory, I have stored a few, should you wish to hear one."

Wren tilted her head. "What kind of stories?"

Elric leaned back with an exhale, gazing to the tops of the trees as if musing. "'The Age of Stars'? Or 'The King of Wishes'?"

Wren's eyes widened a fraction. "How many bedtime stories do you have committed to memory?"

"Some call them stories. Others history. A few say legend. Me?" he shrugged. "I simply like them."

Wren laughed softly. "Okay, then. 'The Age of Stars'?"

Elric smiled. "A personal favorite of mine. The Age of Stars was the first age of Breteria. The founders of this world, the Awduron, all woke upon the realm at once, save one—those born from stars. Legend states that when the five strands of magic and the stars collided in the heavens to create our land, the humans who still believed in magic were caught up with them. They awoke beside the Awduron and were called the Elérynd, and while magic lived within their hearts and souls, they possessed no magic to sustain their life here. The stars then intervened on their behalf, coming down from the sky to provide stability for the Elérynd to live and thrive. The stars were given the name Isteriaeth, for they were the embodiment of magic and a gift to the world. Some were powerful stewards, carrying all five forms of magic. Others bore a few, but most only one." He paused, and when he spoke again his voice was wistful. "Breteria was a much different place when the stars walked upon the world."

"What are the five strands of magic?" Wren asked, thankful that the darkness hid the embarrassment burning on her cheeks. Her curiosity piqued at the connection, but she couldn't help but feel foolish. Discussing star-beings and magic was not something she imagined she'd be doing...ever.

Elric sat up now, excitement dancing in his eyes with the light from the flames on his face. "Well there is atmospheric magic, which gives the ability to conjure items out of the air itself. There is magic of form, bestowed upon beings able to forge their form into whatever they wish. There is elemental magic which bestows power over the four elements. And then temporal which defies time, halting it and bending it to the user's will."

A long pause filled the wood before Wren finally spoke. "I know I'm tired, but that was only four."

Elric shifted in his spot, rolling a small ball of snow, watching it grow. "The fifth form...is tenebrescent. Dark magic. It is the strand we do not readily speak of—and the one that ushered in the end of the Age of Stars and brought about the fall of the Trifolium Thrones."

Wren felt the weight of his final five words, as if the mention of it caused the entire wood around them to still in solemn respect. She wanted to ask more about it, but at the same time didn't want to know the tale that made the very air itself mourn.

She hadn't realized her eyes were heavy until they drifted shut, but even closed she could see the flakes of snow dancing before her, and just beyond them, a sandstone castle with banners waving from four turrets.

Banners that bore the same gold clover etched upon her ornament.

CHAPTER EIGHT

The sky was still black above them when they swept fresh snow over the remains of the campfire. The flakes fell steadier, and although the sun was now high in the sky, the cold felt as if it were seeping into Wren's brain—clouding and sealing it in a mist of fine frost. She did not force words, concentrating all her energy on moving the limbs that were beginning to stiffen both from the dive in temperature and the full day of walking they already had behind them.

She stopped when she was told to stop, ate when food was slipped into her hand, and drank when she was reminded to. It felt strange placing her well-being in the hands of two men she'd met only days prior. Even if they were kind and likable, it felt irresponsible to trust them. Yet she recognized that there would be no surviving this forest on her own. She resolved to keep her guard up, but also accepted that more than ever before she needed them to survive.

The sun had set once again and this time the trees were thinner, allowing faint moonlight to illuminate the snow around them. Wren's body screamed in protest, begging her to pause for the night with each step she struggled to take through the ever-deepening snow. If she didn't know any better, she'd think they were venturing farther into the woods—or worse yet, somehow deeper into winter.

A familiar hold on her elbow brought her to a halt, and when she opened her mouth to speak, Timothius threw her a warning glance. His eyes were hard, the same unmovable stone they had been the day he killed the rat guard. They flicked to Elric who was walking ahead, and she watched his steps slow, each one made carefully on silent boots. It was then that Wren heard heavy footfalls crunching in the snow beyond them, their weight shaking flakes from the boughs overhead.

Timothius moved in front of her, slipping her from one hand to the other behind his back. He strode gingerly toward a slightly thicker copse of trees to their left, guarding her, and never once letting her go.

His fingers wrapped around the hilt of his sword, prompting her to draw an arrow from the quiver on her back. She could barely feel her fingers, but she slid the bow from her shoulder to her hands and managed to nock an arrow despite her stiff and aching joints.

Now to see how much skill she had retained after nearly twenty years.

Elric appeared by Timothius's side, and though he was weaponless, he shielded her body with his own. He slowly slipped his gloves off, tucking them away in a pocket beneath his cloak.

Timothius angled to face him, and Wren realized that, with their backs to the trees, they had effectively hidden her. She didn't know who or what was coming, or what could prompt such a strong reaction from them, but she found herself wishing once again that this were somehow only a nightmare.

The steps drew closer. So close that Wren could feel the

THE CADENCE OF CROWNS

presence just outside of their sight. So close that Timothius silently unsheathed his sword. So close that Elric stepped back and leaned close to her ear.

"Stay behind us. Mind your aim, but do not hesitate to use that."

A horrifying scream, wild like the cries of a coyote or the screech of an owl, broke them apart before Wren could answer. Instinctively, she dropped her bow and ground her palms against her ears. The sharp, shrill violence of the sound, like long fingernails being drug down a chalkboard, sliced into her head and made her jaw ache.

"Get down!" yelled Elric the same moment that Timothius surged forward, swinging his sword in an upward arc.

Wren fell to her knees in a pile of skirts, the snow shocking the skin of her calves and seeping into her clothes. When she looked up to see what possessed Timothius to swing with such force, a scream lodged in her throat.

Something akin to a werewolf, only less wolf and more monster, towered over Timothius. Its eyes were yellow and slitted like a cat's, its ears—tall, pointed, and cylindrical— resembled an owl's, and it had a long and pointed wolf's muzzle. Its gangly arms and legs were covered in fur dark as the night, and extending from each of its ten fingers and toes were taloned claws, yellow like bone but honed into points sharper than any blade she knew their company possessed.

And its eyes were locked on her.

Elric spun in front of Wren, and the world around her fell into darkness. She would have been panicked were she not instantly surrounded by the scent of cardamom. It tugged at her memory, and when she inhaled, she realized that it smelled faintly like—

"Do not move," Elric muttered in her ear, the weight of his hands releasing the snow-dampened fabric. He had thrown his cloak over her. She held her breath, but the sound of Timothius's sword clanging off claw and the screams of the monster caused oxygen to sneak out.

Desperate to see what was happening around her yet not wanting to draw attention back to herself, Wren closed her eyes tight. She felt helpless, like a child lost in the fray, separated from safety by a chaos she could not escape.

I want to go home. I just want to go home.

A thud shuddered the ground and something heavy collided with Wren's back, knocking the air from her lungs and sending her sprawling in the snow. The impact tore the cloak away, revealing her to the night, and when she whipped her head around, she was met with the sight of Timothius sliding across the snow, Elric's cloak pinned beneath his body. The monster had thrown him and was now bearing down on them.

Or it would be, were it not for Elric standing between her and the beast. Arms straight and hands outstretched in front of his body, he faced the creature and uttered words Wren did not understand. Her eyes widened at the low glow radiating from his palms, illuminating the fine mist they were emitting into the air. No, not mist. Was that...*dust?*

The monster fought against it, staggering forward on its bowed legs, swiping at the air as if for purchase in the fight. It advanced one horrible bound at a time, but still Elric held his ground.

Looking back to Timothius, she saw his eyes widen. "Do something!" she shrieked.

He shook his head. "I cannot get between them. His magic is too unpredictable."

Wren shook her head in disbelief, and when beast took another step closer to Elric, she snapped into action. Snatching up the bow, she retrieved a new arrow from her back and nocked it against the string. Exhaling slowly, she raised it, pulled the string back until her thumb reached her eye, and then, after taking careful aim, she let the arrow fly.

Straight and true, it dug into the animal's core, too low to have pierced the heart or lungs. Stringing another arrow, she let it fly, lodging it squarely beside the other. The animal screeched, its maw foaming and eyes shining red.

Taking a risk, she nocked her final arrow, and tracking the beast carefully, she let go and watched with satisfaction as the arrow found its mark in the beast's throat.

It stopped, and though it didn't fall, it did not advance either. The magic dust surrounded it, twisting around its limbs and cinching like a tourniquet. The monster dropped forward on all fours, resembling a wolf now but easily the length of a sedan. Its eyes found Wren and spittle flew when it howled. She saw the hunger in its face, the horrors it promised, and when it cried out for her again, she slid backward in the snow.

Elric's magic vanished in half a heartbeat and, as if shot from a cannon, the beast lurched for Wren. She screamed in panic, but Timothius stepped in front of her, and in one swift motion, cleaved the monster's head from its shoulders.

The body collapsed in a heap, its head lolling across the ground, and where blood should have stained the snow thick darkness seeped through the frost and vanished from sight.

The forest fell silent once more. Wren tore her eyes away from the lifeless mass before her and stared breathlessly at the slightly winded Timothius, who broke her gaze only to glance at Elric.

"Well. So much for not being tracked," he remarked. "We won't be hiding this mess."

Elric smirked. "I'm afraid not all of it. But we will do our best and then get far from here. That carcass is sure to attract more wealdwolves. Or worse, soldiers." He moved to the body and started to flex his hands, twisting up what appeared to be a cloud of dust filled with strands of glittering light that entranced Wren.

"My lady." Timothius's voice snapped her out of her stupor, and she looked to where his hand was extended to her. She took it and rose, but though she loosened her grip, he did not. "Are you all right?"

She nodded. "I— I think. What was that thing?"

"A wealdwolf," Timothius confirmed, his voice grim. "They haunt the Deorc Weald. The forest beyond Inflamel City."

"Is that near here?" she asked faintly.

Timothius shook his head, his eyes betraying nothing. "It is not."

"Then why was it here?"

"I'm afraid I do not know," he replied.

Wren swallowed, and she didn't know why, but she dropped her voice to only a whisper between them. "It kept looking for me. I could feel it staring at me, like it wanted me."

Timothius slowly nodded. "I believe you are right."

Wren met his eyes. "But why?"

He was silent for a long moment then finally released her hand. "I do not know, my lady. But I fear the magic your crystallum contains runs much deeper than we thought."

The words resounded in Wren's mind, and something clicked into place. "You!" she snapped, rounding on Elric who froze with the monster's head suspended in midair between them. Its gaping mouth faced Wren, and she gagged a little, walking a wide circle around it to make eye contact with him. "You have magic."

Elric looked as if he wanted to deny it but then realized that the magic in question was holding up half of the creature in front of him.

"So you are a-a *star*?"

He pursed his lips and bit back a cough, but Timothius was

the first to burst out in laughter, startling Wren and causing her to turn on her heel.

"Is something funny? I must be missing something because I haven't laughed once since showing up here. I've been chased and tied up and nearly eaten, and I am just not finding the humor in any of it."

Timothius was still chuckling as he yanked the wealdwolf's body toward a thicket of bushes, but Elric recovered faster. "We cannot discuss this here," he chided. The authority in his tone gave Wren pause, and with a flick of a finger, the wealdwolf's head vanished into thin air.

Her jaw dropped at the effortless power, but before she could speak, Elric was directly in front of her. "The crystallum. Where is it?" he asked in a low voice.

She dug a hand into her pocket, feeling the orb immediately —but her relief was short-lived as her fingers were once again met with shards of glass. Yanking it from her pocket, she examined it closely but found that other than now being royal blue and etched with swirls of silver and gold, it was perfectly intact.

"I guess this happened when we were attacked," she said hesitantly.

Elric shook his head. "I would venture to say this is what led the wealdwolf to us."

"But how? We were just walking, nothing happened to break it."

He paused, staring at it intently, and then his eyes returned to study Wren with concern floating in their depths. "I do not know. But I believe whatever magic binds it is also binding something within you. I think you are the key to either unlocking or breaking each other."

Wren stood in disbelief. "You're saying you think that I have *magic?*"

Elric hushed her, looking around to ensure they were still alone. "I would not endanger you in such a way," he murmured, his eyes wide and earnest. "Magic is not safe to possess. Not in Breteria."

A dozen questions flooded Wren's mind, but they stood quietly until Timothius returned. After covering the scuffle and any sign that remained of the wealdwolf's untimely demise, they continued on in silence. Only this time, Wren kept a firm hold on her bow.

CHAPTER NINE

*W*ren's entire body begged for rest by the time she came to a stop beside Elric and Timothius at a thick tree line. They had walked without stopping and barely any speaking since the wealdwolf attack to reach the highway, which turned out to be no more than a dirt road that would have barely accommodated two vehicles side by side on a modern roadway.

The flakes of snow floating past her and out of the Brumal Forest melted on impact when they touched the ground, and when Wren surveyed the trees beyond, she noticed the wood was devoid of snow and the trees bare save for vibrant green buds curling from their gray limbs.

She blinked a few times, unnerved at how she was standing in the middle of winter and gazing at spring, but the sound of boots pounding the ground quickly interrupted her thoughts.

A group of soldiers marched past, their strides long as they scanned the surrounding forests. Like the ones she had already encountered, these men wore full face masks, each one in the likeness of a—

"Rat," she whispered.

"Mouse, actually," murmured Timothius. "It is their king who is the rat."

"Why do they wear masks but you and E do not?" Wren asked, meeting his eyes and suddenly realizing how close they stood, the fog of their breath mingling in the air between them.

Timothius seemed to realize their proximity at the same time. His eyes dropped briefly to her lips, and a chill ran across Wren's skin that had nothing to do with the frigid weather.

"We are not what you'd refer to as loyal subjects of the king," Elric answered, breaking the spell between them.

Wren shifted back and faced him, a twinge of fear striking her heart and reminding her that she knew the men beside her as well as she knew the soldiers before her. In truth, she did not know a single thing about them.

"Then what are you?" she asked bluntly.

An arrow whizzing past her face was her only reply.

Timothius pulled Wren away from the road and back into the wood in an instant. "Run west," he said urgently to Elric, releasing her to him. "When you reach a narrowing of the highway, cross without delay. I will meet you in the Elfin Domain."

Wren's eyes widened, but Timothius turned on his heel and fled in the opposite direction before she could speak.

"You first, my lady," said Elric, grasping her wrist and delicately twisting her beneath his arm to his opposite side, as if they were dancing. "I am with you every step of the way. "

Wren didn't wait for a second request, tearing forward parallel to the road as fast as silent steps would allow. Elric's feet fell in time with her own, and when she tried to glance over her shoulder, his firm hand around hers spurred her onward. The soft *thwack* of arrows scattered the branches above them, dropping crystals of snow and errant pine needles on their heads, and Wren pulled his arm forward until they were running side by side.

Elric glanced toward the road a few times, and after a moment, she heard him whisper, "Ah!"

She halted and turned to face him. His eyes were bright when he pulled a handful of stones the size of smooth eggs from within his cloak and pressed them into her hand. He drew out more—small glittering stars falling from his palm as he did— and nodded in a way that told Wren without words to watch closely. Then he spun and hurled the stones into the forest with as much force as he could muster.

Wren followed suit, drawing her arm back and hurling the stones into the trees, sending snow, ice, and rock clattering to the forest floor. Elric's hand around her own prompted her to move forward as he continued to send more stones whizzing over their heads. The commotion echoed deep into the wood and soon the pounding of boots and twang of bowstrings lessened at their backs, drawn away by the confusing chorus of noise. With a quick glance, Elric threw his last stone, clasped Wren's hand, and broke into a sprint once more.

"Here," he whispered after a few moments, stopping short of the tree line once again. There were no soldiers on the road as far as the eye could see. "When we reach the other side, do not stop running until I give the word."

Wren nodded, gulping in air before they set off again. "Got it. On three?"

The urgency on Elric's face broke long enough for his forehead to furrow. "What is 'on three'?"

Wren stifled a smile. "I'll count and then we run on three. One...two...."

The moment the last word left her lips, they took off, exploding out of the forest like children in a relay. In a few long bounds they were across the road and barreling through the towering oaks. The farther they delved into the wood, the more the dry and dormant ground came alive, increasingly littered with petals of white and blush. The once sparse branches filled in with bright-green leaves and flowering boughs, the trees taller and wider than Wren had ever seen—as if they had stood for lifetimes.

The misty air was still frigid, their panting breaths nothing but puffs ahead of their stride, but beams of sunlight streamed through the branches, cutting the chill and casting a warm glow to the forest before them—a promise of spring to their winter-weary bones.

Side by side they raced deeper into the wood, and when Wren glanced at Elric, she found him taking stock of her as well. His gaze held a measure of respect, but the challenge sparking in his eye gave her a renewed burst of speed. She nearly forgot they were running from anyone. All she felt was alive, the scent of dew-softened earth and the tease of warmth in the air reviving her.

It was almost as if she were a child again. Running through the wind, laughing without reason, no worries burdening her. It was a feeling she had forgotten—one she had never imagined she would feel again. Yet, here she was.

Beside her, Elric smiled, and when they skidded into a small clearing, the sun warming their skin, he finally halted.

He approached a tree to their right and moved his hand along the front, causing the bark to ripple beneath his touch. Wren ducked inside and sat, prepared for the slide down this time, and when Elric finally reached the floor beside her, they both lay in relieved exhaustion.

"I can't move," Wren huffed. "I don't want to move."

Elric laughed. "That is a good thing, as there is nowhere to go."

She heard him rise and a flame lit the lamp above them, illuminating the room they were in—if it could be called a room. It was a circle roughly eight feet in diameter, as if the tree above them was completely hollow straight into the ground.

Elric waved his hand, fingers dancing in the air, conducting an orchestra only he could see. Plumes of what appeared to be smoke gathered before him, and in the dim light, Wren could have sworn she saw something sparkle within it—like he had conjured a cloud from the midnight sky and filled it with stars.

Two blankets appeared, followed by two pillows, and her jaw fully dropped when a bag plopped onto the small patch of open ground between them, smelling of roasted meat and something richly seasoned with garlic.

"How…. What…. *Why* did we not have this in the winter forest?" she moaned, forcing herself to a seated position.

"We did," replied Elric, sitting on the ground beside her and opening the sack. He handed Wren a leg of meat and pulled out a small parcel filled with fingerling potatoes before lifting another leg for himself. "I call that home, where we started. We have one of these in each forest. This is the safe point for the Vernal Wood."

Wren hesitated, considering what was happening in the world above them. "Will Timothius be safe?"

"I assure you, my lady, he can quite handle himself. He is our leader for a reason."

Wren stilled. "What do you mean leader?"

Elric fixed her with a firm and intent stare, every bit of the boy she felt she had been running beside replaced by a powerful man capable of conducting the night. "As I'm sure you may have surmised, we are rebels against the king and crown. Timothius is a vital part of leading that charge.

"I am about to place a good deal of trust in you, my lady. This is not anything you asked for, I know, and I do not expect anything from you. I extend it to you as a means of safety, for you have placed great trust in us at your own expense. Now, in return, I shall provide you with a truth of our own that may protect you, should you feel the need to use it."

Wren blinked slowly, taken aback by his words. "I…I don't

understand. I can keep your rebellion secret if that's what you're asking. But who *are* you?"

"I'm Elric," he replied calmly. "That is who I am. As for what I am, I am an Isteriaeth."

Wren's mouth fell agape, but before she could speak, Elric held up a hand. "Allow me to explain. All that I have told you of our kind is true. Our power, our magic. You have now seen the dhust that I possess. And it is also true that Isteriaeth do not gather here any longer. We were among the first magical beings to walk upon this realm. We, ourselves, were each birthed from our own star and because of it we are woven into the magic that formed this world. The tale I mentioned to you, the fall of the Thrones? The day the last Throne fell, here in this very realm, was the final stand of the Isteriaeth. With the loss of our true rulers, no more stars descended, and those who were already here were no longer safe. Many were captured and enslaved to evil, our power manipulated and used for the worst atrocities. Others fled and hid with those who were loyal to the Thrones until they, too, fell. I, myself, narrowly escaped capture in the kingdom to our north—my homeland. I was the lone survivor there, smuggled on a ship across the Strait to Inflamel. And I have been in hiding ever since."

Wren blanched. "How old *are* you?"

"Isteriaeth are made of stars and dhust, my lady. Age does not have power over us when we helped form the ages."

Wren nodded, feeling slightly faint. As if sensing it, Elric flicked his wrist in the air, conjured up a skin filled with what smelled like sweet wine, then handed it to her. She did not hesitate to take a long swig.

Elric smiled and continued, "That is how I knew what you possessed, and how I confirmed that more than one Isteriaeth forged it. That is how you came to wear magic boots. I am the last of my kind, and I—with Timothius—lead the charge of the rebellion against the Rat King and his horde of masked demons."

Wren's perception began to clear. "The soldiers in the forest, the one who attacked me the day I arrived, they were following Timothius. It's why he was there, wasn't it?"

Elric nodded. "It was either he or I who was seen. He often leads their attention away from me to avoid me using magic in plain sight. No one can ever know what I truly am, or else I will be claimed for the king."

Wren hesitated. "Claimed sounds like more than just imprisonment."

A shadow passed over Elric's eyes. "It is. But I do not wish to discuss that for as long as it may be helped."

A twinge of suspicion pricked the edge of Wren's mind, but a softer understanding led her to nod in acceptance. "Thank you for trusting me." She considered her words for a long time, and then added, "I don't know what it is like to be the last of my kind, but I know what it feels like to be hidden. To never be seen, even when I wish I could be. Maybe now we can be invisible together?"

Elric's smile broadened, and it brought a smile to her own face. "I would like that very much, I think. Thank you, my lady."

"Wren," she reminded him. "Call me Wren."

They finished their meal in silence before shifting as best they could to allow themselves room to sleep uninhibited by the other, Wren with her back curved into the wall facing Elric who was mirrored the same.

He reached up and extinguished the flame with a midair pinch of his fingers, and Wren marveled, realizing that he had lit the candle not with a match but with magic alone. And even as she fell asleep, still hoping she would wake once again on the chaise in front of the tree at her grandmother's house, she found herself looking forward to a new day and new discoveries in this world of rebels, enchantment, and kings.

CHAPTER TEN

"So when you said Vernal Wood, you really meant spring?"

Elric laughed softly, kicking at stray dandelion clusters while they walked through the trees, the branches thickened with buds that complemented the sky's various shades of pink from the setting sun. "Yes, spring. There are five forests in our kingdom and so far you have been in three of them—this one, the Brumal Forest where it is an eternal winter, and the outskirts of the Autumnal Wood which is where you met T."

Wren wrinkled her nose. "That explains a lot. Autumn is always gray and gloomy where I'm from, and that was definitely not anywhere I wanted to stay. Although the cold isn't my favorite either. I honestly think I like it here the best."

Elric smiled to himself. "You'd be surprised, my lady. You can gaze upon many different sides and angles—some ugly and others beautiful—and find that you have been viewing the same thing all along."

Wren picked a dandelion and blew on it gently, watching the wisps float across the grass. "So is there a summer forest, then? I'm willing to bet I'd like that more."

"The Aestival Forest is certainly summer, but not in the manner you would think. Let us say it has teeth all its own."

"Does it have creepy mutant wolves too?"

Elric stiffened. "It does not. They reside in the fifth forest which lies beyond Inflamel City on the eastern coast. The Deorc Weald is a forest you never want to find yourself in, my lady."

"I don't know, it sounds lovely," Wren replied drolly.

Elric's head twisted nearly off his shoulders, his bright-blue eyes the size of moons.

"I'm kidding." Wren smiled, swallowing her laugh. "It sounds terrifying, I'll stick with the seasons, thanks."

Elric seemed appeased by the answer but walked a bit closer to her, as if worried she might take off for whatever nightmare forest he had described. After a moment, he stopped and glanced around the clearing. "On the subject, I believe here is as good a place as any for a break."

Wren paused and turned on her heel. "We were being chased by guards yesterday and now you want to take a break out in the open?"

Elric dropped his pack on the ground and unclipped his cloak, draping it over a low-hanging branch and sending petals drifting gently to the ground. "The Guardian possesses elemental magic. While one would think it useful for control over earth, wind, air, and fire alone, it may also be used to bend those elements—to conceal what must remain hidden. Now that we are near the Elfin Domain we are within the bounds of that protection. Anyone who may pursue us will reach the edge of the coast and turn away long before they ever find us here. And as it stands, I believe we have a far more pressing matter at hand."

"Such as?" Wren asked, shedding her own cloak and enjoying the far warmer breeze as it rustled her skirt against the grass.

"Honing your skills with the bow and blade," Elric replied

simply. He withdrew his sword and flipped it deftly, offering it to Wren handle-first.

Another glistening blade appeared in his opposite hand, and Wren had no choice but to reluctantly accept the weapon. It was heavier in her palm than she anticipated, and she was forced to grip it with both hands to keep it from dipping to the ground. "I think I'm good with my bow, thank you very much."

Elric scratched his upper lip with his thumb, trying and failing to hide his smirk . "You must know how to protect yourself by whatever means necessary. You have proven to be a strong runner, but one can only flee so far. Arrows are useless in close quarters and there cannot always be an endless supply. Therefore, you must be familiar with a sword."

The edge of his blade met hers, running down the length and supporting it. He held it steady, balancing the weight for Wren to gain a better grip. "If I can barely hold it, what makes you think I can fight with it?" she asked.

"If you can hold it, you can swing it. And in the heat of battle, sometimes the ability to slice away at the air around you is all you need." He slowly slid away, leaving the sword held aloft firmly in Wren's grasp, and shrugged. "And quite frankly, it is better than nothing. It is a skill I would feel better knowing you possess."

"Oh, because you're worried about me now?" Wren asked, releasing one hand from the hilt and quickly replacing it when the blade became unsteady.

"Yes, I am."

The frown fell from her face and she let the tip of the sword fall to the grass. The earnestness on the Isteriaeth's face disarmed her. "But you barely know me."

Elric considered her words, grappling with a weight behind his eyes that she could not fully grasp, and then softly spoke. "Be that as it may, why does one need knowledge to care for another being? You knew next to nothing about me or T and yet you did not hesitate to fight back against the wealdwolf. Your fiber is woven from a strength I admire—one I remember seeing in my own kin, before they were lost to me. I could not offer them safety, but I can extend it now to you. I do not wish to see you come to harm."

His honest vulnerability nearly caused her to drop the sword, but she recovered it quickly and cleared her throat. "I guess I didn't think of it that way. Where I came from, it was always me against the world."

"And it may be yet," Elric replied, squaring his stance. "But as you said, for now we are invisible together. So you best let me teach you a thing or two before you go chasing monsters into their haunted wood."

They covered a few techniques and had barely sparred for ten minutes when the Isteriaeth forcefully sheathed his sword, his cheeks puffing and reddening in frustration. "You are terrible at taking instruction."

"And you are a horrible teacher," Wren retorted, throwing her blade on the ground at his feet.

He picked it up, cleaning the dew from the steel and glowering at her. "I have corralled felines more attentive than you."

Wren gave an offended gasp. "Then it's time for archery practice. Send for an apple so I can shoot it off your head."

Elric barked a laugh and tipped his head over his shoulder. Wren glanced around him and saw red orbs glistening from the trees, each one seated on top of the branches at varying distances. She dropped her arms, her trembling muscles already dreading the thought of pulling back the string of her bow.

"Be careful what you wish for around an Isteriaeth, my lady," Elric said with a triumphant grin, and when Wren quickly let an arrow fly, he had the good sense to duck.

❄

AFTER SOME TIME, and far too few felled apples, they stopped. Wren took the opportunity to observe her companion closer, watching in wonder as Elric traded his borrowed sword for two skins of water.

She didn't mind traveling with him. And now that she could see him for what he truly was, she was fascinated. The way the dhust in varying shades of deep blue mixed with stars, swirling about him like a tornado trapped within his personal orbit was beautiful and made him look equally so. It also made him appear powerful. And not in any way she had seen men carry power in her various business circles. This was a brand all his own—ancient and proud, yet kind.

"You can cease your ogling of me, I am spoken for," he said, perusing his sack before sitting on the ground beside her.

"Don't flatter yourself," she muttered. "I was admiring your magic."

"Not the first time I have heard that explanation, I'm afraid," he said, mischief in his eyes. "You will have to do better than that, Lady Wren."

Wren rolled her eyes. "It's just Wren. And I mean it. I've never seen anything like it. The way the blue gathers to contain the stars. It's like you hold a storm of starlight."

He paused then and the teasing left his gaze, leaving quiet stoicism behind. "It is quite like that, actually. Blue is the color of the dhust associated with my power—atmospheric magic. It has been bestowed for so long that I have forgotten what it looks like to someone who is not familiar with it."

"Bestowed? How long have you had your magic?"

"Our strand—the form of magic we will carry—is bestowed in our first decade of life, while we are still children. Our schooling begins then and does not end until our dhust comes to life in our hands. Since I was in hiding, my training was cut short, and my magic suppressed instead of being cultivated and explored. So while I have possessed my dhust for twenty years, my magic has been bestowed for over three centuries."

Wren blanched. "You were a ten-year-old for three hundred years?"

Elric laughed. "One might say that."

"And this…atmospheric magic. It gives you power to do whatever you want? Like move things and make them appear?"

"Ah, that is where I must be creative. I have the ability to summon what I desire, and may summon them to specific places, but I must picture it exactly so. Such as last night. I do not have power over the elements, yet I summoned the flame of the candle from the wick to myself in order to extinguish its light."

Wren, while amazed at his words, couldn't help but voice the question burning in her mind. "Then why didn't you just summon the Guardian to us in the tree?"

He chuckled. "I am not all-powerful, my lady. I cannot call beings to myself, only things. Returning to your question of my age, the strength of the magic that flows through an Isteriaeth's veins determines the length of our years. We do not age according to the days that pass, but rather mature beside our power as it is honed and expanded. I was one of the final stars to be sent from the clouds to the kingdoms. And I was only a child when the Thrones fell. Though I have been alive far longer, I did not start to age physically until I found safety here and my knowledge of my own power began to deepen. That is how I appear your age yet have walked the earth longer than any being I know."

Wren snapped her jaw shut, unsure of when it had fallen open. "I…am not sure what to say to that."

Elric smiled, a slight blush pinking his cheeks. "If I may be forward, I would be more afraid if you did have words to speak on the matter. It is a lot to take in, but you are very bold, my la—

ah, Wren. You say what you are thinking and while it is some-thing I quite enjoy, it is also rather terrifying."

Wren couldn't stop herself from bursting out in laughter, stifling it quickly as the sound carried out through the trees. It struck her then just how relaxed she truly was in this world, even despite its dangers and impossibilities. There was no one to tell her she was being too immature, too unprofessional, too *anything* for that matter. The more she learned of the world around her, the more it felt like a fever dream, and yet she felt more seen than she ever had in her life.

A thought occurred to her. "When I came here, T mentioned that your Yuletide holiday had been two weeks prior. Mine was only two days. Do you think this means that every day in my life equals a week in this world?"

Elric was thoughtful for a long moment. "How frequently do you observe a full moon?"

"Once every month."

His face paled and Wren's stomach plummeted. "Then I'm afraid you may be on the trail of something, for we see a full moon every seven months."

Wren's spine slumped and her eyes fell. She attempted the math inside her head, but her racing thoughts wouldn't allow her to keep track of the numbers. She found comfort in the notion that time may be moving slower in the real world, but it only fueled the adrenaline driving her to return home as quickly as possible.

"Will we reach the Guardian soon?" she asked.

"We shall arrive tomorrow, my lady," Elric replied, standing once again. He extended a hand to Wren, and she accepted it, rising to her feet. "The elfin folk went into hiding after the fall of the Thrones, and they are allied with the rebels against the king. The domain itself is also concealed. And that concealment is of the utmost importance."

Wren nodded thoughtfully, then nudged his shoulder with

her own. "Well, you can feel free to mention that to Wren. I'm not sure if *my lady* is willing to make any promises."

Elric's brow furrowed for a moment until Wren's mischievous smile registered. "Understood...Wren. Now, shall we find a place to make camp for the night? Or do you have more questions you wish to pester me with?"

Wren looked up and noticed stars already twinkling in the twilight overhead. She wondered what Elric saw when he looked at them. Did he see the night sky? Or faces he once knew? Did it bring him comfort? Moreover, why did the thought make her so sad?

She pushed the notion away and followed him deeper into the wood. "Tell me about your King of Wishes. Is he a long-lost brother? A second cousin or something?"

Elric let out a boisterous laugh. "No, actually, this is just a tale. One my nursemaid—an old faery herself—used to tell me every night as I fell asleep, though I fear it is equal halves tragedy and enchantment."

Resisting the urge to ask him about the existence of faeries on top of elfin folk, Wren drained the last of her flask. "Okay, then. Lay it on me."

CHAPTER ELEVEN

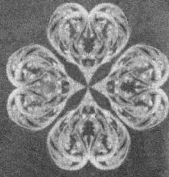

*T*he weather the following day gave way to full-blown spring. The wood, now entirely in bloom, teamed with the chatter of woodland creatures and singing birds. Yet while life thrived freely around them and there were no mouse guards in sight, Wren could not shake the feeling of being observed. The forest was bright, the atmosphere peaceful, but for every inch of beauty she surveyed, she found a shadow lurking—following like a dark cloud, innocently giving shade but lying in wait, ready to unleash a storm.

She assured herself that it was only the adrenaline of the previous days catching up to her, playing with her mind in the serenity of the season's change, and focused instead on the conversation that continued to flow with Elric. It was effortless sharing things about herself—her life and world—with him, and the more relaxed they became around each other the harder the realization was that she would eventually need to say goodbye to him. If they ever seemed to reach the Elfin Domain.

The sun had nearly set on another day when the sight of a riverbank brought Wren to a halt. Elric stopped beside her, quirking an eyebrow.

"My lady?"

Wren stared at the water glistening in the sunlight. "Why can't I hear the water? It's moving, but I don't hear a sound."

Elric smiled broadly. "Because it is a mirage—spelled to deter visitors. They see it and assume the Aestival Forest lay on the other side, so they turn back. But we are to move forward."

Her eyes shot to him in enough time to watch him wrap his hands around the air, pull dhust from nothing, and twist his palm upward, sending its stars off the end of his fingers to ripple against the visage of the water.

Wren took a step back and gasped when the shudder traveled across the trees and up toward the sky, like everything in front of her was no more than a screen blowing in the wind. The dhust began to gather then, forming a churning doorway framed by stars.

Elric stepped up to it and with a single touch, the deep-blue dhust turned diamond white, illuminating a hint of something waiting for them on the other side. Turning back to Wren, he stretched out the same hand he had just used to form the door in the world before them. "Shall we?"

The air lightened around Wren like a fresh breeze when she stepped through the arch, but the world that she entered into felt like a dream all of its own. The grass, the small bushes, the tufts of moss were such a deep green they appeared to have been soaked in dew. The trees stood tall, but their branches bowed low, covering the forest floor in a canopy of delicate vines and branches filled with flowers of soft blush. The river flowed freely now, somewhere ahead yet still out of sight, and when she followed Elric another step forward, the arch behind them vanished, leaving nothing but a reflection of the world outside the domain they had entered.

"Where" was the only word she could utter before a man stepped into the clearing in front of them. Wren was not short by any stretch of the imagination, but the way she craned her neck in order to view his head made her feel as though she were nothing more than a child.

The metal of his helmet and bracers appeared aged, almost like a garden gate of twisted iron that had been exposed to the elements for too long. His midnight-green cloak and tunic were rich against the flat oaken sheen of his boots and trousers and made him seem like a fixture in the garden as opposed to a guard.

He stared at Wren for a long and silent moment and then his azure eyes flicked to Elric. Inclining his head slowly, he dipped forward in a small bow of deep respect, which Elric mirrored in the same way.

"Isteriaeth," he addressed Elric, his voice smooth as silk, singing like the wind in the trees. "Your return is welcome here."

"I shall hold that welcome in highest regard," responded Elric, straightening. "Has Timothius arrived?"

The guard nodded. "He is already in the presence of the Guardian."

Elric nodded. "Right, then. Shall we proceed?"

"Who is your companion?" the guard asked, ignoring Elric's request. His eyes once again rested on Wren, more curious than threatening now.

Elric hesitated for a moment, but Wren stepped forward confidently. "Wren Klaver."

"Of Tauriellis," added Elric quickly, and Wren cast him a glance from the corner of her eye.

The guard nodded once more and extended his hand along the path before them. "May your parting be regarded well."

Elric bowed at the waist. "Your goodwill has been welcome."

Moving once again under the canopy of vines, past the guard, Wren skipped to keep up with Elric's long, purposeful gait. "What was that about?" she asked.

"The guards here are loyal to the Guardian alone. It would be best to conceal where you came from until we have spoken."

A twinge of nervousness pricked Wren's spine, but it only served to harden her resolve. "How soon will we speak with—"

"Ah, Elric. What took you so long?"

Timothius's smirk matched the casual way he leaned against a tree with his arms folded over his chest and his legs crossed at the ankles. Across from him, with long fingers resting gracefully on the rail of a footbridge that spanned a river so blue it appeared teal, stood a woman. The delicate points of her ears peeked out from her voluminous raven waves, and though her skin was a cool, raw-umber that begged for sunlight outside the canopy of trees, it was rich with rose-jeweled undertones that exuded radiant health and vitality.

"Elric." She smiled warmly, her golden eyes sparkling, and she extended her hands to him.

He stepped forward with a smile of his own and accepted her greeting. Dipping to one knee, he pressed his forehead to her knuckles and then rose again in one smooth motion. "Enya, may I introduce you to Lady Florence Klaver. My lady, this is Nelluenya Ravenstar, High Sentinel of the Elfin Domain and Guardian of the Realm."

Wren accepted the Guardian's hand, but before she could dip into an awkward curtsy, the elf placed her other hand upon Wren's wrist, encasing it in an embrace. "Timothius has told me of your appearance here. I trust these men have treated you well since your arrival?"

Wren nodded. "They have, ma'am. I mean my lady. I mean High...Guardian...."

Nelluenya's laughter danced off the trees, melding with the water and running across the garden clearing. "Those are just titles, Lady Florence, which I would be more than happy to explain in due time. You may call me Enya, for we are now friends."

"Then you may call me Wren."

"Ah yes, the *nick* name," Elric interjected, amusing Wren with his emphasis on the first syllable. "A surname shortened among friends."

Wren couldn't help but smile as she returned her attention to Nelluenya. "They say you can determine what magic my ornament has. That you might know how I can return home."

She nodded, her chin bobbing gracefully. "Perhaps. That has yet to be seen. Timothius has told me of your encounter with the wealdwolf and the breaking of the glass. Has it continued to change?"

Wren shook her head, but when her hand dipped into her pocket, she felt in her heart that she was incorrect. Sure enough, the once flawless blue was now lined with cracks, each one splitting off from the next. She tried to remember when she last looked at it but could only recall when it had broken after the wealdwolf's attack. And with all that had transpired since then, she had no way of knowing what may have caused its fracture this time.

"May I?" asked Nelluenya, extending her palms to cup it.

Wren reluctantly released it to her and watched the Guardian's brow wrinkle as she scrutinized the piece.

"And you did not encounter any trouble in the Vernal Wood?" she asked.

"No," confirmed Elric. "Though we took great strides to ensure we were close enough to the realm to escape anything that may have been searching."

"On the subject," interjected Timothius, addressing Nelluenya and startling Wren who had forgotten that he stood quietly behind her. "What was a wealdwolf doing in the Brumal Forest?"

The Guardian stayed silent, examining the crystal for a moment longer before returning it to Wren. "I believe we should enter the house. There is much that bears discussing. I fear there may be a connection to each of our tales after all."

Her dress swirled in the air about her legs when she turned, beckoning them to follow her onto the footbridge. "Come, I shall show you to your guest house."

Elric followed behind her and Timothius behind him, though the latter paused at the base of the bridge and gestured Wren forward. "After you, my lady."

Wren nodded to him in silent thanks, and something deep inside her relaxed with their reunion, as if she had been... worried for him. She tried to brush off the feeling, but after a few steps, she glanced over her shoulder. "Was your trip here uneventful too? You didn't have to trample any more mice, did you?"

Timothius snorted, but no humor danced in his eyes. "No more mice met their demise. Lucky for them, but more so myself. I do not delight in taking lives but pride myself on outrunning the wolves. When I am not rescuing strangely dressed women lost and unchaperoned in the forest, that is."

It was Wren's turn to snort. "That's good, then. I'd hate to know what would happen if I wasn't there to watch your back while you *rescued* me."

A soft chuckle met her ears this time, and when she looked back Timothius was gazing across the water to their left where a large, open-air house stood spanning both sides of the river. The flecks were dancing in his eyes again. "As I said, I am quite lucky."

His gaze moved back to her, and she quickly shifted her focus to the vine growing around the footbridge rails, absent-mindedly stroking the leaves as she walked. This was not the time nor place for flirting. Even if he was both attractive and charming.

The path on the other side of the footbridge turned abruptly to the right, and just beyond the line of trees that blocked a cobblestone footpath parallel to the riverbank, there were several small gazebos. At least, on the outside they appeared to be gazebos, with their round structure, pointed roofs, and half-walls with rails all the way around. Thick curtains covered the top half where the windows would be, some tied down flat to preserve privacy, while others billowed out into the garden.

Nelluenya led them to one such gazebo and pointed to another beyond it. "Timothius has already settled into the quarters over there, Elric. Lady Florence, you may take this housing for your stay. However long you need."

Wren stepped up to the door, glancing back hesitantly at the men and the elf.

"We shall give you time to freshen up and then we will all join Enya in the Great House for a meal and discussion," Timothius said, addressing her questioning eyes. "Keep an ear alert for our knock."

Wren nodded. "I will. And thank you...Enya."

The Guardian smiled. "You are most welcome, Lady Wren. I look forward to hearing your tale. I am sure it is one we will not soon forget."

CHAPTER TWELVE

The inside of the gazebo reminded Wren keenly of a dome tent she had stayed in once during a getaway many years before. Were it not for the massive clawfoot tub filling itself with steaming water, she might have convinced herself she was just glamping at a mountain resort and not in an Elfin Domain surrounded by strangers in a world that seemed too fantastic to possibly be real.

The bath felt heavenly on her aching muscles, and the longer she soaked, the more the temperature adjusted to her needs without once growing cold. She recalled the river she had crossed with Timothius after he had rescued her from the mouse soldiers. It had flowed between the Autumnal Wood and Brumal Forest and yet had been warm. She wondered if the Guardian was the reason for it, if it was the same river, or if perhaps the water itself was…magic.

It couldn't be, she chided herself, and then stopped. *But it is*.

This world and its people were real. Their magic was evident everywhere she looked, and life was no more inscrutable here than it was in the distant parts of the earth she had only read about from history. And now that she was finally alone, she let her guard down and processed the truth. She did not mind being here. In fact, she felt a belonging and a kinship that she had not felt anywhere beyond her grandmother's house. But the thought itself brought reality crashing back in and a bitter homesickness soured her stomach. It did not matter how she had arrived, if she was enthralled by this world, or even why she was there. She needed to return to her grandmother before she, too, slipped away. And hopefully the way home was now within her grasp.

The moment she stepped out of the tub and wrapped herself in a towel, the water vanished, leaving not a drop behind. She crossed the room to a wardrobe and peered inside to find a clean dress not unlike the billowy chiffon gown that Nelluenya had worn. She would have been surprised by its perfect fit had she not met the intelligent water first, and as she surveyed the way its trumpet-shaped skirt and long, bell sleeves flowed off her figure, she couldn't help but smile. She looked like something out of a fairy tale, and in the quiet space while it was only her and her thoughts, she admitted that she was starting to feel like she was inside of one too.

The dress, however gorgeous, was unfortunately devoid of pockets, and after struggling to find a place to stash her ornament on her person where it would both fit and not leave an unsightly bulge, Wren settled for simply carrying it. Maybe then if it continued to break she would see what preceded its change.

Braiding the front strands of her hair back from her face and tying it with a piece of twine she found in a drawer, she heard a light rapping on the wood slats of her door. Sliding into the soft shoes that had appeared beside the bed, she gave the ornament one last reassuring squeeze and exited the gazebo.

Both Elric and Timothius stood waiting for her, and with Timothius leading and Elric bringing up the rear, they continued along the path toward the Great House.

Once inside, a guard identical to the one they'd encountered upon entering the domain led them to the very center of the house and into a large rotunda. The air caught in Wren's lungs at the sight of the painted glass dome above their heads, reflecting shades of rose, ocean blue, violet, gold, vibrant emerald, and soft amber on the stone floor beneath their feet. Though they were inside, it was as if the garden itself had grown through the walls and into the house. Flowers blossomed on every table and beside every chair, and vines grew like garland across the rafters and along the windowpanes. And in the center of the room, adorned with fresh herbs, a great table with nothing short of a feast was laid out before them.

Light streamed in from the open windows looking both out over the footbridge—toward the gazebo homes and other trails —and in the opposite direction, toward the mouth of the river where its teal ripples bled into deep-blue waves. Nelluenya stood by this window, a chalice in hand and the same radiant smile on her face, her lavender gown complementing the outside garden much like Wren's pale-green one.

"Please, sit and eat," Nelluenya implored, crossing the room to take a seat at the head of the banquet. "We have much to discuss."

It was well into the heavenly meal when Elric finally began the conversation. "Where shall we start?"

Wren twisted the ornament nervously in her lap, the only indication of her nervousness—and even then, she made sure it was hidden away below the table where no one else would see her anxiety on display.

"I would suggest with how I may return home," she said, voice steady and confident. This was no different than a business meeting or a board evaluation. It was nothing she could not handle.

Timothius nodded and shifted to face Nelluenya. "It is the leading reason why we are here. Lady Wren carries with her what we believe to be a crystallum. Elric has sensed its magic, though he cannot say what it possesses. We hope you might."

Her brow furrowed. "May I look closer upon the relic, Lady Wren?"

Wren nodded and handed it to her once again. This time, instead of examining the orb, the Guardian held it tight within her fist. Her eyes fluttered closed, and after a few excruciatingly silent minutes, they opened to meet Wren's once again. "The magic within this is far older than I. I'm afraid I will not be able to provide more knowledge of its contents, but I may be able to shine some light on its purpose."

Wren raised an eyebrow, prompting a small smile to toy on Nelluenya's lips before she continued. "For magic that old to be contained until this moment, to be gifted to you and then to bring you here, it is not merely a relic of old magic. There must be something hidden within that is tied to the very fabric of our world."

The Guardian slid from her chair and started to move around the room. "There have been great happenings as of late. Murmurings from deep within the earth. Ancient beings, ancient magic that has not been felt nor heard since the fall of the Thrones has begun to awaken. In the stories of old there is talk of such things coming to pass, but only when the Trifolium Thrones rise again."

"That would mean that the lost ruler, the one the Isteriaeth gathered to save here in this very kingdom, is returning," Elric said, staring at Nelluenya—who had paused her turn about the room.

After a moment, the elf's head dipped in a nod.

Wren looked around at her three companions. "Are you suggesting that the lost royal from your Trifolium Thrones is somehow inside my ornament?"

Timothius cracked a smile and Wren nearly asked what he found so entertaining amid such a heavy conversation, but it was Nelluenya who answered, saying, "I would hope they do not reside within. Maybe if they were a faery, but to be trapped within an orb all these years—that does not seem like something the Isteriaeth would give their lives to carry out. At the very least it would seem that your arrival, the crystallum's arrival, and the stirring in our world are connected in some way, but whatever the case may be, forces are starting to move. They are preparing for war."

"I am aware of the whispers of Kollapsars," remarked Timothius, leaning forward on the table. "What other forces have there been?"

"What on earth is a Kollapsar?" Wren interrupted, alarmed, picturing earthquakes collapsing structures and opening voids to swallow them whole.

Concern marred The Guardian's features. "Kollapsars walked upon our realm beside the Awduron, the authors of our world, yet in opposition to them. As with the Awduron, the Kollapsars take many forms—Axion warriors, formless terrors called Vacare, giant Eoten who possess the strength of ten men, and the winged and monstrous Hrotesk. But they all share one common bond: They must consume magic in order to live."

"So," Wren's mind raced to catch up, "your realm...Breteria... it's made of magic, isn't it? And stars?"

"That is correct," confirmed Elric, pride shining in his eyes at her knowledge.

"And Kollapsars consume...the world?"

Nelluenya nodded. "They breed destruction. They live off the death of those who possess magic, and when they can no longer taste living magic, they destroy the earth around them. The fall of the Thrones claimed their figurehead and weakened their force, so they descended back into the stone, into the darkest depths of our world, and have remained there. Until now."

"And what of the wealdwolf?" Elric asked.

Nelluenya's face fell and she slowly returned to her chair. "That is a different matter entirely, and a threat that has been growing in your absence, Timothius. There is talk of a powerful force residing in the Deorc Weald. A mage of tenebrescent magic. The wealdwolves are her creation, born of her magic to do her bidding alone. And as her power grows stronger, so does their reach."

"Is this mage a Kollapsar too?" asked Wren, barely keeping up with the information swirling around her.

"There are none who know what she is. Those who have laid eyes on her have had enough life remaining to bring word of her to our shores, each perishing with her cursed name on their lips. She seeks to be known, but not to be found."

"I must depart once the sun returns to the sky. I will see what it is that I can learn of her in my travels," Timothius confirmed solemnly. Wren's head spun to him at the declaration, but he continued speaking without looking at her. "If what you say is true, I will certainly hear of this mage along the way. And if the crystallum does in fact carry a tie to the lost heir of the Trifolium Throne, then...."

"Then we may be closer to freedom than we ever imagined," finished Elric, eyes hopeful until they reached Wren.

As if suddenly remembering she was in the room, two additional pairs of eyes found her, but she only shrugged against the familiar sting. "Don't worry, people forget I'm here all the time. I'm quiet when I want to be. So does this mean I'm stuck in your world until whatever is inside this thing comes out?"

She was met with a long pause before Nelluenya finally spoke. "That is possible; however we cannot say for certain. It would be best for you to remain within the domain, in safety, where we can observe it. No matter what lies within, it still contains powerful magic. With any hope we shall be able to harness enough of its force to return you to your home as it returns whatever it contains to ours. But, Lady Wren, you must know, you have returned something precious and vital to our world—to our lives. And if it is truly the key to the missing heir, then we are forever in your debt."

Wren felt unsteady, like she was standing on planks of wood that had not yet been secured to a foundation. She had so many questions but knew voicing them would reveal both her beliefs and doubts, displaying her points of vulnerability for all to see, so she resorted to a small but genuine smile.

The Guardian fell silent for a moment, staring at the ornament before smiling back at Wren. "If I may offer, we do have an artisan who would be more than happy to craft a pendant for you so that you may keep the crystallum close always. You alone should be its keeper. It was given to you, it chose you to bear it here, it must stay with you. As it was made, so it must remain."

Wren nodded. "That would be much appreciated."

An older elf was summoned, and after a few quick measurements around her neck, he vanished from sight with the ornament in tow. Wren felt its absence innately, and though she knew in her heart that it was safe, it felt as though a part of her very soul was screaming to be reunited with it once again.

"I think it is best that I remain here as well," said Elric, rousing from deep thought. "At least until Timothius returns. I should wish to help my lady in any way I can, as I know this separation from your world is not easy."

Wren found veritable comfort in that and allowed her shoulders to relax. "Thank you, Elric. I have to admit, I'd love to hear more of your stories. Just maybe the ones without world-devouring creatures."

He beamed. "I believe we might reach an arrangement."

They talked for what felt like hours more, Wren staying largely quiet and simply listening to the Isteriaeth, the elf, and the man catch up like old friends. It was not long until the craftsman returned with the ornament now fastened to the end of a chain long enough for Wren to wear against her sternum.

The moment its weight rested around her neck, the last of the tension bled from her shoulders and she found that she was overcome with exhaustion. Rising to excuse herself, she was surprised when Timothius stood as well.

"If I may, I will escort my lady back to her quarters," he said with a small bow to Nelluenya. With a clap on Elric's shoulder, he led Wren into the night.

CHAPTER THIRTEEN

*T*he sun had set over the garden well before their meeting adjourned, but Wren was still woefully unprepared for the beauty of the Elfin Domain after nightfall.

Fireflies hovered all around, twinkling as far as the eye could see. The bushes had awoken from their green slumber and now held large, white blooms that shone in the flickering light. The vines that grew up the bark of the trees, across the Great House, and along the footbridge were no longer dormant but instead flowered with jasmine, filling the garden with a scent as ethereal as the glow beneath the starlit sky. Small lanterns lined the walkways, illuminating the path with warm beams that beckoned, promising enchantment.

The soft trickle of the river was the only indication that it still flowed, its teal glass having deepened under the darkened sky, but the flowers drew the fireflies closer, their winking light reflecting against the water, carrying endless drops of gold from shore to shore.

It was not the sort of atmosphere one rushed through, and Wren's pace slowed beside Timothius, whose careful gait matched hers step for step.

"You travel often?" she asked, breaking the still evening air.

"More often than I would like, I fear," he confirmed. "But it cannot be helped."

"Is it to garner support for the rebellion, or to start trouble?" she asked, eyeing him closely.

Timothius smirked. "So Elric informed you. I had a feeling he might."

She nodded. "He evened the playing field. Secrets given for secrets kept. And don't worry, your secrets are safe with me. I don't know your king or want any trouble. I just want to go home."

"Consider yourself fortunate. The Rat King stands as the most powerful figure in the kingdom, but like so many who rule Breteria, he wields that strength selfishly. What he cannot claim, he destroys. You are better off far from this place." A long silence drew them closer to the gazebos, the words like a ghost haunting the space between them, before Timothius spoke again. "What is it you miss the most? Have you left behind family? A great love?"

Wren nearly missed a step at the words, harkening back to their conversation in the Brumal Forest. "I guess you could say a bit of both? My grandmother is my great love, and she—" She stopped herself, unwilling to voice the words. She had rehearsed them so many times in her mind, but saying them aloud to another being made them feel too real. Too permanent.

"She is unwell?" Timothius asked, his tone as soft as it had been when he'd asked her to start again in the tree home.

She nodded. "Very. I just want to spend time with her. However long I can."

"I understand."

Silence crowded the space between them once more, then Wren found herself speaking. "You mentioned you are solitary by choice. Your family...are they the reason you fight against this king? Like Elric?"

Timothius's face grew shadowed, his eyes stormy, and Wren rushed, "I'm sorry, that's too forward of me. You don't have to answer, I shouldn't have asked."

He stopped walking then, and Wren paused, turning on her heel to face him as he surveyed the river glistening in the light beside them. "The short answer is yes. I never knew my true parents. I do not know if I share any siblings. I have no memory of a time with them. And that in itself is the long answer. I fight for them and for all they never had—for what I will never know."

His admission stunned Wren, and when she opened her mouth, she found there was nothing to be said. She pressed her lips together and worked the inside of her bottom lip between her teeth, looking out over the world again. It was beautiful to her, yet it held so much darkness for the man at her side. Elric's words came back to her, how there could be so many different sides and angles, so many perceptions, all of the very same thing.

"You have been alone for so long." And as the words slipped from her lips, she knew it was just as much a confession of her own as it was an acknowledgement of the truth Timothius had shared.

It was his turn to gaze into the night. "Lonely, yes. But not alone. Never alone."

"You're lucky, then. To be alone is far worse," Wren replied, her voice a rasp through the emotion tightening her throat.

She felt Timothius survey her intently. "You recall your grandmother fondly, yet your eyes say that you understand what it is to be alone. How can one so determined to defy both logic and time suffer such a fate?"

Wren soaked in the question, drawing in the sweet night air with her own bitter resolve, then met his eyes. "Be grateful that you have a choice. So many of us are not given one. When I say goodbye to my grandmother, I will be alone. I would rather remain lonely in the middle of a crowded room than be isolated, out of sight and mind."

Timothius shook his head. "Loneliness is the fog we travel in when we do not see and cannot fathom what we are missing. To be alone and not know love or companionship enough to understand its absence is the truest form of pain."

Wren's eyes snapped back to the river and she shrugged, beginning to walk again. "Sometimes I wish I didn't know what I'll be missing. That kind of ignorance can help you survive. It's the kind of fire that burns long after it gets dark."

"And it may maim you still," Timothius warned softly.

"But at least it will keep you warm at night," she tossed over her shoulder.

The garden was silent for a heartbeat and then Timothius's voice stopped Wren in her tracks. "I have seen what I cannot reach. I have brushed what I cannot keep and touched what cannot be mine. I would rather be taunted with its loss at every turn than see love as only a distant dream."

Wren glanced over her shoulder, but Timothius had already resumed walking. His long strides carried him past, the air churned by his movement rustling the ends of her hair, brushing her skin and raising small bumps along her arm.

"I'm sorry," she said, and this time her words stopped him. "Agree to disagree. The fact that either of us even understand this conversation is a tragedy."

Timothius snorted. "Tragedy is for fiction, my lady. This is merely life. Though I am sorry your short years know this pain too."

"You don't mean to tell me you are a few hundred years old too?" she groaned, shifting the conversation and returning to his side.

Timothius laughed now, the sound deep and warm, like it wasn't heard often but when it rang it filled the spaces it touched. "I am not. I am two and thirty."

"And do you have any kind of magic?" Wren asked curiously. They began to walk again, slower this time, and Timothius shortened his strides to match hers as they followed the path beyond the trees to leave the riverbank behind.

"None, save the magic we all have in this realm. The air we breathe, the food grown from our land, the game raised and hunted all exist from the dhust that brings us life. But no, I hold no power. Only the will to try to do what is right."

Wren nodded, and they finally came to a stop at her door. "How soon will you be back?" she asked, the words sounding more vulnerable than she intended.

"I cannot say. I hope to return sooner than later, though I fear the power rising in the Deorc Weald will complicate matters."

"Will your travels take you there?"

Timothius stiffened. "I surely hope not, yet oftentimes the unknown is safer than the danger you are prepared to face."

Wren nodded. "If I am able to figure out what is causing this ornament to break, maybe it can change things for all of us. Maybe that unknown will be easier than facing a wealdwolf."

Timothius smiled. "The wolf was your unknown and yet you faced it bravely anyway."

She crinkled her nose. "I hid under a cape until I thought it would kill us."

"You disguised yourself as a boulder and ambushed at the exact moment needed."

Wren snorted. "Whatever makes you feel better."

Timothius chuckled, and Wren could not help but smile in return. Placing a hand on the door to push it open, she met his gaze. "I hope to see you again, but if I do not, thank you. For saving me, for helping me, for believing my story. I am glad to have met you."

She turned to enter the gazebo, but Timothius's hand at her elbow gave her pause. Turning back, she found his eyes fixed on her, their flecks dancing in the golden warmth. Slow enough to be mistaken for a reflex, his fingers gently caressed her skin. Time itself seemed to stop, and Wren's heart tripped in her chest, stunned again by how close they stood. The air died between them, replaced by the soft notes of amber and suede consuming her senses, and the world stilled. Everything around them held its breath, awaiting what came next.

His words were quiet and gentle, only for her and the night to hear. "Face your unknowns bravely, Lady Wren, and may they fall at your very presence."

Releasing her arm, he stepped away, the air flooding back into Wren's lungs and the sounds of the garden coming to life once more. He bowed to her and then, with one smooth turn, strode into the night.

CHAPTER FOURTEEN

The garden was alive with the sound of birds calling to each other, the soft hum of dragonfly wings, and the buzz of bees gathering as much nectar as their bellies could carry. A breakfast of fig jam on pastry that was too thick to be a crepe and too thin to be considered a pancake, yet not flaky enough to be a biscuit, waited for Wren along with fresh water for a bath.

After savoring the food and preparing herself for the day, she ventured out into the garden and inhaled the aromatic florals that surrounded her, each note nourishing her soul. She was tempted to have a look around, and investigate the world for herself in the first place safe enough to do so, but ultimately decided to seek out Elric. There were certainly tales he would be able to tell her about the domain and its inhabitants, and she could not wait to hear them.

She was nearly to the entrance of the Great House when hushed voices stopped her in her tracks.

"And how certain are you that she will be understanding?" Nelluenya asked sternly.

"I am not certain," Elric replied. "I hold to the hope that our kindness will be endearing and that she will come to understand. And that in understanding she will seek to help us."

"I do not think this wise," The Guardian cautioned. "To withhold information from a stranger is one matter, but to willingly keep her in the dark if she is who we believe her to be would be incorrect in morality and ethics alike."

"What other choice would you make, Enya?" Elric asked, irritation in his tone. "Would you bring her here under the guise of help, learn such information, and then inform her of her fate? Her trust has already been betrayed in learning that rebels harbor her, more revelations would not end well."

"And how shall it end when she discovers you have lied to her? That we all have. The girl only wishes to return home. The correct action should have been to right the wrong the moment you suspected."

Their footsteps drew closer, and Wren ducked into a small grove of bushes. Sweat beaded on her forehead and her heart raced, an icy fear sinking deeper into her bones than the cold of the Brumal Forest had. Elric paced into view, and she held her breath, afraid to hear what would come next but needing to know. "Do you think I have not considered this? I could not risk her being lost. I could not chance her not reaching the domain. We needed her contained, or else she would run."

"And you do not believe that she will flee the instant she learns?" Nelluenya pressed, unrelenting. "The truth will always make itself known. It is not a matter of if but when. You would do best to tell her before she discovers on her own."

"I will tell her when the time is right," Elric returned, his tone growing heated.

"We have long since passed the right time."

"Enya, you know we need her safe. Breteria needs her safe."

"And what do you plan to say when she realizes that none of us intend to help her return home?"

Pain lanced through Wren's chest and her eyes slammed

shut. She could not believe her ears, yet it was impossible to deny the clanging truth in those words. In Elric's words, of all people. He had been a convincing actor—Timothius and Enya too—but she had been such a fool, blinded by her longing. She had beheld her own loneliness, drawn too close to its fire, and now everything burned.

Chills coursed down her spine, an electric current trapped inside a runaway train, making it impossible to gain control of the thoughts hurtling through her mind. Her breathing came in short gasps through her constricting throat, and she willed her pulse to slow. Elric's steps grew closer, and when he finally stopped, he exhaled deeply.

She drew up enough courage to peek through the bushes at his face and saw his many years in the weight on his shoulders, in the heaviness behind his eyes. She wanted to feel satisfaction that his lies burdened him, but all that swelled in her heart was the bitter sting of betrayal. "All she need know is that the crystallum carries great magic and that we require her help. Nothing more. Not until we know for certain what we face—until her true purpose is revealed."

No more.

Wren shifted back on her heel, retreating slowly on shaky legs. She had been lied to. They hadn't sought to help her at all. They were rebels, pretending to care for her so they could steal the magic and perceived power held within her ornament. And now here she stood, even deeper in their world and no closer to discovering a way out.

Her stomach churned and her nerves frayed, unraveling beside her misplaced trust. Where did she go from here? If she had walked into a trap, was there another way forward? Could she find someone to turn to who might truly help her? And if she did, would it be possible to trust them knowing that she had already fallen straight into the wrong hands?

The wrong hands.

She stopped midstep, the words harkening back to her first moments in Inflamel. As Timothius had so aptly stated, she was a risk until she chose a side. But he had underestimated her. The only person she would side with was herself, and when a plan began to form in place of the building panic, Wren felt a new certainty surge with the adrenaline through her veins. She was going to find her own way home.

Her steps quickened in time with her racing thoughts. The rebels had shown their true colors, but all she knew of the king was what they had told her. He was selfish, known to be a rat, but he was also the most powerful being in Inflamel. She knew there was a decent chance that he would seek to use her as well —that the devil she knew would be better than the one she had not met—but unlike before, she was now armed with enough knowledge to make herself valuable to him. And she was not afraid to negotiate until she had what she wanted.

She closed herself away in the gazebo and hatched her plan until Elric arrived. Gone were his worries and the lines that had wrinkled his forehead. Even Nelluenya appeared jovial, no sign of hesitancy in her eyes as she took Wren on a tour of the Elfin Domain. Wren matched their calm demeanors, all the while burning inside and taking note of everything she was shown— every path, every boundary, every entrance and exit concealing them from the world at large.

The day itself felt as though it lasted a hundred years, but when night finally fell—well past the hour when the owls began to call to one another in the trees—Wren rose from her bed.

Packing away the few dresses she knew would be sensible for travel, she fastened her cloak, slid into her boots, and disappeared into the silent garden. Hurrying down pathway after lantern-lit pathway, she reached the grass and stole through the trees, careful to avoid the places she thought guards may hide until she arrived at the shimmering boundary. Darkness met her eyes, and though the trees on the other side were lush and at the height of their summer blooming, she couldn't help but feel a prickle of fear.

She didn't doubt they would know the moment she set foot outside of the boundary. And even if she did escape undetected, they would surely discover by daybreak when they came to retrieve her. Yet in her mind, there was no remaining here. She could not return home on her own, but she would not be held captive either. She could only push forward.

It was just a matter of reaching the castle.

Wren swallowed hard, trying to erase the dryness in her mouth. She was desperate to forget the kindness she thought she had found in Nelluenya. The kindred spirit she discovered engaging with Elric. And she hated to admit that she had felt a sting at Timothius's departure, but she was thankful for it now. There was no doubt in her mind that he would have been on her trail before she could set foot into the Aestival Forest.

It was now or never.

The sensation of cold layers being peeled back from her skin was the only indication Wren had that she'd exited the Elfin Domain. The river glistened and flowed through the night, but again, when she stared at it, it failed to make a sound. She set a swift yet sustainable pace in the thick and humid summer air, moving along the bank of the river on silent feet. She didn't know how far she would need to travel, and it was a shot in the dark to head in the direction she thought they had come from on the other side of the embankment, but if she were able to reach the highway, the soldiers would surely take her to the city —and hopefully not as a prisoner.

The sky started to lighten, the fading stars sparkling off the river, when the rhythmic thud of boots and the clang of metal upon metal broke the still night at her back. The elfin guards were coming.

Wren broke into a run, fleeing directly into the trees. She had only gone a few paces when something sharp ripped across her cheek, biting into her skin. She gasped and brushed at the spots of blood, but when she tried to move again, another sting like a needle bit into her ankle. She stepped back, away from the pain, but her skirts remained, pinned in place by the vines that had assaulted her.

There was barely any light to see, no breeze to rustle the trees about her, but still Wren squinted, gingerly reaching out. What met her fingertips were not thorns or vines or even vegetation at all, but instead the petals of a large, velvety rose.

Eyes finally adjusting to the inky dark of the forest, she made out more blooms, light enough to stand out against the greenery that they sprouted from in earnest. She realized then that she was in the middle of a thicket of rose bushes, their thorns surrounding her on every side and their vines climbing the trees like dangerous, beautiful garland.

Shouts from behind urged her to continue forward, but when she did, the bushes tore at her more. Wren bit her lip to keep from crying out, her rising panic and the dense heat of the forest inducing a frenzy in her mind. It did not matter what way she turned, how she moved or where she tried to run, everything her body touched was either an unmovable tree or a shrub waiting to nip at her skin, as if the trees themselves had trapped her in their snare.

Though miserable in the unrelenting heat, she tugged her sleeves down over her hands, pulled her cloak tighter around her body, and pressed on deeper into the forest. She prayed that the brutal flowers would deter her pursuers, but she could still hear them moving behind her.

She pressed on, plunging through brush and vines, the sound of the elfin guards growing more distant with every step. The trees around her opened to a clearing, and she broke into a run, skidding suddenly to a stop and throwing her hands out in front of her face to barely avoid a collision with a massive wall of thick bark.

The pre-dawn sky brightened enough of her surroundings to reveal a felled tree towering feet above her head and long enough to disappear from sight to both the right and left. Thinking quickly, Wren dug her fingers into the bark until she found grooves deep enough to support her grip. She did the same with the toes of her boots, wedging them in until her feet left the forest floor.

Arms screaming under the strain, she continued to climb the side of the tree, all the while urging herself on. If the elfin guards believed she had tried to find a way around the tree, it might buy her valuable time. She just needed to reach the top and she would be away before they knew it.

Her limbs trembled and sweat poured down her face and spine, cleansing the fresh cuts on her hands and causing them burn alongside her muscles. The thick, sticky humidity clung to her skin, but she finally hoisted herself to the top, pausing to catch her breath. She lay for only a heartbeat and then rolled as carefully as she could muster to a seated position. Dropping down the other side of the tree, Wren landed flat on her feet and the force sent her lurching forward into more brush.

With a grunt, she straightened once more and pushed farther into the forest, her cloak pulling and ripping as the thorns frayed it apart. Dizziness from fatigue and what she was certain was building dehydration set in, causing her to stumble and nearly fall. If the heat was this oppressive before daybreak, she would never make it if she continued at this pace in the afternoon sun.

The sky brightened even more as she ran and it was not long before sunlight poured through the trees, its beams illuminating her surroundings enough to reveal the roses growing from every surface in the forest. But for each stunning bloom the shadows thickened, threatening to swallow all that fell in its path. They crept closer, hemming Wren in and blotting out the sky overhead. Every time she slowed, it pressed closer, corralling her forward. She chased the shreds of brightness that remained, each a beacon of dying light along a twisted breadcrumb trail.

There was no sign of life—no animals or birds. Not so much as a single mushroom or cluster of berries could be found anywhere. She had run away, recklessly without food or water, and was well and truly lost.

Darkness began to play at the edges of her vision, and when she stumbled next, she was unable to catch herself. Collapsing to her hands and knees, the soft grass broke her fall, but the thorns caught her and held. She ripped her cloak from around her body and let it drop, allowing herself a small whimper before sinking to the forest floor beside it.

Curling up on her side, she cradled her knees to her chest. She was alone in the thick of the forest with the sun rising high in the sky. At least it felt like the thick of it, having lost what little bearing she had. There was no way of knowing which direction she was running or how far she would have to go to exit. She didn't even trust that she was heading in the direction of civilization anymore, be it castle, river, or road. And right now, she didn't care who found her first, so long as someone did.

Wren did not know how much time passed when commotion to her right caused her to jump. She tried and failed to stand when a pair of black boots appeared in her view, followed by another pair, and then another.

She looked up and met the beady eyes of a gilded mouse mask, the soldier's hand wrapped about the hilt of a sword, though thankfully it was not drawn.

"You found me," she breathed, relaxing in exhaustion.

"Who are you?" barked the man. "Identify your purpose in these woods."

"Lost," Wren rasped. "I must see the king. Please, I need to speak with him."

The soldiers released their swords one by one, two gently moving to either side of her and helping her to her feet. Now standing even with the face of the soldier who had addressed her, she watched him tilt his head, somehow looking even more mouselike than before. "What business do you have with the king?"

Wren thought for a long moment, catching her breath, buying herself more time. Finally, she drew herself up and met the shrewd gaze of the mask in front of her. "I believe that I may have something he wants."

PART II
THE REBELLION

CHAPTER FIFTEEN

*T*he trek through the rest of the forest to the highway was a blur, and Wren found herself even more grateful for the soldiers that located her. Still weakened from exhaustion and dehydration, she was half-carried by a guard on either side. Others cleared their pathway, keeping the thorns at bay but ruthlessly cutting down the roses in the process. She couldn't help but feel a tinge of guilt watching them be crushed. It was as if she were to blame, and though she recognized that she felt too deeply about flowers, she refused to entertain the notion that it may in fact be guilt manifesting over her aban-donment of the *friends* that had sought to help her escape the clutches of the very people accompanying her now. Or at least they had helped before they decided to lie to her.

Upon reaching the road, she was hoisted onto the back of a horse and later transferred to a small wooden carriage filled with additional weapons, supplies, and—to her amusement—masks.

After being given a food ration and water, she allowed herself to sleep for a spell, the creak and rumble of the wheels on the highway lulling her into submission. When she awoke, it was dawn the next day. There were still trees on either side of them, but the presence of soldiers had increased substantially. It wasn't until the sun was high in the sky that the tree line out the window vanished and she realized they were almost to the castle.

The carriage came to a halt, and when Wren stepped from it to mount yet another horse behind a wolf-masked guard, a small gasp escaped her. With the forests now behind them, the highway continued forward through a rolling meadow that spanned miles between the trees and the city, stretching out on either side for as far as the eye could see. To her left, the roses of the Aestival Forest peeked out from the shadows of their thick, viny foliage, and to the right, leaves the color of fire glowed beneath the sun, but at the center—with spires towering above the world—stood a castle, proudly built into the great stone wall of a city. It was medieval and majestic and breathtakingly beautiful.

The horse carried them forward, running parallel to the glittering sea that Wren could see when squinting at the horizon line well past what she could only assume was the Autumnal Wood, and they at last reached the highway's end. They stood before a moat surrounding the perimeter of the city, closing it off from the rest of the world. High above them, guards stood ready upon the rampart, stretched out in intervals with a few strolling the battlement, and after a moment, the drawbridge began to lower.

The city within was old, slightly run down, yet bustling with life. A cobblestone road paved the way to the castle and parted the dirt ground in half. One side appeared to be largely residences—two-story buildings built from wood with slatted roofs and clouded, dirty windows. The other side was filled with shops and businesses, most single-story structures crafted of stone with small courtyards or dingy alleyways that separated them from the road.

The drawbridge groaned and rose behind Wren, and a tingling of nervousness crept across her skin, like the tips of fingers walking along the edge of her resolve. *You chose to come here of your own free will*, she reminded herself. Yet now, inside the impenetrable walls of the city, she found herself wondering if she had made the right decision.

The wolf-masked soldier dismounted, and the crowd parted for him to lead the way through the city, walking ahead of Wren and the two soldiers that now flanked her from behind. She kept pace with them, their steps maintaining a monotonous beat along the road as it bent off to the right. The gatehouse came into view ahead of them with the castle's spiraling turrets —one significantly taller than the other—rising high above the city and wall below.

The castle itself was a sight to behold, towering above them in pride and beauty. Its arched stone windows and beveled glass caught the sunlight and reflected it back out over the city like a diamond, and Wren could not help when her lips parted in awe.

The closer they drew, however, the more she noticed that the soldiers lining the rampart all wore one of two identically gilded masks, either mouse or wolf. Her brow furrowed and she surveyed the faces of the people moving within the city. Sure enough, every last one of them bore a mask. Theirs were not ornate, most appeared to be made of some sort of leather, wool, or even wood, but they were all fashioned to look like the face of a different animal. It was almost as if she had wandered into a zoo.

The soldiers ahead of her stopped short, bringing her to a halt at the center of their group. One of the men stepped forward, addressing the guards stationed before the gatehouse. After a moment of conversing, they moved aside and allowed Wren's party to enter the castle through a single door that looked like a miniature portcullis.

The moment Wren set foot inside the heavily guarded door,

the warm light vanished, replaced by a cold, dim entrance hall lit only by torches lining the walls.

Unable to see ahead of her, Wren kept close to the guard in the lead. They came to another door—this one surprisingly unguarded—but when three of the four guards accompanying her strained against its weight, she understood that it did not need protection.

Once it was open far enough to allow the sunlight to reach them again, their party slipped through to the other side. Wren squinted in the sunlight, coaxing her vision back by surveying first the hem of her skirt and then her feet and then finally the tile that her boots clicked against. Just ahead, plush carpet—dark in hue with gold threaded throughout—brought the world back into focus, and when she lifted her eyes, the air caught in her lungs.

They stood at the head of a great foyer with half a dozen columns towering on either side of the carpeted hall. On the right, light streamed in from windows that were nearly as tall as the columns, while rows of doors mirrored them on the opposite wall. Affixed between each were enormous portraits, ornate and ancient, though there were no pictures within the frames.

One in particular caught Wren's eye—a frame molded in curls of gold—and she took a small step toward it. Her knees suddenly buckled and gave way and one of the soldiers grasped her elbow, steadying her. Wren closed her eyes against the dizziness overtaking her. But when she opened them again, she stood alone.

People hurried past, women with rosy cheeks and silken skirts. Men wearing uniforms decorated with embroidered embellishments and rows of buttons lining their jackets. A small group of individuals strolled by, laughing together, their cloaks swishing and kicking up star-laced dhust. Children ran past, followed closely by a laughing woman, her delicate ears pointed and her gait graceful. And upon every being that passed, not one mask was seen.

Instead of frosted panes, the windows were replaced by shaped panels of glass stained in various colors, each one casting a rainbow across the white, tiled floor that shone brilliantly under their light. But what drew her eye the most were the banners displayed on the enormous columns. The pennants hung proudly, each a deep emerald edged in gold, and embroidered in the center of every one was a single clover.

Its leaves stood to the north, south, east, and west, all dimpled at their tip and thinned at their root. Each was brocaded in gold filigree, its central design wrought and woven into feathered twists and interlocking curls. Attached only at the very center, the leaves stood independent of one another, yet connected at the heart, forming an ornate clover, bold yet delicate and sparkling in the light as if the thread were truly spun gold.

Wren blinked once and the banners vanished. The colors disappeared from the floor and she was once again standing on the rug in the dimly lit hall amid the soldiers in their expressionless masks. Yet her eyes stung with unshed tears, and there was a radiant warmth in her chest that welled with pride.

Before she could utter a word, a door at the opposite end of the foyer swung open, slamming into the empty frame behind it. A short man strode their way, his silver hair flying out every which way around a mask crafted to look identical to the face of an owl. He marched straight to the soldiers and stopped directly in front of them.

His eyes, visible through the mask, narrowed on Wren. "A strange-looking woman says she has something His Majesty wants and you march her straight to our door without so much as a question? If I tell you you're a bird, would you seek to fly from the top of the east tower as well?"

The guards shifted on their feet, but Wren only straightened and stepped forward. "This strange-looking woman holds a relic containing magic. But if you'd rather me leave, then I suppose I will be on my way."

The owl-man's eyes were beady through the holes of their

ornate cage. Finally, they flicked to the guards. "Leave us," he crowed, and without hesitation the guards turned on their heels and strode away.

Wren faced the small man, her posture betraying no concern. He circled her, reminding her oddly of a fowl circling its prey, and her eyes followed his every step—head swiveling to his position, unwilling to back down.

He finally came to a halt in front of her again. "You are a foolish girl, but not easily frightened. We shall see what you feel gazing upon the face of our great king."

Turning on his heel, he strode away. "Come along," he tossed dismissively over his shoulder, as if she were nothing more than a dog.

Wren followed, bristling at the summons.

Instead of returning through the door he had used to enter, the man led her to an arch toward the end of the hall, up a grand stairwell, and down a series of corridors before finally stopping in front of a pair of large, wooden doors. Two guards were posted outside, each bearing the same wolf mask.

The guards parted for the owl-man, and he paused long enough for the doors to be opened. Wren followed him into the room, but when the doors closed behind them, the man stopped and bent at the waist in a low, sweeping bow.

A long table stretched in front of him with maps strewn about, and at the opposite end stood a man. He had a prominent chin and strong cheekbones, and his amber eyes were keen and sharp. He was younger than Wren had imagined and far better looking. His svelte figure was chiseled beneath an opulent waistcoat, and lean muscles rippled against the tapered trousers that hugged his body. He was still older than she was, as his dark to luminescent silver hair would attest, but his skin was as smooth as a youth's might be. And on his head rested a crown, its four tallest spires crafted into a shape that caused Wren's eyes to widen—dimpled four-leaf clovers.

To his right, standing silently in the corner, another man towered over the room, his very presence shrouding the space in hushed fear. His boots were blemish-free, his trousers pressed straight, and his jacket crisp and black while its embroidered gold bars stretched across his chest, their fasteners catching the light from the torches along both walls. Tassels stitched onto the shoulders gave way to the white collar that rose about his neck, barely kissing his fully masked face. Only this guard was no animal. His mask was that of a man, eyes hollow, lips carved into the ivory, and stress marks cracking the skin. It would have been frightful were it not for the delicate gold filigree on either side, framing the lifeless facade like horror trapped in art. His dark hair was combed straight back, and while he stood at ease with a gloved hand on the pommel of his sword, it was clear that this soldier was set apart from the rest.

The sight of him chilled Wren to her core.

"Musannulos. What have you brought me?" the king asked the small man, though his eyes did not stray from Wren.

The owl-man, Musannulos, straightened and stepped aside, extending an arm to Wren. "This woman was recovered in the Aestival Forest. She claims she is in possession of something Your Majesty requires and has requested an audience."

The king's eyes surveyed her, appraising her in a way that made Wren's skin crawl and looking down his nose disapprovingly at her general presence. He glanced back to Musannulos. "Leave us," he commanded. With a bow, Musannulos was gone, closing the door firmly behind Wren yet again.

The king straightened, every bit the height of the soldier at his side, and turned to stroll down the left side of the table. As if tethered to his motion, the soldier moved as well, stalking step for step with the king down the right.

Wren centered herself, certain she did not want to turn a shoulder to either of the men, but still her posture remained relaxed. She was used to influential, self-assured men standing over her. She had never once bent for them, she would not begin now.

"Your Highness," she said, dipping into a curtsy. "I have come here to offer you something you may have use for. But I have also come to ask for your help."

The king laughed, the sound rich but also deadly, cracking the confidence surrounding Wren's heart. He was devastatingly handsome, but there was a darkness about him she could not deny. "And who are you, a *woman*, to demand an audience with the most powerful being in the realm?"

"I'm a *human* not of your realm who believes the most powerful king can help her return home."

The king stopped before her, and Wren glanced out of the corner of her eye to see the soldier had done the same to her right. They both stared at her, the king with a face of stone and the soldier with a mask of deadly calm. "And what, pray tell, could you offer me in exchange for this great favor?"

Wren smiled and slipped her hair behind her ear. "Ancient magic strong enough to bring back the true rulers of this world," she replied unflinchingly. "Help me return home and I will give it to you. Deny me and I will make sure it is your undoing."

CHAPTER SIXTEEN

*T*he king stared at Wren and she could see every reason why the rebels referred to him as a rat. His eyes were ravenous, and she was certain that if he were not regal, he would bare his teeth at her.

"And you think it wise to come into my presence and give me an ultimatum?" he asked, a smile playing on his lips. "Tell me, what stops me from having your blood splattered on my walls and your magic stolen as my own?"

Wren only smiled demurely. "What is more curious to me is that you took me at my word without question. The magic is hidden where only I can find. If you kill me, its location dies with me. But, if you help me, my last action here will be to surrender it to you."

The king eyed her closely. He flicked his eyes to the soldier beyond Wren and back again. A strong hand instantly clamped her upper arm and another wrapped around her throat, gripping it like a vice.

The air rushed from Wren's lungs with a gasp, and the king stepped into her vision, blocking out the room entirely as black spots danced before her eyes. His eyes bore into her own, casually stripping her soul bare one layer at a time, and then he spoke slowly. "I am inclined to believe you are not from this world, but with such a knowledge, how do I know you are not one of those filthy rebels sent to draw me out?"

The grasp on Wren's throat loosened enough to allow words. "I do not know—what rebels—you speak of. But I will— I will remain here. In the castle. As your loyal subject."

The king chewed on the words, his stare gnawing at her resolve. Finally, he stepped back and gave a small nod. The soldier released Wren, and she slumped forward, gulping in air. Dizziness overtook her, but to her shock, soft hands came around her own.

She looked up and found the king himself steadying her. "There, there, my dear. You must know that this land is dangerous. Not many friends can be trusted, let alone a stranger. But you are lucky to have come here and fortunate to have sought my favor. I will grant you safe harbor within my court. But I am afraid I cannot do as you ask at this time."

Wren's heart sank, but the king pressed on. "Because my rule is contested, I cannot readily draw from the power my throne should afford me. And if you insist on withholding the ancient magic that you claim to possess, then I am without option. I may only grasp at the threads of magic when the moon rises full in the sky. I will return you home, but it will be some time until then."

She rubbed her throat where she could still feel the imprint of gloves stinging her skin. "When is your next full moon?"

The king laughed haughtily. "We just passed the third-quarter moon."

"So that would mean...."

"The full moon shall return greater than three months from now."

Wren did not allow her inward flinch to reflect on her face. She would be trapped in this castle, in the court of the Rat King, away from her world and home, from her grandmother, for three months. It was a painful reality, one she had hoped to avoid at all costs, and she struggled to wrap her mind around it, though she knew she had no other choice. She nodded, forcing down the bitter pill of resolution. "Very well. Then I accept your invitation and will stay here, where you can keep watch, for three months. And on the night you help me return home, I will turn over the magic to you."

The king smiled broadly, and to Wren's surprise he took a step back and sketched a low bow. "Then allow me to be the first to welcome you to my court. I am King Phillipae Vasileio, first of my name. And you are?"

Wren placed her palm back in his outstretched hand. "Lady Florence Klaver. Thank you, Your Majesty, for your hospitality. Especially during these dangerous times."

The king pressed a kiss to the back of her hand and straightened slowly, his eyes a burning ember. "Dangerous times indeed."

He clapped his hands together twice, and the door swung open far enough for Musannulos to scurry in. "Musannulos, please escort Lady Klaver to the guest quarters on the eastward wall. Send up Lady Poultney, as well as the royal modiste so that she may be fitted properly for court."

Musannulos bent into an exaggerated bow, so low that the beak of his mask nearly brushed the floor. "Yes, Your Majesty."

Wren moved to follow the small owl-man but jumped back when she found the soldier still towering over her. His blank, unseeing eyes twitched slightly, and it was then that Wren realized they were his eyelids, closed to create unnerving voids, and not a part of the mask itself.

She side-stepped him and made for the door, but the king's voice stopped her once again. "Lady Florence? Do know that if you are lying to me, I will find out. One way or another, I always do."

Wren pasted a gracious smile on her lips. "Understood. And thank you, Your Majesty."

He nodded in dismissal, and Wren turned, following Musannulos from the room without so much as a glance back at the king or his terrifying bodyguard.

They moved back through the castle, Wren trailing behind the man who scurried along on short legs, and returned to the same stairwell they had climbed moments before. After ascending a few more flights of stairs, Wren felt the air in the corridors grow warmer. Soon enough, windows became more frequent and the halls brighter, signaling that they were closer to the outer walls of the castle. Finally, turning down a long, carpeted hall, Musannulos stopped outside a single door.

"Your quarters, Lady Klaver. I shall send your lady-in-waiting along shortly with the royal modiste to collect your measurements and fit you with your mask." He turned on his heel and disappeared back down the hall without waiting for Wren to utter a word.

She opened the door and surveyed her quarters in pleasant surprise and awe. Large, oval windows allowed warm, natural light to flood across the floor of the spacious room. She was at a high enough elevation to not only overlook the half-moon shaped bailey that lay between the castle and the rampart, but she could also gaze out over the meadow all the way to its distant edge where it met the sea.

A four-poster bed stood proudly against one wall, its canopies drawn back, and along the other stood a dresser beside a full-length mirror. Off the main room was a modest bathroom with a wash basin, a chamber pot open to a deep hole that disappeared well into the depths of the castle, and a large soaking tub devoid of water.

A small desk and a stool rounded out the living space, but before Wren could even sit down, a rapping noise sounded at the door.

"Come in," she called, and the door swung open to reveal a woman in a rose gold mask with the pointed ears and snout of a fox. Closing the door behind her, she dipped into a low curtsy and tipped her face to the floor, revealing coiffed locks of golden hair pinned into a shimmering net at the back of her neck.

"Lady Kathrina Poultney, my lady. I shall escort you for the duration of your time here at court."

Wren smiled and dipped her head as the woman rose. "I'm Florence. It's a pleasure to meet you. And since we're in here, can you remove that thing or does it really have to stay on everywhere?"

She heard a muffled noise, like a swallowed giggle hidden by the mask. "His majesty requires his people to remain masked, so we obey willingly."

Wren nodded with a sigh. "Well…that will be fun."

The small laugh came again, but this time the woman reached up and released two pins from her hair. She slid the mask off her face, and Wren was met with cheeks flushed from the heat, rose-colored lips, and dancing green eyes. "This is much better," Kathrina said, breathing a sigh of relief. "But the masks must stay on when in the presence of another, or outside our own quarters. To be found without is a punishable offense."

Wren frowned. "You'd be punished for not wearing a mask?"

Kathrina smiled but there was a tinge of sadness in her eyes. "His majesty is benevolent and kind, and he asks that, in return, we offer our subservience to him."

"And you do that by wearing the faces of animals?" Wren asked bluntly.

Kathrina nodded in earnest. "We do. It is a reflection of our reverence for him as our lord and king. We defer our humanity to his own and thereby swear fealty in word and deed."

"That is…" *Creepy*, Wren thought. "Admirable," she said instead.

Kathrina nodded, her smile unmoved, though a single eyebrow lifted as if she questioned Wren's sincerity.

A knock sounded on the door once again, and Kathrina slid the mask back into place moments before it opened to reveal a tall, rail-thin man. He wore the enamel face of a goat, the mask's long beard chiseled from the same pewter as the horns that twisted above his head. Wren could not help but grimace slightly, thinking of how terribly heavy it must be, and made a note to be careful which mask she chose.

Two additional individuals followed—each with similar masks featuring the curled horns of a ram—carrying a long case that was locked tight at either end.

"You may select your mask from the royal collection," he said, an accent thick on his tongue. "I shall fit you for your gowns. They are to be delivered in advance of the ball."

"Ball?" Wren asked, turning to Kathrina.

The lady fox nodded. "His majesty holds a ball each night. The seven dances are when his court gathers before him in entertainment and merrymaking so that he may delight in our pleasure."

Slightly unnerved by the words, Wren turned her attention back to the case that had been laid across the desk. It was so long that the ends hung off either side. The locks snapped apart at the behest of the ram-masked stewards and the lid was lifted to reveal rows upon rows of gilded masks.

"You may choose whichever speaks to your heart and your loyalty to our king," the modiste said, a note of pride in his voice as he extended his hand to the collection.

Wren stepped forward and surveyed the display, which appeared to be organized by species and size. Foxes and bears, rams, goats, and sheep, saber-toothed cats and long-horned gazelle, but notedly absent were any masks that resembled mice, rats, wolves, or even an owl. And certainly none that looked like the face of a human, let alone the man who had nearly strangled her before the king.

Mirrored shards caught her eye, and she reached for the mask, untangling it from the mass of ribboned ties. She delicately removed it from the box and held it up to her face. Turning to the mirror, her breath caught in her throat at the sight.

The mask covered her chin and mouth entirely in a smooth, brushed-silver fabric laid upon what felt like stiff wax. However, circling the eyes, sweeping up the right side of the forehead and down across the left cheekbone were layers of mirrored feathers, giving her face the sleek appearance of a glass swan caught in flight.

"The king would allow part of her face to remain?" Kathrina asked the modiste, indicating the skin that would be revealed both above and below the wings of the asymmetric design.

"Musannulos carried his word that it may," he replied. "She is His Majesty's honored guest."

Kathrina murmured in affirmation. "You are quite lucky, my lady. It is a great honor."

Wren held the mask in place, a cold feeling settling over her that she could not quite place. Something about it called for her, begging her to keep it close, while at the same time it felt so very wrong. "A great honor," she echoed.

The modiste took her measurements and left swiftly, his assistants in tow, leaving Kathrina to show Wren how to fasten her mask with pins in a way that would not apply too much pressure or strain on her face and head after long periods of time.

She had just placed the finishing touches on Wren's makeup, embellishing her eyes with a shimmering powder, and was wrangling her too-short hair into coiffed submission when the door opened once again.

Lady's maids, each with the face of a peacock, streamed in

the room carrying armfuls of dresses in—to Wren's surprise—only a handful of colors.

When the door clicked shut once more, Kathrina removed her mask and beckoned Wren over to the piles of skirts, beginning to organize them in the wardrobe one color at a time.

"His Majesty commands us to wear gray within the city walls. Our clothes are simple and indiscriminate so that our masks may shine. However, in return, he gifts us with the most opulent designs in his given colors for the dances every night. There is no limit to the number we may have, no restriction to the design, as long as we remain in the correct color."

She held up a selection of dresses in shades of shimmering gold and blush. "These are for the Dance of the Sun." Nudging them to one arm, she pointed to a pile of velvety amethyst and lavender silk. "These are for the Dance of the Roses."

Some of the gowns that followed were pale blue, while others were soft cream, but all were elaborately decorated with glittering embroidery and brilliant diamond gemstones. "These here are for the Dance of the Frost."

Next to those were flowing, ethereal dresses in layers of forest and dewy green organza. "Those are for the Dance of the Faeries." The next group appeared to be ballgowns of delicate black lace and smooth ivory silk. "These belong to the Dance of Midnight, and all of the dresses in crimson and silver are for the Dance of Storm and Fire." Coming to the end of the line, she beckoned to the lengths of copper and sienna finery. "And lastly, we have the Dance of the Harvest."

Wren was awestruck as she surveyed the dresses being loaded into the wardrobe, and her mouth fell slightly agape when Kathrina tugged the selection of crimson skirts back out. "Tonight is the Dance of Storm and Fire," she said with a spark in her eye. "Shall you be the storm that ignites the flame? Or will you burn with a raging fire?"

Wren selected a gown of deep red, its fitted bodice a soft

velvet and its full skirts tulle, giving the illusion that she was half princess and half ballet dancer. Kathrina laced up the corset, its silver embroidered and sequined accents fitting Wren's curves like a glove. Straps roughly an inch wide sat on her shoulders but quickly slid off—unnecessary with how well the bodice held her in place—leaving her neck bare to the ends of hair that had been left to curl against her collarbone.

Finally stepping back to admire her handiwork, Kathrina nodded. "A perfect fit for court. Both you and the dress. I must hurry now to change, then I shall return and we will greet the evening. I hear it is to be a wonderful celebration."

CHAPTER SEVENTEEN

*W*ren wasn't quite sure what she expected, but it wasn't for the court to be a full-blown ballroom. Her heeled slippers clicked across the marbled floor, the sound muffled by the conversations already underway, and she was grateful for the mask that concealed her open-mouthed expression.

She turned in place, taking in the warm glow from the dozens of small lanterns suspended all over the room. The space itself was bathed in red and orange and streaming down from the ceiling were sparkling strands of what looked like spun silver, giving the illusion that the room was ignited in flame by a storm of lightning.

Tables lined the walls with many a reveler already seated, enjoying the copious amounts of food and drink that had been placed everywhere for their merriment. Still more guests turned about in the center of the floor, dancing in time with the music and one another, and a band played off in a corner beside the dais where a single large throne sat.

The king was already there, reclined with his bloodred regalia on full display against the brilliant silver and onyx of his hair. Posted beside him, clothed in dark gray and flashing silver like an oncoming storm, stood the same soldier in the same mask—his eyes like hunks of coal, lifeless and cold—somehow looking even more severe in the room of brilliant reds and jovial animal faces.

Wren stood in awe, speechless at the opulence of the puppets commanded by a king who gave them no alternative. The court barely resembled the humble city she had been led through or the elfin folk cloistered in their domain—and certainly not the rebels who lived beside warm hearths within trees.

"What is this place?" she wondered aloud.

"His Majesty beckons, Lady Florence," Kathrina murmured from her side, and when Wren turned, she was already being whisked away by a man with the face of a lion.

Wren spun on her heel to face the dais and saw the king staring directly at her, his finger crooked in summoning.

Navigating a path around the dance floor, Wren dipped in a curtsy before the throne.

The king smiled broadly and stood with his arms outstretched in welcome. "A swan. How delightful! You fit in my court as if you were meant to belong, Lady Florence. Tell me, what do you think of my ball?"

"It is beautiful, Your Majesty," Wren said honestly, and when the king continued to stare at her she realized how difficult it was to flatter him with her face half hidden. "I have never been anywhere like this," she pressed on, painting an enamored glow across her eyes. "It is truly one of the most stunning places I have ever seen. I cannot thank you enough for the dresses as well. Your graciousness knows no bounds."

The king's face softened, though his eyes remained shrewd, and he sank back into the throne. As if noticing the presence of the soldier standing at attention by his side for the first time, he absentmindedly ran his hand down the arm of his jacket, picking lint from his glove and treating him as no more than a drape or tapestry hung against the wall. "You flatter me, Lady Florence. I do hope that our encounter today has not left you ill at heart in any way. Sometimes my soldier can be a little...heavy-handed."

His choice of words was not lost on Wren, and for the first time she was glad a mask concealed the thoughts she was certain were evident all over her face. "I am quite well. Thank you for asking."

The king nodded, a possessive hand still on the man frozen like stone by his side, when his face lit up. "Ah! Your first partner of the evening approaches. I shall let you fly away now. Dance for me well. I do love a good display."

Wren's brow furrowed but when she glanced to the left, a man with the face of a horse was bowing at her side. She stammered out her protests, but he took her hand anyway and spun her onto the floor.

Panic bloomed, overtaking her mind, causing her limbs to lock and her muscles to go taut. She had never danced before— at least not like this. Family weddings and proms were hardly the occasion for ballroom dancing, and she found herself far more alarmed at this prospect than she had anything since the wealdwolf.

Her partner was gracious, though she could feel his reluctance to continue dancing with her as they navigated the floor. She tripped over his feet as well as her own, moving her arms a solid beat behind the other dancers in clumsy, awkward gestures. Sure enough, the moment the song ended, he relinquished her hand and disappeared into the crowd.

Wren slowly searched the room for a vacant seat and came up empty. Deciding she would rather lean against a wall than suffer through another dance, she had just reached the side of the room when a hand caught her arm.

She turned, coming face to face with the snout of a fox. "You must dance," whispered Kathrina, looping her arm through Wren's in a feigned turn about the room.

"I cannot dance," Wren murmured in return.

"Then you must learn. The king will not be pleased if you do not dance. These nights are his gifts to us. His kindness. You are new at court and mustn't appear ungrateful."

As quickly as she had appeared on Wren's arm, Kathrina vanished again into the throng of dancers. Wren watched them for a moment, trying to grasp the concept of the dance or at the very least to connect with the music. She clasped and unclasped her hands, nervous energy coursing through her body, willing her to ignore Kathrina's warning and leave. But her senses made her painfully aware of the attention she was drawing from the dais, and though she wished otherwise, she understood that she was no more than a pretty pawn on a lavish game board. She did not determine the moves here. And it was better to learn and follow the steps than be controlled and directed without agency. Taking one long, deep breath, she pushed down the cold uncertainty and took to the floor again.

This dance felt simpler, and with couples being exchanged hand to hand in repetitive movements, it made it easier for her to relax. She was certain she was making a fool of herself in front of an entire line of dancers, but at least she was not stepping on the feet of just one single person. It was a small win, but she would take it.

The song ended and a new, mid-tempo piece started up on the strings. The line broke apart into couples, and Wren's chest filled with unease when a firm hand snaked around her waist. The opposite gloved palm slid against her own, guiding their hands up and turning her with grace and ease into the arms of her partner for the next dance.

Wren sighed to herself, sorry for the poor soul, but when she lifted her eyes, she was grateful that his hold kept her steady. The king's guard stood before her, his half-doll, half-human face now close enough for her to make out every swirl and filigree ornately crafted down the sides of his mask. Only this time, instead of the dead, unseeing eyes, she was met with a familiar hazel, their green flecks piercing her disbelief with venomous daggers.

"You," she hissed at the same moment Timothius uttered, "Traitor."

Wren was aghast. "*I'm* a traitor? Are you serious right now?"

The hand on her waist tightened. "You must dance, my dear swan," he said, voice low and deep, warm and threatening all at once. "And be aware that the steps will move quickly."

Wren rolled her eyes. "Wonderful. At least I won't feel bad stepping on your toes."

"I was about to suggest that," said Timothius matter-of-factly. "My boots are walled with steel. Stand on my feet."

"Stand on your fe— Are you crazy? What makes you think I want to be that close to you?"

"It is not uncommon for dancers to grow closer on the floor. Beyond that, the king is watching. And there are things we must discuss."

"I have nothing to discuss with—"

Timothius hoisted her from the floor and rested her toes upon the tips of his boots. Sure enough, they felt as solid as the floor and did not sag or bend in any place. And to Wren's relief there was still a hair's breadth of space between them, despite it vanishing when Timothius's arm locked around her waist and pulled her flush against his body.

She glared at him and though his eyes were embers burning back, something other than anger and disgust lit the flame—a different kind of heat that stirred deep within Wren's core and caused the room to feel much hotter.

The music cut a lively pace between ballad and folk tune, and with effortless strength, Timothius widened his steps and covered the dance floor in remarkably graceful strides, bringing Wren along for the ride.

He refused to look at her now and she tried her best to ignore him, though remaining in the prison of his arms made him inescapable. What did avoiding eye contact matter when the scent of dark amber and suede was cementing its place in her memory forever? And what good were masks when the only thing she could see when she glanced at him were light freckles, soft curls, and a smirk that made his eyes dance?

"Was it your intention all along to betray those who sought to help you? Or did you decide to take part after you had been fed, clothed, and provided safety?"

And then he had to open his mouth.

"I'm sorry, I thought this time was for dancing. Surely the king's right-hand man would have a more suitable place for interrogations. Do you torture people on the rack here or has that not been invented yet?"

"I am not the king's right-hand man, I am—"

"A liar? A double agent? A phony? Does Enya know where you are? Who you are and what you do when you're *traveling*? Does Elric?"

"Do not speak their names here," Timothius replied tersely, and Wren found herself thankful that their masks concealed their mouths. There was nothing to betray their conversation or outward disdain for one another save the tension bracketing both their postures.

"Were you a part of their lies, or were you too busy sneaking away to hide your own? E is in on all of this too, isn't he?" she accused.

"He is not related to my affairs, he merely keeps my secret."

"And why would he do that? It couldn't be because the rebel leader stands side by side with the man he insists on overthrowing, could it? Do you plan to stage a coup? Take the throne for yourself?"

"You know nothing of what you speak," Timothius all but growled, his tone reminiscent of the one he had used when he first spoke to Wren. When he had asked her what king sat on the throne.

"And I don't need to know," she said dismissively. "The king will help me. I just have to be patient and wait. And apparently learn how to dance."

The grip on her palm tightened, the arm about her waist cinching tighter, causing her spine to arch gracefully with the music. Timothius tipped her back only slightly and her chest rose and fell rapidly between them. His eyes flicked down at her for a moment and then he quickly straightened, loosening his hold enough for her back to straighten as well.

"The king does not help people," he rumbled. "He does what he wishes to get what he wants. You have flaunted something that he desires, and he shall entertain you long enough to learn the truth of what you claim to possess. When he finds out, he will take it from you and leave you to bleed out on the floor."

"He will? Or *you* will?"

Timothius's eyes were unflinching, and though he did not utter a word, his next step faltered ever so slightly, bringing a triumphant smile to Wren's face. Too bad he couldn't see it. "Oh, did I strike a nerve? I'm so sorry. I assumed you enjoyed being commanded to do things like choke out innocent women. My bad."

"I will say again, you know nothing of what you speak," uttered Timothius, his voice lethal.

"I know enough," Wren retorted. "And I know enough to get myself home, so thank you for your help. Even if it was just to hide me away until you could figure out if I was any use to you. I can take it from here, just stay out of my way."

The song ended sharply, and before a new piece could begin, Wren stepped down from Timothius's boots. Gathering her skirt in her hands, she sank into the lowest and most elaborate curtsy she could muster on already fatiguing legs. "Thank you for the dance, Master Liar. Enjoy the rest of your evening."

She straightened, turned on her heel, and strode away with all the pride and confidence she possessed, feeling the soldier's stare burn against her back the entire way.

Catching her arm, Kathrina spun her into a small cluster of women gathered beside a table and pushed a flute of sparkling liquid into her hand. The other women—already intoxicated, loud, and quite oblivious to their presence—provided them with the perfect cover.

"What was the meaning of that?" Kathrina asked, shock coloring her tone.

"The meaning of what? The dance? He offered to teach me a few steps, that's all."

"The King's Glaive teaching someone how to dance? Now I've seen it all."

Wren felt uneasy and when her eyes rested on Timothius once again standing beside the king, she asked, "Who is he? What does a Glaive do?"

Kathrina took a healthy swig from her flute. "No one knows who he is. He is above us and favored by the king, silently waiting by his side to do his bidding. He stands where he is told, moves when and where is permitted, and in return is allowed the only human face apart from His Majesty himself. We might be the pets on display in the royal sanctuary, but he is nothing more than a plaything, always within reach of the king to toy with as he sees fit."

She paused, sliding closer to Wren and lowering her voice before continuing. "A glaive, however, is a weapon. A sword upon the end of a pole. It is deadly and allows those who wield it to stay a safe distance away. So that is what the people call him. The king does not lift a finger. He does not exact judgment or punishment. He keeps his hands clean and his merciful nature assured while his toy soldier carries out justice with his blood-drenched gloves."

The disdain was not hidden in Kathrina's tone, and while she sipped the last of her drink beneath her mask, Wren could not help but ask, "Do you not care for the king?"

Kathrina stiffened. "I am loyal to His Majesty. I am grateful for his benevolence and the roof he has placed over my head. But I do not agree with all of his actions. I have seen too many lives cut down on rumor and suspicion." She glanced around the room. "But find me the person who can agree wholeheartedly with their leader all of the time. It is not possible, or else the world would be free of wars and rebellions."

Wren nodded, the woman's choice of words not lost on her. "I think you are right," she said, draining her own glass in a single swig. "And I say that is plenty of discussion for one night. But before we go back to dancing, will you do something for me?"

Kathrina dipped in a small curtsy. "Anything, my lady. I am here to serve you."

Wren grabbed two full flutes from the table and pressed one into the fox's hand with a smile she knew her eyes would convey. "Call me Wren."

CHAPTER EIGHTEEN

The lights were far too bright and the sound of her own pounding head was excruciatingly loud when Wren awoke the next day. Lying on her back, she stared at the canopy overhead and followed its swirls, each one resembling its own small constellation.

Her thoughts wandered over everything that had happened since her arrival in this strange world, homing in especially on her choices in recent days. She liked Kathrina and trusted her well enough, but not to the extent that she had bonded with Elric.

It stung recalling his words in the garden. Should she have confronted him? Yes, she knew that. But she had been betrayed and taken for a fool. And she had been too stubborn to face it.

Arriving in this world had been jarring and very little had made sense, but over time she had come to appreciate the second chance it offered her. The taste of what it felt like to be known and remembered. She had never experienced a life in which she was so visible to everyone, and now that she was, she was not sure how she felt about it. But when she spoke to Elric within the tree, and even to Timothius the night before he left the Elfin Domain, she had felt understood—accepted without effort. She had been drawn into the arms of their false security and had started to feel safe there.

Then the moment she realized she had been exploited by her own unspoken longing, all sense of rationality and fledgling empathy for them flew out the window. She had exercised her right to control her own fate, and look where it had landed her. Essentially, a prisoner to a man who clearly had a superiority complex and his assassin who the court mocked and referred to as a toy, all on the tentative truth of—

Wren sat up straight, hand flying to her neck.

Where is my necklace?

Swinging her legs off the side of the bed, she ignored the dizziness that was causing her sluggish movements and rushed to where her dress lay in a heap on the floor. Rummaging around her skirts, it took a moment, but she finally came up with the orb clutched in her hand. To the eye it looked unharmed, but its jagged cracks were now driven almost clear through the center.

She had hardly been in the castle a day and it was nearly broken again.

Slipping the chain over her head, she tucked it into her nightdress, thankful for its weight resting against her skin. It was her lifeline. And not just to her return home, but to her grandmother.

Her heart ached at the thought of remaining in this world for months. She was hopeful it really was a lesser span of time in her world, but time itself was not on her side where her grandmother was concerned. She needed to get home.

She began to untangle the pins from her hair and her thoughts drifted to the ornament and its prospective breaking— of the magic it was rumored to release. What would it do to this world? Who would it aid in the end? And what *would* become of her? She wished she knew, but the side that had sworn to help her only wanted her for the ornament, and the side she currently resided on made it clear they only sought to obtain its power. And somewhere in the middle of them all, playing with fire, stood Wren. She had come to this world begging for it to be a nightmare and she was perilously close to her wish coming true.

The best she could do was pass the time and guard the orb with her life. She was here for one purpose and one purpose only. She did not care what happened between the rebels and the Rat King, she just wanted to return home. And the ornament was her key to getting there.

A handful of lady's maids swept in the room moments later, laying out a crisp gray dress and drawing her a bath. To her dismay, they stayed to help her get ready for the day, even though she longed to rest in the warm bath for hours on her own. Once she was dressed, however, they merely curtsied and moved to exit.

"Wait," she said, stopping the last maid before she could leave. "What am I to do today?"

The maid looked bewildered. "Whatever you wish, m'lady. Guests of His Majesty hold no tasks, they simply attend court."

With a quick bow, she exited the room, leaving Wren alone to her thoughts.

Whatever she wished?

Wren couldn't recall the last time she had the time to do what she wanted. She struggled to remember the last time she let herself slow down for more than a day or a long weekend.

Snapping from her thoughts, she rushed to the door and stuck her head out. "Miss?"

The maid stopped and turned again.

Wren cleared her throat. "I would like food sent here to my room. And wine. A bottle, if you don't mind."

The maid dipped into a curtsy. "Yes, m'lady."

By the time Kathrina entered the room ahead of the nightly

dance, Wren was dressed in a gown made of copper silk with an empire waist and long sleeves split open at the shoulders and down the length of her arms. With a small giggle, she drained the last of her second bottle of wine and draped an arm around Kathrina's shoulders, sliding straight off at the lack of resistance from the fabric of her dress.

"Another night, another ball!" she declared. "Shall we?"

❄

THE NEXT DAYS followed in the same way, with Wren's afternoons spent languishing and her nights a blurry fog of dresses, dancing, and lords and ladies. And at every dance the king presided over it all with his toy soldier at his side, his mask motionless but his eyes following Wren's every move.

The avoidance left Wren feeling uneasy, yet also placated. The ornament was no longer cracking or breaking, and each day's routine lulled her into a comfortable stasis. A week ticked down, and then another, and then more, moving time closer to the full moon and her return home.

It was one such night—her satin dress dripping from her body in draped sheaths of gold, concealing the ornament in the folds hanging about her neck—that she felt Kathrina begin to pull away from her.

"What has gotten into you?" she asked the lady-in-waiting beside her.

"I am concerned for you, my lady," she replied, face grim and eyes serious. "You spend your days in the bottle and your nights the same. Merriment is one thing, but where it does not end, there is danger."

Wren snorted around her glass. "Danger seems to have no issue finding me. If it decides to show up in a bottle, at least I'll feel good when it does."

Sorrow filled Kathrina's emerald eyes. "What a sad way to live out an existence."

"And what a harsh judgment to pass when you don't have to walk in my shoes," Wren fired back. She drained her glass and deposited it on the table with a *clink*.

"I mean no judgment," Kathrina said quietly for only Wren to hear. "If it is distraction you seek, then accompany me to my tasks each day. Let me show you the kingdom and its people. I know it is not your home, but joy can still be found in the waiting."

Wren considered it, the thought sparking an excitement in her that she had not felt in some time, but she pushed the notion down. There was too much at stake. She just needed to keep her head down and make it to the full moon.

"I can't," she answered, shaking her head with genuine remorse. "I'm sorry."

She left Kathrina at the table and cut into the circle of dancers on the floor, beginning to spin beside them. She had become an adequate dancer, the intoxication relaxing her enough to learn without overthinking, and though she hated to admit it, she quite enjoyed the varying themes and the music that differed with each night's ball.

The band had just begun to play a new piece, the notes long and the tempo lively, when a strong forearm met her own and diverted her course.

Gloved fingers pressed lightly against the skin inside her elbow, sending a familiar warmth zinging through her veins. Arms parallel, she rested her hand on a jacket sleeve of deep copper. Its golden tassels, the exact shade of her dress, caught the light as Timothius moved around Wren like she was the sun and he an eclipse.

"You are drawing attention you do not want," he said in a low voice.

Wren snorted. "Clearly. You're here."

R.V. WILBUR

She spun with the music, Timothius doing the same, but this time she encircled him. "That is not what I meant," he replied. "Not everyone's intentions at court are honorable."

Wren smiled broadly, allowing it to reach her eyes as she completed her rotation. "As I said before: *Clearly*. You are here."

She heard him exhale and the dance carried them a step toward each other's right and then back again, repeating the motion to the left. Only instead of stepping back, his arm came around her waist. Lifting her clear off the floor, she was forced to grip his shoulder with one hand and the flex of his bicep with the other. He turned in a circle in smooth, even strides, keeping her face just slightly above his own.

In an instant, Wren was back in Brumal Forest, on the edge of the highway, nothing between their faces but chilled air and soft breaths. For a moment, she thought he may have had a similar memory, his eyes meeting hers finally, but when he spoke, his words were devoid of emotion. "Has it broken since you left the domain? Have there been any changes?"

Wren shook the memory away. "It has not changed, but I have. I am not a pawn in whatever game it is that you are playing, and you will not keep me here. The king will help me return home, but I will be taking the magic back with me. It will not fall into any of your hands because it will stay in mine."

Timothius lowered her to the ground before him and began his orbit again. "It was never our intent to trap you, but the magic did complicate things. And you must know the king will never let you go. Whatever he has planned for the full moon is a trick. You mustn't stay here."

Wren mirrored his steps, so close that their hips brushed when she passed. Nearly imperceptible tension lock his spine. He was the perfect soldier now, frozen at attention.

Coming back around to face him, she laid her hands on his shoulders and stepped onto the tips of his massive boots, rising

164

up on her toes to reach his ear. "You're right, you know," she whispered. "I mustn't stay here. Have a good night, toy soldier."

She stepped off to the side and slid by him, a small glance over her shoulder confirming that he had remained in place long after she walked away. A tall man in a gold cravat accosted her by the beverage table, plying her with drinks and dance for the next few hours until she could barely stand.

He suggested they adjourn to her room, and she was aware of him escorting her from the ball; however, when she looked around the hall, the walls were too bare and the carpet too old to be the one leading to her wing.

"Just a bit farther, my lady," he said with a slight hiccup.

Wren slowed, allowing him to walk ahead before stopping entirely. "Let's play a game," she challenged. "Catch the princess, get a kiss."

The man stumbled and turned to face her as she slipped out of her shoes and began to walk backward down the hall. "And who is the princess?" he slurred.

"Me!" she exclaimed, and then turned and ran down the hall as fast as her dress would allow. "Catch me if you can!"

She took corner after corner with surprising sobriety, his steps tripping across the floor behind her. The air was frigid in her lungs, indicating that she was near to the city's wall, and she worried about how she would find her way back to a familiar part of the castle once she had lost him.

She could no longer hear his footsteps, the sound of her own labored breathing the only noise filling the corridor. When she turned the next corner, the hall ended, but she smiled in relief at the sight of the walls lined with tapestries that stretched from floor to ceiling.

Perfect.

She slipped behind the farthest one, and once it billowed back into place, concealing her from view, she exhaled and allowed herself to slump against the wall. But instead of cold stone, it felt soft to the touch, and instead of supporting her, it gave way.

Wren landed squarely on her backside with a *thump*, a cloud of dust puffing up around her face and sending her into a coughing fit from the musty carpet that had barely cushioned her fall. Rolling onto her hands and knees, she could hardly see a thing save for the dim light creeping around the tapestry that had hidden whatever this place was from the rest of the castle.

She stepped into the dead-end hall again, peeking around the corner to ensure there was no one in sight, and removed a torch from the wall before carefully peeling back the tapestry.

A portrait. She had torn through a large portrait.

She took in the faded figures of a family, their faces long erased by time, and something within her stirred. Stepping back through the frame and into the hidden room, she raised the light and let it fill the space. Her breath caught, and all at once— like a rush of wind—the scene unfurled before her.

CHAPTER NINETEEN

*G*old flickered in the firelight. The clover banners shuddered with every beat pounding against the stone walls. Dust and rock fell from the roof above and plumes of smoke snuck in through the broken windows.

A man stood hunched over a desk, one hand on its surface, the other hiding his face as his shoulders shook with deep, silent sobs. She rushed to him and threw her arms around his neck, drawing him to her. He embraced her, enveloping her entirely in his warmth, thawing the chill that had poisoned her bones for too long. She felt it then—the inconceivable pain that was her very heart and soul being ripped into three parts that she would never see again.

"I have failed you," he whispered.

She pulled back, cradling his face in her hands. "No, my love. We were failed. The Trifolium has broken. The kingdoms are falling. You have done what you could."

"And it was not enough," he uttered bitterly.

"And yet it was everything," she replied, pressing a long kiss to his lips.

A sharp knock sounded against the door, and a tall man with a long, auburn beard appeared in the doorway, blood dripping from a wound in his temple. His eyes were filled with fury and starlight.

Pressing a hand to his heart, he fell to one knee. "My queen."

Her hand lifted, beckoning him to rise. She felt so much love for him. So much worry. "Errol, you must flee. Your family in the north will need you. There is not much time."

He shook his head. "There is no time, my queen. Obarian has fallen. We are all that remains."

Her heart thundered and tears stung her eyes. "No...."

Errol's hands wove dhust between them, his concentration bringing a fresh wave of blood trickling down the side of his face, running into his beard and cascading to the floor. Five more figures entered the room, one by one, taking their place in the storm of starlight gathering from his palms.

When the last had entered, he released the tempest in a surge of air. The door slammed shut and the room filled with clouded dhust, blacking out the world in a midnight blue that sparkled as though they stood in the night sky itself.

The breath caught in her throat. "What is this?"

The five men bowed to her, tears streaking down each of their faces, bloodshot eyes unable to hide their grief any longer. Horror bloomed in her chest, drawing lines across her face and leaching the warmth from her skin. She took the hand of her love in her own and gripped it tightly.

"We, the last of our kind, for the memory of our sons and daughters, bind our magic to thee," Errol said, his words steady but his voice breaking. "Your Majesty will not fall. Neither you, nor our king. You will be sent from here, never to return."

She clasped a hand to her mouth, tears dripping from her wide eyes as her heart fractured. "No...."

"You will not," Errol continued. "But you will usher in one who will. Your magic will sift from your body like the sands of time, but before your days are spent, you will bestow your power on one created for this world. They alone may return. They alone may save us."

"But the Thrones," she choked. "My brothers and sister have fallen. What will become of our world?"

Errol shook his head sadly. "That is not for us to know. We may yet fall, but we leave our home to those that follow. May their paths be clear and their futures be blessed."

She turned to the man beside her, burying her face in his chest. He held her, grieved with her—for a life, a future, a kingdom lost.

Taking a deep breath, she drew herself up. She removed the crown from her head and lay it on the desk, encircling the kingdom at its center. The heart of their world. Her home. Inflamel.

A second crown joined her own, only his was placed in the north, encircling the mountains and cliffs where a single castle resided, for it was the place that had held both his heart and his life.

Hands clasped, fingers entwined, they faced their inevitable future. One they never could have expected, yet one they knew they would live out together.

Errol nodded in reverence, and she reciprocated, her eyes conveying her resolve.

They were ready.

Placing a hand on his chest, fingers taut, Errol shut his eyes and summoned his magic. Starlight glistened on his skin and collected over his heart, gathering and churning, growing and spinning, and when his body started to tremble, a flash of brilliant light formed from the very life draining from his heart. His hair whitened, his skin withered, and as his body bent, it broke under the strain of age.

The next four Isteriaeth followed, stripping their own life, magic, and immortality from their beings to encircle his own—every one forming a new layer of crystalline light on top of the other—before they fell to the ground.

The fifth and final Isteriaeth did the same, and with his last bit of strength, took the orb in his hand. Stumbling forward, he placed it in the palm of his queen and laid the king's overtop.

Though his spirit was broken, his smile was triumphant, bringing force and passion to his final words. "Your Majesty, it has been our greatest honor serving and dying for you. May your days be long, and may you live to see the Thrones rise again."

She could not speak. Could not form words adequate enough to encapsulate the immeasurable sacrifice she had witnessed. But she did not have time to try. The world exploded around them, drawing them straight out of the room and far from the castle. Tugged on a tether high above the kingdom and beyond the realm, she would have believed her flesh was being ripped from her bones were it not for the orb firmly in her hand and the man beside her who refused to let go.

It was then and only then that she allowed herself to break. To grieve the loss and failure. To mourn the lives sacrificed to preserve her legacy. To cry for the world she would never lay eyes on again.

She had come to the end.

❄

WREN BLINKED. A sharp *crack* burst against her skin and glass rained upon the floor. Tears streamed down her cheeks, and her breaths heaved in shuddering gasps.

The light in her hand trembled, casting shadows across the capes strewn about the floor. The desk overturned in the corner. The map, singed and frayed, pinned beneath a broken chair.

She sank to the floor, unable and unwilling to move, and tugged the crystallum from the folds of her dress.

It was smaller now, the size of a golf ball, and a shimmering onyx with thin, gold bars that formed small crosses, like stitching on a canvas.

She grasped it in her palm and looked up, her eyes searching the space. On trembling legs, she rose and moved across the room to lift the sagging banner from where it was torn in two— pulling it together until the gold leaves of the clover met once again.

She didn't know what to think. Didn't know what to feel.

Was uncertain of what she had even seen, apart from the fact that she had been inside that woman's mind—the queen's mind. She had felt every emotion, seen the sacrifice, smelled the castle burning, and tasted the iron as she'd worried her own lips. Even now, Wren's lip ached from where she had pinned it between her teeth during the vision.

That was what it had been, right? A vision?

She turned and crossed the room—careful not to disturb the cloaks encircling the floor—and after finding a sconce on the wall to affix the torch to, she tugged the map free and spread it out on the ground.

Inflamel sat at its center, a river running through the middle with its city to the east and forests to the west. To its north was Obarian, the capital marked by a castle, with towns strewn from its valleys to the mountain range that separated it from another castle perched on the mountaintops, overlooking the sea.

She could faintly make out the words Grimoira on the westernmost country that had been largely singed from the map, and though all that remained was a *T* on the southernmost country, she recalled Timothius mentioning Tauriellis after her arrival.

But it was the castle in the mountains that her eyes returned to, and the words etched beside it, visible even through the soot.

The Trifolium Keep.

Trifolium Keep. Trifolium Thrones.

Wren looked to the banner, then back to the world splayed out before her, and finally to the orb hanging around her neck.

Reaching up, she brushed a trembling hand across her cheek, her fingers coming away soaked from her tear-drenched face.

She didn't know how or why, but she knew for certain that it had not been a vision.

It had been a memory.

CHAPTER TWENTY

*I*t took Wren far too long to find the way back to her room, but she made it in enough time to fall into bed and a deep, exhausted sleep. Now well-rested, sober, and ready for the day, she waited for Kathrina to arrive. It did not take long, and as soon as the woman entered her room, Wren stood.

"Kathrina, I am so sorry," she began, pausing for the woman to remove her mask.

Kathrina eyed her cautiously and then shook her head, her face softening. "You have been under much stress, all is forgiven. Was there something you needed?"

Wren smiled tentatively. "Do you mind if I join you today? For your tasks?"

Surprise shone in Kathrina's eyes and then gave way to a smile that took up half her face. "I would love that. Today is a good day for it too. I will be venturing outside the city proper. We have a harvest to collect."

Moments later, Wren was following Kathrina down corridor after corridor until they reached the spiral staircase of the shorter of the two main towers. The farther they descended, the

more the temperature plummeted, and Wren could not hide her shivering.

"Why is it so cold in here when it is warm outside?" she asked.

"Oh, that is because of the well system," Kathrina replied. "The water from the moat funnels beneath the city and through the castle before it travels to the sea. But unlike the river between the forests, which is rumored to be enchanted, the water here is frigid. It is pulled up through cisterns and heated in the kitchens for cooking, cleaning, and bathing. We are close to the well house now, actually."

Wren tugged her cloak tighter around her arms, and within a few moments, they emerged in a musty room filled with random items used by the castle's household. Handing Wren a basket and taking one of her own, Kathrina pushed the door ajar and—passing two guards posted outside—emerged into the sunlight.

It was late morning and the city's streets were already full. People acknowledged them as they passed, men tipping their hats and women nodding from behind their gilded shrouds. It unnerved Wren, and she was thankful for her own face cover-ing. She did not know how to respond, how to react, and decided finally on a small dip of her head.

What would she say if they spoke to her? She had never felt so noticed before, exposed, like she was naked and on display instead of just walking through a market. If she was ever to believe in magic, this would surely be a sign. Among family and even at work when she addressed people, they startled, rushing to catch their bearings and respond, as if she were immediately out of mind the second she was not within view. It had made so much discontent rise up within her, but now she found that she missed the comfort obscurity brought.

The women made for the drawbridge, and after confirming

her identity and intentions outside the city wall, the guards allowed Kathrina through with Wren by her side.

Once across the moat, Kathrina veered off the road to the left and began to stride knee-to-waist across the tall grass of the meadow that surrounded the city. Wren took the opportunity to look around—to look back on the rampart, the shorter and taller spires where the castle was, then out across the countryside.

The space was wide and open to both the left and right, but when Wren looked forward, she saw nothing but saffron and scarlet leaves.

"So that's the Autumnal Wood," she remarked.

"It is," Kathrina replied. "Did you not travel through there?"

"I didn't, I came…." Wren hesitated, realizing she needed to choose her words carefully. "I got lost in the Aestival Forest. Admittedly, I slept most of the carriage ride here, and by the time we moved to horseback, I was not looking back."

"Well, you'll have a chance to be up close and personal with it," Kathrina said, a smile coloring her tone. "The Flugés' house is just on the edge. They provide the castle with—"

Her sharp intake of breath was the only warning Wren received before a face appeared in the grass directly in front of them. Shoulders, a small torso, and gangly arms followed as a young boy of at least seven stood, giggled, then bounded away.

A shout carried on the air, echoing from across the meadow, and when Wren glanced over her shoulder, she saw another boy approaching. His eyes were a deep blue and his hair was a sun-lightened brown. Though he was far taller than the boy who was now running away at breakneck speed, he could not have been more than thirteen. The stern look on his face, however, gave him the appearance of being older and far wiser.

"Milo Penrith! This is not the time for tricks. You come back here and apologize to the ladies," he scolded, the youthful chime of his voice not matching the gruff words.

From beside Wren, Kathrina giggled. "He's quite fine, Reggie. I'm only glad I didn't step on him this time!"

"This time?" Wren echoed, highly amused.

Milo's face popped out of the grass by her side, causing her to jump. "You almost stepped on my face," he stated matter-of-factly. "But I'm too fast. No one can catch me!"

Kathrina laughed. "And what are you today, Milo? A rabbit? A snake?"

"A mole!" he squealed with glee, dropping to all fours before popping back up out of the grass on his hind quarters. "I'm a meadow mole."

"And you'll be dinner if I catch you," muttered the elder boy. He turned his face to Wren then. "I'm sorry, my lady, I don't believe I've seen you 'round the city."

Kathrina patted her arm. "This is Lady Florence. I am accompanying her during her stay at court. She'll be leaving on the next full moon, but for the time being, she is a guest of the king. Wren, this is Reginald, a dear friend of mine and often-times Milo's unfortunate babysitter."

Wren extended her hand to Reginald, but he turned it over, fumbling a moment before bowing and pressing a kiss to her fingers. "My lady," he said, adjusting his jacket nervously as he straightened.

Wren smiled, keenly remembering the way it felt to be uncomfortable within her own skin at the same age—to feel as if the very body that had kept you alive your whole life was suddenly a stranger. And she had no doubt that this boy, though awkward now, would be a dashing gentleman someday.

"It is such a pleasure to meet you, Reginald," she said warmly. "Is Milo your family?"

"Our mothers were cousins," he replied. "I am the only child in my family."

"Then we have that in common."

It was Reginald's turn to smile, his eyes reflecting thankfulness to have found common ground with his new friend. He looked back to Kathrina. "Are you off to the Flugés', Lady Kathrina?"

"Yes, Reg, and please, just Kathrina. We do not need such formality outside the city."

Before he could reply, a shout came from the wall. "You there! Boy! Where is your mask?"

Reginald paled, patting his pockets as if one could be stashed in his old, faded trousers. A small hand shot up from the grass, the wooden face of a rabbit clutched in its grasp.

"Ah, here it is," Reginald exclaimed loud enough for the guard to hear. "The ruddy strap broke again. I'll have the milliner fix it."

"See that you do," the guard barked with warning.

Reginald quickly fastened the mask to his face, tucking the long strap, that did in fact look as though it had been replaced, behind his ear. "Thanks, Milo," he said softly.

Milo's sigh could be heard and then he, too, stood, wearing his own mask—a small dove.

Wren's face fell behind her mask, but Kathrina only knelt to the smaller boy's level. "Would you like to escort us?" she asked. "I've heard there are ferocious moles scurrying about, and I would feel far more at ease if there were strong and capable men to accompany us the rest of the way."

Milo puffed out his chest, and Wren stifled a laugh, hearing Reginald do the same. "It would be my honor, my lady," Milo said with a bow. Taking Kathrina's hand, they continued on their way across the meadow with Wren and Reginald falling in step behind them.

It was not long until they came upon a waist-high wooden fence. Milo rushed ahead, clamoring over it, and Reginald picked up his pace to open the gate for the women. The ground within had been cleared of the tall grass and was instead lined with rows upon rows of crops thriving in the sunlight. Beyond the garden sat a small cottage with a pointed thatched roof, the thick, sweet smell of berries rising from the chimney.

Wren stopped in her tracks, the scent bowling her over. In an instant, she was in her grandmother's living room, the same candle burning with all three wicks alight. And though she never knew its name, she would know that scent in the dark.

"Mauri!" called Milo from the front stoop, banging his small fist on the door. "We're here for a visit!"

The door swung open and a short, plump woman with dark-gray hair swept off her neck in a braid twisted about her head greeted them. Wearing a threadbare dress and a stained apron, she spotted the group trailing behind Milo and smiled warmly. "Come in, loves, I was just canning some preserves. I've got loaves about to spoil as well if ye wanted to dip in and test the taste for me."

Reginald's pace quickened at her words and even Kathrina's steps picked up speed, prompting Wren to shake off the sense of déjà vu and share in the excitement.

Stopping outside the door, she paused, allowing the boys' and Kathrina's chatter to distract from her absence. She slid the crystallum from where it was tucked in the pocket of her dress, and after staring at it intently and running a finger over the surface in every direction, she returned it to its hiding place. She could not shake the feeling that there was something new she was close to discovering.

And she did not want to miss its change this time.

CHAPTER TWENTY-ONE

*T*he inside of the cottage was small with a living area in the foreground and a kitchen in the back. The kitchen by far commanded the room with two large wash basins, ample counters along the wall, an island erected in the middle, and a table long enough to seat nearly a dozen people separating it from the living space. Every available surface held a jar, their mouths agape, either filled with thick, sweet jam or waiting for the berry preserves that were bubbling in a massive cauldron over the fire.

No sooner had the door clicked shut behind them than the boys ripped their masks back off their faces, Kathrina's following immediately after.

"And who might this be?" the woman called Mauri asked, peering at Wren as she revealed her own features.

"This is Lady Florence," replied Kathrina, shuffling to the cupboard and pulling four plates from it. "Wren, this is Mauritania Flugé. And her husband Gerard is around here somewhere."

"And where do ye hail from, Lady Florence?" Mauritania asked.

"I, um...." Wren hesitated, mind racing. "Tauriellis." It was a shot in the dark, still knowing next to nothing of the country, but there was no hope in explaining her real home. Not again.

Mauritania nodded slowly, considering her with knowing eyes. "Tauriellis. Lovely this time of year, though its waters have become lawless. Best be careful trying to return on ye own. They will trade in whatever they can get their hands on. Those ports are no place for a lady."

"She is here until the king can aid in securing her safe passage home," Kathrina said, plating slabs of bread and passing each dish down the table. "We have become fast friends, and I am grateful for her time here."

Wren's heart swelled, the earnestness of the sentiment taking her by surprise, and she nearly missed how the older woman's eyes narrowed at the mention of the king. But whatever had crossed her mind was quickly covered by a wide smile when a tall man with salt and pepper hair strode through the door.

"Well now, a friend of our Kathrina is a friend of ours," he said, removing his hat, "but it would appear that we have an infestation of urchins, Mauri. Best haul out the torches, we'll be needing to smoke 'em out."

She laughed above the boys' chorused protests around their mouthfuls of bread. Kathrina threw them both a glare and laid a bowl on the table with a large spoon resting across its rim.

"Help yourselves," she said, spooning a large helping of berry preserves onto her own plate and allowing the bread to soak in the sweet, sticky liquid.

Milo reached for the handle, but with a swift swipe, Reginald stole the spoon and handed it to Wren. "Ladies first," he chided the smaller boy, and Wren had to hide her smile at the boy's impish grin. She spooned both her helping and Milo's onto their plates and handed the spoon back to Reginald, who thanked her with a tip of his head and a brilliant smile.

184

"Now, what have ye lot been up to today?" asked Gerard, hanging his hat from the spindle of a chair before sinking down in the seat with the sigh of someone who had just released a great weight.

"Getting in trouble for not wearing masks. Again," replied a sullen Milo. "You never wear one and you don't get in trouble."

"Aye, but I spend most daylight hours farming between here and the wood. Even Mauri wears a man's getup while tending the harvest. No rat guard dare approach us for indecency on our own land, given to us by the king or not."

Wren blinked. "Did you say rat guard?"

"Rat, mouse, they're all the same," Reginald said, anger glowing in his eyes. "They do nothing for the people outside the court. They just scurry about and bite when we step a toe out of line. It isn't what a good soldier would do."

"And what do you know of good soldiers?" retorted Milo.

"I know enough to know we need more of them," Reginald responded earnestly. "Upstanding men who will protect and defend, not oppress and cut down. Someday, I'll be one and I'll make a difference."

"My sweet boy," said Mauritania, laying a hand on his shoulder. With an emotion Wren could not read in her eyes, she turned back to tend the cauldron above the fire. "Ye would make a fine soldier. But I do not wish for ye that fate."

"I don't believe they are all bad," Kathrina replied. "It is hard to differentiate between uniforms and masks, but every person is not the same beneath them. You cannot judge all by one."

"But you can judge them by the one in charge," said Reginald with disdain. "They are a reflection of their leader and he is the worst of them all."

"Surely you don't mean the king?" Wren asked, though she knew it would not be far from her own limited experience with him.

Gerard laughed. "No, my lady. While we do not care for the

guards, I can assure ye on our duty as royal harvesters given to us by His Majesty, we do not partake in treason casually over afternoon dessert. Reg refers to the Glaive—the king's executioner."

A cold sweat prickled across Wren's skin. They were talking about Timothius. "Is he—"

"The only one of us good enough to be seen as a human?" replied Gerard. "Aye. The king rules with justice in his mind. Mercy, yes, but justice, though his hands remain clean. The Glaive is the blade he bloodies, and in return he is honored by being the sole face His Majesty accepts aside from his own. Even if he is a hollow and soulless being."

"But you are all human. We all are."

Wren's words brought silence over the room, the only sound the distant calls of children in the field and the bubbling of the preserves over the fire.

"We are. And we are not," replied Gerard softly. "We have life in our blood and magic in our bones, but we are subjects of the king. And he decrees his loyal servants know their place. So this," he raised Milo's mask from the table, "is the way of it."

"All this talk of kings and masks and soldiers is too sour for such sweet treats," declared Mauritania. "Ye boys best finish up and get along yer way. Ye will never make it halfway to the sea and back before sundown at this rate."

"We're picking up a supply boat today!" declared Milo, unfazed by the weighty air in the room.

"We are retrieving supplies from a boat," corrected Reginald with a sad smile. "But someday, I will have a boat. If I cannot be a guard, then I shall let the world guard me. Sail until I find somewhere without masks. Where I can feel the sun on my face every day."

Mauritania laid a hand on his shoulder. "Ye deserve a full life of adventure, thrill, freedom, and love. Though love will bring them all to ye with no room to spare. So above all, I wish ye love."

Milo snorted. "Love is gross. I just want a boat so I can sail where I want when I want."

Gerard chuckled and cuffed the boy on the head. "And ye would do well on a boat, young sir. The dangers of the sea do not compare to the trouble ye'll find yerself in if ye're drawing the ire of the king's men before ye've seen eight summers."

Talk turned to the sea and travel, and the boys departed not long before Kathrina gathered the fresh herbs from the Flugés that she had been tasked to retrieve for the castle's storehouse. As they crossed the meadow once again, Wren looked back at the small cottage and found herself thinking of Reginald's words, wondering what kind of life could truly be had within the prison of a mask.

CHAPTER TWENTY-TWO

"*K*athrina. Why would a king who is considered just put his people in animal masks?"

Kathrina's hands stilled where they were plaiting small strands of Wren's hair back from her face with a thin lavender ribbon that complimented the strands lacing the corset of her deep amethyst ball gown.

"I know we haven't known each other long, and I don't want to make you speak poorly of the king, but it feels...wrong," Wren added. She had no apologies for being so blunt, but she did wish there was an easier way to ask. Or to at least explain why the answer was important to her.

Slowly, Kathrina began to work again. "King Phillipae's family took the throne when our world was at its darkest, but it was not until he bore the crown that the city and castle were rebuilt to what you see now. He cared for us in that way and is seen as a savior by many because of it. However, the memories passed down from the fall of the Thrones have undoubtedly influenced his rule, and as a result, he despises magic."

Wren's brow furrowed, wondering why a king who hated magic would be so interested in using it to help her—and why he would do it in exchange for more. "How can he despise something that is everywhere?"

"He refuses to embrace anything that may draw the loyalty of the people from himself. And when it was revealed that the people held tighter to the legend than his rule, he decreed that Inflamel forsake its roots in magic. The consequence was to become lower than him, so in his sight, we are his menagerie. Here for his entertainment, forsaking what we are truly made of."

Is that why a rebellion is rising against the king? The words were on the tip of Wren's tongue, but she could not bring herself to put her newfound friend on the spot any longer. And she certainly would not put her in danger.

"What kind of magic do you have, then?" Wren asked, changing the subject.

Kathrina smiled sadly. "My mother was an Elérynd, so I am one as well. My father, however, was a form forger. He could forge his form into a bird of prey and fly high above the world. Had he married another Awduron, I would possess magic. When I was a child, I would pretend to carry elemental magic, green like my father's eyes. Now I only daydream of it when I work. It helps me pass the time—the daydreaming. I believe that's how many of us survive every day."

She excused herself to dress for the evening, and the moment Wren rested her own mask firmly in place, she let her face fall in the safety of its shadow.

Kathrina's words weighed on her. The revelations regarding the king were unsettling, but it was her final words that left a sour taste in Wren's mouth. Every day in the kingdom was a game of survival—one that led children to speak of reform and grown women to play pretend in order to endure. Wren was at a loss trying to comprehend the helplessness of every soul around her yet awed by the hope they still possessed. But what shook her the most, leaving her exposed and unsteady, was her own failure to recall the last time she had put aside her own bitter resignation for the courage to dream.

❄

WISTERIA HUNG like grapes from the vine strung around the perimeter of the room. Small lanterns dangled in their midst, emitting a brilliant silver glow upon the Dance of the Roses. Their soft light flickered against the petals of the white and lavender roses blanketing every surface, reflecting off the brocaded masks and from the jewels that dripped down skirts and bodices. The king was nowhere in sight, but as he was every night, Timothius stood like a statue beside the empty throne, surveying the revelers below, his suit a vibrant blue and his onyx gloves matching both his trousers and boots.

A flute of lavender champagne was pressed into Wren's hand, but she set it down immediately. She knew better than to think Timothius had not noticed her entrance. She was able to recall their conversation the previous night, and she could only hope her belligerence had not been enough to keep him away all evening. As he enjoyed saying, there were things they needed to discuss. And she was ready to talk.

It took approximately three songs for the dancers around Wren to hush and the man in the deer mask before her to bow and flee like the animal he portrayed. She smiled to herself, but quickly let it fall, turning with the music into a waltz with the King's Glaive.

"You have quite the reputation around here," she said quietly.

Timothius said nothing, but she saw his eyes dance with irony.

"Do you prefer to go by soldier? Toy? Glaive? You're so stiff up there you could probably pass for a piece of the decor."

"And your dancing this evening could nearly pass for sobriety."

His voice was low, colder than the man who had assured her of safety in his home within a tree, yet still one and the same. She found her skin prickling at the sound and her sense of challenge rose to the occasion. "I wanted to know what it felt like to let loose a little, but I've had my fill of fun."

"And did your partner last night convince you of this?"

The bite in his tone nearly made her miss a step, and she was grateful for the dip in the music, signaling his next move. He took the cue and turned her in three quick circles, sending her skirt out in waves that broke against his leg like he was the shore catching her sea. Facing each other once more, she relaxed in his arms and allowed her fingers to slacken in his grasp. It was not lost on her how natural, how right, it felt to not only be dancing but to be dancing with him, but she dismissed the notion.

"My dear soldier, are you *jealous*?" she asked, tone dripping with a sweetness so thick it rivaled Mauritania's preserves.

"Jealousy is for men who crave what they cannot have," he replied stonily. "There is nothing for me here."

"What about Timothius?" she asked.

It was his turn to nearly miss a step. He released Wren and circled the floor around her, the men surrounding them doing the same. But while they glided about their partners, Timothius stalked with a purpose. She watched them all move about, but from behind her, a warm breath tickled the back of her neck— the softest exhale escaping from beneath the mask that was far closer than what she saw exhibited by the other dancers. His dance was not to corral, or even to revere, it was to lay a boundary—to ward off anyone who might dare approach.

He was staking his claim.

"Do not say that name here," he uttered into her ear before completing his turn and continuing their glide about the floor.

Wren swallowed, trying not to overthink how much closer they were now. How their elbows aligned and their forearms touched—how her skirt wrapped about his legs with every turn. Their hands, instead of being folded one in the other, were twisted together, her pale, delicate skin entwined with his long, gloved fingers like lovers tangled in bedsheets.

"Why?" she asked, unable to hide the tremor in her voice. "Are you afraid you'll become an animal like the rest of the people you conspire to protect? He already has you groomed into one, what is the difference if you lose your face?"

The hand within her own tightened, and they stopped moving. Timothius stepped so close she could see the places the paint had cracked on his mask with age and wear.

What kind of life could truly be had within the prison of a mask?

And he had been inside that mask for so long....

"I fear nothing," he said, eyes flashing. "And I will keep my mask until the day the animals' teeth become strong enough to provide me freedom from this prison once and for all. But what do you care? Swan or Wren, either way you are only a bird that will fly away."

His words were meant to cut, but Wren threw them on the flames building within her chest instead. They began to move again, their faces inches apart—his stone facade and her fiery spirit threatening one another from across the chasm open wide between them—yet all the while they continued their dance, orbiting each other like planets about the sun.

And that is what they were, she realized—two enigmas too powerful to collide yet imprisoned and unable to break free of the proper order. At the mercy of the universe they had been thrust into, they were resigned to this fate until one of them dared challenge gravity, forcing their course to either bend or break. And with all she had seen and heard, Wren was ready for a collision.

"Memories," she murmured, the word flung out like a lifeline across the gorge separating them.

His eyes widened slightly, moving back and forth between

her own, and she drew herself to her full height, daring him to move with her—to defy order and cease their monotonous orbit.

To bend.

To break.

"Memories are releasing the magic within the crystallum."

Timothius didn't speak. His motions continued seamlessly through the end of the dance, but Wren could have sworn the man stopped breathing. The song came to a close, and though he relinquished his hold on her and took a step back, he kept her hand and bowed low.

His words drifted up to meet her ear. "We cannot discuss this here. Meet me tonight. I shall send for you."

Then he dropped her hand and was gone.

CHAPTER TWENTY-THREE

*W*ren was still in her gown when the rap sounded on the door. She had slipped away from the dance unnoticed, and though she did not know what Kathrina would think when she realized Wren's absence, she knew well enough to don her mask once again and open the door.

She startled at the sight of a wolf-masked soldier before her. His face looked exactly like the one she had encountered in the wood, even if his build indicated that he was not the same guard.

"This way, my lady," he groused, turning on his heel and stalking away, leaving Wren to keep up behind him.

He led her halfway down the corridor and up a few flights of stairs, exiting a door that—to Wren's surprise—opened within the city wall itself. The night air whistled inside slatted, open blocks within the rampart that were wide enough only for an arrow to be nocked through. Its frigid bite sent a shiver coursing down her body, but its cry, howling up and down the stone corridor, chilled her to the core.

The torchlight danced with the threat of plunging them into darkness, doing nothing to ease her mounting nerves, so she picked up her pace behind the guard who had also increased his speed, appearing to enjoy the walk as much as she did.

They had reached the juncture of the rampart and one of the castle's main turrets when the guard stopped just short of it, turned to a single door, and tapped loudly.

It swung open to reveal none other than Timothius still in full uniform and mask. He nodded at the soldier who tipped his head in a bow and then strode away, his footsteps echoing back down the abandoned corridor.

Wren walked inside and Timothius shut the door firmly behind her, locking the bolt in place.

His quarters looked far more like an apartment than the guest room Wren resided in. The sitting area was spacious with a fireplace, sofa, and a small study area with a desk and credenza. A partially open doorway that lay beyond led into what she was certain was a private bedroom if the discarded uniforms slung over a chair in the corner were any indication.

"You may remove your mask if you so wish," said Timothius, crossing the room to pour a single glass of what appeared to be wine.

"Will you remove yours?" Wren asked, already sliding it from her face.

"No. I do not show my face here."

"Ever?"

"Never."

She hesitated, thinking through her own assumptions about the man before her. Timothius offered her the glass, and when she took it, he gestured toward the chair closest to the fire. She accepted it, the radiant heat thawing her chilled skin. Timothius sat on the sofa across from her, the light of the fire reflecting off the gilded filigree in his mask, flashing like fireflies.

"I'm sorry," she said finally, and she did not need to see his face to notice the surprise that stiffened his body.

"Whatever for, my lady?"

"For what I said earlier. About your position and your mask. Especially what I said about the king. It was wrong and I shouldn't have said it."

He was quiet for a long moment and then spoke, all cold hardness melted from his tone. "You were not far from the truth. And I do not fear because I have already accepted that which I fear most."

Wren studied the man in front of her, his eyes conveying a sadness his mask would not reveal.

"He's the reason you have the scars on your back, isn't he?"

Her words fell into silence, but the slight bow in Timothius's proud spine told her both the shame and the memory were never too far from his mind.

"How long?" she asked.

"Since I was a boy."

Wren flinched. "He has abused you since you were a boy?"

"The discipline stopped some time ago. As you so succinctly pointed out, I am now groomed."

Wren's mouth grew dry, her wild inaccuracies scalding her cheeks with guilt.

Timothius tilted his head, the sight eerie, prompting Wren to picture him how she saw him in the wood—the man with the curly hair and the dancing eyes. "Have they told you who I am?"

She shifted in her seat uncomfortably, setting her glass on the small table and wiping her palms on her skirt. "They say you are the Glaive of the king and you carry out his wishes. His hands are clean because yours are bloody."

Timothius leaned forward. The light no longer illuminated the gold, and instead allowed a shadow to cover half his face, giving him a sinister visage.

"And have they told you what I am?"

Wren watched him closely, unwilling to answer. She did not need to wait long.

"I walk the floor—these halls—and though humanity is

stripped from everyone but me, I am the one who remains invisible. People will readily look upon the mice and wolves and woodland creatures before they dare turn their head in my direction when I pass. I am the ghost of every soul I have taken. I am often jury, seldom judge, but always executioner. There is more blood on my hands than there are waves upon our shores, and every life I have taken has cost me my own. I am despised. I am feared. I am respected by requirement, but I am shunned by choice. The ones forced to look upon me are those who take their last breath by my hand."

Wren's mind was a jumble of mixed words and misguided feelings. Part of her longed to retreat to the security of her quarters, but she found herself desperate to stay in the company of one of the few people who knew her truth. She was so torn by her conflicting feelings that she jumped when Timothius's soft voice broke the silence. "And you. I am seen by you. And it is threatening."

She stared at him, at the vulnerable honesty dancing in his eyes, and allowed her shoulders to relax. Her lifeline had been tethered, and from across the chasm she couldn't help but smile at the man reclined so stoically before her. "If you think me just seeing you is threatening, you don't want to come between me and food when I'm hungry."

Timothius chuckled, and Wren saw his shoulders sag, the air in the room shifting and venting their tension.

"So how did this happen?" Wren asked. "You're leading a rebellion but are also the king's prized possession? Does anyone know?"

"Elric is the only one outside the city walls. At least he was meant to be until you appeared."

Wren bristled at the slight irritation in his tone. "It's not like I planned on dropping in your forest and then accidentally following you here when I was trying to go in the complete opposite direction of you and your rebel friends. I knew I was being lied to, but how was I supposed to know you'd be here? You did nothing but keep things from me, all while asking me to trust your help."

"Trust is a bridge with two sides. How was I to know you would flee friends and safety and run straight into the arms of the enemy?" he volleyed. "Furthermore, when I saw you enter that room, how could I have known you would not tell the king everything you had seen and heard?"

"Since you're bringing that up, I didn't appreciate you manhandling me, thank you very much," Wren interjected, eyes narrowing.

"Regardless, these are not the memories you came here to speak of, are they?"

It was Wren's turn to pause. She was still not ready to give in. "If the king is your enemy and you are his personal guard, how do I know you are trustworthy with knowledge of the crystallum?"

"If I were not worthy of your trust, I would have snapped your neck, removed the crystallum, and presented it to the king before your body could lose its warmth," Timothius replied, unflinching.

"Well, that's comforting."

"Quite."

Silence fell once again and Wren swallowed her pride and most of her anger. "You would have killed me that day?"

Timothius was quiet for so long that Wren thought he may not answer at all, but then he spoke in a voice so low she had to lean forward to catch the words. "I was prepared to do what was necessary to keep you from sharing your knowledge with the king. But when you denied knowing anything.... I would have sought to save you somehow. I gave you my word that you were safe here. I will protect you."

"Because I didn't betray the rebels?"

"No, because I admire your strength and the boldness you

have shown in the face of every adversity you've confronted thus far. I believe we may help each other yet."

Wren shook her head. "All I want is to go home. I cannot, I will not, stay here and help you stage a coup."

"I would never ask that of you. As you have so artfully thrown in my face, I intentionally kept the knowledge of our plans from you—and beyond that I have given you my word. But it cannot be denied that you may be the key to freeing us all."

He stood and began moving about the room, picking up and examining his belongings absently like he were perusing them for the first time.

"Three hundred eighty-five years ago, our world was governed by four great rulers who reigned from the four Trifolium Thrones in the northernmost reaches of our realm. Each Throne, each ruler, represented one of our four great kingdoms—Obarian just beyond the mountains, Grimoira in the west, Tauriellis across the southern sea, and Inflamel at the heart of them all. There was peace within the kingdoms and magic thrived among their people.

"No one is certain where it began, but an uprising grew from darkness. An unrest unlike any our world has ever seen. Magic so unnatural and dark that it began to take hold of anyone it touched—poisoning mind and body first before consuming magic and life entirely.

"One by one the Thrones fell, save one. When Inflamel sent its people from the city to safety, they instead stood their ground, knowing they could not avoid their fate. No one knows what transpired within the castle, only that when the final Throne was lost, it sent a tremor of magic through the sky so powerful that the demons themselves fractured into pieces.

"The story has been passed down from parent to child through the ages. The legend we hold is that our ruler was cast from this world and—by the magic that protected them—they will someday come back and usher in the rise of the Trifolium Thrones and the reclaiming of our land. No one knows in what form they are to return, no one knows how, but a crystallum in the hands of a mortal from another time and space is a great indicator that our hope may not be in vain. Whatever the case may be, your ornament is the key."

"And that's why you all lied about helping me find a way home. Because you need the magic."

Timothius's eyes fell shut. "To keep you in the dark—to lie to you—was not what we should have done. But can you assure me that you would not have fled the tree home the moment we sought to claim the one thing connecting you to your land? What wouldn't you do to regain what you have lost? What wouldn't you do to reclaim your life as your own?"

Wren was silent, considering everything, and then she spoke in a slow voice. "The Isteriaeth. Six of them. They sacrificed themselves for their queen. They made the crystallum and sent her away with their dying breath."

Timothius froze, staring at her, and Wren swallowed hard before continuing, "I found where it happened. I saw it all, I felt — I felt their pain. They had lost everything. There was no way out, so they sent her away. To save her. Under the banner of a clover."

"The Trifolium sigil," said Timothius reverently.

"I think the crystallum is showing me and I think my knowledge is meant to help you," Wren said, voice no more than a whisper. "I don't know how, I don't know why, but I think once I do, your ruler will return and it will take me back home."

"If what you say is true," said Timothius slowly, "then you must know the danger you bring upon your head. To speak the name of the Trifolium Thrones is to commit treason. Their history has long since been destroyed, their memory wiped from our walls—"

"And yet I still found them."

The room stilled at Wren's words, and after a heartbeat, Timothius crossed the floor. He knelt in front of her, resting a forearm on his knee and taking her hand in his own. "The king suspects you are more. He lies when he vows to help you. There can be no good in you waiting for the full moon. Would you truly risk your life to aid a people who are not your own?"

Wren absorbed the earnestness in his eyes, letting the life within them breathe into her and fan the flames within her chest. "Do I have any other choice?"

Silence fell in the space between their stares, only this time Wren did not face the stone wall. She faced the man.

"Then I shall help you in any way that I can," Timothius answered softly. "And for your bravery, I swear on my life that I will see you return to your home. Death may find you well along in years, in the comfort of your homeland, but it will not touch you here. Not while I stand guard."

Wren nodded, not allowing her face to betray her nerves at the task that lay ahead—or the fluttering his words had brought to her stomach. "Well then, I guess tomorrow I hunt for more memories."

CHAPTER TWENTY-FOUR

*W*ren tried not to appear too eager when speaking with Kathrina over breakfast the next morning. After declining an invitation into the city, she had inquired about the castle, its age, and if there were any parts of it that had been rebuilt—and if so, where the oldest parts still stood.

Kathrina had raised an eyebrow but directed her to the bailey between the castle and the rampart where a few stone buildings had been erected in the shadow of the monolithic structures.

Wren found herself standing in one now—a long-abandoned cottage that had fallen into disrepair. It had been gutted, no sign of its former use, occupants, or even a trace of life remaining in its walls. Why its shell still resided there, she didn't quite understand.

Moving to the next one, she was met with a space not unlike the Flugés' cottage that had been repurposed into a greenhouse. A cat wandered in and out from between her legs, but when she paused to stroke its fur, it nipped at her and ran off, ears flattened against its head. That was her cue to move on.

The next building was by far the largest of the three and the most intriguing with its boarded windows and barred door. Wren glanced behind her causally, surveying the other people in the courtyard—a handful of soldiers, a few ladies carrying bushels of linens from the base of the rampart where the wash houses were located, and another equally grumpy cat. None were paying her any mind.

Wren slipped around the corner of the building and along its wall, looking and feeling for any sort of crack or space that would allow her entry. It was not until she reached the back of it that she found another door, but instead of iron barring her from entry, it was only nailed shut with five wooden planks— and two of them appeared to be quite loose.

One gave way quickly, the rotted wood disintegrating under her fingers, but the one above it proved to be a bit trickier to pry free. Glancing around once more to make sure no one could see her either from the rampart above or the courtyard beyond, she propped a foot on the side of the building and yanked with all her might.

The board swung harmlessly to the side and sent her tumbling backward in a heap to the stone. But now there was just enough space for her to unlatch the door, push it open, and shimmy her way through the new opening and inside the building.

It took her all of a few seconds to realize that—with boarded windows and doors—there would be no seeing the inside. She cursed herself for not thinking of it sooner, and for the first time since arriving found that she actually missed her cell phone.

It made her pause. How long had she been here again? She didn't even remember. She had counted the days so faithfully when she'd arrived, but now? She thought of her grandmother every day, longed to return to her, but there was not a single other thing she missed.

And both the realization and the acceptance of that fact stunned her.

Shuffling carefully along the floor, she was only a few feet into the room when she felt another door. This one, however, swung easily and allowed her to enter a wide-open room with thin beams of light trickling down from gaps in the roof.

She stood at the end of a long aisle, rows upon rows of round-backed wooden pews lining each side, their velvet cushions still intact, though most were knocked askew. A window to her left had a board missing, a corner of red glass peeking through, revealing that the window beneath was stained-glass. And just ahead, beyond the end of the aisle, pages upon pages of sheet music were scattered about a small platform where a lone pedestal stood.

A chapel. This building was a chapel.

Wren walked slowly down the center aisle, unsure if it was magic stirring to reveal something to her or reverence she felt being in a place that was equal parts beautiful and tragic. It had been many years since she had set foot in a church as old as this. She had felt awed by its timelessness in the same way, only that structure had been preserved in loving, painstaking detail. What could have befallen this one to be so neglected? To be so hated?

She did not need to go far for the answer. A table stood at the foot of the platform with broken glass strewn across its top. Peppered among the shards were dried stems, perfectly preserved. Carefully, so as not to disturb its surroundings or cut her finger, Wren lifted one right in front of her eyes, twisting toward the nearest beam of light so that she could see better. She gasped.

Pinched between her fingers was a four-leaf clover.

Something tugged on her mind—echoes of cheers, thick curls beneath a modest veil, hands raised, heads tipped together in a kiss, crowns sparkling in sunlight, urging her, beckoning her forward. She inhaled deeply, and then—

"You are a foolish, foolish girl."

Jumping nearly out of her skin, Wren dropped the clover. Only the silver beak of the owl mask reflected in the barely illuminated room, the short stature of the man behind her confirming his identity.

"I— I'm—"

"Trespassing," Musannulos crowed. "You are a guest of the king, in his court, and you repay him by trespassing where even his most loyal subjects dare not tread?"

"It's just a chapel," Wren murmured, slowly recovering from her shock. "We have...where I'm from— In Tauriellis there is history. We learn through history—books and old places and ruins and...and recounting the past. I wanted to see if I could learn more about where I am."

Musannulos stomped toward her, the effort he was throwing behind every step failing to eclipse the power held in a single stride of Timothius's boot. "We do not recount our history here, girl. We call upon our future," he spat. "And it is a bright one indeed with Our Majesty leading us. I dare say it will be brighter still when you no longer dim our door."

"I'm sorry, did I do something to you?" Wren asked, stepping toward him.

"To me, no, but know that should you try anything against His Majesty, I will know. There is something about you I do not trust."

"The king clearly does," she replied. "You would dare disagree with His Majesty?"

Musannulos bristled and sputtered. "Do not attempt to twist my words into a trap lest you prove me right, here and now."

Wren smiled innocently, allowing it to reflect beyond the mask in her words. "It was just a question."

The man stepped directly in front of her, and she had to look down to meet his beady eyes, but before he could say a word, the loud *crack* and *pop* of wood breaking sounded from beyond the entryway. A second plank snapped, the third following soon behind. The door swung open, light flooding in from outside illuminating a tall silhouette, and though Wren blinked in the sun, she did not need to see clearly to know exactly who had arrived.

"It is not unlike owls to glide about in darkness, but a swan as well?" Timothius's voice echoed, shunning the silence itself and leaching the air from the room.

"This trespasser was seeking out history to learn more about us," sniffed Musannulos, sounding displeased at the interruption. "Rather suspicious, if you ask me."

Wren opened her mouth to speak, but Timothius's smooth laugh filled the space, sending an apprehensive chill down her spine. "Suspicious is the excess of the king's rations vanishing between the kitchens and His Majesty's table. Suspicious is why the coffers are always empty, even though his people give dutifully. Suspicious is why the king's advisor is not beside him and is instead following a woman who is under the protection of His Majesty's court."

He stalked across the floor, each heavy footfall like a thunderclap in the silence, and walked straight up to Musannulos, stopping directly in front of him and blocking the light entirely. "Do you have any thoughts upon my observations, Musannulos? It is my duty to exact His Majesty's judgment, after all."

Musannulos drew himself up as best he could before the guard towering over him. "Not at this time, Master Soldier. Have you any on mine?"

Wren felt Timothius's eyes on her. "It has been many weeks since His Majesty extended his good will to Lady Klaver," he said slowly, calculating. "Should she wish to see more and learn more of us, I would be happy to ease your concerns and accompany her on a walk about the wall. That way you may return to your duty."

Wren wished she could see the rage on the owl-man's face, but the outline of his mask just tipped to Timothius in acquiescence. Turning on his heel to face her once again, he bowed at the waist, but when he rose, he hissed, "Take care, girl. Take good care."

Wren nodded back to him, and he scuttled wordlessly around Timothius and out the chapel door. It was only then that Wren exhaled a sigh of relief. Timothius turned on his heel to leave, extending an elbow out to her. "Until your eyes grow accustomed to the light. And mind your step. We shall need to bar the door again. It would appear the planks fell off."

Wren bit her lip against a giggle, clasping his elbow and allowing him to lead her out of the chapel and into the daylight. She moved along the building beside him; however, the second they rounded the corner, he pulled out of her reach. "You will need to walk on your own. I am a weapon, not an escort," he said coldly.

She tried to focus on him, blinking against the sun, and nodded. His tone of indifference was jarring, and while it would have grated her nerves before, she found that it did not bother her coming from him now. They all had a part to play, and she needed to keep her own mask in place.

The shade of the rampart cooled her face, giving reprieve to her eyes so they could open fully and adjust to the light. Timothius pushed a door open and stood, allowing her to enter the base of one of the wall's towers, then followed her up the stairwell.

"Holding a door for a lady seems rather escort...ish," Wren remarked.

"Being a gentleman does not require affection," Timothius said, shutting the door and plunging them into darkness. "Simply good manners."

"Oh, that's right," she replied, ascending the stairs carefully with a hand resting on the wall. "You did mention that you forgot what it is to be a gentleman. I'm so glad I can help keep it at the front of your mind."

Silence filled the stairwell, but Wren smiled to herself, loving the way she could get such a reaction out of him—regardless if it was fond recollection of the memory or annoyance with her sass.

"So what should we say to people who ask why you're walking me around the entire wall of the city if you're not escorting me?"

She heard Timothius's steps slow a fraction. "To be escorted by me means death awaits you. To be watched means you are marked."

"Then am I dying or marked?" Wren asked, her hand reaching the frame of a door and prompting her to stop.

To her surprise Timothius continued forward until he stood on the last step beside her, causing her to lean back against the wall. Her chest brushed the gold ties that hung from the front of his uniform jacket, and she looked up to where she knew his eyes would be dancing across her face—the only sign of life behind his frozen facade.

"You are quite alive and incapable of enjoying silence," he answered, tone dry but amused.

"Would you have me any other way?" The words escaped Wren faster than she could catch them. Heat immediately rose to her cheeks, and she wondered why on earth she had even said it. She had never been one for flirting, why did getting a rise out of him bring her so much joy?

Timothius allowed himself a single laugh and then swung open the door, stepping into the daylight at stoic attention and folding his hands behind his back. Wren stepped out beside him, grateful for the clouds giving a reprieve from the sun, and looked up and down the battlement.

"Which way do we go?" she asked.

Timothius did not speak, instead extending a hand forward, indicating that she would choose and he would follow. She turned and started to walk, hearing his boots upon the stone match her step for step.

"Marked," he said, so quiet she nearly missed it. "I have my eye on you."

She stopped herself from turning to look at him, not wanting to draw the attention of any soldiers standing guard or already walking the rise. At least not any more attention—they were already giving them a wide berth, and she knew it had little to do with her and everything to do with the enigma behind her. Everyone deferred to him, mouse and wolf alike. And though there was inherent fear in the way they regarded him, she could not tell if it was born out of respect...or terror.

"What is the difference between a wolf mask and a mouse?" she asked, pausing between clusters of guards to look out over the meadow.

Rather than stand by her side, Timothius came to a halt directly behind her. "The mouse represents His Majesty's army," he replied with quiet, clipped words. "The wolf commands them."

"But they all defer to you," she confirmed.

He did not reply, and Wren took the opportunity to glance back at him—to truly take in his commanding stature. The unmoving, emotionless pallor of his mask, his straight spine and rigid limbs. His flawless uniform, the enormous boots that she knew must be unbearably heavy on his feet, and the way not a single hair on his head was out of place, even in the breeze.

He was formidable. Powerful. A honed and flawless weapon. But inside he was a gentleman, light on his feet with unkempt hair and dancing eyes. And she knew then she would never see him another way.

Wren resumed her stroll, taking in the views of Inflamel from both inside and outside the city.

She had to admit it was somewhere she herself would have loved to call home, especially up here where the air felt as though it were carrying life back into her bones when she drew it in. There was a timeless quality to the kingdom, and she noticed that for every extreme there was a balance. The warmth of the day countered the night's chill, the wide-open spaces surrounding the moat contrasted with the buildings nearly on top of one another inside the city. The grandeur of the castle and its grounds paled in comparison to the majesty of the rampart—a city unto itself—that protected its people. And of course, the striking contrast she witnessed now between the Autumnal Wood and Aestival Forest in the west, and the Deorc Weald in the east.

Now, laying eyes on it for the first time, Wren understood how creatures such as wealdwolves could thrive there and why talk of a dark mage residing there would instill fear. The trees— their highest points level with Wren on the top of the wall— were so barren, so black, it appeared as if the whole expanse had been burned. Yet she saw leaves rustling on the branches and rolling across the ground with the mist. She realized then that Elric had ample reason to be concerned, as she found herself equal parts terrified and thoroughly intrigued.

A shout from farther down the battlement sounded, drawing her attention. A guard pointed across the meadow toward the Weald, and though Wren could not make out what he was saying, she could see exactly what had raised the alarm. The hulking shape of wealdwolves, some standing tall on two legs and others streaking across the meadow on all fours, bled from the Deorc Weald drawing a thick cloud of glittering black dhust in their wake.

Timothius was before her in an instant. "Inside the castle. Now," he uttered, the words betraying no emotion.

He did not move, his eyes the only thing that followed her to the nearest tower, and even as Wren slid the door shut behind her—concern causing her to hesitate with a sliver of it still open —she saw him stand guard, watching and waiting until the dark stole him from her sight.

CHAPTER TWENTY-FIVE

imothius did not attend the ball that night. Wren had tried not to look for him—attempting to occupy herself with dancing—but she could not escape the worry that rotted in the pit of her stomach knowing that the last time she had seen him was on the wall facing the wealdwolves.

"You are distracted today," Kathrina remarked over breakfast, jolting Wren from her thoughts.

"I am," she admitted. "I think I need air. Are you going into the city today?"

Kathrina's smile was wide. "I was not planning on it, but we shall go as soon as our meal is complete. I think a little adventure may not hurt for the morning."

Wren had reservations about pausing her search for connections to the past—the Trifolium sigil still fresh in her mind—but she was unsettled and restless and needed something to distract her until the next ball began.

It was not until she and Kathrina were deep in the heart of the city that she felt herself relax, her nerves easing and her heart warming just before the bobbing heads of both a rabbit and a dove approached them on the cobbled streets.

"Lady Kathrina. Lady Florence," said Reginald, greeting them with a small bow. Milo quickly mirrored his actions and then bounded over to Kathrina, wrapping his arms around her skirt.

"And what are you boys doing inside the city today?" she asked with a smile in her voice, patting the head of the boy hugging her legs.

"Do you not live here?" Wren asked curiously.

"I do, my lady," Reginald replied. "With my grandfather. Milo stays with us most of the time; however, his parents live days across the meadow on the edge of the sea. When I am not working beside my grandfather, I am ferrying goods between the ships and the town. The goods and Milo, that is."

"We were leaving to go fish in the moat," Milo said excitedly.

"We were, but the guards at the gate informed us that we are to stay within the city today. All citizens are," added Reginald.

"Why must we stay in?" Wren asked, looking to Kathrina.

"I have no idea," she replied. "I have been inside since yesterday, but business seemed as usual. Unless something happened—"

A commotion sounded from the square just ahead, a crowd shouting and beginning to gather. Wren took a step forward, but Kathrina placed a hand on her arm, stopping her.

"You there," she said, tone commanding as she addressed a woman hurrying by in a doe's mask. "What is happening in the square today?"

The doe-woman stopped and dipped on her knee. "My lady, have you not been out this last day? A specter from the Deorc Weald cleared the rampart. It has hidden somewhere within the city. They have been searching high and low all night, but during their search they found something even more menacing —an Isteriaeth."

The blood in Wren's veins turned to ice. Elric could not be in the city. Could he?

"Thank you," said Kathrina nervously. She grasped Milo's small shoulders and knelt before him. "You best go home with Reg now. And Reginald, straight home. Do not come back here."

Her tone was so motherly and firm that even Wren found herself wanting to go home at the behest. Reginald did not say a word, only took Milo's hand and continued down the road in the direction opposite the crowd.

Kathrina stood beside Wren, but by the time the boys vanished from sight, she was already moving toward the melee. Skipping to catch up beside her, Wren asked, "What is happening? What do they mean by specter?"

"There is rumored to be a mage who lives in the Weald. They say she sends her magic into the city, looking for people with darkness in their heart. It infects those it comes in contact with and possesses their mind. They, in turn, infect until the entire city becomes nothing more than monsters, eternally bound to her will."

"And what do Isteriaeth have to do with this?"

"I do not know. I have never heard of an Isteriaeth residing within Inflamel City. So let us hope it is simply rumor and not an innocent life about to be claimed."

They hurried, making their way through the growing crowd until they could move no farther. Wren saw nothing, but as she readied to make one more push forward, she caught sight of a familiar smooth, gilded mask of a soldier poking above the clamoring crowd.

The throng fell silent and still, Kathrina craning her neck to see when Wren touched her shoulder. "Ti— The Glaive is here," she whispered.

Kathrina froze then, dropping back on her heels. She did not seem to know what to do with her hands, wishing to cover her mouth or eyes but unable to around her fox's snout. She pulled at her sleeve, wrung her fingers, and then finally clasped them together against her skirt.

"Kathrina, are you well?" Wren asked, but before she could answer, a loud shout came from the front of the crowd.

"*ISTERIAETH!*"

The cry echoed across the assembly, not demanding judgment or even in anger or terror. They sounded mystified—in awe of the being in front of them—and somewhere among the hushed tones, Wren heard a woman gasp.

Just beside Timothius, two guards bearing the faces of mice hoisted a man up on the block at the center of the square. A hood covered his face, and though dhust leaked from his palms in a shimmering green, confirming it was not Elric, Wren felt her heart break all the same. Yes, Elric had misled her, but he had also shared so much of himself with her. More than she needed or deserved to know. And to see someone of his line—to see his very fate playing out before her eyes—pierced her heart like a fiery arrow, leaving white-hot rage in its wake.

"We shall deliver the fallen star to the king," a soldier in a wolf mask declared. Turning to face Timothius he bowed. "May His Majesty smile upon us in favor."

Timothius was still at first, but then he strode forward, a commanding power in every step. Wren found herself holding her breath when he reached up and ripped the hood off the Isteriaeth in front of him. The man's eyes were wide and vacant, his skin the sickly pallor of the magic rolling from him, and when he opened his mouth to speak, all that came out was a gurgle. Bright-red blood bubbled from his lips, running down his chin and sending a gasp up from the crowd.

The dhust turned to black, its cloud fading at his feet, and he slumped in the arms of the soldiers holding him. When Timothius turned, he withdrew his dagger from the Isteriaeth's stomach, pausing to wipe it across the dead man's tunic.

No one questioned the actions, none spoke, and Wren still found it difficult to breathe at the casual act of violence.

The wolf-masked soldier stepped toward Timothius with

purpose, but the flat of the still-stained knife across his heart ceased his movement.

Loud enough for his voice to echo across the square, yet low enough for the words to carry a deep, unnerving darkness, Timothius spoke. "This was no Isteriaeth. You nearly led a specter into the castle," he seethed. "None approach the king—not while the mage lurks in our shadow."

"She shall not lurk for long," a woman screeched from the crowd.

A shudder ran through the people, and many rushed aside, leaving a wide berth around an old crone whose eyes were fixed wholly on Timothius.

Timothius turned to the woman, but before he could take a step, she began to chant, her sing-song shouts toeing the line between excitement and madness.

> *"He plays with his toy while his kingdom's destroyed.*
> *She comes from despair, dark revenge soaks her stare.*
> *Leave your crumbs for the mice lest you suffer death*
> *   twice.*
> *Toll the end of rat's age, and mark her rise...*
> *The Isperi Mage."*

Swords sang as they were ripped from sheaths, but a single fist raised in the air by Timothius commanded both silence and stay.

The old crone laughed maniacally. Raising a bottle of wine to her lips, she drained it then smashed it against the cobble-stone. It exploded in a cloud of deep violet dhust laced with curling black shadows that sent the crowd running from its fumes.

As quick as it appeared, it was gone, the shattered glass lying in the street the only evidence left of the crone.

"Order!" the wolf-masked guard called. "There will be order!

The specter is gone. You will disperse immediately and carry on the king's business."

Wren wasn't sure at what point she had clutched Kathrina's arm, but she loosened her grip on the woman about the same time that Kathrina did the same.

"What just happened?" Wren asked breathlessly.

"I don't know," Kathrina answered, her voice trembling and uncertain.

"Let's return to the castle," Wren said, keeping a hold of Kathrina's arm and guiding her back toward the gates as quickly as the crowd moving with them would allow.

Stealing a glance over her shoulder, Wren found Timothius staring out across the crowd, his dead, black eyes telling her that they were shut seconds before he spun on his heel with a growl and ripped the blade of his knife across the dead man's throat.

CHAPTER TWENTY-SIX

*W*hile word of the events in the city square had not seemed to reach the court, Wren found herself still subdued when she walked into the Dance of the Faeries. Upon their return to the castle, Kathrina had excused herself, and while she had attended to Wren, helping her prepare for the dance, she had retired to her room for the evening soon after and was excused from the nightly festivities due to illness.

Wren wished she could have done the same, longing to be in bed instead of the forest-green gown she wore now. It was soft and plush against her skin, almost comfortingly so, which was why she had chosen it. The lace formed a lattice across the bodice with mauve roses embroidered at each intersection, giving her the feeling of being a faery princess.

Retreating to a table, she found herself accepting a flute of sparkling liquid, if only to have something to occupy her hands. She glanced about the room, taking in its elaborate decorations in various shades of green and brown, accented by soft pastel florals. The lights in particular caught her eye. Instead of the lanterns she was accustomed to illuminating the room, there were hundreds of diminutive orbs suspended in midair, dotting the space between the dancers and the ceiling like starlight in the middle of a forest.

"May I have this dance, dear swan?"

Wren nearly dropped her flute at the sound of Timothius's voice. She first glanced up to the dais where the king sat on his throne, a goblet in hand and his head thrown back in laughter, and then directed her attention to Timothius. "You're here."

"I am," he said. "I had business to attend to within the city last night, but it has reached an end."

"A rather bloody end," she said before she could stop herself.

Timothius froze at her words. "You have heard something."

"I didn't need to hear," she replied simply. "I was there. I watched you—"

Raucous laughter from the table beside them cut off her words. She opened her mouth to continue, but Timothius stepped forward and gently touched her elbow.

She could not help but flinch at the contact, and she saw pain flash in his eyes. His gloves were rough, but his touch soft when he started to sketch soft lines against her skin. The same hand that had claimed a life only hours prior was now the familiar, gentle caress of the man who had sworn to protect her. "May I have this dance...Wren?"

Her name on his lips was so soft that she almost missed it. This was not the King's Glaive asking a lady of the court to dance. This was Timothius asking Wren.

She nodded and rested her flute on the table, then placed her hand in the crook of his elbow and let him guide her to the floor. They fell into step with the music, silently flowing through each motion when Timothius spoke again. "Not all murder is violence. Sometimes it is mercy."

Her eyes met his, and he continued, "I know why you flinch. I understand why you fear. But I cannot say that I did not warn you of what I am."

Wren was silent for a long time, the dance carrying them

apart, and it was only when they came back together at the center of the floor that she asked, "And if what you are is an executioner, whether in violence or mercy, then why are you not up there beside the king who has given you that power?"

"Because I would rather be here. Dancing with you."

She paused at that. "Why?"

Timothius was pensive for a moment, and then hurriedly answered, "I apologize deeply if I have made you uncomfortable, my lady. I don't expect you to understand—"

"I do," she replied softly, their pace slowing with the change of song. "At least, I believe I do. I know what it feels like to be invisible in a crowded room. To be forgotten until you are needed. To be ignored and unwanted. Sometimes a reprieve seems like giving up—a long and silent death. But sometimes it does feel like a mercy."

She watched her acceptance of his words—of him—echo behind his hollow facade, sinking deep into the flesh and marrow of the human within. And slowly yet surely, the tension eased from his limbs. "There are many small deaths before the end," he said quietly. "Some are silent, others loud. And all of us are left with the power to choose. I cannot imagine you ever embracing a silent death."

"And I cannot imagine you choosing anything but mercy."

A long silence filled the air between them, the notes of the newest piece commanding its empty spaces. It was delicate and longing, allowing no room for separation.

Unable to bear the weight of Timothius's eyes on her any longer, Wren asked, "How did they make the lights? I know you don't have electricity and the king doesn't want magic, but they almost look like...."

"Faery light," Timothius replied solemnly.

Wren's eyes widened. "Each one is a faery?"

"Every one," he confirmed. "Faeries are one of the Awduron —an original race of magical beings that settled our world.

Others exist still, Isteriaeth, form forgers, and elfin folk, but they dare not make themselves known lest they suffer the same fate as the faeries. Their purpose here was to mine magic from the earth. They cultivate and protect it, and that makes them valuable—a commodity. The king purchases them from illegal traders and imprisons them, bringing them out only when he tethers them in the sky above the dance mocking their honor, or when negotiations require a bargaining chip."

Wren's mouth fell open. "He sells them? But they're human. I mean, they're people. I mean, they're not, but they're living, breathing things, and he—"

"Did you expect better from a ruler who would see his people as no more than animals or an object to use in whatever manner he sees fit?" Timothius asked, irony dripping from his tone. "There is no hope to be had for a single one of us here. Every being under the rule of such a king—from the faeries to his favored—is trapped and tethered to a fate they cannot change. Sometimes we cannot even bear to dream beyond it."

The fire in her heart raged again, burning back sinew and bone, leaving it wide open with compassion for the people around her. They were not her people, but they didn't need to be. There was not a single soul that deserved to face such a helpless existence. Not when the dead were treated with more mercy than the living.

She watched Timothius closely, taking in every facet of him as his eyes scanned the room. He was the man she had met in the forest with sun-speckled skin, soft curls, fluid and graceful movement, and a laugh that lightened the forest beside his friend, but that man, in turn, was imprisoned in the shroud of a being whose humanity had been stripped away. His movements were stiff, his expression cold, all life and freedom staunched into submission down to the very hair on his head smoothed into slick, frozen waves. He was not tethered, bought, nor sold, but he was a prisoner all the same.

"What do you dream of?" she whispered.

Timothius was caught off guard, stiffening at the words. "What do you mean?"

"When you are alone in a crowd, when no one looks at you, when no one knows your name or your face…. When you have to fill that void, what is it you dream of? What carries you far from this place?"

His throat bobbed, and when he spoke, his voice was raw, as if he'd failed to swallow the emotion choking his words. "I dream of a home. A real one far from here. One I may call my own. Where the sun hits my face and the air fills my lungs and I can dance when I want to dance and laugh when I want to laugh. A place where I am unburdened. Where I do not carry the weight of duty, and where I can rest knowing that my friends are safe and that I have done all I can to protect them. Somewhere where I may rest."

Wren's eyes stung and she let them fall shut. She could feel every bit of longing in his words. Could see the picture he painted for himself. But what broke her the most was the way that it was not unlike the dreams she had for her own future. They existed worlds apart, yet they were one and the same, longing for a safe place to land and call home.

"What do you dream?"

Her eyes flew open, meeting the earnest hazel orbs that floated so close to her face. The storm that had begun building within her chest—the one that demanded she defend herself from all vulnerability—froze in the air, falling as nothing more than soft snow upon her heart. His unspoken understanding, the way she was seen by him, quieted her soul and prompted her to answer.

"I dream of forests and fields. Of wide-open spaces. Of mountains and an endless horizon. A place where I can swing high and run free like a child with no cares and only silly worries. Somewhere away from burdens and responsibilities, where life can be unplanned and breathing easy. Where I don't have to be loud because I am always seen and heard and loved unconditionally."

Their eyes met again and held, and with a small lift of the arm around her waist, Timothius raised her onto the front of his boots and pulled her closer. Their hands were still positioned for the dance, their posture mirroring the couples surrounding them, but the way he touched her—encasing her at every point in the same way that his gloved hand cradled her fingers—made their embrace feel like the hug it truly was.

In that moment, it was easy to forget who and where they were. It was natural for Wren to wish she could lay her cheek against his chest. For them to dance, to rest, and to dream.

They did not speak the remainder of the night, content to simply enjoy each other's company. And it was not until well into the pre-dawn hours that Wren awoke from a deep sleep and sat straight up in her bed, notes of dark amber and suede still lingering in her hair.

She laid a hand on her racing heart, recalling the dream of laughter and dancing in the forest—of happiness, affection, and a warmth unlike any she had ever known. Of a home and a quiet life beside Timothius, surrounded by peace and nestled in love. And there, only there in the dark and invisible silence, did she allow a new dream to break the stillness around her.

"And you. I dream of you."

CHAPTER TWENTY-SEVEN

*T*he grass of the meadow was still speckled with dewdrops, the cool breeze carrying the scent of the moist earth that compressed under Wren's boots as she walked beneath the gray morning sky outside of Inflamel City.

Not wanting to risk the chapel again, she had tried to walk along the top of the rampart and was quickly turned away by wolf-masked guards. Now, with Timothius nowhere to be found and Kathrina having departed early for errands ahead of the evening's ball, she found herself wandering her way to the Flugés' cottage.

She gazed across the meadow as far as her eyes could see. The Strait was ahead, somewhere on the other side of the fog. It had been easy to spot from the rampart, but she could not see it from the ground. And somewhere beyond that lay another country. Would more memories lie there? How far would this really take her? And if it did lead her beyond Inflamel, how would she ever get out?

She reached the place where the moat released into the deep stream that ran all the way to the coast, not nearly as sizable as the river that flowed through the Elfin Domain, but still impressive. She knelt on a rock at its edge and dipped her hand below the surface. A shuddering chill seized her fingers, and she yanked her hand back. As she'd suspected, it felt like ice.

Lost in thought, she did not hear anyone approach until an amused voice rumbled, "You should not be out here alone."

With a small shriek, Wren jolted and lost her balance. She tried to grasp onto the long grass, but it snapped off between her fingers, sending her toppling sideways into the water. Blessedly shallow at its edge, she popped back up as quickly as she had fallen, her locks sending channels of water from her shoulders down the gap in her bodice to her navel.

Gasping from the shock, she pulled her legs back under herself and stood, whirling to face a masked Timothius whose normally erect posture was slightly curved at the shoulders—shoulders that were shaking in a small fit of laughter.

"I...I feel like a soaking-wet fish," she gulped through chattering teeth.

"I fear that's a little redundant. And a minor understatement," Timothius replied, warmth and teasing filling his tone.

She scowled, feeling her ears redden under the scrutiny. "No one asked you."

Timothius stilled, his back straightening. "Are you angry with me?"

Wren didn't answer, instead glaring at him while wringing her skirt out, her arms and legs shaking from the cold.

"You're truly angry," Timothius stated, concern marring his words as he stepped forward.

"No, I'm not," she retorted. "I— Why are you even here?"

"I saw you walking alone. Can I not check to ensure that you are all right? Are we not friends?"

Wren eyed his sincerity with scorn. The word *friend* sent an unnecessary pain to her heart after her dream the night prior and embarrassed her even more. "I'm fine. Just go away."

Instead, he took another step forward. "You're soaking wet

and you're fighting with me," he said, hesitation coloring his tone. "Surely anger and agitation mean the same thing in your world as it does in mine. You simply cannot be fine."

Wren loosed a sigh, threw her hands in the air with exasperation, and cursed herself for landing in a world where men did not accept *fine* as an answer. She looked to Timothius then, only a foot away from her, his uniform and mask pristine, his boots flawless, but his eyes wide with concern and his posture that of a boy who had been caught with his hand somewhere it should not be.

She snorted, instinctively looking away, but as soon as her gaze returned to him, she laughed again. And try as she may, she could not stop. It felt *good* to laugh. And she couldn't remember the last time she truly had, either in this world or her own.

Timothius eyes held bewilderment, but the harder she laughed, the more his muscles relaxed and his stance eased.

He closed the gap between them and released a clasp near his neck, swinging his dark cape with deep-red lining from where it lay against his back. Draping it over her shoulders, he pulled it tightly, paused a moment, then reached up to slip his thumbs beneath her hair. His gloves ever so gently brushed the skin below her ears until the ends slid free to rest outside of the cloak.

Memories of her dream came rushing back, and heat rose to Wren's face for an entirely different reason. Had what transpired between them the night before—their raw honesty, vulnerable trust, and innocent secrets—somehow affected him the way it had shaken her to her core?

Her mouth suddenly dry, she swallowed and watched his eyes dip to her bobbing throat, lingering a moment too long, but when she opened her mouth to speak, a shout sounded from the drawbridge and broke their spell. Timothius snapped ramrod straight and turned, moving away from Wren in long strides.

"Wait," she whispered. "Your cloak."

"Keep it," he said, pausing in the grass. "I was not using it anyway. Head to the Flugés'. Away from here. Now."

Wren only had time to take a handful of steps in the direction of the cottage when hoofbeats thundered around the drawbridge, leading a charge their way—though it was not the king at their head but Musannulos who reared his horse in front of Timothius.

"His Majesty waits for you," he said, voice dripping with disdain from behind his coquettish owl mask.

"And am I to walk to His Majesty while those beneath me proceed on mount?" Timothius snapped, both his voice and demeanor returning to the deadly cold Glaive.

"In fact, you are," replied Musannulos in a clipped tone. "You departed on foot with your cape in tow. I assumed you preferred to travel in such a manner. It is such a lovely day for a stroll." Wren dared not look at him directly, but she could feel his eyes boring into her and his stare locked upon the cloak wrapped around her body.

A low rumble slipped from Timothius, somewhere between an angered growl and a frustrated grunt. "The kingdom for a horse," he muttered, stalking past Musannulos and cleaving through the center of the other soldiers gathered behind him.

He was well on his way back to the castle when the mouse-faced guards began to titter among themselves, mocking him. Wren glared at them all, though only the wolf-masked soldiers took notice, turning their snarling maws on her.

She started to leave, but her heart sank when she heard, "Fancy meeting you here, Lady Florence."

Sighing, she turned to face Musannulos and forced a smile into her voice. "As you said, nice day for a walk."

"And with His Majesty's toy soldier yet again at your side. It is peculiar. I have known him since he was a boy and he has never sought the company of a single living soul in the kingdom, save you."

She didn't allow her thoughts to linger on what part the owlman must have played in Timothius's *discipline*. Instead, her mind raced for words—words that would not get herself or Timothius into any more trouble.

He is kind was on the tip of her tongue. Because he was. Timothius, despite what he thought of himself, was a gentleman. And no matter how he felt about his position, he had the strength and fortitude of a thousand men.

"He is keenly observant," she replied. "It is unnerving how he is always near. Much like you."

Musannulos stared at her for a long time and then finally clicked his tongue. His horse began to turn, and with the motion, the guards behind him did the same, departing toward the keep.

"I am the ears and eyes of the king when he is not present," he said over his shoulder, the words chilling Wren far more than the water had. "You would do well to remember that." And with a slight buck, his horse carried him away.

Wren made it to the Flugés' gate in record time, pausing for only a moment to catch her breath. She had just unlatched the gate when the nagging sensation of being watched caused her to freeze. Glancing over her shoulder and across the field, it was strangely empty, other than the few merchants headed to the city gate, but it was when her eyes crossed the top of the battlement that she caught the sun glint off something gold in the tallest spire, high above the castle—and the silhouette of the king where he stared down upon the meadow.

Heart hammering an unsteady rhythm in her chest, Wren gathered her skirt but instead of entering the gate, she walked around it and toward the tree line. She regretted leading the king's eyes anywhere near the Flugés', but if he somehow believed she were just wandering about the wood, maybe it would ease his suspicion of them and focus it solely on her.

She stopped to pick up a few mushrooms along the way and intended to only step far enough into the Autumnal Wood to enter the Flugés' home from the rear garden, but as soon as the world vanished behind the first line of trees, she felt reality fall away.

The wood was unlike anything she had ever seen. Every surface surrounding her was blanketed in the same vibrant colors dressed upon each tree. They were mostly orange, with some reds and golds high in the boughs where the sun shone the most, but every last hue extended to the ground at her feet in a carpet of freshly fallen leaves.

Visually, and to the touch when she knelt, the leaves were soft—still dew-moistened and velvet with not a crack, curl, or withered spot to be found. There wasn't a speck of brown in sight beyond the tree trunks and few spots of dirt that had been worn down into a trail most likely used by wildlife. The forest was perpetually fall. Not the death of summer nor the promise of winter, but a living, golden autumn bathed in warm sunlight with only the hint of a crisp breeze whispering that a change was coming.

Wren rose, but when she lifted her eyes, the world dimmed ever so slightly, carrying a premonition on the wind and causing her skin to tingle with anticipation.

A small girl with dark curls surrounding her face ran through the leaves. Pausing in front of each drift, she looked around with a keen eye and then dove into the pile by her side. A loud YELP sounded, followed by a torrent of giggles, and an older boy rose with the girl wrapped in his arms. They shared the same nose, the same color eyes, and the same lustrous curls at nearly the same length.

"You found me, Em! But can you catch me?" he teased, dumping her unceremoniously into the pile of leaves before darting off through the trees.

Her shrieking joy chased him, but no sooner had they vanished into the forest did they reappear again, this time running from the opposite direction. The girl was well and truly a teenager now, her hair still wild and her youthful face still flushed with vibrance and freedom. The boy was considerably taller, his voice deeper when he chided her for being so slow. The girl said nothing but instead slid her boot from her foot mid-stride and hurled it at his head. Her aim was true, and he lurched forward with a thud, rolling to his back and howling with laughter. She tumbled over him, threatening him with the other shoe, but ended up collapsing harmlessly at his side in a torrent of giggles.

"I don't want it to be me," the girl said with a sigh, the words sobering them both in an instant.

The boy wrapped his arms around her and pressed a kiss to the top of her head. "If it had to be one of us, it needed to be you. You are strong—made for this. And you will never be alone. You may gain three more siblings in magic, but I am still the brother who loves you most."

She smiled, her eyes glistening with unshed tears, but when she looked up at the face that mirrored her own, she slapped him with the boot still in her hand and shot up, arms pumping through the air as she ran away with all her might.

"Oh no you don't, you terrible creature," he yelled, taking off after her.

The discarded boot still lay in the leaves, or at least it appeared to. The shuffling of feet drew closer and closer to it, but the girl was alone this time. Her childish features were gone, her hair neatly restrained, and on her head sat a glittering circlet devoid of any ornamentation.

Kneeling, she brushed away the leaves to reveal not a boot but a small stone with words etched into it that were already beginning to wear away and fade into time.

"I'm not sure why you wished to come here, of all places," she said, rising and looking over her shoulder. "We get precious few moments together and yet you wish to spend them here."

She extended a hand behind her and a man took it, weaving his fingers through her own and lifting them to his mouth. With the other hand, he cupped her cheek and wiped the tears away. "Thank you for bringing me here," he whispered.

She was overcome with emotion, yet still smiled and nodded. "Why?" was the only word she could speak.

The man beamed, the love in his eyes outshining every color in the golden wood. "Where else would I go? There is none whose presence would be better."

The woman was confused, but when the man sank to one knee, her mouth opened and her eyes glowed with the same happiness that had echoed through that very forest when she was just a child.

"Em, with all that I am, I am yours," the man vowed, looking up at her earnestly. "I do not wish to have a moment of time for the rest of my days that is spent outside of your love. Will you allow me to take your hand, will you give me your heart.... Will you become my wife?"

Her smile broke the dam that held back her tears and all thought of regal pretense was lost as she fell to her knees and threw her arms around his neck, kissing him until they both lay breathless on the blanket of leaves. They remained there, talking of forever, whispering of a promised future.

With a sad joy, she blew a kiss to the headstone, and on the arm of her love, left the forest for the last time.

Wren gasped for air, unsure when she had stopped breathing. Her eyes stung and she wrapped an arm around her stomach, shuddering from the raw emotion coursing through her. It nearly caused her to vomit, but it was the brilliant cold against her skin beneath the cloak that brought her world back to its calm center.

Pulling the crystallum out, she surveyed its deep-rose shade. Now the size of an acorn, there was no design on its surface, but it was almost as if something churned inside it, thrumming with the beat of her pulse.

Desperate to return to the castle but still deeply jarred by the strong emotion within the memory, Wren made for the Flugés' back door. Their small wagon was gone, signaling that they were more than likely in town, but when she entered the back door and closed it firmly behind her, she was shocked to find that the house was not empty.

And with a sheepish grin from Kathrina and a nervous smile from the man who had his arms wrapped around her, Wren let out a slow laugh and removed her mask. "Well, well, well. Hello again, Elric."

CHAPTER TWENTY-EIGHT

*E*lric had the good sense to look nervous at Wren's appearance, though she wasn't entirely sure if it was due to their reunion or the woman in his arms.

Wren, however, smiled warmly at the epiphany. "You're his K."

Kathrina nodded, her cheeks flushing a beautiful pink at the words. "I am. And I don't believe I have to explain why we have the need for secrecy."

"No. And now it makes sense why you were so sick at the thought of an Isteriaeth being captured yesterday." Wren closed the door behind her and moved to sit at the table where a small candle was lit and two dishes were waiting, each with a slice of pie. "So does this mean you've been reporting all my actions back to him?"

"Actually, no. This is the first we have seen each other since before the last moon."

Wren looked between the two, the longing in Kathrina's eyes and the tinge of sadness in Elric's softening her heart. "You've been separated for months."

"We are not able to see each other unless it is here," Elric said quietly. "And even then, we do not dare endanger Gerard and Mauritania."

"You know them too?"

Elric pressed his lips together, appearing disconcerted by his secrets unraveling left and right.

"So which side of you do I get to see now?" Wren asked, lifting a spoon and casually taking a bite of the pie closest to her. "The sweet, loved-up side, or do I have to be worried that you're going to tell me a bunch of stories, then trap me here?"

"*Trap* you? That was never my intent. I meant to—"

"To keep me *safe* until you decided whether it was me or the crystallum you needed. One, I don't need anyone to keep me safe, and two, next time just listen to the woman in the conversation. She's trying to make sure you don't do something dumb."

"What woman were you having a conversation with?" Kathrina asked, her tone playful but her words pointed as she swiped the other slice of pie from the table.

"Enya," Elric replied with a sigh and then addressed Wren once again. "I suppose I know what made you run now. I only wonder why you could not have spoken with me about what you heard."

"If you thought someone was trapping you—if you believed you were a prisoner—would you talk to them? Or would you run the first chance you got?"

A shadow fell over Elric's face, and he nodded in silent understanding.

Wren surveyed the sorrow in his eyes and the remorse weighing on his shoulders. And after all she had come to understand since fleeing the Elfin Domain, she could not keep him out in the cold. Her heart had grown a soft spot for the Isteriaeth, and now that more truths were coming to light, she found herself concerned for him. "Elric, why are you here? This is so dangerous, if you were caught...."

"She is worth it," he replied, his eyes never once wavering from Kathrina's face.

Her eyes glistened, and she moved back to his side and pressed a kiss to his jawline. "We see each other sparingly. Thrice in a calendar if we are lucky."

"How?" The word felt like an old familiar friend tumbling from Wren's lips. "How do you have a relationship? How could you have met if he is…what he is?"

"We have known each other since we were children," Kathrina replied with a smile. "It was the Flugés who found him when he arrived on our shores. They took him in and raised him. We played together in the fields and grew close. When his magic was bestowed, we were forced to part, though we never separated. We steal the spare moments that fall into our hands until someday we can claim them all."

Wren's eyes met Elric's, her wordless question conveyed as he nodded. "Yes, she knows Timothius. In return he watches out for her, but none can know they are familiar."

"He is the reason I serve in the court," Kathrina said quietly. "When I was fourteen, a sickness took nearly half the city. My parents were among the dead. I had nowhere to go and no family to turn to, save the Flugés, but in those times, it was hard enough to feed one mouth, let alone three. I was tending to their deliveries when the palace steward approached and invited me to serve within the castle staff. I found out later that T had pointed me out as a strong worker with ties to the royal harvesters. My future has been secure since."

Wren was silent for a long moment, desperate to ask the question burning in her mind but knowing it was not their story to tell.

"Ask," said Elric softly, coming to sit beside her.

Wren eyed him, allowing her stare to grow cold. "I'm still mad at you, for the record."

Elric chuckled. "We can discuss your misunderstanding and

my misleading more once you say what is on your mind. Seeing that you are on more familiar terms with my friend than when we last saw each other."

Wren felt her ears heat beneath her chilled, damp hair. "That's a bold assumption," she said dryly, taking another bite of pie.

"Not nearly as bold as you wearing his cloak," Elric replied, swiping his finger across the cream dolloped on top of her pie and licking it clean with a triumphant smirk.

Wren pulled the plate closer to her, inwardly cringing but outwardly rolling her eyes. "If Kathrina was fourteen when Timothius secured her job in the castle, then how long has he lived there? How did he become what he is, and how did you all come to know each other?"

"That is a simple answer with a rather long explanation," Elric replied, easing back in his seat. "Timothius is the Flugés' son."

Wren's jaw dropped, but Elric continued before she could speak. "Biologically, the Flugés have never had children of their own, however they have been parents to many over the years. When the Lady Drossel was widowed with Timothius in her womb, and then she herself passed only moments after childbirth, her midwife—Mauritania—pledged to raise the infant as her own. In the same way, when I washed up on shore, they did not hesitate to take me in as his brother. We were raised side by side, inseparable and bound by the common hand dealt to us in life. So when my power was bestowed, it was Timothius who walked straight into the wood, searching for a place where I might hide. He stumbled upon the tree home instead. We were young, on the cusp of manhood, but we stole away in the night. He ensured that I was safe, lingering with me there before leaving and promising to return. Only he never arrived home."

Kathrina rested her plate on the counter and pulled the chair out next to Elric, quietly sitting beside him. He took her hand, his long, delicate fingers matching her own, bleached white from how tightly they held onto one another, already dreading the moment they would need to let go. "The Flugés do not know what became of him. The sickness settled in not too long after, and they accepted that even if he somehow had survived the forest, or been taken, the odds of him being both alive and still within our kingdom were slim. I, however, could not accept it. I waited years to be strong enough in my magic and then stole into the city, masquerading as a peddler and hiding on the streets, searching high and low for any trace of him.

"I had been on the hunt for days. The night was frigid, the rain miserable, and I thought I was concealed enough to summon a meal. But a passerby reported my use of magic and I was arrested. The guards dragged me to the castle, but outside the throne room, his newest soldier apprehended us. Instead of taking me before the king or even down to the dungeons, he ferried me to the bowels of the castle and released me into the night."

Elric paused, fighting back the emotion overcoming him, shadowing him like the dhust he could pull from the air. "I will never forget the moment I saw his face again. It had been ages since he left me in the forest, promising that he would find a way to save us all, and then I lost him. When he removed the mask and revealed himself, we could do nothing more than hold each other and weep. That was when he told me his plan. The rebellion was born that night, and we have been mustering our forces ever since."

"What do you mean by his plan?" Wren asked with trep-idation.

Elric's eyes were solemn when they met hers. "I know him to be Timothius. That is how you first learned of him. Yet the kingdom knows him to be the King's Glaive—a lackey and a plaything, a ruthless, murderous weapon. He remains that way to ensure the rebellion succeeds. We would not have nearly the mustering we do were it not for his efforts. But he, himself, does not intend to see freedom. He has secured unquestionable loyalty to the Rat King in order to deliver his demise when we are ready, and in turn, he has sealed his fate. The rebellion will not let him live and if he is the one to dispose of the king, neither will the castle guard. Our success will cost him his life."

The fog within Wren's thoughts began to clear, like smoke fading from a glass window. She fully understood now what was at stake—what she had fallen into, and what she was an intricate part of whether she wanted to be or not. And beside her, at the center of it all, was Timothius. Doomed to remain in his mask, his personal prison, even after everyone else found their way home.

"There is no excuse for the way I misled you," Elric admitted. "But we had to know you were protected. We are still unsure of how you came to be here, but we cannot lose you. If history itself is on our side—"

"Then you might be able to save him too," Wren finished.

Elric paused. "I do not know," he said honestly. "But I still have hope where he has none left. You have complicated our mission, but you have brought us that hope."

Wren was at a loss for words. She barely knew what to think. But the silence unnerved her. "I've been seeing visions. Memories from the time of the Trifolium Thrones. Timothius has been helping me. There are people close to the king who have been watching. He's endangering himself to protect me."

Elric nodded resolutely. "Despite the part he plays, he feels that he bears the burden of saving everyone. I would even dare to say that the things he has seen, the things he's done, only increase that desire. And that now extends to you."

"But," interjected Kathrina, a mischievous glint in her eye, "I would not discredit his protection of you as duty alone."

Wren snorted. "I don't think he sees me as anything more than another task to keep track of."

Kathrina shook her head, a wide smile commanding her face. "He never danced before he met you."

Elric's gaze shot to her. "What do you mean?"

Wren stilled. "What *do* you mean?"

"He never left the dais," Kathrina replied. "Every night at every dance, he never once moved from the king's side. Until your first night at court. That is how I knew there was more to your appearance here."

"Why would he do that?" Wren snapped. "He's drawing unnecessary attention to himself and to me. It's dangerous and reckless and he should know better."

Elric, recovering from his own surprise at the revelation, looked to Wren with the same softness in his eyes that she saw when he spoke of Kathrina or the stars themselves. "If you knew you were close to ushering in the end, would you not steal a moment of joy? What then would he truly have to lose?"

Wren did not want the words to sting, she did not want to care, and yet…. "So he knows me being here is going to launch the rebellion. He's running out of time and choosing to pass it with me. Leading me on so he can be a martyr and I can go home knowing that I helped free an entire people but lost him. I thought magic meant everyone lived happily ever after?"

"Wren, you are making him happy," Kathrina said with a sad smile. "I have never seen him so happy as when he is with you."

"And what about me?" Wren asked bitterly.

"I thought all you wished for was to return home?" Elric asked quietly.

Wren snapped her mouth shut. That was all she wanted. It was the only reason she was even helping any of them.

Wasn't it?

"Do either of you know anything about the rulers who came before the Rat King?" she asked, abruptly changing the subject. "Was there a queen, a princess, anyone relating to the throne who would have been referred to as Em?"

Kathrina shook her head, looking to Elric whose brow was knit tight in concentration. "When the Thrones fell, those left behind went to great lengths to ensure that the Trifolium rulers were wiped from time. Their names were not passed down."

"And none are allowed in the royal library, the king ensures that," Kathrina added.

Wren paused, an excited awareness rippling up and down her spine. "There's a library inside the castle?"

Kathrina nodded. "It is still filled with books, from what I hear, though none know what kind."

Wren grinned again and finished off Elric's pie with a flourish. "Then I guess I will need to find a way in."

"I don't think that is wise," Elric cautioned, but Wren only stood. Her clothes, still damp, raised bumps across her skin and she pulled Timothius's cloak tighter. All she had learned of him still stung, but she could not dwell on that now. Not until she had time to figure out when he had begun to mean so much to her.

"It probably isn't," she admitted with a shrug. "But I guess you're just going to have to trust me."

Elric looked at his empty plate with disappointment, but then rose as well. "I do trust you, Wren. Truly. But I fear for you." He paused for a moment, emotion thickening his words, but still he forced a smile. "You're abysmal with a sword, how will you ever defend yourself?"

Wren laughed, but the vulnerability of his words struck her core, and before she could rein herself in, she wrapped her arms around his neck. To her relief, he returned the hug, holding her tightly. It struck her how much she had missed him. They were both stubborn, wise in ways that did not encourage attachment, yet the unlikely bond that had formed between them remained. They did not speak the words, but neither needed them to voice the emotion locked within their embrace—quiet apology and unequivocal forgiveness.

She understood then why these people, despite all the missteps and half-truths, would risk it all for one another. They were family. And the determination to care for and love them in the same way became the overwhelming strength that made her whisper in his ear, "Hold on to hope, E. I'll find a way out of the castle. For all of us."

CHAPTER TWENTY-NINE

The Dance of Midnight was already Wren's favorite of the seven dances. There was something both ethereal and menacing about the way the black and silver melted against one another, no two colors dancing together but both pressed so closely they may have been mistaken for the moon dancing with her shadow in a darkened sky.

So when an onyx-gloved hand slipped into her own, it brought a smile to her face without hesitation. Timothius's solid black uniform cut a striking contrast to the white of his mask, causing its cracks to stand out more. He was intimidating, frightening even, but he was the one person she looked for when she entered the room—not to track his movements, but to beguile him with her own.

"We have a lot to talk about," she said, dipping into a curtsy as their dance began. Her ruffled ivory skirt sashayed beneath the asymmetric layer of black lace that draped over it from her strapless bodice of the same material, giving the illusion that it was wrapped around her very skin.

Timothius tipped his head to her, his eyes dancing even before his feet moved. "I was about to say the same."

A sudden apprehension settled into Wren's bones. "Is everything all right?" she asked quietly.

"I am not sure," Timothius replied, but after a beat, he added, "I seem to have misplaced my favorite cloak."

Wren laughed and the sound rang out across the floor, startling her and drawing a few stares. She placed her arms on his, and they fell into step together. "And I guess you want it back?"

Timothius shrugged absently. "I would if I knew where I had left it. But if it has found another home, I suppose it may stay there. It looked far better on its new owner anyway."

Wren blushed, but Timothius continued, "Were you able to find safety after? I did not see you reenter the city."

"I was. I saw...something else. There was another change. And then I ran into an old friend."

A flash of concern brightened his eyes for a moment, and then recognition. "They take far too many chances," he muttered.

"I would hardly call three times a year too many."

"Three is gracious compared to none when they are found out."

The concern, worry, and hurt all knotted in his tone stung worse than the pointed jab of his words. Wren pressed on. "I need to find a way inside the library."

Timothius hummed. "I believe I can assist you in this."

"But I can't let you help me any longer."

The words were nails dropped inside a tin bucket, ear-piercingly loud, making way for deafening silence. It made her uneasy, and when she dared meet his eyes, they were intensely still. "The king was watching earlier. When you gave me your cloak," she rushed.

"He is not watching now," he chided, citing the Rat King deep in his cups with a bear-masked woman perched on one knee.

"I saw him in the tower. And that is the second time Musannulos has seen us together. I know you never danced with anyone before me. You are taking too many risks, and I can't let you keep doing this."

"They are my risks to take," he said tersely. "My choices alone."

"But you are not truly alone, are you?"

A slow and steady exhale flowed from beneath his mask as his eyes fell shut. "What did E say to you?"

"Nothing that I did not ask him first. I will not put you in any more danger than you are already in, and when I have what I need and can leave the city, I am taking you with me."

Timothius chuckled humorlessly, the sound lighting a fire of indignation within Wren's chest. "Is something funny?"

"Oh, dear swan, I am laughing at you," he replied, voice hard. "You are fearless in the best and worst ways, but you do not know when to turn from a battle. I am yours to save now as much as you were mine in the forest. We can both take care of ourselves and meet our futures as equals."

"But you do not need this future. You deserve—"

"I have chosen this," he interrupted, ceasing movement in the middle of the floor and bringing Wren to a halt beside him. "I have had choice after choice stripped from me since the moment I was claimed for the king. I have done what was required in order to survive. I have become what was expected to gain liberty. But I will not allow another to decide my fate for me. My choice is my power, and I shall use it as my strength."

Wren opened her mouth, but no words came out. She tried to fight, tried to refute his words, but she could not bring herself to do it. In her heart, she knew there would be no changing his mind and she would not push him away—she did not want to push him away.

"Now," Timothius said quietly. "Do you wish to see the library?"

Wren nodded.

"Good. Then you will have to play the part."

She did not dare ask what part that would be when he took her hand and led her from the floor. He guided them out a small door along the side of the room opposite the grand entryway she typically used each night. It was not until she was through the doorway that her eyes widened to what lay ahead.

Windows were open to the night, the cool air lifting the curtains and sending their sheer lengths billowing out in waves. Whispers floated on the breeze from shadowed alcoves, carrying sighs off the plush benches that lined a hall veiled with shadow yet bathed in moonlight.

Wren could not look anywhere without seeing lovers in some form of embrace—some bashful, while others decidedly not. Each was a die waiting to be cast, rolling so quickly their monochrome blurred into gray and the lines between them became little more than a dare awaiting fulfillment.

Every mask was a piece searching for completion, racing to find its match hidden in the shadow of the lunar glow. But the dark was more than concealment—it was solace, found both within another and in the finite moment of obscurity before the sun rose to illuminate them all.

Timothius paused for a heartbeat and pulled her flush to his side. One hand curled about her waist, holding her close, while the other cupped her elbow, tracing small circles against her skin and leaving goosebumps in their wake as they strolled down the hall.

"What are we doing?" she whispered, trying to keep all hint of nerves from her voice.

"Playing the part," he murmured, breathing the words beside her ear.

They followed each curve and bend of the hall, walking by couples with no care or notice of who may be passing, and then he stopped again. This time he turned so that they faced one another.

She looked up, their masks only inches apart. Even in her heels he towered over her. Grasping her elbows, he stepped forward, aligning their bodies in a clash of light and shadow, and then, ever so slowly, he guided her back toward the wall.

Wren's heart hammered faster, threatening to beat out of her chest, and she feared that he could feel it through his jacket, beneath her dress and caged within her ribs. She was starting to think that's where he resided—under her skin. And she wondered if there was a way she had burrowed in his too.

The curtains folded around them, hiding them from sight, but the moment her back touched a solid surface, Timothius released her elbow and reached up to pull aside what turned out to be a pocket door. Wide enough for one person to enter sideways, Wren stepped through first, and he followed, sliding it firmly shut behind them.

Motes of dust hung in the air between the cases of books taller than she and Timothius combined. Cobwebs swayed back and forth in the light that shone through missing stones in the ceiling, bathing the library in moonlight. Wren found herself wondering how radiant it must look under a full moon, but the thought brought along a sobering fear, anchoring her back to reality.

Turning, she sank a punch into Timothius's shoulder. He absorbed it with a small snort. "I did nothing to warrant that."

"You could have told me we were just sneaking in here."

"I told you I could arrange your being here. Exactly what did you think we were doing?"

Wren opened her mouth but quickly shut it. "I— Never mind. Let's go, this is going to take forever."

Moving farther into the library, she scanned the spines of books, most in languages she had never seen in her life.

"And what exactly are you looking for?" Timothius asked, following her closely, his hand resting lightly around hilt of his sword.

"Are you expecting trouble?"

"This room is forbidden. Should anyone enter the front or back doors, we would need to run. And should you need more time, I would need to provide a diversion."

Wren gaped. "I don't want anyone dead in this library. It's too beautiful for murder."

Even in the dim light she saw him roll his eyes, the sight making her stifle a laugh. "Incapacitation, not murder. I am a gentleman, remember?"

Wren snorted. "That's right. Sorry, it slipped my mind when you were being *gentlemanly* in the hall."

It was Timothius's turn to snort. "You are rather prickly tonight."

"Swans bite," Wren said with a shrug, coming to a halt at the end of the first row of shelves. There were at least a dozen of them, and she had no idea how deep each one extended within the room. It was less of a room and more of a sanctuary, and she did not want to imagine how long it might take to lay eyes on every shelf.

"I need to find history. Genealogy. Anything," she added, already exasperated.

"Then I would start there," said Timothius from directly over her shoulder, causing her to jump. His arm came around her, finger pointing up to a placard high on the bookcase with simple letters hammered into it:

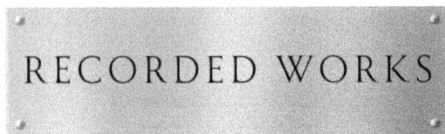

RECORDED WORKS

Wren threw him a shrewd look. "Thank you, oh wise one, for your service."

Timothius's voice conveyed his smile. "And you did not wish for my help."

Wren ignored him, instead continuing down the aisle to the row of shelves holding stacks upon stacks of tomes. Opening one, she could see that they were in fact handwritten records. Some were of property, others of livestock and goods, still more of crops, seeds, and trade. On and on she carefully removed and flipped through book upon book until finally she reached what appeared to be census records.

"This is what we're looking for," she said excitedly, "But it would need to be records of someone connected to the throne. A lady, someone of royal birth. And I believe her name would start with *E*. In the memory I saw, both her elder brother and her lover referred to her as Em."

Timothius nodded and crossed to Wren's other side, retrieving a folio and perusing the pages encased in velvet and coated with layers of dust.

She lost track of time and was starting to lose patience with the search. She was about to voice her nagging concern when Timothius asked, "Are you certain her name would have begun with an *E* in order to be called Em?"

Wren faced him. "Yes. What else would it be short for?"

"It would not be short for anything. But the letter *M* itself would stand for something."

Turning the book in his hand, he laid it in front of Wren. "Born to King Midreik II and Queen Seredyna of Inflamel: A son called Kenric the Cavaliere, heir to the Crown of Inflamel. He died at age sixteen of a wasting illness," he read aloud.

Wren's heart hammered, looking at the portrait of the royal family painted within the pages of the book. They did not need to be perfect for her to see the likeness between the boy on the page and the one she had seen laughing and running through the wood with his sister. Excitement flooded her veins, tightening its hold on her lungs as she kept reading, but the words brought her entire world to a stop.

With trembling fingers, she flipped the page, and though she knew what she would find, she was thoroughly unprepared to see it.

The inscription bore the words: Marionaldi of Clovers, Princess of Inflamel and High Queen of the Trifolium Thrones, and Sir Vincienti, Regent King of Inflamel. But the words were not what stole Wren's breath. It was the portrait of the couple— older than the memory she had seen in the forest, yet younger than the couple she had seen thrust from their world. And now that she saw them side by side, their names aged with time, she knew.

Somehow, Marionaldi—the last Queen of Inflamel and the lost ruler of Trifolium Throne—was her grandmother.

CHAPTER THIRTY

S omewhere to their left, a door banged open. Wren jumped away from the book as if the pages had burned her, and Timothius snapped it shut, swiftly sliding it back into place on the shelf.

He took her hand and wordlessly guided her toward the door they had entered—and then stopped dead in his tracks. With a firm tug on her arm, he whipped down an aisle, pulling Wren deeper into the library, and she nearly collided with his back when he paused at the end.

"Can't have gone far," a mouse-face guard muttered. Light flickered against the shelves, slowly moving from row to row. "Every week it's the same thing, couples wandering where they shouldn't be."

Wren looked at Timothius with wide eyes, but he was gazing at the shelf beyond her head. He removed a small book and tossed it over the shelves to their left, the cascade of rustling paper preceding its *thunk*. The scuffle of boots grew closer, echoing in the row beside them and signaling it was time to move. Exiting the row, they increased the space between them and the guards before Timothius turned sharply down a new aisle and began to walk in long strides, bringing Wren along behind him.

They reached what appeared to be the main entrance doors, which had been left ajar by the guards. He glanced out, then in one swift stride, pulled Wren around the corner and into the hall. His pace nearly doubled in speed, and she rushed to keep up with him, looking around at the unfamiliar portion of the castle.

"Where are we?" she whispered.

"The king's private wing."

Wren blanched, but Timothius continued down the hall to the stairs, unruffled. His pace did not slow until they were nearly two floors below; however, at the sound of voices, he whipped into a room toward the middle of the hall and quietly shut the door behind them.

The curtains were drawn back on a small drawing room, its large windows allowing light from the night sky to filter in on a high-backed chaise, writing desk, and a pianoforte.

"What do we do?" Wren hissed.

Timothius faced her, and for the first time that evening, concern flashed across his eyes. "We are no longer near the king's quarters, but this is not a part of the castle that guests frequent. I cannot leave you here, but I cannot be alone with you without reason."

Wren swallowed, looking around and thinking for a moment before turning back to him. "Sit on the chaise."

Timothius blinked at her.

"Oh, just sit," Wren said, walking to it herself.

He still looked perplexed but did what she asked, sitting rather awkwardly on the upholstered couch. Wren gathered the hem of her skirts above her knees, fumbling with them as her nerves started to get the best of her, but she did not hesitate to approach him. Placing a knee on the cushion by his side, she scooted forward and then hoisted herself up on the other knee to straddle his thighs. Adjusting her skirts to cover her legs, she finally allowed herself to sink down on his lap. She instantly regretted the decision, her undergarments and his uniform pants keeping very little from either of their imaginations.

Timothius's eyes widened. "Wren...."

She shrugged with as much nonchalance as she could muster. "Just play the part."

Timothius paused for a moment, and then quietly started to chuckle. Wren shoved his shoulder playfully, but the rumble grew into silent, body-shaking laughter that Wren found too contagious to resist. Unable to contain her own giggle, she steadied herself on the back of the chaise. They tried to hush one another but could not help but laugh softly through the tension, fear, and awkwardness that had encompassed the entire night.

Wren's breathing started to slow, and she finally regained composure when Timothius lifted his arms from where they rested at his sides. He clasped Wren's wrists and removed her hands from the back of the chair to place them on his shoulders. Gently gripping her waist, he pulled her closer—dragging her across his body—and she could not keep her lips from parting on a breathy inhale.

She slid her hand down, stopping where his heart raced with her own, and when she met his eyes, she found them waiting for her. "To play the part you must look the part," he said, voice low and rough.

She nodded and was about to say something to diffuse the different sort of tension mounting between them when he continued, "You laughed again."

Wren paused. "I do that from time to time. I'm not always rude."

"You said in the Brumal Forest that you had not laughed since arriving in our kingdom. But you did yesterday, and again today. Twice."

Wren frowned. "And your point?"

"I would like it greatly if you continued to do so. You illuminate the room when you do, and the sound...it is its own form of magic."

Wren cheeks heated beneath her mask, and to her own mortification, she felt her eyes begin to sting. "I'm sorry," she said, voice raw. "I am so sorry. You deserve so much more than this."

He shook his head. "You are quite possibly the only person I know who can go from being a hero to none to being a hero for all. You are a dreamer, but rarely even in the happiest tales do all make it out alive."

"What if my tale can only be happy if you do?"

The words were raw and honest, hovering in the small space between their heaving chests and longing eyes.

Timothius's hands, usually so unwavering, trembled as he lifted them, unclamped the pins, and removed Wren's mask from her face. She didn't think her heart could beat any faster, but now—unable to hide—it felt as if it might burst from her chest.

Laying the mask on the cushion at their side, he reached up and ran his thumb along the impression it had left on her cheek.

Before she could second-guess herself, Wren laid her hand over his and removed it. Holding his palm gently, she worked the fingertips of his glove free, one by one, until the fabric slid away. She replaced his hand, and it conformed to the contours of her face instantly, his cool touch easing an ache left by her mask that she hadn't realized was there.

Resting his opposite hand in her lap, she did the same thing, sliding the glove free, laying them both beside her mask, and meeting the intensity of his stare once again.

"You are drawing attention you do not want," he said, voice barely above a whisper.

Wren shook her head and subtly burrowed further into his

touch, though she knew he was aware by the way his hand caressed her skin.

After a moment it fell away, returning to her waist, and she did not hesitate to reach up and grasp either side of his mask. To her surprise it was not secured by ribbon or pin, but instead was molded to his face so perfectly it did not move—a prison held in place by pain.

Timothius moved to stop her, but she was faster. Pulling the edges away from his skin, she felt it succumb to gravity and become nothing more than a weight in her hand. She was met instantly by small bruises along the line where the mask gripped his face, but also his faded freckles and soft, smooth complexion. His hair was still slicked straight back, the curls waxed into waves of submission, but one errant curl now tumbled against his forehead.

Resting the face of the soldier beside the swan and discarded gloves, Wren returned her hands to his shoulders, but this time she slid them behind his neck, drawing their bodies even closer.

"I don't want the attention of anyone but Timothius," she whispered in reply.

His exhale was shaky, matching her unsteady heart, but his grip tightened on her waist as if concerned that she might slip away at any moment. He cleared his throat, though his voice was still thick. "I'm afraid I am no longer playing the part. And even so, I might kiss you."

The flame heating Wren's skin became an inferno beneath the fresh coals that his words added, feeding oxygen to her soul that was desperate to burn.

His eyes fell to her mouth, and she leaned forward in a silent invitation. He did not hesitate to erase the hairsbreadth distance and claim her lips with his own. They were soft, but his kiss was hard, an intentional promise of more.

Wren would have gladly begged for more, but there was something about his reverence in holding her—how he tipped their faces to deepen the kiss and the way his hands slid up her back, his fingertips meeting the skin exposed between her shoulders—that held her desire for him at bay.

She was used to ravenous consumption, but this was deeper. *More.*

She wanted to savor him.

Voices sounded from the hall outside the room, causing them to jolt apart. Rushing to replace their masks, they did not have time to stand before the door flew open and Musannulos stormed in.

He stopped short, eyes somehow even more bulbous within his owl mask, and took in the sight of Wren upon Timothius's lap. She knew they both looked guilty, and she couldn't help but let out a short laugh, realizing that while they had intended for their appearance to look suggestive, they were in fact in a compromising position.

And when Timothius took her hand, steadying her as she rose back to her feet, she caught a glimpse of every inch of compromise she had felt growing from their touch.

"You of all people should know better," Musannulos spat at Timothius. "The best of us acting like a rutting beast."

Timothius rose in a smooth motion and moved to stand in front of Wren. "I do know better, but even toys are allowed to play together. What better than to do so with someone who is not meant to remain?"

Reality slammed down like a damper in Wren's mind, extinguishing all flame, leaving nothing but ashes and smoke in its wake. She knew it had been more—that he was not dismissing her like something to be played with—but the truth was she would be leaving. *More,* no matter how badly she longed for it, would always have a finite amount of sand falling through the hourglass.

"And you." Musannulos rounded on her, his voice breaking through her thoughts. "You are a—"

"You will not address her." Timothius's clipped words cut the owl-man off, his mouth snapping shut beneath his beak. "I will escort Lady Florence to her quarters, safely, as I do every night, and then I will retire to mine. You will continue flapping about and searching for lovers lonely enough to invite you to stay."

"One never grows too old for discipline. I would watch your tone if I were you," Musannulos growled, his voice growing deeper and taking Wren aback.

"Yes, of course, you did always enjoy watching that too. But you would be correct, you are not me," said Timothius, coolly stepping forward to meet him. "And you would do well to remember that."

A long silence followed, and finally Musannulos began to shake his head slowly, a low chuckle sounding when he took a step back. "Be careful, Master Soldier, lest one think you are growing too soft. Broken toys are worth no more than rubbish in the bin. One would hate it if His Majesty needed to find a new one."

It was Timothius's turn to laugh, and though his voice held no humor, it was deep and dark with an edge that raised bumps along Wren's skin. "There is none who could replace me. But, a valiant try."

Taking Wren's hand in his own, he strode past Musannulos. They had just reached the doorway when the owl-man said, "Master Soldier?"

They froze, and Timothius turned, his stare sharp enough to eviscerate a lesser man on the spot. Musannulos grinned triumphantly. "Don't forget your gloves," he said, holding them out.

Timothius made no move to collect the missing piece of his uniform, and instead led Wren wordlessly into the hall.

They did not speak again until they were in front of her quarters. She watched him, ready to ask a thousand questions, but he silenced her with the look in his eyes. There was no regret, no remorse, only longing and something deep she dared not try to name.

"Goodnight...Wren," he whispered softly. Bending forward, he pressed her hand to his mask's cold, unfeeling lips.

He spun on his heel and was gone before she could reply, but watching him leave, she realized that no matter what came next, Musannulos had been right about one thing—Timothius was the best of them.

CHAPTER THIRTY-ONE

*W*ren sat alone at breakfast the next morning. She had not seen Kathrina since the night prior, and for the moment, she was grateful. Her head was muddled, her thoughts a mess, and the further back she looked in her mind, the more difficult it became to see anything at all.

Her grandparents—Vince and Marion Klaver—were King Vincienti and Queen Marionaldi of Inflamel. And more than that, her grandmother was the missing ruler of the Trifolium Thrones.

She stared at the crystallum where it lay against her palm, its deep-maroon glass untainted and insides churning darkness.

Had her grandfather served in a war? Was it the war here? Had her mother known she was a princess of a world she had never seen? Of the stories Wren had heard growing up, how many walked the tightrope between truth and fable? And most importantly, why had her grandmother given *her* the crystallum? And why now?

A commotion outside the door prompted her to straighten, and she tucked the orb back in her bodice moments before a loud knock sounded.

"Yes?" she called as she rose.

"All members of the court are summoned immediately at His Majesty's behest," a gruff voice called. She heard boots move down the hall to the next door, a loud rap, and then the same message repeated.

Suddenly feeling lightheaded, she ran for the door and cracked it open before turning on her heel and running back into the room for her mask. Checking to ensure her dress was smooth and her hair at least presentable, she joined the rest of the hall exiting down the stairs toward the throne room.

Wren had never had a panic attack, had never allowed anything close enough to her heart to shake it so badly, but it beat loud in her ears while she walked. Every pull of air became more difficult than the last, and each step took all her concentration not waver on her feet.

She glanced up, trying to look beyond the line funneling into the throne room, but only saw the columns and the ghost of the green banners rippling, their gold clovers shimmering in the light pouring through the stained-glass windows.

Blinking, she put her head down and closed her eyes. The world spun even in the dark, flashing a different time, a different life, through her mind

She was Wren, but she was Marion.

She was watching from the walls, but she was hurtling through time.

She was there, but she was here.

She was invisible and yet there was no denying that every last detail was real.

This was real.

Two hands wrapped around her arm, and she jumped, nearly pushing the figure aside until she was met with the rose gold fox mask of Kathrina.

"Thank goodness you are safe," Kathrina murmured, holding on to Wren as if her life depended on it.

"What happened?" Wren asked, voice low.

"I do not know. The king only draws the court when he feels the need to affirm our loyalty—when there is a new edict or punishment to be paid. You left the dance early last night and did not return. Neither did T. And when Musannulos arrived for a word with the king.... To wake to this news, I was sick with worry for you."

Wren's heart skipped a beat. Was Timothius safe? He couldn't possibly be punished on the word of a courier. Could he?

"Kathrina, how much danger am I truly in here?" She didn't want to know the answer, but she could not go another moment holding back the question.

"I fear we are all on borrowed time."

They remained silent, stoic, following the rest of the throng into the throne room. Settling in behind another group of lady's maids, lords still wearing their regalia from the night before, and various cooks, stable hands, and workers from all areas of the castle, Wren's eyes skimmed the crowd.

Where is—

A door at the back of the room slammed open, Musannulos scuttling in with as much authority as a short man in a feathered mask could carry. "His Majesty, King Phillipae I, King of Warriors and Warrior of Kings."

Phillipae strode in behind him, the silver at the temples of his onyx hair glinting in jarring opposition to the golden crown tilted back on his head. Following behind him with powerful and even strides was Timothius. The leather belt about the waist of his gray coat sheathed his sword on one side and a long, coiled whip on the other. His eyes swept the room like a scythe.

Passing the rows of people each taking a knee in his presence, the king reached his throne but stopped short of sitting down. Timothius halted on the floor beside the dais and turned to face the crowd, his unseeing black eyelids on full display.

"My people," the king said, a smile on his face and his arms outstretched. "It is a fine morning, is it not?"

"It is, Your Majesty," the people said, their echoed voices rippling about the room.

"And last night! Last night's festivities at the highly favorite Dance of Midnight, they were wonderful, were they not?"

"They were, Your Majesty."

The king beamed but his face froze, and Wren felt a cold awareness rise in her heart the moment that his face descended into fury. "Then tell me why any one of you would abandon my favor for madness?" he bellowed.

A hush fell over the crowd, only a few daring to whisper.

Phillipae's hands dropped to his sides. "Do you not know what I am talking about? Did none of you see the wavering of your fellow man? The disunity and ungratefulness breeding in the shadows of this great city? Did none of you raise the alarm and speak of the treason happening under our very noses while you ate and drank beneath my gracious banner?"

"This will be bad, I fear," whispered Kathrina, her voice filled with terror, but Wren could not speak. She could not tear her eyes from Timothius as the king pressed on.

"A tyrant leader, a cruel leader, a disgraceful rat of a king, would make every last one of you pay. He would lock these doors until the floors ran red with blood and your screams were no more, and then he would replace you with beings that would appreciate his goodness. Who would worship the ruler that has given such unworthy and lowly souls a life as comfortable as this." He paused his pacing and turned slowly, as if musing to himself. "In fact, I believe that's exactly what I shall do."

The doors slammed shut around the throne room. Guards with faces of both wolf and mouse moved to block them, four men deep. Men shouted, women screamed, and swords were drawn from their sheaths, ringing in the air. Kathrina cried out, clutching on to Wren, her breaths whistling through her lungs too fast.

With wide, panicked eyes, Wren turned to look toward the dais and found hazel eyes fixed on her, his gloved hand clenched around the hilt of his sword.

"Although," Phillipae drolled, holding up a hand to silence the shouts, though sobs could still be heard about the room. "You have been good for so long. Such well-behaved pets. So worthy of your lives here. Maybe I shall give you another try. Maybe I can find it in my heart to give you one last chance to come to your senses."

The door at the back of the room opened, and the soldiers parted for a figure to be dragged in, hood concealing their face and chains locked around their wrists and ankles.

"Do you think I am blind and deaf?" the king demanded. "That I am too high in my castle to know that my own people dare rise against me? That I am unaware of the Awduron being hidden from me? Or maybe you know my awareness and seek to protect your friends and neighbors?"

A soldier shoved the prisoner to their knees in front of the king, merely feet from Timothius. Kathrina buried her head against Wren's shoulder, her silent tears dampening the fabric, her whispered pleas a desperate song.

"Either way," the king continued, "it would seem that you all could use a reminder of exactly why they call me the Warrior King. I am a victor and my reign will be unending. I alone am the very reason any one of you continue to breathe. And none shall dare forget it again, lest they learn exactly what it means to forget what I am capable of."

He looked to the soldier behind the prisoner, and with a single lift of his chin, the wolf-masked guard leveled a kick into their back, pitching them forward onto the floor.

A woman's cry filled the room, stealing the air from Wren's lungs and causing Kathrina's head to shoot up. Timothius did not move, but Wren could see his eyes close once again, and though he held himself in full control, his chest rose and fell a little too fast.

The guards tugged the prisoner upright, ripping the hood back, revealing the pale face of Mauritania Flugé—dressed in men's clothing with her braids pulled loose about her face—and it took nearly everything in Wren's power not to lose her breakfast on the spot. Kathrina shoved her hand against her mouth and bit down, the blood trickling from her skin a display of the force it was taking to stay silent.

"Mauritania Flugé, you and your husband have been convicted of treason against the crown for plotting rebellion. The sentence is death by the method in which you chose to betray me—steadily and over time. Do you have any final words before you are escorted back to the dungeon to join your husband for the final time in this life?"

Mauritania lifted her chin proudly, her eyes shining brilliantly with tears, defiance, and pride. "Long live the kings and queens of old. Long live the Awduron. Long live the Trifolium Thrones. May ye watch them rise over yer grave, and may the five strands of magic crush yer dry, dead bones to dust."

The king began to tremble, unfettered rage consuming his face, and he strode forward, ripping the sword from Timothius's belt and bringing it down in an arc against her spine in a near-fatal blow. Her body went limp in the arms of the guards holding her, but they hoisted her back up and began to drag her down the aisle, leaving a slick of blood in their wake.

In a flash of movement that wrenched a gasp from Wren, the king turned on Timothius and shoved the pommel of the sword squarely into his gut, causing him to buckle with a grunt that put them at eye level.

"They do not die until I say they do," he seethed, his voice growing louder with every word.

"Do not think I have not heard whispers of your edge

growing dull from this very court. If I cannot demand subservience by your example, then they are hopeless," he shouted, throwing the sword to the ground and stretching a damning finger toward the court. "This day, Inflamel will remember exactly what you are. *My* weapon. *My* pawn. *My* possession. You have nothing. You are nothing but a shell and a shadow. And that is all you will ever be apart from me. Remind the city that a hollow toy carries no heart and an iron weapon no weakness. Prove your loyalty to your king. Prove your worth to this court. Serve their execution well."

Wren watched in horror as Timothius stepped back and took a knee, bowing his head low to the king with a hand clasped on his heart. Rising with eyes dark as night, he picked up the sword—its blade still dripping—and stalked through the room, his boots leaving an impression in the blood already spilled on the floor long after he was out of sight.

Phillipae released a dejected sigh. "Well then. I hope this lingers in your memory the next time rumors are heard. Your secrets belong to me, the air in your lungs is only there by my mercy, and you will remain loyal to me and me alone or your life is forfeit. You are all dismissed. And someone clean this before it stains. I will not have a rebel's blood defile my throne room."

CHAPTER THIRTY-TWO

They escaped the room and barely made it through the door to Wren's quarters before Kathrina lost the contents of her stomach and collapsed upon the floor, her body shaking from her sobs.

Wren tucked her friend into her own bed, sitting beside her and stroking her hair, allowing silent tears to fall until Kathrina grew still. She was not sure what was worse—believing for a short moment that it could be Elric below the hood or the moment they knew who it was. The moment Timothius knew.

The example being made of him, whether the king knew the extent or not, raised a manic anxiety in Wren that she had never felt before. How would he endure this? How could any of them?

The sun had barely set, the hour of the dance arriving, and Wren sat Kathrina on the stool in front of her small mirror. Brushing her friend's golden locks free of tangles, she braided it into a halo about her head—like Mauritania always wore—and pinned it into place with brilliant silver pearls. At the sight of the bloodred dress, her stomach turned, so she pulled a gown of silver velvet with a tulle skirt from the wardrobe and helped

Kathrina change. The last step was to apply fresh makeup, and then finally she handed Kathrina her mask.

Kathrina stared at it silently, a question in her eyes, like the fox might come to life and help make sense of it all. Wren could not help but embrace her, and the woman clutched her back. They remained that way until the last moment and then Wren rushed to dress in a one-shoulder gown of pewter chiffon, catching her hair up in a charcoal net and securing it with ruby pins.

She corrected her smudged makeup sparingly and took one last look at herself in the mirror. Her eyes shone bright against the black kohl lining her lids—beautiful, yet severe and threatening to burn anyone alive who dared approach them that night. Her pain was deep, but she could bear it. However, the agony she knew her friends carried was unforgivable, and she would not stand idly by and watch them suffer more.

The mask affixed to her face made her look every bit the cold beauty she channeled. She was a swan frozen beneath the ice, biding her time and waiting for her anger to thaw it so that she could take flight and sear her revenge across the heavens.

After a moment of silence—one last second to catch their breath—she held tightly to Kathrina's arm and they made their way to the Dance of Storm and Fire.

The room was bathed in red, as it had been her first night at court, though very few revelers wore any shade of the color, nearly all having opted for silver, flint, iron, and smoke. The king presided over them, his wine flowing and his dark smile full of pride, looking down on them from his throne.

Timothius was nowhere to be seen.

The minutes ticked down, two hours fell away, when a hush descended on the crowd. A small gasp sounded and then utter silence as even the orchestra ceased playing. Kathrina sucked in a sharp breath and Wren turned to face the door, her jaw dropping at the sight.

"I cannot stay here," Kathrina whispered to Wren. "I will come to your room in the morning. I cannot do this."

Wren squeezed her wrist reassuringly, and as swiftly as she had arrived, Kathrina exited the room with a handful of other dancers. The doors were shut behind the newcomer and the king stood to his feet.

"Please, please, do not stop your merrymaking on *his* regard. The night is still young. We have hours to spare." He clapped his hands sharply. "Dance." It was an order, and when the notes began again, the crowd took to the floor leaving a path for the figure to reach the dais.

Timothius wore the same gray jacket he had that morning. His weapons were absent from his belt and his hands appeared clean, but they were the only thing. His sleeves were soaked through, his pants stained, and his mask splattered in a deep red that had nothing to do with the theme. He stood straight, stiff, but with no pride in front of the king whose garb matched his throne adorned in crimson.

The king stepped down to walk around him, completing a circle. "Well done," he said on a laugh, and he pulled a handkerchief from his pocket, dragging it across Timothius's mask. It did nothing to clean the blood, instead smearing it down his face.

He looked at the stained rag in his hand and smirked, tucking it into Timothius's pocket and returning to the throne.

Wren did not realize she had moved until she was before the dais, her rage barely checked when she dipped in a curtsy.

The king raised an eyebrow but nodded to her. "Lady Florence. The full moon approaches."

She stood. "It does, Your Majesty. Time flies. We would do well to number our days better, don't you think?"

The king's stare was like ice, but Wren only tipped her head and approached Timothius. Stepping up on the dais beside him, she slipped her arm through his, swallowing hard against the smell clinging to his clothes. She tried to lead them toward the floor, but Timothius remained rooted to the spot.

"Dance with me," she whispered. "Please."

"I cannot," he said, the hoarseness in his voice that of someone who had screamed it raw.

"You can and you will. Dance with me. Dream with me."

His steps were slow, reticent, as if at any moment he might turn on his heel and return to his post, yet he stayed beside Wren all the way to the edge of the floor. She could feel the king's stare burning holes in her back and hear the whispers of unease and disgust from the court around them.

Timothius's smudged eyelids fluttered shut.

"No," she said, placing his hands on her waist and stepping into his arms. His eyes opened—a bloodshot, pain-ridden hazel —all light having long since died within them.

"Eyes on me," she said softly. "Only me. You don't need to look anywhere else. No one else exists. It's just you and me."

He did not speak, did not agree or decline, but when she took his hand and they began to move, his eyes did not leave hers for a single heartbeat.

"What do you dream?" she whispered, her voice cracking under the weight she could not lift from his broken spirit.

He did not blink. He did not speak. He only gazed upon her face and danced. The kohl on his lids ran and his hands trembled against hers. That's when she noticed the blood still staining his skin, caked beneath his nails, highlighting his fingerprints, and she knew....

His punishment had been inflicted with his bare hands.

Wren took a deep breath. "You once told me that death was silent or loud. You are still here. You are with me and you are alive. Do not go quietly. Their death was loud and it will be heard for ages, but your life must be louder. Your name must be louder. Who you are matters, not what you have done."

His steps faltered, his eyes falling shut, tears spilling over, and she watched him desperately grasp for composure inside the hell he could not escape.

"I see you," she whispered. "When I dream, I see you. Far beyond here, we're dancing just like this. I'm in your arms, your mask is gone, and we are happy. The lanterns are bright with color, and the faeries dance around our feet on a floor bathed in starlight. Do you see it too?"

A shuddering exhale was his response, but his steps grew more certain.

"Dream with me," she begged. "Far beyond this place. Do you see me?"

"I see you," he whispered back, gravel dragging out his words. "I only see you."

Wren nodded, her own tears sneaking down her face in relief. "Stay there. Live there. Dream there. It's just you and me. Stay with me."

Timothius nodded once, and Wren took the opportunity to step closer. Lifting to her toes, she perched herself on the ends of his boots, forcing him to hold her, wrapping her arms around his neck.

They did not see when the king removed himself from the party. They did not care that the dancers gave them a wide berth. They did not notice that by the time they parted, Wren's dress was as bloody as his uniform.

And when it came time for them to depart the dance, when Timothius tried to look away, Wren gripped his hand and led him straight back to her quarters.

In the doorway, she removed her mask and laid his hand against her cheek, turning her lips to press a kiss to his palm.

"You must leave, Wren," he rasped, the words stopping her heart.

She shook her head. "No. Not when we are so close."

"You do not have a choice. You must reach E. It is the only way you will be safe."

"And what of you? Who will take care of you?"

"If you care for me, then you will leave now. You are not just in danger here, you are a danger."

Wren stepped back, but the look of defeat in Timothius's eyes gave her anger pause. "You don't mean that."

"I do," he continued. "You are a danger to me, for there are few things I would not do for you."

The tension fell from Wren's face, her lips parting at the confession, at his earnestness. "And what would you do for me?"

Anything, she longed for him to say. *Dream with me, stay with me, promise me anything.*

His silence was deafening, eclipsed only by the broken pieces of her heart plinking like glass upon the floor. Wrapping his arms around her, he held her to his chest, burrowing his hand in her hair while she rested her cheek against his heart.

He pulled away first, stepping out of her arms and further from their dream. But as he stepped backed, his mask bleeding into the shadows of the hall, she heard him answer. A confession in the form of goodbye.

"For you, I would run."

CHAPTER THIRTY-THREE

*I*t was well past noon, the sun high in the sky, and yet Kathrina and Wren sat huddled beneath the same blanket in the beam of light streaming through Wren's window. Wren's skin was still pink, tender to the touch from the furious scrubbing she had given it in the bath the night prior, and her eyes still burned from the tears she had finally let fall as she fed her dress to the fireplace. From the looks of the woman across from her, Kathrina's night had been much the same.

"I don't know what is worse. The relief I felt knowing it was not Elric bleeding before the king, or the pain at watching a parent die again," she confessed, eyes sparkling with tears.

Wren grasped her hand. "Both are valid. To have avoided unbearable loss only to be faced with this…. It's shocking, Kathrina. I don't think it has fully sunk in for me yet."

Kathrina shook her head. "I don't believe it ever will for me. I have always had a way out. T made sure I could find my way in the dark. But I…."

A cold pang stun Wren's heart. "You have to know this was not his fault. He was, he is, so broken by this. If there had been any other way—"

"I know," she replied, grief choking her words. "I wish I could have been there for him. I wish he did not have to endure this alone. We all knew there would be losses. But I never imagined the Flugés." Her tears spilled over, falling on her trembling lips. "Did I do this, Wren? Did I bring this upon them meeting Elric there?"

Wren shook her head. "They were not home, Kathrina. None of us had seen them. I have a feeling they were captured before we even met there. You could not have had anything to do with this."

But when the words left her mouth, bile rose in her throat. She believed wholeheartedly that Kathrina and Elric did not have anything to do with the Flugés' arrest because she was confident that she did.

The memory of the Rat King watching from his tower had haunted her the whole night before. The spectacle that had been made of Timothius and the unspeakable hell he'd been forced to face all came back to her. To her presence in Inflamel.

But that, in turn, led back to the Trifolium Thrones. To her family line and the crown that rightfully belonged to her. She realized then that she'd not had the chance to tell Timothius about her discovery. There had been no time and now that he had asked her to leave, she was not certain she would have the chance to divulge it to him.

Unless he made good on his word and left with her. She would make sure he did. She would not leave him there. Not in a thousand years.

"My grandmother is the reason I'm here," Wren said softly, admitting it to herself as much as she was confessing it to Kathrina. Her friend's eyes widened, but Wren pressed on. "The crystallum was hers, made for her by the stars themselves on the day the Thrones fell. She was queen of Inflamel and a High Queen of the Trifolium Thrones."

Kathrina's mouth fell open, her tear-stained face relaxing

into something akin to hope. "You came back for us," she whispered in awe. "You have come back for the Throne."

Wren took a shaky breath. "I haven't. At least not on my own. I think my grandmother sent me, and the throne is what everything points to. But I...."

Silence filled the room, warm and still. Wren closed her eyes, basking in the light, and for a moment she could imagine she wasn't there. She was sitting in her car and the sun shining through her windshield was blinding off the snow piled high around her grandparents' house. But the vision did not bring her any comfort. She did not want to be there, but she could not bear the thought of remaining here. She had grown up a girl alone, in her own world and invisible to everyone around her. Now she was seen by all and it made her fate inescapable. There was nowhere to hide and no rest. Not for her.

"Elric told me you have seen the Elfin Domain," Kathrina said, changing the subject and cracking the first smile Wren had seen on her face in days.

She nodded. "I have. I feel bad for how I treated them and for leaving like I did. But I don't regret coming here. If I hadn't, I wouldn't have met you."

Kathrina smiled broadly now. "And when we leave, we will both go back and you will show me all there is to see."

Wren couldn't help but grin at the woman's girlish excitement. "I take it you've never been there?"

"Never," she replied. "I've never been anywhere but here. But Elric has told me all about the small houses. Of the Great House and the river and the color of the water against the trees. We plan to be married in the garden where moss carpets the ground and vines frame an altar of lilacs in bloom. The moment I escape, as soon as I am free, he will meet me there and Nelluenya will marry us beneath the trees with the elfin folk bearing witness. He could not ask for my hand with a ring, I would not have been able to conceal it, but we have dreamed everything down to the home we will keep until Inflamel is free of the Rat King once more. Then he will know freedom too and together we will grow our family and a future for the stars."

Wren had no words for the beauty, the happiness she saw in the woman beside her. A woman she had grown fond of without knowing her full name—for her love of stories and her mind that never slowed. She could see it now, evidenced before her, but instead of filling her head with stories, she was filling her heart with a future more beautiful than any dream or fantasy.

"Timothius wants me to leave," she confessed. "I will not leave him here, but I'm afraid I may not have a choice. I don't think the king intends to let me live past the full moon. But if I go—"

"Then I will be by your side," Kathrina affirmed, facing her with eyes as fierce and solemn as a vow. "I will serve you, as my queen, to the very end of this fight. And when the Rat King is gone and you are seated on the throne, I will look from afar with love and pride at the woman who sacrificed all she knew to save a people who were not her own."

Wren shook her head. "I can't see myself as a queen. I don't see myself on a throne. I can barely see myself in any future at all."

Kathrina hummed, a sage affection warming her eyes. "I believe we all see such days, at one time or another. When I found myself at a crossroads between losing Elric, then T, and then my parents, I sat there for a while, refusing to be moved, refusing to even glance ahead. And then one day, I stood up. I still look back, but I do not stop moving forward. And if my path were to change again, had it been Elric under that hood, I don't doubt I would sit between grief and acceptance and wait some more. But there is always a way forward. We must never forget that."

Wren nodded and this time it was Kathrina who reached

over and clasped her hand. "I am so grateful to have met you, Wren."

She met her friend's smile and allowed her own battered heart to bleed love—to reach out, accept the hand up, and begin to walk the path forward, though still glancing back all the way. "And I am so grateful to know and call you a friend, K."

CHAPTER THIRTY-FOUR

*T*he ballroom was flawless, decorated in seamless perfection to complement the Autumnal Wood and the Dance of the Harvest. Wren uncomfortably twisted the flute in her hand, watching the layers of lace along the skirt of her copper gown flutter from the air being kicked up by the dancers twirling on the floor around her. But it was neither the dress nor the drink nor even the dancing that brought about her discomfort. It was what she found missing.

The throne was empty. And so was the dais.

Kathrina, on the floor and doing her best to appear engaged after her early exit the night before, glanced over every so often. Her fox eyes would focus on Wren, flit casually past Timothius's empty post, and then back again.

Where was he?

Another song concluded and the next began with the scratching of strings, jolting Wren from her thoughts. Setting down her glass, she moved to the floor and chose a partner, dipping into a low curtsy while he bowed in return. The music picked up—a quick, staccato rhythm—and though the tempo was harrowing, they started to dance.

The room spun about them and Wren kept her head tipped back over her shoulder, her body angled away from her suitor and her eyes searching every corner of the room for a mask she could not find—a face she did not see.

Her distraction caused her to miss the change in step, and when her partner released her, she stumbled. A new pair of hands caught her, one at her waist and the other clutching her hand. She glanced up and stifled the startled cry that stuck in her throat at the sight of the man before her.

"I sincerely hope you do not mind me cutting in," King Phillipae said with a smooth smile.

"Not at all, Your Majesty. It is quite the honor," she said, forcing her easy and confident smile to reach her eyes. The floor had cleared around them, their fellow dancers trying to continue on as if nothing was amiss, but all looking over at the king who never came down off his throne.

Wren relaxed in his grasp and though the dance led her around him—his hand guiding her pirouette—she circled him with purpose. A predator surveying her prey.

She became keenly aware of his touch when his arm swept about her waist, hoisting her into the air and back down again with the swell of the music. It was not brutal, but not gentle either. It was commanding, like he believed she belonged within his grasp—belonged to him—and something inside her reared its head at the thought.

"I do hope you are well after last night," he said, turning her until her back was pressed against his chest.

"I was quite well last night," she replied smoothly. "Whatever do you mean?"

"I am referring to the point you felt needed to be proven in front of my court. With *my* soldier."

Wren bit down on her tongue. *I will not engage. I will not—* "I apologize, I do not recall seeing your name on him." She turned out of his arms and flashed him a brilliant smile, priding herself on at least attempting to stay silent.

The king's expression was unmovable. "I thought it was he who bore reminding of his purpose here, but it would appear that I was in error. It is you who needs to be taught the ways of my court."

"I believe you made your ways clear when you ran a member of your household through with a sword after threatening a full-scale massacre, Your Majesty," Wren returned pointedly, meeting his iron with fire.

He released a heavy sigh. "I do hate that you needed to witness that. It is...difficult bringing so many to heel. Rabble tends to flock together. Herd mentality and all that. One may never spare the rod when ruling a country."

Wren did not reply as the dance once again moved them away from each other. She continued her desperate search about the room for Timothius, dreading the moment her steps returned her to the king.

That moment arrived again all too soon.

"He is not here," the king tutted, freezing the blood in Wren's veins.

She looked to him slowly, ensuring a dismissive front was firmly in place and her emotions hidden behind the curtains of her eyes. "Is he not? I hadn't noticed."

One second she was standing in front of the king, their feet marking steps around each other, and the next she was jerked forward onto the tips of her toes, mere inches from his face. "Do not play coy with me, Lady Florence," he snarled under his breath. "The full moon is nearly here, and if you still wish for my help, then you will accept your role as my loyal subject until your departure. Have I made myself clear?"

Wren's anger snapped, hissing and spitting as it burned through her carefully composed facade and she allowed just a sliver of hate to reach her eyes. "Crystal. Now, where is he?"

The king smiled and she could have sworn his eyes grew darker. "I'm sure you've been here long enough to discover that I have a bit of an issue with a mage wielding dark magic. Rumor has it no one has met her eyes and lived to tell the tale. Naturally, I could not go looking for her myself, but my toy is so useful for such things. He is capable in most everything, though I did hear that he struggled to deliver the final blows to those traitors yesterday. It was a shame to learn today that they were innocent after all. I did inform him of that, of course, before he departed—a morsel to stew on for the road. I don't doubt he will bring back word of the great Isperi Mage's whereabouts. Unfortunately, it is quite the undertaking and will occupy him for some time. I forgot to mention that to him…. Nonetheless, their convoy is prepared for the journey. I don't expect his return before the next new moon at least."

A fury unlike anything she had ever felt boiled beneath Wren's skin at the king's arrogance. She refused to believe he was one step ahead of them—she would never allow herself to accept it.

With her forearm still locked in his grip, she leaned closer to hiss a response, when a weight tugged on the skin at her neck. Her eyes widened only a fraction at the exact moment the king glanced down to the crystallum dangling from its chain in the air between them.

Wren emptied her mind and thoughts as quickly as she could, desperately trying to slow her heart and steady her pulse. She would not allow him to feel her panic. She would not let him smell her fear. And she would certainly not reveal the crystallum as anything more than a bauble.

Not to him. Not now. Not ever.

The king's gaze finally broke from the orb, and when he lifted his eyes to lock with Wren's, she could not stop the small gasp that escaped her lips.

His pupils had blown out—consuming all the color and

spreading cracks and fissures of the purest black across the white of his eyes—yet somehow that was not what startled her the most. It was the darkness that churned at the center, endless and fathomless, emitting pulses of shadow and sparks like an explosion of a thousand burning stars.

Wren's eyes widened and her mouth opened in horror, but the moment he blinked, they returned to normal.

The king released her as if nothing had happened and took a step back. To her surprise, he sketched a low bow and then turned, pausing to smile at where she stood still frozen in horrified silence. "It has been a pleasure dancing with you this evening, Lady Klaver. And do take care to number your days."

CHAPTER THIRTY-FIVE

The full moon was less than a month away and every day that passed was marked by tension within the castle and the city. Wren felt the strain echo in her chest and though she left her room to tend to the chores with Kathrina, her trips to collect food and herbs all remained within the city and were not enough to distract from the burden.

News of the Flugés' fate had spread through the kingdom like wildfire. Word had reached Milo and Reginald before Kathrina could, and when their paths crossed in the city under the watchful eye of the guards, it took everything in Wren's power not to run and embrace them. Dark shadows marred the skin beneath Milo's eyes, the weight of forced maturity slumping his shoulders and stealing the bounce from his step. But what she saw reflected in Reginald's face haunted her more—hardened determination and a fire that lit a thousand undimmed torches all raging for justice.

She found excuses and ways to steal outside the wall, visiting with the boys as often as she could. They kept shorter, light-weight blades stashed in a hole dug beneath a rock on the edge of the Autumnal Wood, just out of sight from the wall, and

Wren found that she greatly preferred sparring with them as opposed to the weighty sword that Elric had lent her. She trained with the boys from time to time and Reginald turned out to be quite skilled with a blade. He was considerably more patient than Elric, and in a few days' time, he helped Wren learn enough technique to disarm him a time or two.

Their afternoons always ended too soon, ushering in another dance, and on this particular night, Wren lingered at her window only long enough to look out once in the direction of the Flugés' house and then to the Deorc Weald where the sun itself seemed to die.

It had been two weeks yet there was no sign of Timothius or word from the Weald, and though she and Kathrina planned to wait until the last possible moment, Wren knew that moment was nearly upon them. She swore to herself she would not leave the castle without him, but they were running out of time.

She descended to yet another dance—her gown of deep plum expertly matched to the roses Kathrina had woven into her hair—and when she looked up at the dais, her heart tumbled into the pit of her stomach. Standing beside the throne in a uniform of flawless royal blue was Timothius. His eyes were on her, marking her just as he said he had all those weeks ago, but it wasn't until then that she realized something had changed.

It was not long before he left the ball, stalking away alone against the storm of revelry. The king's voice rang in her head, accompanying the warning bells already clanging, but she could not stop herself from following.

Reaching the doors, she looked both ways and barely caught his shadow disappearing around the bend in the direction of the staircase leading to the rampart.

Wren grasped her skirts and followed, pursuing as quickly as she dared and throwing herself upon the door to the stairwell as it closed on his heel. She swung it open far enough to slip through and then shut it quietly, looking up into the darkness after the sound of his boots.

"Timothius?" she whispered urgently, yanking the mask from her face and pulling tendrils of hair free in the process.

The steps halted and she climbed the stairs until her hand found the sleeve of his jacket.

"You're back," she whispered. "I was worried—"

"You have no need to worry," he murmured, voice stoic and cold as ice. "Return to the dance, you will be missed."

"By the king? Yes, I know, we had a little chat while you were away. But I don't care. I just needed...I needed to...."

His arm disappeared from beneath her hand and instinctively she took a step back against the wall. The dark somehow became deeper, the air more stagnant, and she felt his hands rest on either side of her face—his towering figure drowning out even the night.

"Needed to what, dear swan? Needed to appease your own conscience? You've embraced your savior complex quite nicely, but I do not need watching or protection, even from you. I am beyond saving. My place is here and yours is far from it. I suspect you already know this, but it would seem you need the reminder."

The words fanned flames of anger yet stoked icy tendrils of fear, both fighting for purchase in Wren's heart. "Did he get to you too?"

"He did not need to. You must remember who we are in this game and that while we fight the same battle, we play for opposing sides."

"Stop it," she hissed. "If that were true, you wouldn't have kissed me."

"Playing the part requires commitment," he replied matter-of-factly. "As I've said, I am a gentleman. I am committed to my future, as you should be to your own."

"And what if my future is different?" Wren asked, demanding an answer. "What if it's changing?"

"You do not mean that. And if you begin to believe that it is better for you to remain here than to leave for safety, then I have done you the greatest disservice by misleading you with my intentions."

"You have not," she snapped. "You remind me...of home. And of what I'm fighting for. You remind me of who I am, and you give me the confidence to be who I'm meant to be. I need you, Timothius. Do not abandon me when you are the only constant I've had since the day I set foot in this world."

His hands fell from the wall and she felt the cold stillness build between them. After what seemed like an eternity, his fingers brushed the strands of hair that had escaped against her cheek. They vanished again and then moments later, a soft exhale warmed her lips. Hope bloomed in Wren's heart with the realization that both their masks were gone and she did not stop to think of the consequences when she reached up to rest her fingers against his cheek, causing him to inhale a sharp breath.

"Do not give up," she whispered. "Not yet."

He said nothing, the stalemate stealing every last bit of their oxygen, and Wren begged the heat of his breath on her skin to thaw the wall of ice he had erected between them. But her answer—like a death all its own—came silently when his warmth slipped away from her.

He remained quiet, and she knew the mask was back on his face, fixed firmly in place when he turned and walked away. She stayed, her back against the wall and her bitter tears falling, tasting like salt on her lips, until the *thud* of his boots reached the top of the stairwell. A soft light trickled down from the door when he opened it to the night.

And as she dried her tears, he left her without a word.

❄

"IF HE IS AVOIDING YOU, it is for your safety," Kathrina assured her, pulling back a small section of her hair and securing it with crystal pins, giving it the appearance of snowflakes resting upon her head.

"I know," Wren admitted. "It's just the silence. The cold shoulder. How do you live with it?"

Kathrina patted her arm, and Wren met her eyes in the mirror. "I scream loudly and often," Kathrina revealed with a tired smile. "Now come, let us show him what he has missed these last weeks."

The ballroom was encrusted in silver and white, as if preserved in a midwinter storm that encased the room in splendor. It reminded Wren of the first days she had spent in this world. Of the Isteriaeth who told stories of his people. Of the man who saved her life over accidental loyalty and a mistaken identity. Every star had aligned perfectly to bring her here, and now she stood in a castle, surveying a sea of pale blues and creams, crystallized gold and glittering diamonds, wondering where the time had truly gone.

Not unlike its theme, the room was chilled, and Wren was thankful that her hair had grown long enough to cloak her neck from the air. Her dress rested just off her shoulders in a stunning shade of ice blue, its fabric gathered delicately to give the illusion that it had been draped across her skin and sewn to fit her figure. Its full tulle skirt rustled around her legs, kicking up gently as she traversed the room and looked casually at the empty dais before scanning the many masked faces of her fellow courtiers.

But there was still one missing.

"May I have this dance, my swan?"

The deep timbre of Timothius's voice caused her heart to

leap. She turned too quickly, nearly launching into the arms of the man in front of her, but held back at the last second.

He was once again not dressed in the colors of the night's dance, but instead wore a formal red uniform. The shirt beneath was the only hint of blue and the gold braiding across the breast of his coat matched the tasseled plates on his shoulders, in turn complementing the gilded filigree on his mask. His pants were slightly darker than the silver frost about the room—the color of the snow at dusk—and his onyx boots shone without blemish. He was the picture of perfection, set apart in every way from all others, and Wren could no longer ignore the truth. He was well and truly nothing more than a decorative toy, placed on display for the court to admire and fear through the glass. And it broke her heart.

She slid her fingers into his hand and allowed him to lead her to the floor. A new piece started, the plucking of the strings forming a minor melody set to the cadence of a waltz. Timothius's palm rested warm and firm on her waist and he raised their joined hands to chin height before stepping into her, pulling their bodies flush, and beginning to dance.

"Where is the king?" she asked, nearly breathless. "If he sees you, will he—"

"You must leave. Tonight," interrupted Timothius, and though their bodies met at a dozen different points that Wren felt intimately, his eyes scanned the room above her head, as if both looking for something and refusing to look at her.

"What happened?" she asked.

"Nothing yet, but something has changed in my absence. I left the king in his chambers where he is issuing the order for your arrest. You are to be taken tonight, but you will be held until the full moon. I do not dare to wonder what fate he has planned for you then. You and Kathrina must go tonight. Go to the domain, and—"

"I'm not going anywhere without you," Wren challenged.

"And if staying here until you can leave with us endangers my safety, then that is a risk I am willing to take."

The room somehow grew colder when Timothius's hardened eyes met hers. "It is not one I am willing to take any longer."

She stared at him incredulously. "That is not your decision to make."

"It became my decision the moment your lips touched mine."

Wren's mouth snapped shut. He was really trying to send her away. He was going to cut her off as he had with everyone else in his life and return to his plan—to his own sacrifice. She would never allow it. "Do I need to leave for my safety? Or because you're too concerned about the softness of your own heart?"

He looked away, and though his face remained hidden by the blank facade, she could hear the iron set in his jaw when he spoke. "Allow me to worry after my heart. You do what is required to ensure your own continues beating."

Everything within Wren longed to protest. To rage and beg and fight. But she knew deep down that he was just as stubborn as she was, and if he refused to fight, he would not be moved.

"You said you would run for me," she whispered, allowing a plea to bleed into her words. He remained unmoved and something within her broke, a small tether to her composure that had frayed beyond its ability to hold. "Timothius, look at me."

At the sound of his name, he flinched, but then his eyes slowly dropped to her face.

"If you will not run now, will you run before the end?"

He did not reply right away, but he did not need to. She knew his answer before he could form the words. She closed her eyes and let her face fall, but his gloved hand touched her chin and gently tipped it up. Wren forced her eyes open and found his waiting—wide, empty, and broken—holding back emotion but unable to hide the defeat. "In every dream, I will run with you. I shall look for you there until the very end."

The music drifted toward its final phrase, and as she felt their dance coming to an end, Wren hardened her resolve. Their time of dreaming together was over before either one had learned how to say goodbye, yet it could not stop her from stealing one more.

She dreamed what it would be like to look upon his face one last time. To grasp the lip of the mask and pull it away—to remove it from his sight and far from his mind. She would feel his hands flex on her waist, holding her closer still, and she would reach up and brush that errant curl back from middle of his forehead. Then she would kiss him one last time.

She saw every resignation within her own heart reflect in his eyes, a regret for each moment they had wasted dreaming instead of fighting for a future where they could have remained in each other's arms.

The final strains of music died, and Wren stepped back. Her composure slipped, but when she turned away, Timothius held her fingers fast. He pressed them to his lips, their cold, unfeeling affection matching the numb resoluteness that Wren willed into her heart, and when he let her go, she whispered, "I will dream without you, but it will always be of you. In every dream, I will dance with you."

CHAPTER THIRTY-SIX

*K*athrina was a flurry of skirts appearing in Wren's room. "We do not have much time. Your departure from the dance was noted and the king has been summoned."

Wren fastened Timothius's cloak around her neck, took a moment to ensure the crystallum was safely tucked against her chest, then faced her friend. "I'm ready. Let's go."

She reached for her knapsack, but Kathrina shook her head. "We take nothing. You will not want to be encumbered."

Wren stilled, but when she opened her mouth to question, a shout echoed from outside the room. Kathrina whirled and cracked the door, peering into the hall before turning back to Wren. "They are in the stairwell. We must run."

Wren did not hesitate another moment and followed Kathrina from her room, locking the door and pulling it closed behind them. "Hopefully, that will buy us some time," she whispered.

They broke into a run toward the staircase furthest from the voices that were drawing nearer, but to Wren's surprise, they only descended to the floor below. Kathrina scanned the hall cautiously from the landing, then nodded to a vacant room at the opposite end.

Wren dared not breathe until they were safely inside with the door fastened behind them.

The noises grew louder within the castle—shouts, pounding boots, and the scrape of metal against walls as their owners rushed forth. Running into the adjoining dressing room, Kathrina shoved open a door beside the tub. "Here," she said and disappeared inside.

Wren followed her carefully into the dark, her toes dangling off the side of a step immediately.

"The scullery corridors," Kathrina whispered. "We go all the way down."

The stairs felt endless, the dark oppressive, and the cold setting into Wren's bones was the sole indication of where they may be within the castle. With hands on the wall to either side, she steadied herself as the stone beneath her feet became slick with moisture and the steps lessened in height.

Kathrina slowed to a near stop, and Wren bumped into her with thankfully little force, catching herself against the curve of the wall. "Down we go," her friend quipped, and as suddenly as Wren had felt her back on the next step, she was gone.

Wren stepped down; however, when she searched for the edge with her foot, there was nothing—only a smooth slope downward. Sucking in the cold air, she sat, and the moment she scooted forward, she began to slide down the frigid rock, hurtling through the darkness in an increasingly vertical drop.

Without warning, the chute opened up, and she was dumped onto a pile of linens—towels, bedsheets, curtains, and gowns. Kathrina had already wrestled herself from the pile and was looking around at the gaping holes in the floor.

Wren fought to her feet, her eyes adjusting to the torchlit room. They were still inside the castle, but from the looks of the water basins and wash racks, they had to be within the wall just above where the water flowed from the city into the moat and beyond. The room smelled of damp earth and a heavy moisture hung in the air around them. It reminded Wren instantly of pools inside luxury hotels, but it lacked any and all warmth that those rooms held, especially through the winter months.

Kathrina made a murmur of approval, stopping beside the pit nearest the outside wall. "This is the largest one. It is the width of a stallion until about four yards down and then it narrows to the width of a skirt's hoop until it empties into the water roughly eight below that. We shall need to clear the jump down and swim to the bars at the base of the wall that allow the water to flow freely into the moat. From there, we'll go down river until we are able to make a run for the Flugés' house. There is a satchel concealed there containing a blend of dhust from the faeries themselves. It will take us to the border of the Elfin Domain."

Wren nodded but her mind spun when she looked down. The cold within the pit blew back at her and all was dark save the sound of the water lapping somewhere below. She tried to convert the measurements in her head, surmising that it would be a near twelve-meter dive. With no room for error between them and the unforgiving stone wall that is what it would have to be—a dive.

"Do you know what you're doing?" she asked Kathrina who was already stripping the weightier top layers off her dress.

"Not in the slightest, but to stay here is death. I would rather break my neck and drown than face the Rat King. They may remember me fondly as the fox who escaped her den," she said, voice trembling but optimistic.

She threw her mask down upon her heap of clothing beside the door and helped Wren with her own buttons and stays. The instant Wren threw her own mask beside Kathrina's, the pounding of boots reached their ears.

There was no time to hide before the door swung open,

sweeping back their dresses and crushing their masks beneath its weight. Whirling in a circle, Wren grasped for a method of self-defense of any kind and came up short, but her heart stilled when the torchlight glinted off the filigree of Timothius's mask in the doorway.

He did not hesitate to remove it, though his face was not any softer beneath as he surveyed the shivering women and the cavernous hole behind them. "Are you certain you can make it?" he asked, looking to Kathrina.

She nodded, eyes burning with a determination that stood in such contrast to the softness of her nature. "You have prepared me well for this. I know the path ahead and I am ready. It has been long enough."

Timothius nodded once, then strode forward. Clasping her shoulders, he pressed a small kiss to the top of her head and then pulled back, smiling warmly. "Elric will be waiting. And next week there shall be a wedding."

Kathrina beamed, her eyes welling, and she gave him a quick hug before turning to Wren. Throwing her arms around her friend's neck, Wren sent every ounce of confidence and excitement through the embrace that she could muster. She would not be afraid. She would not let her friend feel her fear. They would be free, come what may.

"I will see you down there," Kathrina whispered, stepping away.

Wren watched her turn and gather up her skirts, throwing them about her shoulders and pulling them tight like a cloak, shielding her bare arms. She took one deep breath, rose up on her toes, and pointed one foot out into the center of the hole. With the strength of a woman who had been dancing every night for over a decade, she leaped into the center, locked her pointed feet at the ankles, and fell like a pin into the depths.

Rushing to the side, Wren looked down. She saw nothing, heard nothing, until the splash at the bottom—and then a moment later the sound of Kathrina breaking the surface once again.

Turning to face Timothius, every nerve in Wren's body twitched from the cold and the nervous tension coursing through. "I-I'm going in differently. I trained as a diver for a few years and this is the only way I am comfortable." She recalled another time that she had spoken those words, moments before she departed a tree home, accepting a familiar form of security from the same man in front of her now. It felt like a lifetime ago, yet it had all led them here. And it would continue forward, no matter what happened next. "It is what I know," she added, forcing confidence into her voice. "I can make it this way."

Timothius nodded, his eyes slightly too wide and his breathing a hair too quick. She felt her own heart race, and fear cut through, overtaking her—the worry that this could be the last time she saw him.

"Marionaldi is my grandmother," she blurted, watching the revelation land and sink into his skin. "I never had a chance to tell you. I don't know how and I do not know why but— But it was not accidental. I am meant to be here."

He remained frozen for a moment, then stepped forward and clasped her fingers in his own. Eyes never once wavering from Wren's, he pressed a hard kiss to them and then fell to a knee. With one hand on his heart and the other holding on tightly to her, he vowed, "I will see you on the other side of this."

Wren lifted her chin, fighting the relief that threatened to break her composure. "Swear it. On my life. On yours. Because no matter what you say, I will worry about your heart. It belongs to a part of mine. I'm too afraid to face the future without you, so do not sacrifice yourself for this—for me. I need you more."

He nodded. "I swear it. By the Trifolium Thrones, I swear it."

Wren nodded back, unable to contain her trembling. "Good. I will be waiting for you."

Slipping her fingers from Timothius's hand, she faced the well, looking down and positioning herself along the edge at its very center. Turning slowly so her back was to the hole, she rose onto her toes and allowed her heels to feel the air off the side of the pit below. Exhaling, she closed her eyes and lifted her arms high above her head.

An arm caught her around the waist, as it had so many times in dance, pulling her into a chest that smelled of amber and suede. Her eyes flew open and she let her arms fall around his neck, clutching him tightly to her as he cradled the back of her head, burying his fingers in her hair.

"Take care, my heart," Timothius whispered in her ear, his voice cracking on the final words. Her eyes slammed shut at the raw emotion, the unbidden love and fear that made it impossible to truly accept their parting.

He loosened his hold on her enough to allow a fraction of space between them, and when a traitorous tear snuck free from the corner of Wren's eye, he caught it, wiping it away and leaving his warm caress in its place. Their chests heaved against one another, and Wren held his gaze, tilting her head forward in a silent indication of what she longed for more than anything.

There was no hesitation this time. Timothius's mouth claimed hers in a blistering kiss. For every passionate tryst Wren had ever known, none had set her on fire like feeling his stone facade fall around her. She did not know the exact moment it had happened, but she knew without a doubt that she would give anything to be by his side for as long as time would allow. And Thrones be damned, she *would* have the chance to kiss him like this again.

They broke apart and she saw a fire in his eyes—a vibrant, burning life that confirmed he felt the same. Before either of them could think or speak again, Wren stepped back, raised her arms, bent three quick but strong times at the knees, and flipped back, diving headfirst into the abyss.

She fought her muscles' urging to bend, to twist, to flail her way to her doom and locked them straight as the air tightened around her. The distance made her stomach drop ever so slightly, and a small panic set in when the water did not meet her as quickly as she'd expected, but once the well's walls vanished and the air opened around her, she allowed her limbs to relax and plunged headfirst into the depths of the water below.

CHAPTER THIRTY-SEVEN

The shock of the cold felt like a thousand needles plunging into Wren's body, and it took every discipline she had to not gasp for air before her head broke the surface. Once above water, she quickly gathered her bearings and located the barred opening in the wall to the right where she could see a head bobbing and arms arching forward. Kathrina was almost to freedom and she needed to catch up.

She had always been a strong swimmer, and it didn't take her long to meet her friend at the bars. They slipped through, and when the cold night air struck, Wren knew this would be unlike any test of endurance she had experienced so far. They swam side by side as quickly and silently as they could, clearing the wall and traveling up the river parallel to the Autumnal Wood. Shouts rang out from the rampart, followed by the twang of bowstrings and the plink of arrows piercing the water behind them.

Wren's heart began to hammer again, her limbs nearly unable to function, but she pushed past the cold, panic, and fatigue all dragging her down and increased her speed.

The moment the small house came into view, they made for

shore. Wren forced herself to her feet and pulled Kathrina straight up beside her. Stumbling and tripping across the tall grass, they fell through the open gate of the Flugés' house, but it wasn't until they saw the door ajar that they knew they'd made a massive miscalculation.

Glancing back, Wren could already see the drawbridge of the castle beginning to lower, and the soldiers' torches flickering from the other side. She plunged inside the house behind Kathrina, slamming the door in their wake. They surveyed the wreckage within—cabinets ripped from the walls, dishes shattered, and furniture upended—and then looked at one another.

"It's here. We must find it," Kathrina gasped, gulping in air. "Search everywhere. It's a small, green satchel."

Wren glanced back out the window at the soldiers now growing closer by the second and rushed toward the dining table that had been thrown onto its side. "Grab the other end, we'll bar the door."

With strength fueled by adrenaline alone, they managed to wrestle the table in front of the door, drawing the tattered curtains as best they could across the windows before frantically searching through the mess—and coming up empty.

Wren took a deep breath, the cold beginning to stiffen her body. "We'll have to make a run for it. Into the woods. We have to do something. We have to keep running."

"In what?" Kathrina asked frantically, her composure fraying as she threw glasses from a cabinet that rested in the sink. "We will die if we go into the forest this wet and barely clothed. We don't even have shoes. We're trapped here. We're going to die."

The words snapped Wren back to reality, and she stormed across the room, grasping her friend by the shoulders. "Kathrina Poultney, you are one of the bravest women I know. If we are going to die, we will die running and fighting for our lives, not rotting in the prison cell of a rat. We are fighters and we will go out fighting."

Kathrina nodded furiously, but when her eyes diverted over Wren's shoulder, they widened and she let out a shriek. Wren spun on her heel, watching her friend run across the room and rip the face off the clock on the mantel, revealing it to be a hidden door that swung open on squeaky hinges. She tugged on silken strings, and a small satchel fell out into her hand.

Shouts sounded from outside the cottage and horses' hoof-beats slowed to a stop at the front of the house.

"What do we do with it?" Wren hissed as Kathrina struggled with frozen fingers to untie the cinch. The back door flew open, and Wren spun, snatching a broomstick from the floor, but at the sight of Elric's face, she nearly cried from happiness.

Kathrina whimpered in relief, and when he ran to her, she shoved the satchel into his hands. "Hurry, please," she begged, but Elric already had a knife in hand, slitting the bag open. Shimmering dhust sifted out, clouding the room, and he wrapped an arm around Kathrina, waving to Wren with the other.

"Come on," he shouted above the splintering front door. The windows shattered all around them, torches swiftly following, sending fire and smoke billowing inside.

Wren coughed and stumbled forward, falling to her knees and reaching out blindly. Elric sought out her hand, wrapping her fingers tightly in his. The air began to thin, the world blur-ring. Plumes of violet dhust and star-laced magic rose to push back the smoke, but when Wren looked up, she saw the door crack in two and a guard peer inside. He rested his crossbow on the side of the table that barred his entry and steadied it, centering his aim.

With a snap, the bow released the bolt, sending it soaring directly at Wren's heart.

She held her breath, closed her eyes, and braced for the pain of impact. Something slammed into her, the force thrusting them all backward, but instead of hitting the floor, they continued to twist and free-fall in an endless downward spiral. They spun through clouds and starlight, beyond the event horizon into blessed nothingness, and there—deep at the heart of the dark oblivion—emotion with the force of hundreds of years slammed into Wren's heart.

It was anguish and loss being undone. It was a bitter parting being removed from memory. It was raw, nagging, endless pain finally healing—missing pieces now restored. And just as quickly as it all rushed through her, it passed by, and her feet hit the forest floor with an impact that sent all three of them toppling over in a heap.

Elric groaned beneath Wren, and she rolled off him onto her side. She waited to feel pain, expected to see blood everywhere, but when she looked down, she found no wound. Her dress was not even torn. There was no trace of the arrow. Her eyes widened, but when she sought to make eye contact with Kathrina, she noticed that the woman was the only one of them who had not yet moved.

And that was when she knew.

"Kathrina!" The sound ripped out of her throat like the cry of a woman possessed, echoing into the night.

The color drained from Elric's face and he sat up quickly. Crawling to Kathrina, he gently lifted her into his arms, but at the sight of the arrow lodged within her chest—burrowed deeper still from the fall—his hands faltered.

Cursing himself loudly for allowing her to slip, he wrapped his arms around her and pulled her into his lap, cradling her like a child with one hand below her head so that it did not loll.

"Kathrina," he bit out, deep agony carving lines across his face. "K, please. You must stay, you must wake up."

At his words, Kathrina's eyes fluttered open. A small trickle of blood fell from her lips, yet still she smiled. "Oh, the way I love you," she breathed.

"No," Elric grunted, shaking his head. "No. I waited three

THE CADENCE OF CROWNS

hundred years to know your face. I will not live without you. I cannot."

Kathrina's eyes began to leak, tears mixing with blood across her cheek. Life, death, and pain becoming one in a single moment of time. "You will love still," she choked. "You were the greatest love of my life. But I am not meant to be yours. Only the first." Her breathing became labored, but she moved her hand enough to clasp his shirt. "Promise me you won't forget. Promise me you will love. Promise me."

Elric's tears streamed, flooding his face, pouring through the anguish etched across his skin, but he nodded. "I will love you forever."

Kathrina's eyes fell shut and her gasps grew shorter, her lungs struggling to expand—struggling for air. "Remember me forever. But love again. Please, Elric. Love always."

A cough bubbled up in her chest, her breaths rattling an imminent death. Wren turned away, unable to bear witness. She had seen it once before—these last minutes of life. The final moment shared between a love so strong that it should have been enough to cheat death. Love was truly the strongest force the world could ever know, but from it she saw the same pain, the same cleaving apart that she had seen in her own grandparents the day that her grandfather closed his eyes for the last time.

Love could sustain anything. It could withstand anything. It could supersede everything. But in the end, it was finite. Nothing lasted forever.

And this…. This was where it ended.

"I love you," she heard Elric cry.

"And I, you," Kathrina echoed.

And then her chest fell silent.

There was a heartbeat in the forest where nothing moved. Nature paused in mournful reflection and even the wind in the trees whispered an elegy for the love that had died before their very eyes.

Then an anguished scream broke the night from the heart of a shattered man who just lost everything.

Wren was not sure how long they sat there. She didn't know when the elfin guards surrounded them, or when they lifted Kathrina's body onto a stretcher made of soft wool. She just stared as they laid a sheet of lilac muslin over her, covering the wound but leaving her pale face—now peaceful in an eternal sleep—turned toward the stars.

She didn't know where they took Elric, only that she would recall his haunting screams for the rest of her days. She was unsure of when she broke—the weight of everything finally cracking her facade, allowing the agony within to surge out in crippling waves of her own loss. And she didn't know at what point she closed her eyes and surrendered to the magic that eased her into a dreamless sleep.

Time finally stopped then, and though Wren wasn't sure when it would begin again—though she was not ready for it to resume—she knew it would. And she would face what came next.

And as she slept, there was one final thing she knew for certain: she never wanted to watch another person she loved die.

She would wake and allow time to march on, but only if it brought her the opportunity to destroy the Rat King once and for all. If it gave her the chance to spare anyone else the unfair ending she had witnessed tonight. But if it did not, if it cost her everything, she would happily lose it all if it meant she burned his world down around him too.

PART III
THE RISE

CHAPTER THIRTY-EIGHT

*W*ren sprang up from the bed, chest heaving and tears rushing to her eyes as they searched the room for a friend she knew in her heart would not be there.

The gaze she did meet stilled her grieving heart, yet caused her nerves to alight.

However, when Nelluenya crossed the room with outstretched arms, Wren did not hesitate to fold into them.

"I am so sorry," she rasped. Her head pounded and her throat felt as if she had swallowed fire, but nothing compared to the stinging memory of the last time she was in the Elfin Domain.

The Guardian shook her head. "Your return is welcome here, and the apology belongs to me. Your Highness."

Wren pulled back at her words, finding Nelluenya's eyes were also misty in the spring dawn.

"As Guardian of this realm I am duty bound to defend what is honorable," she continued. "I should have divulged the truth of what we suspected that very first night."

"I would not have accepted it," Wren admitted. "I would have only run sooner. It was something I needed to find for myself. Except…."

Nelluenya rested her palm on Wren's arm. "Kathrina's loss is not on your shoulders."

Wren shook her head furiously. "She pushed me back. She shouldn't have done it. She had her whole future ahead of her. I am meaningless, destined to be forgotten no matter where I am."

The Guardian's eyebrows drew together. "Is that what you believe?"

"What else is there?" Wren could hear the hopelessness in her own voice—the vulnerability—and she despised it. "And that is not self-pity, it is an honest question. I am a vessel of memories and magic here, but I do not belong to the world I came from. What choice is there for me? What future do I have that is not already decided?"

Nelluenya was silent, surveying Wren for a moment, then she stood and crossed the room to a small table in the corner. Removing a box from its surface, she turned to Wren once again. "When the Trifolium Thrones fell, the four leaves of the clover were lost. One was consumed by darkness, another fled, and still one more hid. But the fourth—Inflamel's queen—was saved by her people. She was hidden by magic and only with magic would she return to us. It is what we have believed and held as truth for centuries. And we were wrong."

She returned to the side of the bed and rested the box in Wren's hands, pulling the lid back to reveal the chain not with the crystallum hanging from it, but a golden shard the length of a sewing needle and the width of a penny whistle. Its edges were jagged and sharp, but its color was flawless, the surface unblemished.

"We were wrong," Nelluenya continued softly, "because instead of returning to her rightful place, she sacrificed it all and bestowed it on you. Breteria's magic—our magic—flows through their veins. You have always belonged here.

"What you hold is a piece of the Trifolium Throne itself. The bond that the four rulers formed in the Thrones lives within this shard. That is what the Isteriaeth came together to preserve. Its strength is beyond any of the five strands of magic and its power is unmatched—created by the ultimate sacrifice of the original rulers. Whatever flesh it pierces, whatever magic it draws in, it binds. Magic, power, souls, lives—it becomes one."

Wren stared at the shard, then gasped. "This is how we defeat the Rat King."

Nelluenya was quiet, pensive for a moment, then said, "It is hope. You are our only hope. This is the dawning of a new future. Your magic awaits inheritance should you accept it, and if that is your choice, the people of Inflamel will ride with you. They will take up the banner of the Trifolium sigil once more, and they will fight for you."

"And if it is not my choice?" Wren asked, looking up to meet her eye.

A single tear fell down Nelluenya's cheek. "Then I do not doubt the strands will release you to your world. But here you will fade from time and we will all do so with honor beside you. It is your choice and yours alone."

Wren tried and failed to swallow the lump in her throat— her heart, body, and mind at war with one another all at once. Silencing them, she cleared her throat and asked the question plaguing her thoughts—the one she dreaded the most. "Where's Elric?"

Nelluenya's eyes fell shut, and when she opened them again, there was no hint of hope left in them. "He is in the west garden. By her side."

※

WREN WAS SURPRISED to learn she had been unconscious for quite a few days, but the shock did not compare to how she felt seeing the scores of people already in the Elfin Domain. Rebel supporters from all over the kingdom were arriving every moment as news of the Rat King's attempt on Wren's life, and her rumored identity, spread. Nelluenya had taken good care to ensure her privacy in the days since her arrival, but Wren was still unprepared to face them, so with the Elfin Guardian's direction, she exited the Great House on the side of the river opposite the gazebos and followed the pathway north toward the coast.

She had not ventured this close to the mouth of the river before, but when the wood opened to a small clearing, she knew the spot immediately.

The ground was a carpet of dewy moss more than it was grass-covered. Vines streamed from the trees that bordered the clearing's edge, hemming it in like a living veil and hiding it from the world. In the center, a fresh plot had been dug, the moss and grass absent and the soil overturned. Freshly planted at its head was a mature and vibrant bush filled with light-purple blooms. Their sweet lilac scent already surrounded Wren, but that was not what caused the air to catch in her lungs. It was what lay on the ground beside the grave—Elric, his eyes shut, with one arm stretched above his head and the other surrounding a book that served as his makeshift pillow.

Wren stood rooted to the spot, unable to breathe. She wanted to be there for him, yet she wanted to flee. She was intruding on such a private, such a sacred moment. Yet she could not bring herself to move.

Elric's eyes opened, locating her instantly and then widening.

Her lips parted and she grasped for words, desperately trying to find the right ones to say. But what could be said? What could possibly begin to address everything that had happened between them? Where did they go from here?

He stood carefully to his feet, wavering on unsteady legs. His clothes were clean but unkempt, as if he had changed when they arrived and not again since. He was a shadow of the Elric she knew, and Wren would have thought he was intoxicated if she didn't see the exhaustion clouding his face like the dhust he wrought from the air. His first two steps were staggered, and he paused to get his feet back beneath him. Growing more confident he tried again, picking up speed and before she knew it, Wren was rushing to meet him halfway.

They collided and held on to one another as if at any moment the earth might open up to take one of them away. Wren clutched the thinnest strand of her composure, but the shaking of Elric's shoulders, the silent sobs emanating from his chest, and the tears flooding from his eyes caused all trace of her pretense to crumble. Burying her face in his shoulder, Wren finally allowed herself to cry.

For Elric, for Kathrina, for her grandmother, for Timothius.

She cried until she could no longer feel tears falling from her eyes. And somewhere along the way, Elric's subsided too. They broke their embrace, but Wren kept an arm about his waist, and his remained slung over her shoulder. Together, they approached Kathrina's final resting place—the very garden she had dreamed of seeing.

They sat beside one another on the ground in silence for a while, and then Elric began to speak. He told Wren about his K. About the first time he saw her, as an orphan lost on the shores of a new world. How she looked like an angel but sang like a frog. How she was by his side the first time he felt his magic stir. How he had proposed by telling her he had no right to ask for her hand without a ring, but she only laughed and said he could have both hands if it meant he would tell her stories of the stars every night. It was why they never waited longer than the moon's rising to see each other.

He told her everything Kathrina loved—the list endless—and all that she hated, which was spiders. He confided things he said he had never shared with another soul about their love, secrets he swore he would hold close to his heart and memories Wren knew he would hide away and pull back out when the days grew cold and the nights too dark to find a light. And all the while, Wren listened—laughing, crying, and celebrating the life of a friend she wished she could have known more. Every fear she had of Elric blaming her, every doubt she had that their friendship would withstand the burden of such a loss, blew away on the wind, bearing lilac petals through the vines and into the clear, blue sky above the water.

They fell silent once again long after the sky had turned golden—the sun sinking and the night opening its starlit eyes on the world. Wren watched Elric look up at those stars, staring unblinkingly until the last of his tears crept down his face.

"Elric, I am so sorry," she whispered. "You deserve the world, and yet you have lost everything."

To her surprise, he smiled, closing his eyes and shaking his head at the sky. He turned toward her and fixed her with an earnest but hard stare. "I have not lost everything. Not yet. My brother is out there and my sister is beside me. Come what may, live or die, I will do so with you both by my side. You are my future now."

Overcome with emotion, Wren released a shuddering breath and returned his smile through streaming tears. "When I was a kid, I used to wish on stars. I never thought I'd come to love one."

Elric wrapped an arm around her once again and rested the palm of his opposite hand on the dirt next to him, letting his fingers sink into the earth as if he could still hold the hand of the woman lost from his side. "Death can steal away life all it wants, but it will never take away love."

CHAPTER THIRTY-NINE

*W*ren's room within the Great House was still dark. The breeze off the water rustled her curtains, allowing the moonlight to flood the space and beckon her closer. She crossed the floor, pulling the fabric to the side. The moon was nearly full. It was what she had longed for—what she believed would take her home. And now, looking upon it, it filled her with an impending sense of dread for the unknown path ahead.

Lights in the wood below caught her eye. They were not blinking as fireflies would, their light steady and in varying shades of blue, red, green, purple, and silver. But they were *dancing*. Spinning and twirling through the air, enchanting her and begging her to come closer.

She slid her feet into slippers and stole down the hall, descending the staircase to the exit. The night was still warm, and the breeze kicked up the skirt of her ivory nightdress, blowing her hair across her face. She gathered the locks to one side to keep it from obstructing her view and crossed the footbridge, stepping off the path and into the wood where the lights grew brighter—larger somehow. Once the trees concealed the river at her back and the moon overhead, the colored lights flared, illuminating the wood in front of her.

Faeries.

Every single light, every shade in all five colors, was its own individual faery. They were not small as they had appeared from her window, but were instead the size of any other person, with lithe, willowy limbs, delicately pointed ears, and wings so intricate and unique she wished she could sit and study each pair in detail.

In awe of their beauty, she stepped forward, but the moment she opened her mouth to say hello, every last one of them vanished.

"Wren Klaver, it is past your bedtime," came a lilting, yet strong voice.

Wren gasped and turned, coming face to face with her grandmother. Only it was not the grandmother she knew. It was her grandmother as she had been in her memories—older than the day she'd pledged to marry Wren's grandfather, yet younger than she had appeared the day she was separated from her home and thrown into a strange world light years away.

"Gran.... How?"

The woman stepped forward, her appearance changing with each step, aging her into the same woman in a soft-yellow sweater that Wren had sat beside under the lights of a tree. Something in Wren's heart broke—a dam she hadn't realized was containing a flood. The fear she held in her heart that they would never be reunited was erased when they wrapped their arms around each other, and she let every pretense fade, laying down her stubborn strength to weep in her grandmother's unmistakable embrace.

"I knew from the moment you were born," she said, brushing Wren's hair back and drying the tears on her cheeks. "Your mother came soon after we arrived on earth, but there was no magic passed down to her—or to any of your uncles after. We had lost all hope. But the moment they placed you in my arms, I heard the Throne call. I felt my magic stir, and I knew.

"You walked as a ghost upon the earth, you grew as any child would, but you did not belong. You did not know what flowed dormant in your veins or what knit your bones together, and there was no way for me to explain away reality. There was only time. And this is your time."

"It can't be," Wren said, shaking her head. "I'm not cut out for this. There are people here far, far better fit for crowns and thrones than I am. I'm not anyone's queen, I am a mess."

"And that is what makes you the most fit to be their queen," her grandmother replied earnestly with all the love in her eyes. "It is those who are the most reluctant to take their rightful place, to raise themselves up and lead, who are the most fit to rule. You fear for them and long for their protection because in your heart, they are already your people."

A fear-filled tear snuck down Wren's cheek. "I can carry the burden of things, but I cannot carry the weight of people. So many who have fought to survive will die, and I cannot watch them die for me. I am not strong enough to face this."

"Alone," her grandmother said with a smile. "You are not strong enough alone. But you are not alone, are you? The love you already hold for this world has nothing to do with what you were born to be but everything to do with who you are. For the first time in your life, your heart is home."

The storm of Wren's thoughts stopped, frozen in the air, then drifted to the ground like snow. Home. Her heart was home. Except, when she thought of home, she did not picture a kingdom or a castle or even the people she had come to love. There was only one thing—one person—that made her heart truly feel at home.

"I don't have him either," she whispered. "I don't even know if he is safe."

Her grandmother inclined her head, mischief dancing in her eyes. "And what wouldn't you do to save him?"

For the first time, Wren relaxed. She did not think five steps ahead, she did not bargain, she did not negotiate, she did not plead. The answer was as clear as the path that had been laid open in front of her—her future. "Nothing," she said, smiling through the tears now welling for a completely different reason. "I would take it all. I would fight the world if it meant he was safe."

Her grandmother's smile was radiant, and all she needed to do was open her arms for Wren to fall into them. Wrapped up in her warmth, in her unconditional love, Wren's tumultuous mind began to ease.

But this balm was more than hope. It was an overwhelming rightness. It was peace.

The older woman pulled away after a long moment, and when Wren looked at her again, she saw the lines of age fade from her skin. As if time itself was turning back the clock, she watched her grandmother become whole, strong, and healthy once more.

"I have shown you the things I could never say," she said. "I have given every last bit of my magic back to the throne that bestowed it on me. And now I am home. It is time for you to rise. Your crown is waiting."

Wren's mind raced—the validation of all she had seen and heard, coming from the one person she believed above all others, fueled a power she had never felt within herself before. And though her thoughts continued to dance, her heart was still. "But what of the Rat King?"

Darkness clouded her grandmother's face. "He is not what he appears to be. The same darkness that took this world, that scattered the Trifolium to the winds, lives within him. And I fear that more of his kind walk the realm—waiting, watching for the

Thrones to rise again. And they will. They will begin with you, but all four kingdoms will unite again under the banner of the Trifolium sigil. Then and only then will you take the Throne and receive your full power. But first you must save our people."

Wren took a shaky breath, drawing on the steady hope growing in her chest. The responsibility. The honor. The love.

The air around her grandmother started to shimmer, a soft halo of light that continued to brighten, though the woman's face started to fade. She was slipping away. And though the pain of facing this goodbye shattered Wren's heart, she viewed it now with fresh eyes. She had spent the last months on a journey with her grandmother, becoming acquainted with her most intimate secrets and preserving her memory in ways she never could have before. Now, with a legacy that would live on in Wren, it was time to let go.

Wren stared at her one last time, felt the soft wrinkles on her skin, drew in the floral and citrus that she would recall for the rest of her days, and let her composure shatter for the goodbye she dreaded most. "I'm going to miss you so much."

The woman smiled back with nothing but pride and endless joy in her eyes. She pulled Wren close to her side like she had so many times before, and Wren knew in her heart that was where she would remain, no matter how long they were apart. "I will see you again, my Wren. The most beautiful and wonderful things can always be seen by those who have eyes for them. It is time for me to rest, but it is time for you to wake. You are ready."

❄

WREN OPENED her eyes and stared at the moonlight reflecting across the ceiling of her room. The tears were still fresh on her cheeks. Her grandmother's scent still clung to her skin. And when she clasped a hand around the crystallum resting against her chest, all that remained was the shard.

She did not think, she only moved. Moments later, with her hood pulled over her head and a bow strung across her back, she crept on silent feet down the open-air corridors of the Great House. Undetected, and with one last glance and a silent apology, she slipped onto the path and out of the Elfin Domain.

The sky was clear yet starless and for that she was grateful. She navigated the gardens, blending in with the rebels settling into gazebos and tents, and avoiding the guard patrolling the edge of the elfin territory.

They were all waiting for war. And she would make sure that it did not touch them.

She felt the shift in the air around her just before the clear night plunged into the darkness of the Aestival Forest. Fear prickled along her spine when she heard life crawling across the leaves and branches surrounding her, but she stayed calm—moving with them as if she were a specter of the night itself.

Carefully navigating the vicious roses climbing upon every surface, she reached the great felled tree and bore left, following its path—

A loud *snap* sounded from the other side of the tree, and she froze in her steps. The tree cracked beneath a boot finding purchase on its side and another followed suit, making way for a towering figure to stand on its top.

Wren ducked against the tree, hiding within its shadow as the figure walked slowly down the length, stopping only once they were directly above her.

"You said you would be waiting for me," a deep and familiar voice said. "It was my error to assume that meant you would be safe within the Elfin Domain and not alone in the forest in the middle of the night."

CHAPTER FORTY

Wren's body slumped in frustration even as her heart skipped a few beats. Pushing off the tree, she turned to face Timothius and ripped the hood back from her head. "We lost Kathrina. Elric is practically a ghost. Rebels are flooding the Domain ready for war. I did not have time to wait before, and with you here now it is only a matter of time before the king comes looking for us all. If he wants me, he will get me. But when I go down, I will make sure I take him with me."

Timothius's feet crushed the leaves where he landed in front of her, and when he stood his unmasked face was mere inches from her own. "I arrived across the meadow and saw the Flugés' house consumed in flames. I reached it to learn that one of my men had fired a bolt into a woman's heart—a woman they could find no trace of when the flames smoldered to ash. I have spent days unaware if you are living or dead and it nearly drove me mad. So no, you will not surrender to him. You will not go alone. This is a war, not a vigilante mission."

"It's personal," she hissed.

"You are not the only one to have lost a friend," Timothius replied, his words landing with a sting.

"No, but I will make sure we do not lose any more."

She turned on her heel and walked once again into the darkness, though she did not get far when a gloved hand clasped her elbow. His touch caused her resolve to falter, her heart begging her to find solace in his arms, but the fear of what would become of them held her prisoner.

"I mean it, Timothius. Let me go," she warned, desperation bracketing her tone.

"Or what, Wren?" he fired back. "Tell me, what do you have planned for the king?"

Though it was dark she could see the challenge in his eyes— the terrifying, burning will of the Glaive. It would have halted the average man, it may have even given her pause a short time ago, but he had made a critical mistake that revealed the weakness in his hand. He had called her by name.

She smirked. "You won't stop me. You may be the most feared figure in this land, but you above all would never lay a hand on me."

"I would not hesitate to lift you from your feet and carry you with one arm, screaming, all the way to the Great House on my shoulder," he rumbled, ice filling his tone and colliding with the fire in his eyes when he took a step toward her. "Now answer the question. What will you do?"

"I will destroy him," Wren spat. "And I will laugh while I watch everything he stands for burn."

Timothius's face faltered for a moment, but he caught himself and maintained control. "You are not a villain, Wren. You are a queen, fated to unite the kingdoms and rule this world in justice and peace. More than that, you are—"

He cut himself off and his eyes fell closed, but Wren was not ready to stand down. "What? I'm what? Are you back to your distant and chivalrous self now that we are outside the castle walls? Do not talk to me about who I am and am not when you know full well the razor-thin line that exists between hero and villain. I didn't come here to be a hero. I came here to find my own way, whatever the cost. And if that cost makes me the villain, so be it."

He shook his head slowly, burning eyes meeting her intensity once again. "You do not want such a weight on your conscience, a guilt so putrid you cannot wash it away for as long as you live. You do not know what it is that you're asking."

The pain in his eyes served to extinguish some of Wren's fury. "I don't. But I'm asking you to accept that I will do this. I am the only one who can. I have a shard from the Trifolium Throne, I can use it to—"

His voice raised. "No. I refuse to accept this. I would remain by your side to the end, I would follow you to the grave if you asked me to, but I will not stand idly by and watch you throw your life away."

She shook her head, traitorous tears stinging her eyes. "It is what I was put here for. I don't exist in my world. The one person who ever truly saw me there is gone. The rebellion will find and elect a new ruler. Let this be my purpose. I will bind the Rat King's life to my own, and then when I die, you will all be free. No more masks."

"And where do you think I could ever find freedom if I lose you?" Timothius shouted, his voice echoing against the trees. He stepped toward her until she could see the rivulets running from his eyes as he clasped her face in his hands. "There is no life for me outside of the one I have dreamed of with you. You do not have my heart, you *are* my heart. I would sooner spend my days seeing nothing beyond the darkness of a mask than go the rest of my wretched life without touching you again."

Wren froze, words unable to form on her lips. Timothius stood silent as well, hands falling back to his sides. The only sound around them was the beating of their hearts, the forest itself holding its breath and waiting for one of them to lay down their arms. She stared at the soft curls, windswept and run through on the top of his head. She took in his face, full of fire and passion, power and warmth, all melded together in a hazel hue she could picture with her eyes closed.

She could give up everything—her world, her expectations, her comforts, her reality, her life—but could she give up the only man who had ever made her dream of love?

Swallowing the lump in her throat, Wren took one of his hands in her own. His breathing stuttered when she began to tug on the tips of his gloves a single finger at a time. She repeated the motion with the other hand and did not lift her gaze until she held both gloves in one fist. Letting them fall to the ground, she took his left hand in hers and raised it to her cheek, cradling his skin against her own.

He shuddered, his kohl-stained lids falling shut as he cupped her face. Raising his other hand, Wren laid it gently against her chest, right above her racing heart, and his eyes opened once more, a fire of a different kind burning in them.

"I never want to see your face hidden from mine ever again," she swore. "I never want to feel anything between my skin and your touch. And if I am your heart, then know that for as long as it beats, I will belong to you."

Timothius's lips parted—

The sharp twang of bowstrings broke the stillness of the night followed by the sickening *thump* of arrows sinking into flesh.

Timothius lurched forward, and when Wren caught him, she could see wolf masks gleaming from the trees behind him.

Rage tore a scream from her throat when the guards surged from the forest. Regaining his balance, Timothius gritted his teeth and straightened to reach over his shoulder. He ripped three arrows from where they had lodged in his shoulder and cast them to the ground. Unsheathing both swords at his side, he turned and met two guards in a clash of steel, one falling to his blade almost instantly.

Wren stepped back from the fray, catching the glimpse of an arrow being nocked. Her own was in her hands in seconds, and she did not stop firing until she saw the archer fall. Still more guards advanced on her, and though she retreated, she lost the distance needed to fire her bow.

"Wren!" Timothius shouted, and when she looked at him, he tossed her one of his swords. She grasped the hilt tightly, shocked at how secure the weapon rested in her palm despite its weight, and turned seconds before a guard raised his sword to meet her own. The force of the blades clashing nearly took her off her feet, but the sight of his snarling mask sent a rush of potent violence and determination through her veins.

She pushed back and he stumbled, as if he had not expected her show of strength. Wren did not hesitate, lunging for him and striking so fast that she could barely think. She could only move, training all her concentration on the defensive maneuvers Reginald had taught her, and looking for any opening to gain the upper hand. His back hit a tree, and he faltered when his sword arm snagged on a branch. Holding her breath but forcing her eyes to stay open, Wren swung with all her might and released his head from his shoulders.

She felt the man at her back before she heard him and turned, her blade once again scorching through the darkness like a brand. It caught him deep in the stomach and his entrails fell to the forest floor, his body soon following.

Her fury continued on, butchering anything that crossed her path until all that remained between her and Timothius was a single guard. Everything within her stopped and time itself stood still when she saw him fall to one knee. His chest and arms were covered in blood, and no matter how hard she tried, she could not convince herself it belonged only to the soldiers he had brought down. He fought to regain his footing, but his arm dropped against his knee, barely able to support the weight of his sword any longer.

Wren was upon the guard in an instant. "You will not take him from me," she growled, and with two hands, she lifted the sword and cleaved through his arm, sending both it and his weapon hurtling to the ground. The man tipped to the side, into the felled tree, his screams piercing the silent night.

With the tip of her sword below his chin, holding him still, Wren ripped the wolf mask from his face.

"Clover harlot," he spat. "Kill me quickly so that your love may die in your arms."

Wren straightened her blade and shoved it through his throat with all her might. His eyes widened and the gurgling need that echoed his desperation to take a breath was not a sound she would readily forget. "Let him watch your life bleed out slowly while I save his."

She twisted the blade vertically and tore it downward, running him through, and as silence filled the forest once again, she cast her sword aside and threw herself upon Timothius.

Convulsions racked his body, and she pulled him into her arms, steadying his head and cupping his face. "Timothius. Timothius, stay with me. Look at me. Your eyes, I need to see your eyes. Focus on me."

Her voice rose to a fever pitch and cut through whatever agony was consuming him. His unseeing eyes finally found hers, their dull light fading fast, and she forced a smile. "There you are. Now keep those eyes on me. We're going to get you to the domain. You're going to be jus-just fine."

But even though she said the words, she knew they were a lie. The gray pallor of his skin, the blue seeping into his lips told her so. Timothius's breathing was ragged, his mouth grasping for words he couldn't form. She cupped his cheek, stroking it, memorizing how he felt. "Shhh," she whispered, rocking to conceal her shaking. "I'm not letting you go anywhere. Just stay here. Stay with me."

Wetness slicked against her body with every sluggish pump of his heart, and her own shattered within her chest.

Her chest.

Eyes flying open, she released her hold on Timothius long enough to rip the shard from around her neck. She didn't know if it was the magic calling or her desperation driving her, but somehow it was clear what needed to be done. Shifting Timothius to lay flat on the ground, she knelt above him and ripped his shirt to expose the grotesque wounds that surrounded both his heart and lungs.

She took her bodice in her hands and tore it until the fabric pulled away, leaving a deep, jagged *V* between her breasts. Grasping the shard with both hands, she turned it on herself and rested it with the point against the skin just above her heart. She held her breath and then pitched forward, falling flat to the ground and driving the shard straight into her heart.

The pain was a shock, stealing her breath and causing everything within her to slow, as if it could not account for the life exiting her body at such a rapid rate. Wrapping the shard's chain in her fist, she ripped it away, tearing the shard from her flesh.

Her body pumped blood freely now, streaming down her dress and pooling on the ground, but when she leaned over Timothius's cold body, she thought she saw color and warmth return to his skin beneath its flow. With the shard in her trembling hands, coated entirely in her life source, she plunged it straight into a wound left by one of the arrows—directly into Timothius's barely pulsing heart.

The beat was nothing more than a flicker at first, but as the world began to fuzz around Wren, she could have sworn the shard melted in front of her eyes, disintegrating under her fingertips, encasing his heart in a brilliant gold, and staunching the bleeding.

And when she slumped across his chest, she was almost certain she felt his skin warm under her cheek.

Soft skin that now covered where his wounds had been.

Black spots clouded her vision, but in the seconds before her eyelids fell shut, she dreamed that she saw his flutter open.

CHAPTER FORTY-ONE

The light was so bright that, even behind her eyelids, Wren flinched. She took a deep breath and the scent of lilac invaded her senses, sending all of her memories rushing back in. Unable to move, she forced her eyes open, and a shadow crossed the sun streaming in the window, shrouding her in blissful darkness. She focused the best she could despite her pounding head, and then looked up to meet Elric's crystal-blue stare.

"You are back," he said with a smile, his words attempting a jest while the dark circles beneath his glassy eyes and pale skin conveyed his sick worry.

Wren struggled to sit up, making it far enough to rest her back against the wall that supported the pillow. "Where is he?"

"Timothius is fine," said Elric softly. "Well, alive, at least. You saved him."

All tension leaked from her body, her mind relaxing and her chest lightening, making it easier to breathe.

"And you two are...." He didn't need to finish. His lips twitched upward, forming dimples beneath sparkling eyes that completed the question on his behalf.

355

A small snort escaped Wren, as much of a laugh as her body would allow at the moment. "I don't know what we are. I'm not even sure if we are actually a *we*."

Elric threw her a sideways glance. "He left the service of the king, endangered an entire rebellion, and walked night and day through a forest of thorns for the woman who chanced fate by impaling her own heart in order to save his life. No, I would have to agree, certainly nothing exists between the two of you."

Wren rolled her eyes at the sarcasm dripping from his tone, but did not refute him. Smoothing the blanket draped across her lap, she finally murmured, "I saw my grandmother."

The side of the bed creaked under Elric's weight, and when she met his eyes, he appeared utterly perplexed. "I cannot say I've ever discussed grandparents while speaking of romance, but I will give you the benefit of the doubt that these stories connect somehow and it is not the blood loss going to your head."

Wren snapped out of her stupor enough to throw him a blistering look, earning herself the first full smile she had seen on his face since the morning she found him in the Flugés' house with....

"She told me to take the crown," she pressed on. "But I was afraid of losing anyone else. Nelluenya told me about the shard and I thought if I could sacrifice myself that it would give you all freedom. Then you would be able to find someone better suited to lead you. It was selfish, but I'm afraid that what I've done now is even worse."

"How do you suppose that?"

"Timothius's life is now bound to me." The words ringing in her ears somehow inflicted more pain than the thoughts spinning aimlessly within her mind. "He escaped the service of the king, finally left imprisonment and bondage, and now he can never be free. And worse, now if anything happens to me—if the king does come for me—he will lose his life too."

Elric raised an eyebrow. "That is your concern?"

Wren cut him a glare. "What do you mean *that*? I just stole someone's life without their consent. How am I any better than the Rat King himself?"

Elric fell silent and stared at where his hands lay folded in his lap, appearing to think. Wren waited, taking the moment to look at him closer. There was a fragility to his skin. His eyelids were swollen, and red streaked through the whites of his eyes. He appeared older, worn down and gaunt—the ghost of the boisterous, powerful Isteriaeth Wren had come to know and love.

"It was today, you know," he said softly, to no one in particular. "K and I were to be married one week after she arrived here. It would have been today."

Wren opened her mouth, but words failed her. Elric blinked rapidly and glanced away, inhaling deeply through his nose before allowing the air to flow metered from his lips. Facing Wren squarely on the bed, he hesitated for only a moment and then held out his hands, palms up. Wren blinked back her own tears and straightened as much as she could muster to grasp them.

As if the touch was all he needed to draw strength, he nodded to himself and squeezed her hands. His eyes locked on Wren's, their brokenness on full display, yet she watched his courage rise and saw his timeless power flicker deep within them—proof and a promise of life. "If I had thought for one moment that her life could have been bound to mine, that I may have saved her, there would have been nothing to stop me. I would have done anything. I would have died trying everything. Because I loved her. Truly loved her. And a true love is not a selfish love. When you love someone, you do not let them go. You do not allow yourself to lose them. And you never let something trivial like death force you to release them."

Wren opened her mouth but the earnestness in his eyes stole her protests.

"Of all of the magic I have touched in my lifetime, there is not one I recognize more than love."

Love.

She *loved* Timothius? Even as she asked the question, she felt the words resonate in her soul. She loved Timothius. Somewhere along the way, in one of a thousand dances, in learning each other from the inside out, hidden behind masks and beneath cloaks, in forbidden rooms and dark stairwells, she had fallen in love with him. She had never spoken the words, but she knew with everything inside her it was true.

Did he feel the same? He had called her his heart, but did he mean that? Would he mean that even after he learned that his life was no longer his own? She needed to see him, to speak with—

A realization dawned and Wren's body tensed, her chest tugging where a fresh scar lay over her heart. "Elric, you said that Timothius is alive, but you didn't say he's fine. Where is he? What is wrong?"

Elric exhaled loudly. "I'm afraid he's had a worse awakening than you. He is currently in the Great House. The rebels have called a tribunal. He is being tried for treason."

"Treason?" Wren shrieked, rising far too fast from the bed and nearly falling over.

Elric was before her in an instant, steadying her. "How can anyone try Timothius for treason?" she rushed. "He has led this rebellion from the start. He has lost just as much as the rest of you."

Elric nodded sadly. "I know that and you know that, but when he was found in his uniform with the mask of the Rat King's toy in his possession, there was no other explanation."

Wren's eyes widened. "Then why are you sitting here exchanging pleasantries with me? Go defend him right now!"

Elric helped her take a step forward, her legs resembling those of a baby deer taking its first steps more than a rage-filled woman determined to reach the trial. "I tried," he swore, exasperation filling his voice. "I did all that I could, but I am only one word against all of his crimes. They will not listen to reason, and in the end, I cannot intervene for a life. They do not yet know that he is bound to you, and until we know for certain what this means, I dare not wonder what may befall either of you should they make an attempt on his life. His fate, and possibly your own, lies in their hands."

"Fate can go straight to hell. They will not steal him from me," Wren vowed, taking another trembling step forward. "Take me there. Right now."

Elric tipped his head back to look at the ceiling with a groan, but continued to walk backward, guiding Wren across the floor —her steps becoming more certain the closer they got to the door. "Best not invoke Hades on your first day as queen, my lady. The Rat King may seek us, but it will be your mouth that is the death of us all."

CHAPTER FORTY-TWO

*B*y the time they reached the rotunda in the heart of the Great House, Wren was able to walk on her own. Flinging the doors open, Elric at her back, she strode inside. She was unprepared to see it filled with elfin folk, humans, and soldiers all alike, but she paid them no mind and instead fixed her eyes on the man at the center of the room.

Timothius wore a simple white tunic, untucked over plain black breeches. Gone were the heavy, commanding boots of the soldier—replaced with the old, worn pair that had carried him through the wood at Wren's side. His hands were bound in front of him and his tunic had been tussled and pushed aside, revealing a scar on his chest that bore the same glimmer of gold as the line scored above Wren's heart. His curls were piled soft on the top of his head and he looked healthy—no worse for wear. Moreover, he looked like Timothius.

Her Timothius.

Wren strode across the room to him, and he raised his arms so that when she threw her own about his waist, he was able to bring them down around her neck in an embrace. Wren smiled, the longing to have him closer as overpowering as the amber and suede clinging to his skin. Even more commanding, however, was her need to steady herself against him to keep from collapsing.

"Are you well?" he whispered.

"Yes," she replied softly. "But please don't let me fall over."

"Never," he swore and pressed a quick kiss to her temple before raising his arms to release her. He stuck his elbow out to the side, but instead of looping her arm in his, Wren clasped her hands around his elbow, stroking the skin in soft circles that silently proclaimed her love. She turned to face the row of leaders sitting at the table before them.

Looking down the line, she made eye contact with each of the rebels and studied their faces, recognizing none until she came to the amused eyes of Nelluenya.

"Enya," she said in polite acknowledgment, "what exactly are you all doing with my captain?"

Nelluenya's lip twitched in an imperceptible smile and she inclined her head to Wren, but before she could speak, a man at the opposite end of the table stood.

"My lady, this soldier is the King's Glaive. Responsible for the demise of dozens of our friends and family. He is no captain. He is a toy now owned by us. And we seek to exact justice of our own."

Murmurs of affirmation rose around the room, and Wren pursed her lips, nodding. "The last time I checked, your name was not Enya. But thank you for explaining your intent. Now, once again I will ask: *Enya*, what are you doing with my captain?"

The man's brow furrowed, but Wren continued, "I know you do not know who I am. And I know more than anyone in this room that I am entirely undeserving of what I am about to claim, but it does not make it any more or less true.

"My name is Wren Klaver. I was born in a world far from here. One you did not know existed. And one night, during the solstice, I was given a gift that brought me here. I have spent every day since trying to return to my time—my world. But instead, I have managed to find my way home. And that home is where I stand in front of you right now.

"The gift given to me was a crystallum, saved until the perfect moment by my grandmother, Marion. She told me that it was a gift from my grandfather, but recently I have come to learn of them by different names—Vincienti, King of Inflamel, and Marionaldi, Queen of Inflamel and High Queen of the Trifolium Thrones."

A hushed gasp rippled around the room, widening the smile on Nelluenya's face and further confusing the rest of the leaders seated at the table. But still, Wren pressed on.

"The crystallum contained layers of magic, each revealed to me by a vision—a memory—that belonged to my grandmother. It showed me your history. *Our* history. And then it revealed the greatest weapon of all: a shard broken from the Trifolium Throne itself. I sought to use it against the Rat King. To bind him to myself so that he would never be able to touch another one of you again. But I have found that there is something greater than power, crowns, or even justice…. Love.

"When faced with the choice between it all, I chose love. A wise woman once told a dear friend of mine that she wished him love, and as a queen, it is all that I want for my people. It is the only power I crave for myself. But in order to start, I must claim what is mine."

She stepped forward, releasing Timothius's arm, and walked to the center of the room, pointing back to him and meeting the eye of every leader before her.

"This man is mine. He is bound to me in every way. At every time and in every realm, he is the other half of my heart, woven to my soul until we take our final breaths. He is not a possession, he is a gentleman, and he is the man I trust as captain of the guard to lead the rebellion in taking back our kingdom. It is fine if you disagree with me. I will allow it as long as you do not let me hear you speak ill of him. But to threaten him? To take the judgment of a rat out on the one burdened and damned by every loss? I will personally cut you down where you stand. To harm him is to wound me, to revile him is to despise me, and to come against him is to rise up against the queen you have waited for."

Murmurs echoed around the room, and many of the leaders looked to Nelluenya who continued to beam, affirming every last one of Wren's claims. One by one the leaders fell silent, and when the Guardian gave her an encouraging nod, Wren softened her posture and pressed on. "You have hoped, you have dreamed, and you have lost everything waiting for your queen to return. You loved her. But none of you have loved her so much as me. I seek to honor her in accepting the crown and taking her throne. And if you will have me, I will rule faithfully for all of my days, with this man by my side—not as a murderer, but as a defender. Together we will fight, and we will not stop until the Trifolium Thrones have risen and peace is returned to this realm. But you cannot have one without the other. There will never be me without him." She allowed the words to ring out in the room, glancing once more at every face. "So will you have us?"

The room was silent, and Wren was certain everyone could hear how fast her heart raced, yet still she waited, proud and unwavering, with Timothius by her side and Elric at her back. It was the same way they had walked through the snow. The way they had faced the darkness before they even knew what would become of their futures. Together, as one, ready for whatever lay ahead.

The man who had spoken first came around the table and stopped. He surveyed her for a lingering moment, then placed a hand on his heart and dropped to one knee.

"My queen," he said, all hint of anger, all promise of violence gone from his eyes.

One by one, each leader followed, and when Wren surveyed their gazes, their differing emotions caught in her chest. They were people of all ages, hardened by suffering and loss, watching their wildest dream and desperate hope be fulfilled in front of their very eyes. They were filled with joy and a fervent grief. And beneath it all was a fire burning within each one of them.

Every person in the room—elfin folk and human alike—followed suit, bowing in respect and honor until Nelluenya finally approached. Standing directly before Wren, she took her hand, removed a crescent ring from her own finger, and placed it in Wren's palm.

"I have guarded your kingdom to the best of my ability, Your Highness. Inflamel is now in your capable hands." And with a smile of love and pride, she dipped into a bow.

The moment she lowered to the ground, the elfin guard surrounding the room dropped the points of their swords to the floor with a clang, banging them four times upon the tile.

"Hail the Throne of Inflamel," came a cry.

"Hail!" echoed the room.

"Hail the rise of the Trifolium Thrones."

"Hail!" the room cried again.

"All hail the rightful ruler of Inflamel, Queen of Rebels and High Queen of the Trifolium Thrones, Her Majesty Wren of Clover."

The room erupted with rallying yells and cries of triumphant joy, and when Wren turned, she found both Elric and Timothius upon one knee. Locking eyes with Timothius, she smiled, but as she took a step toward him, the world spun. A strong arm caught her just before she hit the ground.

Then, the world went dark.

CHAPTER FORTY-THREE

The sun—high in the sky—streamed in from windows cut into the roof. A steady breeze turned a makeshift fan suspended from the center of the ceiling. Wren knew the room was not her own, but she did not recognize where she was either.

Beside her, reclined in a chair, Elric shook his head. "We must stop meeting like this," he said with a tired but playful smile.

Wren could not help but laugh, and she sat up, though this time much slower. "Where is—"

"Here, my heart," Timothius answered, walking from behind Elric to the side of the bed.

Elric glanced between them and stood, relinquishing his seat to Timothius. "I believe I shall leave you two alone for a moment. I will return soon."

Timothius nodded to him, and they clasped each other on the shoulder, their touch lingering a moment before Elric left the room and shut the door behind him. The room grew quiet, the only noise the faint chatter from outside the Great House,

and after examining the floor for a moment, Timothius's eyes found Wren.

"This isn't my bed," Wren rushed, trying to fill the awkward silence.

Timothius took the chair beside her, absently rubbing his wrists where the rope burns were still present. "It is not. Enya had you brought to her private quarters. As her queen, she wanted to ensure that you were safe, and as her friend, she wanted to allow us a moment of privacy."

Wren nodded and spun the ring that now rested on her index finger. "That is…that's so nice. It's good. That's…."

Timothius's hand came into view, resting heavily on Wren's and stilling her anxious movement. After a moment, she met his eyes. They were wide, imploring and expectant. And they terrified her. "What is it, my heart?" he asked, and her resolve quaked, shattering her composure.

"I fear this may be the worst thing I have ever done," she half-whispered, as if afraid to voice the words. "I wanted to save you. I wanted to protect you and selfishly keep you alive."

"I do not find that selfish. In fact, I am most appreciative," he said with a grin that nearly stopped her heart.

She wanted to smile in return, but she could only shake her head. "For over half your life you have been used. You've been a weapon. You've been manipulated and abused. And I want you to know that I see that. I recognize that in you, and because I do, it will never excuse what I've done. I'm no better than the Rat King."

"You cannot believe that."

"But I do," she cried. "I have put another scar on your body. I saved your life, but I stole your freedom. And I am so sorry."

"Wren—"

"No, you don't need to make me feel better. You may be bound to me forever, but I will not shackle you. We will survive this and I will make sure that you finally have the life you deserve—the chance to be your own person and set your own course in life. You deserve to be free. You deserve the life you've dreamed of."

Timothius was silent and pensive when he released her hands. Leaning back in the chair, he folded them in his lap. "Then I am afraid I was mistaken."

Wren's eyebrows drew together. "What do you mean?"

Timothius looked uncomfortably at the floor. "What you said in the forest. I thought— I had hoped it meant that your feelings for me…. That the feelings you had were…stronger." He swallowed, then added, "That they were closer to my own."

Wren's lips parted but she quickly closed them again, shutting her eyes to hide from the words she was about to say. "My feelings for you are ironclad. I am falling in love with you, Timothius. More every single moment. But it is because I love you that I want your happiness. You deserve the world, whether I am in it or not. I will not see you powerlessly handed from to one ruler to the next."

She opened her eyes and met his steady hazel. "Then you are giving me authority to choose?" he asked. "For myself? Apart from duty or magic vow?"

"I am."

"And you wish for me to decide in freedom, outside of obligation? You want my decision, chosen by my hand alone, to carve my path forward?"

"More than anything."

He leaned forward, and the searing passion in his eyes flushed her skin with heat. "Then, to speak plainly, you wish for me to follow my heart?"

Wren dared not speak. She only nodded.

"Then my answer is simple. I have spent my entire life fighting for an end. Allow me to fight for you—for our beginning."

"Timothius, that doesn't—"

"You wished for me to choose my own path. Do not pretend to change my mind now. You asked what I want and it is you— to never be parted from you for as long as we draw breath together."

Wren shook her head. "But would you have said this before? Would I have been what you wanted *before* I shoved a shard in your heart and bound your life to mine?"

"Unquestionably, yes."

"How do you know?"

"Because since the time we parted in this very domain my soul has begged for you. And from the moment I released you beside that well, I belonged to you. The only thing that has changed is that you no longer carry my heart, you *are* my heart. Every beat, every breath, all that I am is yours."

Wren was speechless, unable to form a coherent response, but still Timothius pressed on.

"There is one thing, however, that you are correct in saying. I do not wish to serve you as my queen." He rested his elbows on the bed beside her and took one of her hands in his own, drawing it to him. "I wish to care for you as my wife."

Her jaw dropped but he continued. "It is soon. Too soon. We have fallen too quickly for any sense, but I will not be moved from your side. I would have remained there for all of my days, and now even in death I am bound to you. I know peace because I need not worry myself with losing you. Where you go, I will go too. And if we do not move past this moment, if we are to remain nothing more than friends, I will happily serve you with the deepest affection I possess. You, too, deserve a choice in the midst of this world you were thrust into and the destiny that has been laid on your shoulders. Our lives have defied all odds and danced parallel to one another from the moment you set foot here. And now, they always shall. But they are not fully bound until we say so."

Silence blanketed the room, and Wren swallowed, her heart

beating an unsteady rhythm. To her surprise Timothius chuckled and rubbed his hand over his own chest. "I can feel your heart racing. It is making me nervous."

Wren smiled. "You don't strike me as the kind to be nervous over much."

"You would be correct," he replied. "However, you have always had a way of balancing me on the edge of a sword ever since I saw one at your throat in the Autumnal Wood."

Wren could not help but laugh softly. "I truly thought this was all a dream. And then I started bleeding and realized I'd made such a huge mistake."

Timothius shook his head at her, the flecks in his eyes dancing in unconditional love. "And yet you faced it all bravely. Every last unknown. You do not need anyone, Queen Wren of Inflamel, High Queen of the Trifolium Thrones. But I know what you dream of, and I do hope you choose to have me."

Wren slid forward and Timothius rose to meet her. She threw her arms around his neck, clutching him to her as if he might disappear at any moment. He held her just as tightly, and she realized then how much loss he had endured. Enough to know the impressive weight that belonging carried—the risk and the value earned in every second spent with someone. He spoke with his whole heart. And he spoke for her too.

"Do not ever leave me, Timothius Drossel," she whispered fiercely in his ear.

"Never," he swore. "I will never let you go."

The door flung open behind them, slamming the wall and forcing them apart.

"I am sorry," Elric said, face lined with worry. "I thought we had more time, but you must come at once. There is a messenger wandering the Vernal Wood. Sent by the Rat King. They are threatening to burn it if we do not come out and meet them."

CHAPTER FORTY-FOUR

*W*ren dressed quickly and walked with a purpose to the rotunda where Timothius and Elric waited with their weapons at their sides. Nelluenya met her at the door and, after securing her own belt filled with delicate blades around Wren's waist, said, "These are to show that you are girded with the might of the elfin guard. We will not step beyond the boundary, but we are behind you. If anything goes wrong...."

"It will not," Wren replied firmly. "I will make sure your home remains safe."

Nelluenya wrapped her in a hug, quickly releasing her and handing her a quiver filled with golden arrows. "Soar straight and true, my queen."

Wren nodded once and then strode to the boundary at the southernmost edge of the domain. She had not seen one since entering the Elfin Domain beside Elric for the first time, but its beauty still struck her. The boundary—and the world that lay within—was extraordinary and breathtaking and all hers. Her home. A part of her. And her heart swelled with pride as it bore that knowledge.

She stopped and turned to face Elric. "I need you to stay here."

His eyes widened and he stopped short. "No," he sputtered. "Not for a second."

"Elric, they cannot see you. Not yet. Your protection is as important as the elfin folk, if not more so because of all you are to me. Please. I am asking you to stand down."

"I will not."

She drew herself up and met his stubborn nature with a firm wall. "As your queen, I command it."

His jaw dropped and from her opposite side, Wren heard Timothius snicker. She whirled on him. "Is something funny? You want to stay in here too?"

He only laughed harder, looking at Elric. "I believe that is the top bed for me tonight."

Elric's chest puffed as Wren glanced between them. "You... what?"

Timothius sighed. "We had a wager on the first moment you would wield your power as queen. He bet you would use it against me first, but I knew it would be him. So tonight, he sleeps on the bottom cot."

Wren, thoroughly amused at the thought of the ageless Isteriaeth and the most feared guard in the kingdom sharing a bunk bed and squabbling above who slept on the top, suppressed her glee over the exchange and gave each one a good-natured shove. "We will talk about this later, but for now you stay," she said, poking a finger in Elric's chest. "And you, with me," she said, pointing to Timothius.

"Yes, mother," Elric muttered, and though she threw him a glare, she wrapped her arms around his neck and gave him one final squeeze, squared up in front of the gate, and walked through.

She didn't need to look, she could feel Timothius at her back, their heart beating steady, calm, and true. She was unsure if it was his rhythm setting their pace or her own, but she was confident that it did so only because of the man beside her. Not because of who he was, but because he was hers.

They traveled through the trees, scanning their surroundings for the first sign that they had traveled outside of Nelluenya's magic, and were surprised to discover they did not need to go far.

When they stepped into a clearing, they met a figure not bearing the mask of a snarling wolf or a sniveling mouse, but of an owl. Musannulos raised his head. His eyes fired daggers as they approached, but Wren just smiled saccharinely.

"You have something His Majesty would like returned," he tittered from behind the mask, tossing his head toward Timothius.

"Shame for him," Wren said in a clipped tone. "I don't like to share."

"No, you only steal what is not yours."

"I don't need to steal what already belongs to me. This world, these people—they are mine. And I am here to take them back."

He sneered but did not reply. Ripping open the scroll in his fists, he read aloud, "His Majesty King Phillipae Vasileio I, Warrior King of Inflamel and Ruler of the Middle Kingdom, hereby demands the surrender of one Florence Klaver, not of this world and scourge on our land. You will come willingly and quietly to surrender the power in your possession and face your fate with honor and integrity.

"Upon your arrival, he shall accept the harbored fugitive and traitor to the crown, one Glaive, to hereby be tried for treason, decommissioned, stripped of identity, and hanged from the wall for a fortnight henceforth. Any beings found to be harbored with the traitor will be drawn out, and in His Majesty's merciful reign, offered a mask of disgrace, forever to be worn as a sign of indentured servitude to our king. Any who refuse will be relegated to His Majesty's dungeon until the end of their days."

He stopped and looked up from the scroll to meet Wren's bored stare. She raised an eyebrow. "And if we do not?"

He paused for a moment, as if surprised she was not tripping over herself to fulfill the king's every wish. Glancing back to the scroll, he continued, "Should these demands be denied, the king shall hereby carry out the execution of a single resident of the esteemed Inflamel City in the number of one per hour and their heads shall be displayed upon the rampart until the rebellion has surrendered."

The scroll snapped shut and he stood at ease, his animalistic stare fixed on her, waiting for a reply. Wren could feel eyes on her. From behind, those who lingered out of sight but were ready to rise in her name, and from the forest before her, hiding and waiting to attack should she deny. They would not let her say no without a fight, but she did not want war here. Not with the enemy this close to a place that held so many people she loved.

"Were we provided a deadline?" she asked, shifting casually from one foot to the other.

Mussanulos's head tilted. "A deadline?"

"To make our decision. Were we given any time to decide our fates or only an ultimatum?"

His shoulders tensed and he mirrored her, shifting from one foot to the other. "No time was outlined. His Majesty demands an answer."

Wren clicked her tongue and shook her head. "That does not sound like a merciful king. Has he forgotten his place with his people? Or are the tales of his benevolence untrue? I mean, everyone forgets something from time to time, so I would understand if he had not remembered to include a timeline. Because I'm sure he meant to. If he hadn't, that would make him dishonest. Untruthful. One might even call him...a rat."

Wolf- and mouse-masked guards alike stepped from the trees, their swords gleaming in the sunlight, and Wren felt her heart thrum faster, though she herself remained calm. It was not her adrenaline beginning to mount.

Glancing subtly over her shoulder, she made eye contact with Timothius who, on the outside, appeared as relaxed as ever, despite his hand now resting on the pommel of his sword. She could feel his readiness, the coiling energy prepared to snap and surge through anyone who might take aim. He looked back at her and raised one eyebrow, awaiting her direction, but she only smiled at him and said, "I am never going to get tired of seeing your face."

Turning back to Musannulos, she stepped forward. "The full moon. In six nights, we will meet the king himself on the meadow and provide our answer. But he will stay executions until dawn the next day. And if we fail to meet him, he may carry out his demands."

The owl-man froze, as if immobilized, considering her words. She did not move to press forward or stand down. She stood strong—bravely—and waited until his hands snapped to his sides.

"Very well," he sputtered. "But if we do not see you in front of our gates under the light of the full moon, the king will exact justice as is his right."

Wren snorted. "I doubt that, but we will be there before he can find someone else to do it for him. It has been a pleasure negotiating with you, but you are no longer welcome here. Now leave."

She waited for him to turn, watched as he walked away, but when he reached the line of guards that stood behind him, he began to laugh. It was a raucous and cruel noise, and though she did not allow her face to betray her, Wren's blood ran cold.

"You believe yourself to be so strong. So ready to face what

377

lies ahead of you," he chided. "But you do not know how to rule from one step ahead. Let this serve as a lesson to you."

He raised a hand and archers stepped from the trees with bows at the ready, the guards at their back holding torches. The telltale pop and hiss of a match being struck was the only warning given before their cloth-bound arrows were ignited. Flames sparked, their embers floating to the ground, and the air filled with smoke. But instead of aiming at Wren or Timothius, the soldiers pivoted in different directions, aimed for the trees and the bushes, then loosed their bows.

Wren's eyes widened and she took a small step back as fire engulfed the leaves, racing down the vines and catching on the grass and flowers surrounding their bases.

Mussanulos's laughter cackled above the crackle of dry branches and the howling shouts of the mouse and wolf soldiers running through the wood with their torches, leaving a trail of fire behind them.

Wren whirled, but the elfin guard was already surging through the gate, some carrying armfuls of thick cloaks and others ferrying pails of water to the fire consuming the Vernal Wood. Wren watched in awe as some cast cloaks on the ground, Timothius joining them in an attempt to choke out the fire before it could spread or burn. She discarded her own cloak and grabbed a bucket, planting herself beside the elfin folk where they sent water arching into the trees to ease the flames.

Enya, she whispered to herself, watching with pride as it refilled with water, ready to be thrown upon the blaze again.

Rushing to the center of the clearing, Elric stood and surveyed the world around them with wide eyes. His eyes found Wren and he was at her side in an instant. "Can you summon a hose or something?" she shouted above the fray. "If I describe it, could you bring one here?"

He shook his head. "I cannot. But…." Slapping his hands together, they sparked and small stars fell from the building sapphire smoke snaking from his palms. Wren watched in awe while the cloud billowed larger and larger in the clearing, blue consuming the air, deep and vibrant against the angry orange, and then just at its edge, it started to shimmer a faint emerald green.

Thunder clapped overhead—loud enough to halt everyone in the clearing, enough to make Wren jump, but only enough for Elric to open his eyes and look to the sky. Thick drops of rain started to fall, splashing off armor and metal, staining cloaks, tunics, and gowns. And slowly, a burgeoning hiss filled the wood with smoke. The fire was extinguished.

Wren stared at Elric with wide eyes. "I thought you couldn't control the elements?"

He looked bewildered, but through his dazed fog, he grinned. "I cannot. But apparently I can summon a raincloud."

Wren stood astonished and then, with a bubbling giggle, she started to laugh. Beside her, Elric did the same, and even the elfin guard surrounding them laid down their buckets and cloaks to let the rain soak their skin.

They took a few moments to walk farther away from the realm, the elfin guard never leaving Wren's side, and it was sobering to take in how much the fire had consumed in the wake of the king's fleeing forces. But even then, beneath the charred earth, green was already beginning to sprout again.

With no sign of wolf, mouse, or owl lurking anywhere, it meant that the clock was ticking. And they needed to act before time ran out.

CHAPTER FORTY-FIVE

"Our forces are small in number, but far stronger than the Rat King would perceive," said Timothius, leaning over the table that had been erected in Nelluenya's private quarters.

It was well after dark, and the Elfin Domain had long since fallen silent. Wren sat at one end of the table, opposite the Elfin Guardian at the other. Between them were Timothius, Elric, the commander of the elfin guard, and a man Wren had learned was called Sir Shelburne—the rebel leader who had led the tribunal against Timothius. She kept a cold eye on him, and though she could sense his discomfort under her stare, she refused to afford him personal space or the benefit of the doubt. Not yet.

"Our disadvantage," Timothius continued hesitantly, "is that the muster of our forces resides within the city walls."

"Then we must find a way in," Wren said. "Is there a way up through the wells? Does the water level ever rise?"

Timothius nodded. "It will be higher under the full moon, but not nearly high enough to climb into the wellhouse. The city is impenetrable, save through the drawbridge gate."

"Would there be a way for us to draw them out?" Wren wondered aloud. "To lower the bridge so we can sneak inside?"

"And go where, exactly?" inquired Sir Shelburne. "It would be hard to walk into the square unnoticed with welcome, it will be nearly impossible to enter undetected."

"Unless you draw them out with enough force to distract them," the elfin commander said deeply. "A sleight of hand."

"And even then, we must realize that the Rat King will not be with his army," Timothius added quietly. "He will not even be on the wall. He will remain inside the castle, cloistered in his quarters. Waiting."

"Waiting for what?" Wren asked.

"Victory," Timothius replied, meeting her eyes. "Or you."

"You truly wish to face him?" Nelluenya's voice commanded the attention of everyone in the room, but her sole focus was on Wren. "Even knowing everything that lies at stake?"

"There is no other way," Wren conceded, a pang in her heart not for her own life but for Timothius's. "But I wish—"

"I would not have it another way," he interrupted, and though she avoided his eyes, she knew he had felt her pain innately. "Bonded or not, I would be by your side every step of the way."

"And you two would face him alone?" Nelluenya prodded. "Even now, understanding what he may be?"

Words failed on Wren's tongue. She had divulged to them what her grandmother had said about the Rat King—that he was one of the fabled Kollapsars of old—but the question remained as to which being of darkness hid beneath his skin.

Would he be Axion, a dark warrior of old, or Vacare, a shapeless demon born of nightmares? It was also possible that he could be less fable and more a monster—Eoten, an impenetrable behemoth, or a Hrotesk with the wings of a bat, the claws of a hawk, and rows upon rows of needled teeth. Or could it be that he was something more? Something as unfathomable as

Wren's own return to this realm. And if he was, who were they to stand against him?

The voice of the elfin commander interrupted her musing. "To split the forces would be a great risk. I do not know if the rebellion alone has enough force to stand in anything other than a united front."

"What do you mean the rebellion alone?" she asked, staring at him pointedly. "Will the elfin folk not be with us?"

Silence descended upon the room, and all focus slowly shifted to Nelluenya, who looked at Wren with sorrow pooling in her golden eyes.

"We have remained safe and hidden for nearly four centuries," she said, shaking her head. "I cannot, we cannot, break with our people to stand beside you. If we were to fall, there would be none other to guard the realm—to foster attempts to return it to its rightful heir."

Wren laughed in disbelief. "I am the heir. What realm will you have left if I fall? You said yourself that you will fade if I do not succeed."

"And yet it is the decision of our people," the elf replied firmly, her eyes downcast. "We shall remain here, protect the people who have taken shelter inside our borders, and if all fails, we shall aid their escape by boat, across the strait and into Grimoira."

Elric's head whipped to the side. "Grimoira has long since closed their borders. They harbor their own and shun all others. There are rumors of why, though none know for certain. But those who enter are never permitted to leave again."

"Obarian, then."

"Obarian does not even care for their own. They will not accept anyone at their border, especially none of Awduron origin. You are currency to them—to be bartered, sold, or enslaved."

Timothius nodded. "It is true. Word reached the Rat King

that they are on the brink of rebellion themselves. It is said that their ruler is ill and his daughter is set to take the throne, but the people are restless and we have inspired them to action. It is only a matter of time before they descend into war."

"All the more reason for us to succeed, then," said Wren, standing. "Admittedly, I don't know much about battle strategy and I do not know anything about war, but what I do know is that we need a way into the city. We are hopeless if I do not breach that wall."

"If *we* do not breach the wall," Timothius urged, and when Wren looked at him, his face was firm. "I will be by your side. Straight to the king."

Wren knew there was no use in fighting it and she doubted she would be any match for the king on her own with what little skill she had. So, as much as it terrified her, she knew that where they went, they went together.

"I can create a diversion," Elric said. "Draw them out and—"

"No," said Wren and Timothius at the same time.

Elric snorted and shook his head. "I do not believe I was requesting permission. For me to conceal myself earlier was sensible, but for me to remain behind while you risk your lives to enter the city is foolishness. I will not sit idly by and allow my friends to die for the freedom of a power I am not able to use. I will not—" He broke off, voice cracking, but he cleared his throat and pressed on. "I will not allow K to die in vain. She gave everything to save you, Wren. I can do no less."

Wren sank back into her chair, unable to fend off the overwhelming defeat settling on her shoulders. She knew it was war. She knew she was out of her depth. She knew that people would die. But she could not see a way in which they could succeed without great risk.

She nodded in silent agreement and looked to Timothius who did the same. "All right," he said, unrolling a map of the city. "What exactly do you have in mind?"

Elric smiled and with a flick of his wrist, he summoned his dhust, the stars now dancing in a sky of sapphire clouds. "Perhaps I can bring in some old friends."

❄

WREN STOOD on the bank of the river with a few hundred able-bodied rebels at her back—men and women alike—all ready to fight for their freedom. She looked upon the gardens that she had come to love, upon people she longed to see again. She couldn't bear to think of what would befall the Elfin Domain and the surrounding wood should she fail.

She could not fail. It was not an option.

Nelluenya stepped forward and extended her hands, which Wren accepted with a squeeze of reassurance and affection. To her surprise the Elfin Guardian was unable to keep tears from spilling over her lower lids. "Wren, forgive me," she murmured.

Wren shook her head fervently. "You have nothing to be sorry for. But please promise me something."

"Anything, Your Highness."

"If we fail, do not stay here. If there is a chance for you beyond me, then run. And do not stop running. Do not stay here and face your fate. Don't give up hope."

Nelluenya looked at Wren with awe and shook her head. "We are fortunate to be led by someone so willing to give of themselves, yet still thinking only of those they protect. Your grandmother would be proud."

Wren blinked back her own tears. "Promise me, Enya."

The Elfin Guardian took a deep breath and then nodded once. "I promise."

With one final bow, Nelluenya released her hands and moved to Timothius at Wren's side. She produced a long ribbon the shade of the water within the domain. "Will you carry my ribbon as a sign of good faith and affection between our people?"

Timothius shook his head. "It is an honor, and one I will carry with me in spirit, but I cannot carry your token. There is but one I will bear in faithfulness and truth, and it is her favor alone that I will wear with pride."

Nelluenya smiled and nodded, turning to Elric. "Will you, Fallen Star?"

Elric inclined his head. "It would be my honor."

She wove the ribbon beneath the strap of his armlet and tied it firmly in place. Leaning forward, she kissed his forehead, and then stepped back, extending her hand to Timothius, who bowed and pressed his lips to the back of it.

"May your parting be regarded well," she said, smiling upon her friends.

Turning once again to Wren, her face was firm and strong, all hints of emotion gone, leaving behind the visage of a fierce Guardian. And when she spoke, her voice echoed on the breeze to every corner of the domain. "With fidelity and courage, may you march to battle. And may you stand beside one another to victory or death."

A cry rose from the elfin folk.

A rally.

A hope.

A fortifying promise.

Wren raised her chin, and with one last look, she led the march from the Elfin Domain toward the castle and to war.

CHAPTER FORTY-SIX

*T*he highway was devoid of any beings, masked or otherwise, causing the fine hairs across Wren's skin to rise with apprehension. But it was not until the rebellion's forces separated—one half going deep into the Aestival Forest and the other vanishing within the gold-and-orange trees of the Autumnal Wood—that she allowed herself to breathe.

They had traveled night and day without incident and now, days later, they stood where the forests met the edge of the meadow and looked out through the trees upon Inflamel City. With each camp settled in on either side of the highway, they took their rest and waited for night to fall once again—the last before the full moon.

Within the Autumnal Wood, Wren could not help but stand for a minute and gaze around, recalling every memory her grandmother had shown her of her time here. So much joy and sorrow, levity and loss. Being there brought her comfort and made her feel closer to her grandmother once again. But it also filled her with a longing fear that she may not live to see her own life beyond the following forty-eight hours.

Everyone had retired quietly, far enough within the wood to

hide them from sight, in hopes that they may rest hidden through the following day. But as Wren lay with open eyes, staring at the roof of her tent, a sharp and keening pain tore through her chest, right above her heart.

Sitting straight up on her cot, she gasped. It was not a pain of injury, and she was certain she was not having a heart attack, but the throb remained and continued to ache deeper and deeper until realization struck her.

Timothius.

She swung her legs off the bed and pulled her boots on, then a cloak over the simple brown dress that she'd chosen to sleep in, just in case they were raised to war suddenly in the night. Peering out from her tent, she found the camp quiet with only the men standing guard surrounding them. But when the groaning in her chest persisted, she moved forward, following a path out of the encampment and into the forest.

Stealing through the night on silent feet, she had never been more thankful for the soft, velvet leaves freshly fallen beneath her boots. They were a far cry from the dried, brown crumbles that had clung to her slippers when she ran for her life in that very same wood.

Just ahead, a hooded figure crossed under a beam of light from the moon that was nearing its peak. She cut sharply to the left and followed him from a distance, concerned why he would be slipping away in the middle of the night. Alone. But it was not until the trees began to thin and she saw a glimpse of the meadow beyond that her heart caught in her throat. Sure enough, she came upon a small gate, propped open, with rows of unharvested crops leading right up to the edge of the wood— and the Flugés' cottage.

Wren hesitated, wondering if she should intrude. She understood now why there was so much pain in his heart and knew he needed this moment. But she also recalled the way he had sought comfort in her eyes, in her words, the night he'd stained her dress with blood while they had danced. And she could not bring herself to walk away from him any more now than she had that night.

She had chosen him then. She would choose him now. She would choose him for the rest of her life.

Stepping into the clearing, she followed the pathway to the house and the back door that was still ajar to the shell of the burned-out home. The rear wall, still mostly erect, served as cover for her to peer inside and find Timothius standing with his back to her, looking around the room.

The gnawing pain in her chest eased just enough to make way for a bittersweet joy, and she wondered what he was thinking. Growing up here as a child? Could he see memories playing out all around like the ones Wren had witnessed from the crystallum? When was the last time he had set foot in his home? Would the love from his past sustain him through the wreckage he stood in now?

Timothius stepped carefully across the floor, righting a chair as he went, and stopped before the mantle to gaze at the clock. With two fingertips, he closed the face on its hinges and then opened the glass that had been fogged and stained from the smoke. He twirled the hands around and around and did not stop until they reached the top of the hour with a melodic chime.

From the clock, two small figures rose. They bowed to one another and then moved forward with soft, mechanical clicks until their outstretched arms met. Their right hands joined beside their cheeks and the left hand of the princess—holding out her skirt at length—left a perfect opening for the hand of the prince to pass through and rest on her waist. The mechanism began to rotate, clicking out the cadence of a waltz and carrying them in twelve circles before it came to a stop, returned the dolls to their starting positions, and lowered them out of sight once again.

Timothius's shoulders hunched and he rested a hand on the mantel. Burying his forehead in the other, his body started to shake with shuddering, broken sobs.

Wren didn't know if the splitting in her heart was her own or his, but she could not stop herself from entering what was left of the cottage, crossing the room, and laying a hand on his shoulder.

To her surprise, instead of freezing or shying away, he turned and embraced her, holding her tightly to his chest as if he needed her to stand. She held him all the same and ran her fingers up and down his back in soft strokes.

There were no words exchanged between them. There did not need to be. She did not need or want to ask what had happened in their final moments—what horrors would haunt him for the rest of his days. She felt his pain, unfathomable and endless, and knew that while she could not change it, she could remain beside him, show him how worthy he was of every good thing, and after each nightmare, remind him how to dream.

They remained that way until the pain in their heart eased and the tears flowing from their eyes slowed. With one final look about the cottage—at his childhood home—Timothius took a fortifying breath and released it steadily. He extended his arm to Wren, and she did not hesitate to take it, walking beside him quietly to the camp. He paused by his own tent, but she continued walking, not letting go of his elbow. And it was not until they were safely inside, the only light between them the glow of what one small candle allowed, that she spoke.

"I do not want you to serve me. And I am not content for you to make me your wife alone. I love you, Timothius. Every part—seen and unseen, broken and whole—and I never want to be separated from you. When we win this war, when we find the Thrones and raise the Trifolium sigil above the keep once more, Inflamel will need its king. So share with me, crown and kingdom. Rule with me. Dream with me. And say you'll love me until our heart stops beating."

His lips were on hers in an instant, their heart racing as one, and he parted only long enough to reply, "I love you, Wren Klaver, and I shall never stop. On the other side of this, come what may, will you become my bride?"

She nodded and her smile threatened to consume her whole. "Yes. Yes, I will."

He kissed her again, deeper this time, and somewhere lost within each other, Wren reached up and began to unlace his tunic.

Timothius gently stilled her hands and broke their kiss, resting his forehead on hers, utterly breathless.

Wren swallowed, suddenly feeling self-conscious, but when she moved to step away, he clutched her waist and pulled her firmly against him. "No, my heart, stay. Stay here, please. It is not you. I do not— What I mean to say is I have not...I have never...."

Realization dawned in Wren's mind and her eyes widened. "I'm so sorry, I shouldn't have been so forward. I didn't think... with my head."

Timothius chuckled. "I should like you to be more forward. I want to do what is right by you, and you are worthy of more than a cot or the flimsy privacy of a tent." His hand slipped to her elbow and they both watched his thumb tenderly trace lines along the inside. The simple action, so natural to them, soothed and ignited a fire inside Wren at once, and when his eyes met hers again, she saw the same heat bringing the green flecks within the hazel to life. "When I claim you, there will be no one near enough to hear. Your heart, your body, each touch, every noise you make, I want them all to be mine alone."

Wren's heart swelled, but she hesitated. "Would it worry you — Would you think less of me to know that I've...already...."

He shook his head firmly. "I do not care. Your choices were

your own. It does not matter now. I could never see you as less than the woman I love."

Wren laughed softly and allowed herself to be drawn back against the curve of his lips. "Do you always say such perfect things?"

He pressed a kiss to the skin along her jaw, another in the curve below her ear, then murmured, "Only to you. You are worthy of every good thing."

She pulled back enough to look him in the eye. "And you are worthy of love. Always. For the rest of our days."

They stood together for a while longer, exchanging soft, quiet, lingering kisses in the dark, and when Timothius turned to leave, Wren held onto his arm. "Wait here," she said, rushing over to her pack.

Digging through it, she found what she was looking for and returned. Looping a long ribbon the color of the lilacs in the Elfin Domain around his neck, she smiled bashfully. "This somehow made it from the castle all the way to the domain. I didn't know why at the time, but I do now. Timothius Drossel, will you honor me by wearing this into battle tomorrow? Will you accept it as a token of my love?"

He stared at her, his eyes soaking in every inch of her face, before he nodded, and in a voice thick with awe, said, "I have found my great love, and it is you."

Recalling the words from what felt like a lifetime ago, Wren smiled and pressed another kiss to his lips. "And you are my endless dream."

CHAPTER FORTY-SEVEN

The rebel infantry stood before the forests' edge, overlooking the meadow and the city that were now bathed in the light of the full moon. Their ranks extended back into the shadow of the trees and they looked on while soldiers lined the battlement two and three deep. The drawbridge lowered slowly and still more poured into the meadow, dwarfing their numbers.

The great door raised with a groan and when it shut with a loud *clang*, the masks of wolves and mice alike began to taunt and jeer.

"My Queen," came a voice to Wren's right.

She startled and turned to face Sir Shelburne.

"The people wait on your word," he said with a dip of his head.

"My word?"

"Yes. You are their queen. They seek to hear from you before they enter into battle."

A nervousness that had nothing to do with the army facing them and everything to do with her own inadequacies came over Wren. "What could I possibly say to them?"

Timothius was in front of her in an instant. "Rally their courage. Bring them hope. You are their beacon, shine radiantly so they may see it in their mind's eye through the darkness they shall face."

She swallowed hard, grasping for protest but coming up empty. "I am not prepared for this," she whispered.

He tipped up her chin, and with her ribbon rippling gently against his collar, pressed a reassuring kiss to her lips. "No, but you were born for it."

Taking a shaky breath, Wren nodded and then turned, squaring her shoulders and walking out before the rebel army— her army. She looked from face to face in the torchlight, from man to woman, their determination, worry, fear, and courage all worn so bravely. So beautifully. It rallied her soul and lit a fire in her bones. These were her people. They had endured, and now they would leave their mark.

"All your lives, you have been faceless. Masked. Treated with contempt. Your freedom, every choice, was stolen and used as a weapon against you. But that ends today," she said, her voice ringing clear and true through the night. "You have chosen to be here. You have chosen to rise up for your kingdom and your queen. For the Trifolium Thrones, and for the generations that will come after us. But there is another decision to be made."

Her eyes flicked to Timothius, to the love and pride glowing on his face, and her words grew stronger. "Someone once told me that there are many small deaths before the end. Some are silent. Others are loud. We do not control when we face it, but we are left with the power to choose how we are remembered. So I ask you now, which will you choose? Shall we go silently, decaying from the inside out beneath a mask? Or shall we go screaming our names to the heavens lest the Rat King dare forget who we are?"

With weapons raised, a mighty war cry resounded across the clearing to the walls of the city. Turning to face it, Wren focused on the tallest spire and drew her own sword. With Sir Shelburne to her left and Timothius to her right, she stood ready and waiting.

She did not have to wait long. An eerie howl mounted on the wind, a baying call that sent a familiar chill down her spine.

Elric had done it. He had summoned wealdwolves.

She glanced to Timothius and he met her wide eyes with a shrug and a smirk. "It would appear they are objects after all."

Shouts of alarm rose from the battlement and soldiers facing the southern side fled their posts in droves. The mouse-masked soldiers already amassed in the meadow looked around in terror, but the wolf-faced guards commanded their attention. Urging them to advance, they began to march as one.

More howls broke the air, their screams deafening, and Wren turned to Timothius. "How many did he bring here?"

Timothius shook his head. "I do not know."

"And what if they come after us?"

"That is not the bridge we are to cross. However...."

Timothius nodded, and Wren surveyed the city once more. The drawbridge had started to lower again. She took a deep breath, looked to Sir Shelburne, and gave him one final nod.

He turned and raised his sword to the rebels behind him, giving the signal for them to march.

Timothius drew his sword, but Wren chose to sheathe hers, nocking an arrow in her bow instead. Weapons pointed to the ground at their sides, they faced each other one last time.

"Remember, they are weakest on the left flank," Timothius said urgently. "We make our way there and when there is an opening, we slip inside the city. The plan is not to fight our way to the castle—we run."

She nodded fiercely. "I am with you."

Grasping her waist, he pulled her to him and kissed her deeply without a care of who stood around or what they witnessed. Breaking apart, his eyes crossed her face with reverence. "I cannot wait to see you upon the Throne," he said, causing Wren to blush.

"Save it for later," she replied with a wink, and together they strode into the heart of the rebel lines.

At the behest of Sir Shelburne, the rebels doubled their speed toward the king's guards who were already running to meet them in a wave of snarls and sharp teeth. Wren let her fear give way to rage, casting down her doubt and insecurity to be trampled beneath the rush of adrenaline and bold confidence. Her people were with her, her heart was beside her, and her crown lay ahead of her. It was time.

There was a heartbeat of silence. A moment where the only thing heard or felt was the second before. And in a collision of iron and steel, might and power, battle cries and dying screams, the past met the present head on and both sides fractured into the unknown.

Wren tried not to count the dying around her—tried not to focus on who was lost and from what side of the fight. With her eyes fixed ahead, where Timothius was carving their path through the melee, she launched arrow after arrow. The quiver on her back, crafted from dhust, afforded her endless bolts, though her muscles burned with every shot. The air ripped too quickly in and out of her lungs, loud in her ears amid the overwhelming turbulence of war. Every yard gained was a struggle, a battle unto itself, but she carried the blood of the Throne—of her grandmother—in her veins, and she refused to surrender.

A man fell behind her, clipping the back of her heels and causing her to trip. It was when she regained her footing that she realized he bore the mask of a mouse. She had been that close to falling to his blade.

Another guard, this one with the face of a wolf, blocked her path. He raised his sword like an axe, ready to bring it down upon her shoulders, but at the last moment, a rebel soldier slashed through his knees, sending him to the ground with his weapon harmlessly at his side.

Fear sank its claws into Wren's mind. Her senses were overwhelmed and everything in her being begged for a respite from the endless shouting, crashing blows, and pain-filled cries being cut off too soon. She took a deep breath, but the moment her fear started to ease, reality rushed back in with a jolt. Whipping around, she searched frantically for a head of curls towering over the rest. She found none.

"Timothius!" she screamed.

Another guard outfitted in a wolf mask broke through the line and made straight for her. Unable to nock an arrow, she hooked her bow to her back and freed her sword, drawing it in time to deflect the weapon arching toward her head. The impact was jarring, but she absorbed it the best she could, holding her ground until he retreated enough to advance again.

She tried to stay focused on his movement and searched for an opening, but it was as if the wall of bodies had closed in around them. There was no air, no life. Her lungs drew in only death, and the world was beginning to blur at the edges under the unforgiving pace of her ravaged pulse.

Finding the mark she had been looking for, Wren attacked, but the guard blocked her sword, locking their blades in the process. In one swift motion, he swiped out with a dagger in his other hand. Wren moved at the last moment, the tip of the knife slitting her skirt but failing to find flesh beneath. He swung again, higher this time, and she leaned back, barely recovering before he swiped again.

An arrow soared over her shoulder and lodged itself firmly in the man's chest, stunning him. Another followed, and then another, fired rapidly with expert precision, passing her with tiny wisps of a breeze.

Wren freed her sword from the wolf-mask guard and he collapsed, motionless. She spun around and met the eyes of Sir

Shelburne. He stood with his bow hanging from one hand and placed his other on his heart, nodding to her with a measure of respect.

Then, to her horror, he fell to one knee.

Wren screamed and rushed forward to catch him, steadying him as he collapsed. That was when she noticed that his side had been gouged open, his blood soaking the very ground that he had stood upon to save her life.

"Sir Shelburne," she gasped. "You saved my life. Let me get you out of here, let me help you."

The man smiled and blood started to trickle from his nose and eyes. "You already have, my queen. You already have."

Tears filled Wren's eyes, spilling down her cheeks as he took his last breath, his pride leaving the peaceful ghost of a smile upon his face.

A rage loud enough to drown out the surrounding battle surged through Wren's body, burning her, consuming her entirely. She had not known him long—she had barely had the chance to learn anything about him—yet he had given his life for her. His loss ricocheted in her chest and loosed the shrapnel already left behind by Kathrina, the Flugés, even her grandmother, all the way down through time to every Isteriaeth, every being who had perished for the fleeting hope of freedom.

She looked to the sky and screamed.

Ripping his sword from his belt, she stood with a blade in each hand, and like a warrior of old, she descended upon the king's advancing army, mercy forgotten and fury in her eyes.

Elric's words of advice from their training so long ago rang in her ears and she sliced the air around her, slashing a path to where Timothius fended off two wolf-masked guards at once. His eyes grew wide taking in the sight of her, a bloodied sword in each hand, but together they made quick work of the guards and when he opened his mouth to speak, a rallying cry rose from the rampart. They both turned to see a fresh wave of soldiers surging around the city and into battle.

Wren's head whipped wildly around the meadow. "Why aren't they heading for the Deorc Weald? We were supposed to draw them away from the battle, not into it."

Timothius searched the meadow. "I do not see wealdwolves or hear them. And I can no longer find Elric."

Wren's lips parted in horror and reality started to creep in, but Timothius grasped her by the shoulders, demanding her focus. "We stay the course. The sacrifice out here is for naught if we do not make it inside that city. We must move."

She nodded firmly and, side by side, they continued to fight their way through the conflict and toward the moat. In a stroke of luck, the drawbridge was lowered; however, the more guards she saw pour from the mouth of the city, the more Wren's hope began to falter. She looked back over the meadow and watched the rebellion's final line descending from the shadow of the trees. They were not even half the might of the fresh-footed guards who had entered the fray from the opposing side.

They were outnumbered, had lost too many warriors, their diversion was gone, and they were still not any closer to finding a way inside the city wall.

As if reading her thoughts, Timothius met Wren's eyes, his own filled with determination. "We will have to fight our way to the drawbridge."

Wren steeled her resolve and nodded, sheathing her sword and gripping Sir Shelburne's blade with both hands. She took a deep breath, closed her eyes for a heartbeat, and then opened them with reignited fervor. "One…. Two…."

Bells rang loud and clear across the meadow. Their pealing bounced off the walls of the city and the trees of the forests alike—echoing all the way to the seas and shaking the ground itself. Every head turned, forgetting the battle at hand, and

Wren and Timothius spun around, still holding on to one another.

There, at the mouth of the road between the Autumnal Wood and Aestival Forest, iron armor twisting and glowing like lightning beneath the blaze of the torches they carried, stood the elfin guard. At their head, wearing a dress of flowing turquoise and armor wrought of bronze—the embodiment of the Elfin Domain itself—was Nelluenya. Her raven hair was woven into long braids down the length of her back, and she held a sword in one hand and a scythe in the other.

And with a cry that shattered a lifetime of imprisonment and a world of estrangement, she led the full might of the elfin guard upon the City of Inflamel.

CHAPTER FORTY-EIGHT

The elfin guard overtook the battle in a wave of graceful vengeance, making quick and effective work of the Rat King's army in a dance that could have only been perfected by ages of lying in wait—preparing for the moment they would breathe the air of the free world again. Wren could not fathom the shift that must have occurred after they departed, but whatever had transpired was enough for the entire force to move as one. In turn, their show of might rallied the failing rebel infantries to rise with new energy and return to their attack with an undimmed fire.

A tug on her arm brought Wren back to the now, and she followed Timothius who led them toward the drawbridge. The soldiers coming from within the city had slowed and the bridge itself was now raised two feet from the ground, the last soldiers leaping from it and into the fray. Timothius ran ahead and jumped on, clearing the edge easily, though it continued to rise higher. Driving his sword into the wood, he anchored his foot against it and leaned over the side. Wren ran to meet him, and dropping Sir Shelburne's sword, she launched high enough to catch his forearm and lodge her own firmly in his grasp.

R.V. WILBUR

Shouts sounded from the rampart, and Wren swung her legs wildly when they left the ground. She grabbed the lip of the drawbridge with her opposite hand in an attempt to hoist herself onto the door rising higher and more vertical by the second. Timothius held her fast, fighting the gravity that threatened to drag her down and trying to wrestle her over the edge while remaining balanced on his blade. Arrows struck and lodged in the wood on either side of Wren, and when one landed beside her hip, a desperate idea took hold. She rested her weight on it and pushed herself up far enough for Timothius to grab her around the waist and pull her over to his side.

"Hold on," he huffed in her ear, and she only had a second to brace herself before they were sliding down the full length of the drawbridge and collapsing in a heap at the bottom.

Guards rushed toward them, and Timothius tore Wren's sword from her belt, swinging it wide and meeting the incoming soldiers head on. He carved space out for Wren, giving her a wide enough berth to make quick work of releasing arrows toward the guards lurking on the wall above. With their backs to one another, they began to move slowly along the wall, away from the drawbridge and into the city.

Wren released another arrow toward the sky when Timothius grabbed her wrist and yelled, "Run!"

Through a gap in the perimeter, they cleared the guards and hurtled down the street. Shouts to halt, boots clashing against the cobblestone, and the twang of bowstrings echoed their pounding steps. Wren could see the castle looming on their right, but they were running along the streets to the left—farther from it.

Timothius took a sharp right down an alleyway and cats skittered in every direction when he started to overturn barrels and rip down lines of clothing in their wake. When they emerged on the other side, he led them deeper into the heart of the city, and though the sounds of pursuit still chased them, they appeared to have gained more distance.

Rounding a corner to their left, Timothius rushed into the courtyard of what appeared to be a milliner's shop, hiding just inside the door and crouching below the large window that had been broken out at some point. Wren struggled to catch her breath and stay silent, watching and following Timothius's methodic breathing as he did the same.

They had made it inside the city. The hardest part was over. Now they needed to survive long enough to somehow make it in the castle.

Somewhere in the back of the shop a door burst open, kicked in by a guard wearing the face of a wolf. Wren wrestled an arrow from her back and tried to get it across her bow fast enough, but to no avail—he was upon them. Timothius stood, sword drawn, but the soldier only paused and laughed. Four more guards entered the front of the shop, and when Wren peered through the window at her back, the courtyard was filled with more.

They were surrounded.

"And who is caught like a rat now?" one of the guards mocked, laughing at Wren and Timothius trapped in the corner of the room.

"You are!" cried a small voice from somewhere above, so familiar that Wren's mouth fell open with a gasp.

The soldiers whirled around, looking every which way to search the room, but no one was to be found. Granules of black dust trickled down from the roof above them, sprinkling on their heads and soft steps ran back and forth. It wasn't until a board in the ceiling lifted and a small hand came into view holding a candle that Wren knew exactly what had rained on them.

A guard looked up in time to see the flame fall, but it was too late. It hit the ground, igniting the black powder that littered the floor and the cloaks of the soldiers standing nearby. Shouts rang out and a group of men burst through the back door with their swords at the ready.

Timothius stretched out his arm in front of Wren, backing her farther into the corner and away from the flames, when a hand tapped her on the shoulder. She whirled around, arrow in hand, and nearly cried with relief when she surveyed the face on the other side of the window.

"Out you come, Lady Wren," Reginald said with a smile, his voice deep and proud. She took his hand, strong and sure, and Timothius helped lift her out of the window and into the boy's waiting arms.

Wren could not help but throw her arms around his neck. "Reg, I'm so glad you're safe. What on earth is Milo doing in that attic? Get him down before the fire reaches him!"

Reginald laughed. "I can assure you he is already down and safely away. We needed a meadow mole small enough to crawl the rafters in order to make the plan work. The king declared that we would die at dawn and said you were a traitor who had left us to die, but we knew you would come. It was lucky that we spotted you in here, or else we would have burned the entire building down with the rats inside."

Timothius clapped him on the shoulder. "It is good to see the Rat King has not hampered your spirit."

Reginald's eyes flashed with a fire far beyond his years. "He has tried. But we knew Wren would not leave us. We trust our queen, and who the queen trusts, so do we. We will do whatever is needed to make sure you succeed."

"We need to get inside the castle," Wren replied.

Reginald grinned and drew his sword, turning on his heel to face the amassing crowd that Wren now recognized as citizens and townsfolk wielding any form of weapon they could carry, from swords and daggers to pitchforks and iron stokers. "You heard the queen," he shouted. "We take the castle!"

A cry rose up and the crowd rushed into the street, their numbers growing as they marched. Wren kept close to Timothius's side, her bow ready to be drawn, but when her eyes scanned the wall, she noticed that most guards had abandoned their posts. And though she feared that it meant they still had one last stand ahead of them, she knew it also indicated a dwindling of the Rat King's forces. And now their numbers inside the city were growing stronger.

The crowd turned the final bend on the road to the castle and came to an abrupt halt. Mouse- and wolf-masked guards stood shoulder to shoulder, both the width of the gatehouse and the depth of at least five men, but when Wren looked behind her —though they were a ragtag bunch—she realized the rebels dwarfed the Rat King's men in numbers. She surveyed the faces of her people and Elric's timeless words came back to her. Only now she knew that each facet of them—while different—was somehow more brave and beautiful than the first.

With a cry, the rebels surged forward without fear, overtaking Wren, Timothius, and Reginald in seconds to meet the Rat King's forces blow for blow.

"Stay close," Reginald yelled above the din. The three of them formed an arrow, with Reginald at the point, driving his way through the heart of the fight to the castle entrance. The sight of it directly ahead of them made Wren's heart leap with joy. They were going to make it.

Out of the corner of her eye, she caught a glimpse of a beaked mask flashing in the moonlight. She turned and locked eyes with none other than Musannulos, shouting orders from where he stood on a box near the door. Fire flooded her veins, but before she could move toward him, Timothius stepped in front of her and strode forward. Musannulos spotted him—a panicked recognition dawning in his eyes—and Timothius's sword arched gracefully through the air, cleaving his head from his shoulders with one smooth, backhanded swipe. Musannulos's body fell in a small heap and his head rolled to Wren's feet, the owl mask still perfectly affixed.

She looked at Timothius with raised eyebrows, but he only shrugged. "I have waited a long time to do that."

She nodded and bent down. Pulling the ribbon at the back of the head, she released the mask from his face, let it fall with a clatter to the ground, then smashed it to pieces with her foot. Glancing back at Timothius, who wore an expression very similar to what her own had been, she flashed him a smile. "Same."

They marched on together, once again falling in behind Reginald whose grace with the sword was as impressive as it was deadly. He made quick work of anyone in their way, and within a matter of minutes—with sweat pouring down their faces—they arrived at the front of the gatehouse.

The rebels formed a protective barrier around them, now guarding the front of the castle against the king's guards who were desperately trying to reach it again. Timothius opened the door and scanned inside, confirming that nothing waited for them in the dark, then he looked to Wren and nodded—waiting.

She took the opportunity to embrace Reginald once more. "You are a good soldier," she whispered. "The very best. Be safe. You still have so many days ahead of you."

He squeezed her back. "Thank you, my lady. I mean, my queen."

Wren pulled away, shaking her head with a smile. "Wren. I will always be Wren to you. Now find Milo and get out of harm's way. That is a command."

The boy grinned, but when he moved to kiss her hand, she pecked him on the cheek instead, causing his ears to burn bright red even in the darkness. And then with a deep and steadying breath, Wren followed Timothius into the depths of the castle and toward their final obstacle—the Rat King.

CHAPTER FORTY-NINE

*T*he weighted door gave way to the great hall that appeared both cavernous and eerie under the light of the moon. They canvassed the shadows together and once certain they were truly alone, Wren turned to Timothius. "Where would he be?"

Timothius looked toward the staircase. "His quarters. The tallest spire belongs to him. It is how he is never involved in anything but sees all. He will know we are coming."

Wren took a deep, steadying breath and nodded. Instead of leading the way, Timothius took her hand, and they raced up the stairs side by side.

They stopped on a landing that opened to a familiar corridor. Wren recognized the doors to the library, but they continued into one of the rooms on the opposite side. She looked around at the large, barren space and realized it was not a room at all but a small wing that led to a far narrower stairwell.

The steps were steep and cold as ice, winders that carried them higher and higher with no light or windows to give any bearing of how far they ascended. After a few moments, Timothius slowed to a halt and faced Wren.

"We are nearly there. I count my steps," he admitted at her confused look. "It is how I find my way so that I do not give in to the madness of the dark."

Wren felt the meaning of his words deep within her heart far more than she heard what he said and stepped up on the stair beside him. Stealing the moment to catch their breath, she wrapped her arms around his bicep and laid her head on his shoulder. His tension eased and her own muscles relaxed, but the moment was short-lived when soft strains of music began to trickle down the stairwell.

The inescapable melody echoed from the stone, the strings haunting and beautiful, and while her heart slowed, the hairs on the back of Wren's neck stood on end. "Is that—"

"He plays to accompany bloodshed," Timothius confirmed, his voice cold and detached. "Death is his muse, even if the act itself is not. I have inspired many a song for him. He quite enjoyed playing them for me."

Chills coursed down Wren's spine as an acerbic loathing boiled in her veins. "I will never forgive him," she breathed, her words a poisonous vow. "Not for all you had to endure."

Timothius was pensive for a moment and then spoke softly. "I believe I will someday. I hope that it is easier to make peace with this life once he is dead and gone, for I cannot rest with him breathing. He is always lingering in my mind, watching and waiting to press the mask on my face once again."

Wren rested her hand on his cheek. "Never. I promise, never again. It is time to live our dream. The nightmare ends tonight."

He nodded and turned his head, pressing a soft kiss to her palm before stepping up, shifting Wren behind his back, and silently climbing the final spirals of the staircase.

The top came into view, but there was no door—only an open frame that led into the circular turret room. The icy air was the first thing that struck Wren, its raw and brutal gusts strangling every ounce of air from her lungs, and she realized that where there were arches in the walls, there were no windows. The night air rushed through the tower at an elevation high enough to chill a human to the very bone. Yet somehow the torches affixed to the stone walls between each window opening stayed alight without the smallest flicker. In fact, while the wind ripped and howled, everything within the room remained perfectly still, giving it an unnerving sense of wrongness.

In the middle of the room, with a violin resting on his shoulder, stood the Rat King. He was dressed in obsidian from head to toe, accenting the perfect slick of his hair and causing its silver strands to glow like quartz in the moonlight. On his head was the crown of clovers with the four golden trifolium blooms —each representing a kingdom stolen hundreds of years in the past. And now Wren would be the first to seize it back.

"Do not linger in the doorway, Daughter of the Trifolium," Phillipae's voice crooned, sliding along the waves of music that held their own against the wind and the echoing carnage below. "You have made me wait long enough."

Timothius stepped into the tower and Wren entered beside him. He tried to shift her behind him, but she refused to be moved. She squared her shoulders against the Rat King, the arrow nocked in her bow ready and waiting.

"Apologies. I had a bit of trouble getting up here," she replied with honeyed sarcasm.

Phillipae laughed with his back still to them and continued to draw long notes from his instrument. Wren tugged on Timothius's sleeve and without either one of them removing their eyes from the evil king, she whispered in his ear. "Something is not right."

The music cut off sharply and the king dropped the instrument to his side. He turned enough to glance over his shoulder at them, and something deep within Wren stirred. She knew a heartbeat before she saw his eyes that whatever her grandmother had feared paled in comparison to the being in front of her. And when he smiled—his teeth long and pointed and his eyes churning, black pools of dying starlight—she felt her own dormant power rise in her veins like electricity seeking a conduit.

"No, Wren of Clovers, all is how it should be," he crooned, his voice like velvet, his visage lethal. "I have waited for you for three hundred eighty-five years. And tonight, under the fullness of the moon, you are mine to consume."

He raised his arm, and Wren barely had time to register the crossbow in his hand before he fired a bolt straight through Timothius's shoulder with a force that pinned him to the stone behind them. She gasped, but Timothius shouted, "Wren, look out!"

A force knocked her from her feet, driving her away from him and across the tower. Phillipae, his hand outstretched, strode toward her with the crossbow in one hand and a thick cloud of onyx dhust billowing from the other. "They robbed us," he said, somewhere between a growl and a hiss, the noise unearthly yet altogether human. "The stars robbed us. They brought life to us—magic that could make us stronger. But then they cast us out. They buried us below the ground and starved us."

Wren ripped an arrow from the quiver at her back and let it fly, but with a flick of his wrist, Phillipae deflected it. Another surge of dhust emanated from him and the bow in her hand disintegrated into nothing more than fine gravel and stone.

"But stars are nothing compared to the taste of pure magic, and our hunger was stronger than their pride," he continued, his steps a death march carrying him closer and closer. "We returned and fought. We swallowed the stars and their magic whole. We devoured kingdom after kingdom, people upon people, but none could satisfy. And then, when we fractured the Thrones, when we deceived the conqueror and broke his spirit, they stole that which we craved most."

He snarled, his silhouette growing seemingly larger as his agitation mounted. "A single taste of the magic held between the Trifolium crowns—a single second to rest upon their Thrones was all we needed to lay claim to this realm. We nearly had it all, but they hid you away. And now that you have returned, we will stop at nothing until we taste the power in your blood. Until your magic is ours."

Wren slid backward, searching the room wildly for anything she could use to defend herself and coming up empty. Her back met the tower wall. "I don't have magic. My parents are both human," she replied, hoping her words might buy her a few more precious seconds from the monster growing in front of her. His skin darkened in pallor now, becoming a shade of obsidian so deep it appeared blue-tinged with a texture resembling that of stone. His mouth widened, revealing rows of pointed teeth, and the shadows expanding at his back solidified into what looked like two wings, filling the room. The Rat King was becoming a Hrotesk before her very eyes.

"A half-truth, half-falsehood," his gravelly voice replied with amusement. "Do not think you may fool me. I know what you are, though you still cannot fathom me."

Defiant anger rose in Wren's blood. "What you are is dead. You will be defeated, if not by me, then by my people."

Phillipae threw his head back and laughed, the noise echoing across the sky itself like a clap of thunder as the dhust of tenebrescent magic extended from his clawed hands. "I shall win either way. You must decide what is a worse fate. Do you let me go and watch me rally my brothers and take back what is ours, or do you somehow destroy me and unleash a nightmare you cannot even begin to comprehend? It does not matter the path you choose, each ends in death."

Wren shook her head and rose to her feet. The dhust surrounded her now, ripping her hair in the wind, swallowing her in a cloud of darkness that was illuminated only by the flash of exploding stars—each one serving to fan the flame of vengeance burning in her veins. Beyond the monster, something silver glinted in the light, differing from the flash of the dying lights and the dhust that was plunging the world into darkness.

And the strong, steady thrum in her heart told her exactly what it was.

She smiled, allowing her own teeth to show. "An entire kingdom, an entire realm fell to you, and you still could not win. What makes you think you could ever succeed when we all rise against you?"

Phillipae howled an evil laugh, fixing his eyes on her, and deep within their darkness she saw the coals flare red. "You think you have won, but you do not realize what you are truly up against, Wren of Clovers. If you were stronger, you would choose to delay your revenge and remove the head at the neck. Instead, you will foolishly cut down the puppet and free the master's hands to raise up an army."

Wren could see Timothius now on the other side of the Hrotesk, his right arm hanging limply and the left holding his sword aloft. In that instant the churning eyes of the Rat King stilled and the red within them burst. Before she could open her mouth, he spun and caught Timothius by the throat with his clawed fingers. Lifting his feet from the ground, she watched in horror as his hand constricted around Timothius's neck.

She searched frantically, her own heart shuddering with Timothius's need for air. In a moment of desperation, she tore her boot from her foot and launched it at the Rat King. It flew perfectly between his wings and collided with the back of his head, knocking it forward and sending his crown clattering to the stone floor.

He dropped Timothius to the ground in an unmoving mass and turned upon Wren. "I tire of you. And I have waited so long. You are mine, Wren of Clover. Mine."

Something clattered across the stone, skittering past the Rat King and colliding with the wall at her side.

Timothius's sword.

She made eye contact with the Hrotesk, and the instant she moved for the hilt, he lunged for her. Fortifying herself against the brick, Wren locked the sword at her side like a javelin and pointed it up. The force of darkness hurtling toward her could not stop, and when his claws met her throat, the blade sank into his skin, cleaving through sinew and bone and tearing out the other side, impaling him directly through the heart.

His claws ripped away from her, down her neck and across her chest, slashing her skin in shreds as it went, wrenching a cry from her lips. The Rat King fell to the floor, convulsing and writhing in pain. The magic bled from his eyes and his monstrous features retreated—vanishing to reveal the sniveling coward of a man who had ruled the kingdom with a hand of terror, stripping humanity from the lives of thousands, all for his own entertainment.

Phillipae Vasileio now lay on the ground before her, stilling, but instead of a silent death, he began to laugh. His eyes met Wren's, rapidly losing their malevolent light, and his final words —uttered on his dying breath—sent cold fear to her very heart. "Thank you, my queen. I look forward...to seeing you...at the end...."

The stars stopped dying in the air around them. The dhust blew away on the night breeze, out the windows of the tower and over the city. The torches all went out, leaving the moon to illuminate the body in front of her as it crumbled to ash and vanished into nothingness.

Wren's chest heaved, pain choking off the air in her lungs. She rushed to where Timothius lay and fell by his side.

He groaned, blood still pouring from the wound in his shoulder where he had ripped the bolt free, and when he tried to sit up, he could not.

Wren tried to speak—tried to say she would rise and go for help—but she found she could not. The air was clearing, but the world was darkening around her. She crumpled to the ground beside her love and in the final seconds before the dark consumed her, she gripped his elbow with one hand and wrapped the other around the crown.

CHAPTER FIFTY

The meadow beyond the rampart was strewn with bodies of the fallen. The city within was in shambles. The castle, which had been fully breached at some point during the battle, was a wreckage—the windows in the great hall destroyed—and the once pristine ballroom was now gutted to house displaced families and wounded soldiers.

Wren stood in the middle of the demolished hall and closed her eyes to the sunlight warming her face. Bandages crossed her body, looping above her left shoulder and below her right, holding the healing ointment against her ravaged skin. Some wounds would mend without a trace, but she already knew that she would bear the scars of others for the rest of her life. A one-shoulder dress covered her right shoulder, trailing embroidered lace flowers diagonally across the dressings—soft beauty laid atop pain—and though she was attempting to learn how to love it, she did not enjoy the weight of the crown on her head. Even if it was a perfect fit.

The sound of voices in the hall roused her, and she opened her eyes once more, turning to smile at Elric. His hands were bandaged and his face was still swollen and mottled, an ugly reminder of the blood vessels that had burst under strain. The physical repercussions of exhausting his magic both fighting for his life and summoning whatever weaponry the rebel and elfin forces could use to aid their onslaught.

Timothius stood beside him, his shirt collar open to accommodate the packing that dressed his shoulder and the sling that kept his arm wrapped firmly to his body. He was otherwise no worse for wear, save the fatigue in his eyes that mirrored Wren's residual exhaustion.

Entering the room behind them were Nelluenya, the commander of the elfin guard, and—to Wren's delight—Reginald, who had accepted her invitation. They all joined her at the center of the hall, greeting each other warmly while Elric summoned a table and six chairs.

Wren took a seat, but glared at him. "You are not supposed to use your magic until you've healed."

He shrugged. "They are small things."

"An entire dining set is what you'd consider small?"

"Yes, actually. I did briefly entertain a few settees with cushions and a footstool, so be thankful it was only a table and a handful of chairs."

Wren sighed and threw him a withering look, but Nelluenya's laugh cut her off. "The orneriness you show our queen, Elric. You must watch that she does not send you back to your tree."

"That is actually the first matter that I would like to discuss."

The table fell silent and all looked to her with wide and questioning eyes, save Timothius who grinned knowingly. They had stayed up late into the night discussing their plans for the future, and this was one of the first things they had decided.

"It is a given that once we have been married and crowned, we will begin our search for the remaining three rulers—my brothers or sisters of the Trifolium Thrones. And we will need a regent here to lead while we are absent," Wren said, looking to

Elric. "One who can also advise us as we rule, just like Errol—your grandfather—served my grandparents. And selfishly, we don't want to be without you, Elric. I know it is a huge risk we are asking you to take, but you've hidden long enough. You have sacrificed enough. Will you come out of hiding and reside here with us as our regent?"

Tears filled Elric's eyes, rapidly clouding their bright blue as he absorbed the gravity of what she was saying. "I...would be free here?"

Wren nodded. "The first free Isteriaeth of this age. We would guarantee your safety within the borders of Inflamel and anywhere you were to travel with us. You are a part of us. You always have been and now you always will be."

Elric's tears spilled over and he leaned forward on the table, resting his forehead on the wood. With his good arm, Timothius laid a hand on his shoulder and clasped it firmly, remaining that way until Elric gained his composure. He lifted his head and nodded rapidly. "Yes. Always. It will be my honor to pester you with questions of your world for the rest of our days."

Wren laughed and shook her head. "Only if you continue to tell me stories. I have so much more to learn about our realm. Though I don't see anything topping 'The King of Wishes'. There's something about the way it—"

Timothius cleared his throat. "We are getting off track. Elric, my brother, you are stuck with us. And now we must discuss the upcoming months and years. Once the city has been rebuilt and the castle restored, Wren and I plan to set out. Word is already spreading to the ends of Breteria, which means opposition will rise. The other three rulers are out there somewhere, and we must find them first."

Wren nodded. "I will not stop until I find them." She paused, and then tentatively added, "I can feel them."

Nelluenya's eyebrows raised. "Your magic? Has it awoken?"

"I don't have magic that I can use, but I feel different. I have ever since the crystallum broke for the final time. It's faint, but there is something there and it has been growing. It calls and responds to magic all around me."

"All the more reason for us to locate the remaining Thrones and ensure your safe ascension," Elric confirmed. "Since you were not born in magic and the magic was instead born within you, I believe it changes things. It may not be fully bestowed until you inherit the power contained within the Thrones, but you cannot remain defenseless. Not when we are unsure of who and what might lie ahead."

Reginald raised a tentative hand, and Wren beamed at him. "You are not a student here, Reg, you're an equal. Speak your mind."

He nodded once and cleared his throat. "What of the Isperi Mage? Was she defeated with the Rat King?"

It was Timothius's turn to shake his head. "The Rat King was desperate to find her—to drive her from our lands. I do not believe he knew her, and there were even moments I would have dared to say he feared her. Elric was able to summon the wealdwolves at the start of the battle, but once they reached the southern side of the city, they vanished."

"Do you think they were summoned back to her?" Wren asked.

Elric nodded. "I believe so. No one has seen or heard of her or the wolves since, but we will need to keep a weathered eye on the Deorc Weald. Our first threat may lie closer than we think."

The words of the crone in the square from what felt like ages ago echoed in the back of Wren's mind, unsettling her nerves. She turned to Timothius. "Did you ever find anything when the Rat King sent you to the Weald? Or was it all a ploy to draw you away?"

Timothius was silent for a long time, his face troubled, and when he spoke, the words seemed to drain the air from the room. "I saw her. The Isperi Mage. We were a day's journey into the forest and had found nothing. Then, like a ghost, she was there in front of us."

"What did she look like?" Reginald pressed, his eyes wide. "Are the stories true?"

Timothius nodded, staring intently at the table. "Her hair was snow white against the branches—the brightest thing in the darkness of the wood. It blew in the wind, covering most of her face and tangling around her arms and waist. Her dress was black, her skin the palest white, and with the bruised dhust billowing from her fist, she looked every bit the powerful mage, residing wild among the trees."

"Did she see you?" Wren asked, fear filling her veins.

Timothius shifted uncomfortably. "She stared at me and I could not look away. Her eyes… They shone like the night, deep and dark but a glowing violet."

Silence stole the air from the room, mouths agape around the table, including Wren's. "Did she say anything?"

He shook his head but looked up from the table with a pale face, like he recalled seeing a ghost. "No. She only smiled."

Chills ran the length of Wren's skin, and beside her Elric swallowed. "To be Isteriaeth is to be magic. To become a mage is to be filled wholly with magic. For her eyes to truly be violet— for her magic to be reflected from her soul and not contained within her dhust alone—is unheard of."

"Violet," Wren said, almost to herself. "What form of magic did you say that was, Elric?"

He hesitated. "Violet is known to be temporal magic. There is no known being that carries the strand anymore. Its origins are from either the faeries who mine the dhust directly from our earth or the Isteriaeth of old whose magic was bestowed temporal."

"Then how can she be consumed by it?" Reginald asked, his face pale with a worry far beyond his years.

"Does that mean she has established a new form of Kollapsar?" Nelluenya asked, her words laying a cold worry upon Wren's chest.

"No," Elric replied. "I am afraid it makes her worse. A Kollapsar exists to consume, to destroy magic. She has given herself over to the magic she consumed, and in turn has chosen to sacrifice her humanity. Her life is forfeit, but her power? It is limitless."

"Then how do we stop her?" Wren asked, determination in her voice.

"I do not know," Elric admitted, anger flaring in his eyes at his own helplessness. "Our hope is to reach the Thrones. To reunite the four rulers—for them to stand united. Their magic is the only force I know great enough to defeat such darkness."

Silence fell around the table, and Wren laid a hand in the crook of Timothius's elbow, his fingers gripping her own in reassurance. "Then it is settled," she said. "We rebuild, we find this mage before she seeks us out and make sure she does not grow stronger or raise any more monsters, and then we locate the rulers of the Trifolium Thrones."

The table nodded in agreement, and when they stood, Wren looked at Timothius and smiled. "But first, we plan for a celebration. One without masks."

CHAPTER FIFTY-ONE

The next full moon arrived and departed. It was the morning after, and the bells were tolling in Inflamel. Timothius walked the rampart, the morning breeze lifting his curls and cooling his flushed nerves. He savored the warmth of the sun on his face, recalling every time he had dreamed of a moment like this. The shadows still hid in his mind, the violent memories trapped behind a proverbial mask that was now visible to him alone.

Him and Wren, that was. His heart was never fooled by his stoic front. Every morning she assessed him, taking stock of the emotions he thought were safely contained. And by the end of every day, she would find a way to pry the prison back off his face and show him the beauty that could accompany vulnerability and trust.

He paused and rested his hands on a crenel within the battlement. The wall outside the gate was strung with garland and the city was open, welcoming the people of Inflamel in with open arms for the celebration. They flooded across the drawbridge from the coast and outlier homes, crossing the meadow with the elfin folk who were all dressed in their finest. Each one

433

bore a flower from the gardens of the Elfin Domain to lay upon the stone before the royal chapel. To carpet the path of their new king and queen.

The long grass of the meadow had withered and blown away, and it was now filled with clover. Each one bore four delicate leaves, and white blooms grew thick and lush in their midst, promising new days and a hopeful beginning. And there, on the very edge of the Autumnal Forest where the leaves drifted out on the breeze, a small cottage stood. It had been rebuilt—fully restored—and though it remained empty, it stood ready to welcome those without home, without family, without love over its threshold and into its nurturing warmth.

The silent hand being laid on his shoulder would have startled a lesser man, but Timothius had heard his friend approach from well down the rampart.

He turned and met the bright-blue eyes of Elric, his auburn hair pulling red in the sunlight. "The hour is nearly upon us. Are you ready?"

Timothius smiled. "To be married, I am more than ready. But to wear a crown...."

The Isteriaeth shook his head and a knowing smile crossed his face, even as Timothius's faded. "You have always been a leader. Every step of your journey, fair and foul, has prepared you for this. You are ready."

Timothius stared down at the stone and nodded, timid at first, then growing more certain. "I do wish there were considerably less people. It is still hard to face them."

Elric clasped his shoulder once more. "It has been difficult for all to come out of the shadows into the light of a new day. The brightness is blinding, the possibilities overwhelming, and the hope for the future staggering. Yet we stand side by side. As one, we learn how to make sense of what was and look to what will be. We hold on to a new understanding, tarrying at the edge of the road until we are ready to take tentative steps together.

The people—your people—will need time for healing and more days to trust you fully, but they look to you to learn the way forward. Show them."

Timothius nodded and drew himself to his full height, not in domineering or commanding intimidation, but in strength and pride for who he was and all he had endured. He clasped Elric's shoulder and pulled him into a firm embrace. No more words were needed between them, and they remained for a few moments longer before Timothius took one last reassuring breath and descended to the courtyard and the crowd that awaited.

Sunlight streamed inside the stained-glass windows of the small chapel. Their colors glowed, depicting the birth of Breteria and the Trifolium Thrones and illuminating the room and those who waited both inside and outside of its walls.

Elric strode ahead to the front of the chapel. His deep-azure robes, embroidered with stars and constellations that none had yet seen, billowed out behind him. Timothius followed, adjusting the golden tassels and straightening the cords on his white uniform. Though his hands were devoid of gloves, they still faltered, his nerves getting the best of him until cool, raw-umber skin broke into his vision.

Nelluenya, her silk gown bright as the sun itself, fixed the twisted cords across his chest and then laid a hand on his arm. "I hope you are ready, my friend," she said quietly, mischief sparkling in her golden eyes. "She is breathtaking."

Nerves of a different kind settled into his stomach, and he took an unsteady breath, releasing it slowly.

Enya beamed and then stepped to the side, beckoning to a pedestal at the front of the room and the bouquet at its center. There were lilacs and a single rose, one sprig of holly, and a stem with soft-pink blooms flowering from the vine.

Looking between the men once again, unshed tears shone in her eyes. "The queen wished for Kathrina to be represented.

And Mauritania and Gerard, and her grandmother. For all of us to be together in witness. I know they would all be proud. You have both done so well."

Neither man kept their composure, and after embracing them both, the Elfin Guardian took her seat in the front row beside a glowing Reginald and a fidgeting Milo.

"Why can't I watch from the outside with the rest of the kids?" Timothius heard Milo grumble. "It's just love stuff."

Reginald flicked him in the arm and gave him a stern look that finally convinced the boy to sit. "Because we have been invited to sit inside as friends of Wren and Timothius. And besides, weddings are more than love stuff. They're quite beautiful."

Milo frowned. "I thought you just wanted to be a soldier?"

Reginald nodded. "I do. And I am one now. But I think maybe I wish for love too." His eyes met Timothius's and widened when he realized that the latter was already watching him.

"Great love is the thing of fairy tales, you know," he said, capturing both boys' attention. "Of dreams that drift close enough to be held in your arms. You are young still, but when you find it, you will know. It is the most powerful magic you shall ever see."

Reginald beamed, and Milo muttered, "Yuck," but then he sat up, straight and still, and with the rest of the chapel's patrons, continued to wait.

Timothius gathered his wit and looked out over the crowd. He surveyed the people who had hated him, the people he had terrified into submission, the ones who would have rather seen him dead only months prior, and he took in their looks of joy and admiration. It was not out of pride, or for his own well-being—for all he had been a part of in protecting their queen and saving their kingdom—but for what he saw.

Their faces.

He would never tire of taking in the faces of every person around him, and he found his throat thickening with emotion when he looked at each one. It was a sight he never thought he would live to see. And one he was grateful he could enjoy by his love's side for the rest of their days.

Seconds later, a hush fell upon the crowd.

From the back of the room, the doors opened once again, and when Wren came into view, Timothius was certain their heart stopped beating the moment their eyes found each other.

She was dressed in a gown of ivory taffeta, its bodice adorned with lace and crystals that sparkled like the stars in the sky. The line of each hem was embellished with golden clover blooms, and her veil was embroidered with dandelion seeds— their wishes floating out behind her as she walked.

She was breathtaking, his heart. And she would leave there his wife.

His great love.

His queen.

His dream brought to life.

His entire world.

She had saved him in every way. And he would live and breathe for only her until the end of their days.

Starting now.

CHAPTER FIFTY-TWO

Of all the things Wren had faced, the aisle before her was somehow the most terrifying, but she made it to the end and finally reached the man waiting there for her.

She could not take her eyes off him when they recited the vows of old, passed down from the stars to the Awduron—spoken from Elric's lips and repeated by their own. Two simple rings woven in gold with the Trifolium sigil etched upon their surfaces were exchanged and then, kneeling in front of the altar, the coronation began.

"Florence Klaver, granddaughter of High Queen Marionaldi of Clover and King Vincienti of Inflamel, do you promise to defend life and protect your people? To seek mercy, justice, and preservation of the five sacred strands of magic from which we are all formed? And do you swear to bear the crown of the Trifolium in love, peace, and prosperity until the last of your days?"

Wren felt tears sting her eyes, but she smiled when she met Elric's gaze. "I do, until the last of my days."

Elric turned and lifted a tiara from where it laid on a pillow of silk. Every filigree and twist formed an unending pattern of clovers with diamonds in between, marking the places where their flowers bloomed and thrived. He rested it on her head and stepped back far enough to bow. As he rose, he caught Wren's eye and smiled through his own tears. "May your reign be blessed from the sea to the stars."

Straightening before Timothius, he repeated the vow, and then placed a golden crown—etched and studded with the same ornamental decoration as Wren's—on his head. He bowed low and then rose, his voice cracking when he said, "My brother. It is an honor."

Facing the crowd, Elric cleared his throat and spoke loudly, his voice filled with commanding pride. "It is my soul's privilege —as bestowed on me by the stars of old—and my heart's joy to announce the presence of King Timothius of Inflamel and Queen Wren of Clover, future High Queen of the Trifolium Thrones. Long may their heart reign."

Jubilant cheers went up from the crowd. The world was a blur around Wren when she took Timothius's arm and they made their way out of the chapel, through the crowd, and across the courtyard. The noise did not begin to subside until they were deep inside the castle and on their way to the walk atop the gatehouse that would allow them to overlook the city and greet their people as king and queen—one for the first time. But when they passed the ballroom, Timothius stopped, bringing Wren to a halt beside him.

He glanced inside, then looked at her with a smile in his eyes. "May I have this dance, my heart?"

Wren's chest swelled, and for a moment, she thought it might burst from happiness. She nodded, and he led her to the floor.

The room looked nothing like it had before. The faeries had all been freed and the candlelight suspended from the ceiling shone there of its own accord. The walls were bright, the curtains drawn back, and the marbled floor was polished to a shine, giving the room a warm and ethereal glow.

There was no music. There did not need to be. It resided within their minds and beat alongside their heart in time with the echo of their dreams.

Every inch of their bodies was perfectly aligned—Wren wrapped tightly in Timothius's arms, her own around his neck in an embrace she would never cease being grateful for.

She stood on her toes, rested her cheek against his, and tilted her head back enough to whisper in his ear. "What do you dream of?"

She felt his smile on her skin. "You," he replied. "For all of our days and nights and the hours that fall in between. For the moments that still lie ahead of us, and for the day of the Thrones—when they rise and the entire realm knows the freedom that we know now. Then I want to steal you away. To go somewhere with open spaces and endless horizons. Where we have nothing to do beyond breathing except to hold and love one another."

Tears of joy trickled down Wren's cheek, and Timothius's hand rose to brush them away. "What does my wife dream of?" he whispered against her lips.

Every last ounce of her resolve failing, Wren melted into him. Their lips lingered, exploring one another and taking their time. The kingdom outside could wait because this dance, to the cadence of their heart, would outlast their crowns. The world would fade, but their love would stand until the end of time.

When they finally parted, Wren whispered her reply. "You. I have and will only ever dream of you."

Timothius lifted her in his arms and spun them around the floor. Their laughter echoed off the walls—their joy filling every corner of a castle that had once been so dark. Ceasing their movement, though still holding her in his arms, Timothius rested his forehead against Wren's. "Will they wait for us if we attend to our chamber first?"

Wren flushed, but laughed. "If we greet them now and then go to our chamber after, we will not have to leave again."

Timothius groaned and drew back to look at her. "But there is a ball tonight in our honor."

Wren shrugged. "I think we've had our fair share of dances."

Timothius laughed, shaking his head, and set her feet back on the ground. "You make a fair point. Let's get on with it, then, so that we may reach the *after*."

He led her from the room and to the stairwell ascending to the top of the gatehouse, but on the first step, Wren stopped, bringing him to a pause on the step above her own. Looking back out over the hall, she took it all in—the colored glass now affixed in each window, the light streaming across the floor, and the deep-green banners, every one emblazoned with the Trifolium sigil—and then she looked back to the man at her side. Her husband. Her king.

"I love you, Timothius Drossel. Beyond crown and kingdom. Until the end of time."

He pressed her hand to his lips, his eyes alight with fire, and then placed it on his heart, her own steady beat hammering out life in his chest. "And I love you, Wren Klaver. My life's great love and my endless dream. Until the end of time."

They reached the doors at the top, took one last breath and stole one last kiss, and then together flung them open—stepping into the sunlight above the city and kingdom they called their own.

Cheers rang out from every road, every home, every building in and outside the city walls in a din of overwhelming joy. Wren's breathing came faster and faster, not with fear or uncertainty, but filled with pride and an all-consuming happiness. She beamed at her people and when her eyes met those of the man standing beside her, she let her welling tears fall, glistening like stars in the radiance of her smile.

She knew then, without a doubt, that she had been made—born and created—for this. Across time and space, between reality and worlds born of stars, every moment had converged with her at this fixed point in time. Every last one of her wildest dreams had come true.

She was seen. She was known. She was loved. And she was going to change this world exactly how it had changed her.

A single dream at a time.

WARNING: YOU ARE ABOUT TO READ THE EPILOGUE

There is no going back once you turn this page.
The book will no longer be wrapped up in a pretty bow, handed
to you beneath twinkling lights with a warm and happy glow.
So if you prefer to end Wren and Timothius's tale with their
happily-ever-after (permanently, or just for today) then I
encourage you to stop here.

However...
If you are a risk taker and a lover of chaos who enjoys plunging
off the side of a cliff for the long scale down to closure far, far,
far at the bottom, then by all means continue on!

Either way, I will see you on the other side♥

A single dream.

It was the echo she still heard in her mind.

It was the epitaph she scratched into the stone above her own grave.

It was the blood under her fingernails; it was her hair, long and unkempt, in her face, and the sole noise she would let inside her head beyond that of her own screaming.

It was the only thing she could bear to remember.

Not the grinding of the castle walls or the groaning of the earth beneath her feet.

Not the screams of the people, the cries of the soldiers, or the desperate pleas of the king at her side.

The king. Her husband. Her soldier. Timothius.

No.

She slammed the book resting in her lap shut and hurled it so hard that it bounced off the ground at her feet.

Not even him.

She could not bear to remember him grasping for her. The wild desperation that consumed the love in his eyes when he tried to pull her close to him—to save and protect her.

She would not remember the shift in the air or the smell of the wind as it changed.

Not the crown as it fell from her head and shattered on the ground. Not her wedding ring or the ring of the Guardian that slipped from her fingers, clinking on the stone as they rolled away, or her gown as it tore and wrapped around her legs to form soft, fleece-lined leggings.

Not the hair ripped from its braids, flying around her in the maelstrom like a hurricane.

Not her own desperation, searching for what had happened and wondering how such happiness, such beauty, came to an untimely end.

How the sun fell from the sky, leaving a storm of darkness in its wake.

How she screamed when the sleeves of her tunic sweater fell around her and her slipper socks bound her feet.

Stop, Wren. We will not do this. We must focus.

Focus not on the prison she lived in now. The family she had returned to, grieving the loss of their beloved mother and grandmother. The ones who had awoken to find her gone, reported her missing, and then forgotten about her. The ones who barely recalled her, and when they did, labeled her insane and turned her out.

She would focus only on the eyes she had found in the crowd below the castle. The ones that locked on hers, hidden beneath a hood that concealed her long, white hair. The violet eyes that glowed with the same force as the magic that fueled the storm coiling around Wren.

Yes, she'd focus on them and not on the last look she exchanged with her husband. The man she still longed for heart, body, and soul.

His heart used to beat in her chest and her own within his. She used to feel him—his desperate pain and longing. But not anymore.

All that remained was the decaying of her own heart. She could feel it blackening and dying, starved for love and begging for light.

He would hate to see what she had become, but there was nothing she would not give—nothing she would not sacrifice. She had not rested until she found the final option, the key to awakening the magic that lurked dormant in her veins.

They had all been wrong. There *were* still traces of magic hiding about her world. Strings that had frayed off a single strand, magic that was whispered about in secret circles but seldom believed to be true.

Tenebrescent magic.

Every day that passed, a more frantic madness—something feral and rabid—settled into her bones. Every rise and setting of the sun taunted her with another week lost.

Another week they did not have together.

Time that had been stolen from them.

But she would not think of that. She was growing stronger. She wondered if he could feel it too. She hoped not, but if he did, she willed with every ounce of her being that he would know it was for him. What she was doing, becoming, was only ever for him. So that she could return to him.

Until then, she would focus on the final promise of eternal love that had fallen from her lips. Not the panic in his eyes or the vow that he swore to find her seconds before his words were lost to the wind.

She would close her eyes and see his face alone. Not the last sight of her world, her life, her kingdom, her friends, becoming nothing more than a dark and triumphant stain of violet and black that scarred her vision like a bruise.

Enough.

Wren stopped then and silenced her mind. *Enough thinking.*

She took a long, deep breath in through her nose and exhaled it in equal measure between her lips.

No. The only thing safe for her to hold on to were those three words—*a single dream*. Though this time they were not a hope or an inspiration.

They were a vow.

An unbreakable vow.

And even as she turned to face the small, pathetic tree stuffed in the corner of her dingy room—decorated for the holiday again—the one-year anniversary of her loss shone from its twinkling bulbs and glared off the ornaments that she had shattered on the ground. But the three words burned brighter than it all.

A single dream.

She lifted her arm in the air, closed her eyes, and opened her hand. A long and silent moment later, the spine of the book snapped into her palm, sending a surge of hot magic ripping through her like electricity, setting her soul aflame.

Yes, she would return better.

Stronger.

One way or another. No matter the cost.

Wren surveyed the room once more and, on the opposite side, caught sight of her reflection in the cracked and dirty mirror.

Her eyes glowed with a rage so hot they appeared violet.

And she smiled.

ALSO BY R.V. WILBUR

ACKNOWLEDGMENTS

Well hello, thank you so much for reading The Cadence of Crowns! Whether this is your first introduction to my writing, or you're returning as a friend I am SO grateful for you and thankful that you've given my words your time, my stories a place in your mind, and my characters room in your heart.

This story was the first book I ever penned some twenty odd years ago. I cut it to a 5x8 size, three hole punched it into a green binder, and stuck it on my shelf beside my favorite books. And though it has grown and evolved so much over time, the one thing that hasn't changed is its place at the beginning— because we're only just getting started.

One of my favorite things about writing is getting to immortalize what I love in words and stories that will live beyond me. Sometimes they're small things, like a phrase with a secret significance or an accessory that is special to me.

For this story, however, it is something much bigger, and I would be remiss not to first thank my Gran. My grandparents were the most incredible people I will ever know. I see their fingerprints all over my life, I feel them everywhere I turn, and there is not a single day that goes by that I don't think of my grandmother at least once. She was magic to me, and now just a small part of her gets to live forever on this side of heaven, tucked into the pages of a book, which was a place she always loved to be.

This book is wholly, entirely, from the ground up written for my babies. A + B you are my biggest cheerleaders, you sacrifice the most in sharing me with all of the demands of this career (on top of everything else), and all you ask for is input on cover colors and when you can read my books. Thank you both for being my critique partners during the proofreading process, and a special thank you goes to my A for drawing out the final placements of the four kingdoms of Breteria with me. Your sketch looked better than mine ever will and I can't wait to see where your art carries you!!

Erik...babe...I don't even know what to say about the ways you've kept me going through this book and this year. We both know I'll continue to spiral a million times over, but it is easier to climb this mountain when I know you're right behind me making sure I don't fall off or stay down for too long. You are my great love, my endless dream, and I love you with every beat of my heart.

To my parents for being my biggest fans, for forgiving me when I make questionable choices with my characters, and for reminding me that there are boundaries to what I can/can't do to them if I want to stay in the will. I will (try to) keep your favorites alive!! And a special shout out goes to my mom who is the only person beyond me to have read this book in both its forms, twenty years apart. We've come so far and I don't know what I'd do without you. I love you, man!!

To Chinah, the absolutely brilliant queen that you are!! I would be utterly lost without you and not a day goes by that I'm not grateful for your passion, your way with names (can I get a hallelujah), and the way you balance challenging and teaching me to be better with every word I write.

To Lex with Selkkie Designs, you took my bare minimum vision for this series and created an entire brand that exceeded my every dream. You are brilliant and I cannot thank you enough!!

Lindsey and Maryia, you ladies are some of the most remarkable artists I know and the way you brought my world to life in two wildly unique styles has made my heart SO happy!! THANK YOU THANK YOU THANK YOU.

To my incredible beta, hype, and arc teams...I have always known that the fantasy community has some of the most dedicated readers, but seeing you from this side has given me an even greater appreciation for your love of these worlds and stories. Thank you for your obsession and your passion. It keeps my author heart going on the hard days♥

Brittany...another year, another milestone, another achievement, another goal, and we're still chasing down these dreams together. This year has been a difficult one, but if I know anything it's that doing the hard things is a million times better with a friend by your side. Thank you for always being one text away no matter what!!

To the Queens of my Chaos, the feets of my heart, and the other 10 turkeys in my soul, love is not a strong enough word for how much I adore every single one of you. Thank you for showing up every day, every step of the way, for laughing, crying, and laugh-crying with me, and for keeping me one Gumby gif this side of sanity. I promise, I PROMISE, I'm writing book two!!

Alex, Alexis, Hillary, Jaclyn, Jenny (mom), Jessica, Nicole, and Vanessa, THANK YOU for being a sounding board, a support system, a cheer squad, and for helping me navigate my way through so many new things this year. There is so much I would NOT have the courage to do alone, and with you I never am. You mean the world to me, thank you!!

To Rory Pond for being my emotional support floof, for purring when I need calm, for being my desk chair buddy, and for laying on my head when I just won't stop panicking. I know I'm still just "other human", but I love you, Floofenheimer!!

And lastly to my brain, Brian (three cheers for autocorrect). Thank you for nothing this year. Absolutely nothing. But you know what? I STILL MADE IT! *mic drop*

ABOUT THE AUTHOR

R.V. Wilbur has been in love with reading ever since she received her first Little Golden Book library at the age of two. A love of words soon followed and, after publishing selected poems, she drafted her first book at the age of thirteen.

Despite all of this she is still somehow terrible at writing blurbs, so this is about all you get. She currently resides in North Carolina with her husband, two children, and of course her black cat Rory Pond. And she's probably drinking coffee.

No, she is definitely drinking coffee.

facebook.com/RVWilburAuthor
instagram.com/rvwilburauthor
amazon.com/author/rvwilbur

www.ingramcontent.com/pod-product-compliance
Ingram Content Group UK Ltd.
Pitfield, Milton Keynes, MK11 3LW, UK
UKHW041941131224
452403UK00004B/335